PRAISE FOR
A Moment on the Edge: 100 Years of Crime Stories by Women

Also by Elizabeth George

A Moment on the Edge

100
YEARS OF
CRIME STORIES BY WOMEN

Edited by Elizabeth George

HARPER
PERENNIAL

HARPER ● PERENNIAL

An extension of this copyright page appears on pages v–vii.

Originally published in 2002 in Great Britain by Hodder & Stoughton, a division of Hodder Headline, with the title *Crime from the Mind of a Woman: A Collection of Women Crime Writers of the Century.*

A hardcover edition of this book was published in 2004 by HarperCollins Publishers.

FIRST HARPER PERENNIAL EDITION PUBLISHED 2005.

The Library of Congress has catalogued the hardcover edition as follows:
A moment on the edge : 100 years of crime stories by women / edited by Elizabeth George.—1st. ed.
    p.   cm.
Originally published under the title: Crime from the mind of a woman.
ISBN 0-06-058821-7 (alk. paper)
    1. Detective and mystery stories. 2. Fiction—Women authors.
I. Title: 100 years of crime stories by women. II. Title: One hundred years of crime stories by women. III. George, Elizabeth. IV. Title.
PN6120.95.D45C75   2004
808.83'872—dc22   2003067608

ISBN-10: 0-06-058822-5 (pbk.)
ISBN-13: 978-0-06-058822-9 (pbk.)

05 06 07 08 09   ❖/RRD   10 9 8 7 6 5 4 3 2 1

ACKNOWLEDGMENTS

"Introduction" by Elizabeth George. Copyright © 2001 by Elizabeth George.

Story notes by Jon L. Breen. Copyright © 2004 by Jon L. Breen.

"A Jury of Her Peers" by Susan Glaspell. Copyright 1917 by Susan Glaspell, renewed. First published in *Every Week*, 1917. Reprinted by permission of the agent for the author's Estate, Curtis Brown Ltd.

"The Man Who Knew How" by Dorothy L. Sayers. Copyright 1932 by Dorothy L. Sayers, renewed. First published in *Harpers Bazaar*, February 1932. Reprinted by permission of the agents of the author's Estate, David Higham Associates.

"I Can Find My Way Out" by Ngaio Marsh. Copyright 1946 by Ngaio Marsh, renewed. First published in *Alfred Hitchcock's Mystery Magazine*, August 1946. Reprinted by permission of HarperCollins Publishers Ltd. and the agents for the author's Estate, Gillon Aitken.

"The Summer People" by Shirley Jackson. Copyright 1950 by Shirley Jackson. First published in *Charm*, 1950. Reprinted by the permission of the agent for the Estate of Shirley Jackson.

"St. Patrick's Day in the Morning" by Charlotte Armstrong. Copyright © 1959 by Charlotte Armstrong. Copyright renewed © 1987 by Jeremy B. Lewi, Peter M. Lewi, and Jacqueline Lewi Byngata. First published in *Ellery Queen's Mystery Magazine*, April 1960. Reprinted by permission of the agent for the author's Estate, Brandt & Brandt Literary Agents, Inc.

"The Purple Is Everything" by Dorothy Salisbury Davis. Copyright © 1963 by Dorothy Salisbury Davis. First published in *Ellery Queen's Mystery Magazine*, June 1964. Reprinted by permission of the author.

"Money to Burn" by Margery Allingham. Copyright © 1969 by Rights Limited, a Chorion Group Company. First published in *Ellery Queen's Mystery Magazine*, April 1957. Reprinted by permission of the agent for the author's Estate, Rights Limited, a Chorion Group Company. All rights reserved.

"A Nice Place to Stay" by Nedra Tyre. Copyright © 1970 by Davis Publications, Inc. First published in *Ellery Queen's Mystery Magazine*, June 1970. Reprinted by permission of the agent for the author's Estate, Scott Meredith Literary Agency, Inc.

"Clever and Quick" by Christianna Brand. Copyright © 1974 by Christianna Brand. First published in *Ellery Queen's Mystery Magazine*, March 1974. Reprinted by permission of the agent for the author's Estate, A. M. Heath & Co. Ltd.

"Country Lovers" by Nadine Gordimer. Copyright © 1975 by Nadine Gordimer, from *Soldier's Embrace* by Nadine Gordimer. Reprinted by permission of Viking Penguin, a division of Penguin Putnam, Inc., A. P. Watt Ltd. on behalf of Nadine Gordimer.

"The Irony of Hate" by Ruth Rendell. Copyright © 1977 by Kingsmarkham Enterprises, Ltd. First published in *Winter's Crimes*. Reprinted by permission of the author.

"Sweet Baby Jenny" by Joyce Harrington. Copyright © 1981 by Joyce Harrington. First published in *Ellery Queen's Mystery Magazine*, May 1981. Reprinted by permission of the author.

"Wild Mustard" by Marcia Muller. Copyright © 1984 by the Pronzini-Muller Family Trust. First published in *The Eyes Have It*. Reprinted by permission of the author.

"Jemima Shore at the Sunny Grave" by Antonia Fraser. Copyright © 1988 by Antonia Fraser. First published in *Ellery Queen's Mystery Magazine*, June 1988. Reprinted by permission of the author.

"The Case of the Pietro Andromache" by Sara Paretsky. Copyright © 1988 by Sara Paretsky. First published in *Alfred Hitchcock's Mystery Magazine*, December 1988. Reprinted by permission of the author and her agents, Dominick Abel Literary Agency Inc.

"Afraid All the Time" by Nancy Pickard. Copyright © 1989 by the Nancy J. Pickard Trust. First published in *Sisters in Crime.* Reprinted by permission of the author.

"The Young Shall See Visions, and the Old Dream Dreams" by Kristine Kathryn Rusch. Copyright © 1989 by Kristine Kathryn Rusch. First published in *Alfred Hitchcock's Mystery Magazine,* July 1989. Reprinted by permission of the author.

"A Predatory Woman" by Sharyn McCrumb. Copyright © 1991 by Sharyn McCrumb. First published in *Sisters in Crime #4.* Reprinted by permission of the author.

"Jack Be Quick" by Barbara Paul. Copyright © 1991 by Barbara Paul. First published in *Solved.* Reprinted by permission of the author.

"Ghost Station" by Carolyn Wheat. Copyright © 1992 by Carolyn Wheat. First published in *A Woman's Eye.* Reprinted by permission of the author.

"New Moon and Rattlesnakes" by Wendy Hornsby. Copyright © 1994 by Wendy Hornsby. First published in *The Mysterious West.* Reprinted by permission of the author.

"Death of a Snowbird" by J. A. Jance. Copyright © 1994 by J. A. Jance. First published in *The Mysterious West.* Reprinted by permission of the author.

"The River Mouth" by Lia Matera. Copyright © 1994 by Lia Matera. First published in *The Mysterious West.* Reprinted by permission of the author.

"A Scandal in Winter" by Gillian Linscott. Copyright © 1996 by Gillian Linscott. First published in *Holmes for the Holidays.* Reprinted by permission of the author.

"Murder-Two" by Joyce Carol Oates. Copyright © 2001 by The Ontario Review Press. First published in *Murder for Revenge.* Reprinted by permission of the author.

"English Autumn—American Fall" by Minette Walters. Copyright © 2001 by Minette Walters. First published in *Ellery Queen's Mystery Magazine,* December 2001. Reprinted by permission of the author and her agents, Gregory and Radice, Agents.

CONTENTS

Contents

INTRODUCTION

by Elizabeth George

Whether the story is a murder mystery, a tale of suspense, a psychological study of the characters affected by a devastating event, the retelling of a famous criminal act, a courtroom drama, an exposé, a police procedural, or a truthful account of an actual offense, the question remains the same. Why crime? Whether the characters involved are FBI agents, policemen and women, forensic scientists, journalists, military personnel, the man or woman on the street, private detectives, or the little old lady who lives next door, the question remains the same. Why crime? Be it murder (singular, serial, or mass), mayhem, robbery, assault, kidnapping, burglary, extortion, or blackmail, we still want to know: why crime? Why exists this fascination with crime and why, above all, exists this fascination with crime on the part of female writers?

I think there are several answers to these questions.

Crime writing is practically as old as writing itself and is consequently very much part of our literary tradition. The earliest crime stories come to us from the Bible: in a jealous rage, Cain kills Abel; in a jealous conspiracy, Joseph's brothers sell him into slavery in Egypt and fake his death for their devastated father; in lustful jealousy, David sends Bathsheba's husband to the front lines in battle so that he might have the winsome woman for himself; in unrequited lust, two respected elders bear false witness against the virtuous Susanna, condemning her to death for adultery unless someone can come forward and disprove their story; fathers lie with their daughters in criminal acts of incest; brothers kill, fight with, lie about, and otherwise abuse their brothers; women demand the heads of men on platters; Judith decapitates

Holofernes; Judas betrays Jesus of Nazareth; King Herod slays the newborn male children of the Hebrews . . . It's a nasty place in the Old and New Testament, and we feed off this place from our earliest years.

Crime is mankind on the edge, *in extremis*, but more than that, crime is mankind stepping outside of the norm. For every Cain, there are a billion brothers who have co-existed throughout the centuries. For every David, there are ten million men who've turned away from a woman they want when they learn she is committed to another. But this is what makes crime so interesting. It isn't what people normally do.

It would be nice to believe that cars slow down on the freeway when there is an accident because of the drivers' heightened sense of caution: everyone sees the flashing lights up ahead, the smoke, the flares, the ambulances, the fire trucks, and hits the brakes so as not to end up in the same condition as the unfortunates currently being extricated from mangled metal. But this is not generally why people slow down. They slow down to gawk, their curiosity piqued. Why? Because an accident on the freeway is an anomaly, and anomalies interest us. They always interest us: have done from the beginning of time and will do till the end of it.

Brutal murders garner front-page space. Kidnappings, disappearances, riots, fatal auto accidents, plane crashes, terrorist bombings, armed robbery, snipers firing on the unsuspecting . . . all of this cuts into everyday life, awakening us to the fragility of our individual existences as it simultaneously whets our appetite to *know*. We grind to a halt as a nation to listen to the verdict in the O. J. Simpson case because there are base passions involved in whatever happened on Bundy Drive, and the base passions of that double killer awaken the base passions within ourselves. Blood spilled cries out for more blood to spill in retribution for the act. We seek a punishment to fit each crime. Crime is as old as humanity. But so is sensation. So is vengeance.

Crime literature gives us a satisfaction that we are often denied in life. In life, we never do know who really killed Nicole and

Ron; we only suspect there was a second gunman on the grassy knoll; we are left to wonder about Dr. Shepherd's wife and Jeffrey MacDonald's capacity for truth or self-delusion. The Green River killer disappears into the primordial slime from which he rose, the Zodiac killer joins him there, and we are left with only the questions themselves: who were these people and why did they murder? But in crime fiction, the killers face justice. It can be real justice, poetic justice, or psychological justice. But face it they do. They are unmasked and normalcy is restored. There is vast satisfaction for the reader in that, certainly more satisfaction than is garnered from the investigation into and punishment for an actual crime.

For the writer who wishes to explore characters, there is nothing so catastrophically catalytic as the intrusion of a crime into an otherwise peaceful landscape. A crime places everyone into a crucible: the investigators, the perpetrator, the victims, and those in relationship to the investigators, the perpetrator, and the victims. Within this crucible of life's most monstrous acts the mettle of the characters is tested. It is when characters confront the most serious challenges to their beliefs, their peace, their sanity, and their way of life that their pathology is triggered. And it is the pathology of the individual character clashing with the pathology of all the other characters that is the stuff of drama and catharsis.

Some of our most enduring pieces of literature have a heinous crime as their backdrop. Hamlet's monumental mental struggle to overcome his conscience and act the part of Nemesis could not occur had the poisoning of his father not happened in a brutal act of fratricide. Oedipus could not fulfill his destiny without first killing King Laius on the road to Thebes. Medea would not be in the position in which she is placed in Corinth— an outcast about to be cast out by a nervous Creon all too aware of her abilities as a sorceress—had her reputation as the master- mind behind King Pelias's death not preceded her. So it should come as no surprise to anyone who reads that crimes continue not only to fascinate writers but also to serve as the backbone for much of their prose.

What a crime does in a piece of literature is two-fold. First, it serves as a throughline for the story to follow: the crime must be investigated and solved within the twists and turns of the plot. But secondly and perhaps more importantly, the crime also acts as a skeleton for the body of the tale that the writer wishes to tell. On this skeleton, the writer can hang as much or as little as she likes. She can keep the skeleton down to the bones alone and tell a story that moves smoothly, concisely, and without deviation or decoration to its revelation and conclusion. Or she can hang upon the skeleton the muscles, tissues, veins, organs, and blood of such diverse elements of storytelling as theme, exploration of character, life and literary symbols, subplots, etc., as well as the specific crime-oriented story elements of clues, red herrings, suspense, and a list of time-honored motifs peculiar to mysteries: the hermetically sealed death chamber (or locked room), the most obvious place, the trail of false clues left by the real killer, the fixed idea, and on and on. Thus, her characters can march hand-in-hand in the direction of an ineluctable conclusion, or they can become sidetracked by the myriad possibilities offered to them through means of an expanded storyline and a more complicated structure.

Why, then, would a writer ever consider dabbling in anything else? There is no reason that I can see. For as long as a writer adheres to the notion that the only rule is there are no rules, the sky's the limit within this field.

This still doesn't answer the question about female writers' attraction to crime literature, and it is indeed a question I've been asked over and over again by journalists, with a rather tedious regularity.

The Golden Age of Mystery in Great Britain and the Commonwealth—which I would consider spanning the years from the twenties through the fifties—is dominated by women. Indeed, their names comprise a pantheon into whose company every modern writer aspires to join. Agatha Christie, Dorothy L. Sayers, Ngaio Marsh, Margery Allingham . . . It's not terribly difficult to sort out why women writers throughout the twentieth century endeavored to join this distinguished company: once one woman made an inroad into an area of literature, other women were quick to follow. The fascination with crime writing on the part of females can thus be explained with ease: women chose to write crime stories because they were successful at it. Success on the part of one woman breeds the desire for success on the part of another.

In the United States, this also holds true. But the difference in the United States is that the Golden Age of Mystery is dominated by men and that women are Janet-come-latelies to it. When we think of the Golden Age in America, we think of Dashiell Hammett and Raymond Chandler, of first-person narratives with tough-guy private eyes who smoke, drink bourbon, live in seedy apartments, and dismissively refer to women as "dames." They use guns and their fists, and they've got 'tude to spare. They're loners, and they like it that way.

Breaking into this male-dominated world required guts and tenacity on the part of women writers. Some of them opted to write kinder, gentler mysteries in order to offer something more in keeping with the delicate sensibilities of the female readers they were hoping to attract. Others decided to barge right in and join the men, creating female private eyes who were as hard-bitten as the men they sought to replace. Sue Grafton and Sara Paretsky proved irrefutably that a female p.i. would be accepted by an audience of both men and women readers, and a score of other female writers began to follow in Grafton and Paretsky's footsteps. Thus, the arena widened in the United States as well, offering women another outlet for their creative energies.

Creating crime fiction offers writers a vast landscape as broad and as varied as crime itself. Because there are no hard-and-fast rules and because those few rules that exist exist to be broken (witness the uproar over *The Murder of Roger Ackroyd* when it was first published in 1926), the writer can choose any setting on earth which she can then people with: teenagers as sleuths, children as sleuths, old ladies as sleuths, animals as sleuths, shut-ins and agoraphobics as sleuths, teachers as sleuths, doctors as sleuths, astronauts as sleuths, and on and on as far as the imagination can carry her. With this as a basic tenet of crime writing, the real question should be not why do so many women write crime stories but why doesn't everyone write crime stories?

This volume doesn't attempt to answer that question. What it does, however, is present for your entertainment a century's collection of crime and suspense stories by women. What you'll notice about this collection is that it includes names closely associated with crime writing—Dorothy L. Sayers, Minette Walters, Sue Grafton, and others—but it also includes some names one doesn't normally associate with crime writing at all: names like Nadine Gordimer and Joyce Carol Oates. I've tried to come up with as wide a range of female authors as possible because a wide range reflects my primary belief about crime writing and that is this: crime writing does not have to be considered genre writing. It is not confined to a few moderately talented practitioners. And most importantly, it is indeed something that can stand, will stand, and has already stood the test of time.

One of the greatest sources of irritation to me as a writer is the number of people who stubbornly consider crime writing a lesser form of literary endeavor. Throughout the years that I've written crime fiction, I've had numerous conversations with people that reflect this very strange point of view. One man at a writing conference told me that he was going to write crime fiction as practice and then, later on, he would write a "real novel." ("Like making tacos until you can graduate to chocolate cake from scratch?" I asked him innocently.) A journalist in Germany once asked me what I thought of the fact that my novels weren't reviewed in a highbrow newspaper that I had never heard of. ("Gosh. I don't know. I guess that paper doesn't have much impact on sales," I told her.) Several times people have stood up during Q&A at the end of speeches I've given and asked me why "a writer like you doesn't write serious novels." ("I consider crime fiction serious," I tell them.) But always there is this underlying belief on the part of some readers and some critics: crime fiction isn't something that should be taken seriously.

This is an unfortunate point of view. While it's true that some crime fiction is lowbrow, formulaic, and without much merit, the same can be said of anything else that's published. Some books are good, some are indifferent, and some are downright bad. But the reality is that a great deal of crime fiction has done what mainstream "literary" fiction only dreams of doing: it has successfully stood the test of time. For every Sir Arthur Conan Doyle, whose Sherlock Holmes still inspires devotion and enthusiasm over one hundred years after his creation, there are thousands of writers whose work of ostensible literature has faded into complete obscurity. Given the choice between being labeled a "literary" writer and disappearing ten years after I hang up my spurs or being labeled "only a crime writer" and having my stories and novels read one hundred years from now, I know which choice I would make and I can only assume any writer of sense would make the same one.

For my money, literature is whatever lasts. During his lifetime, no one would have accused William Shakespeare of writing great literature. He was a popular playwright who peopled his productions with characters who satisfied every possible level of education and experience in his audience. Charles Dickens wrote serials for the newspaper, penning them as quickly as he could in order to support his ever-burgeoning family. And the aforementioned Arthur Conan Doyle, a young ophthalmologist building a practice, wrote mysteries to while away the time as he waited for patients to show up in his surgery. None of these writers was worried about immortality. None of them wrote while wondering whether their work would be considered literature, commercial fiction, or trash. They were each concerned about telling a great story, telling it well, and placing it before an audience. The rest they placed—as wise men and women do—into the hands of time.

This collection of authors represents that same philosophy of writing what you want to write and writing it well. Some of them have done that, died, and achieved a modicum of immortality. The rest of them remain earthbound, still writing, and waiting to see how time will deal with them. All of them share in common a desire to explore mankind in a moment on the edge. The edge equates to the crime committed. How the characters deal with the edge is the story.

A Jury of Her Peers

SUSAN GLASPELL

Susan Keating Glaspell (1876–1948) was born in Davenport, Iowa, attended Drake University and the University of Chicago, and worked as a journalist before turning to full-time fiction-writing in 1901. Her first novel, *The Glory of the Conquered*, appeared in 1909 and her first story collection, *Lifted Masks*, in 1912, but she would achieve her greatest fame as a playwright, culminating in a controversial Pulitzer Prize for *Alison's House* (1930), inspired by the life of Emily Dickinson. From 1914 to 1921, she was a member of the Provincetown Players, a bohemian theatre-based community founded by her idealist husband George Cram Cook. Among the other members were Edna St. Vincent Millay, Djuna Barnes, Edna Ferber, John Reed, and the writer who would become the greatest American playwright of the time, Eugene O'Neill.

After early stories that were popular romances of the local-color school, Glaspell was influenced to adopt a more natura-listic approach, along with socialist political attitudes, by her husband and Floyd Dell. The rebellion of women against the domination of simple-minded males was a continuing subject. One of her plays, the one-act *Trifles* (1916), became the basis for her most famous story, "A Jury of Her Peers" (1917). There's no denying this is a detective story—indeed, in the fashion of the time, one in which amateur sleuths are more perceptive than professionals—but it is a highly unconventional, one-of-a-kind detective story in which the detection is used to make a serious thematic point.

W hen Martha Hale opened the storm-door and got a cut of the north wind, she ran back for her big woolen scarf. As she hurriedly wound that round her head her eye made a scandalized sweep of her kitchen. It was no ordinary thing that called her away—it was probably further from ordinary than anything that had ever happened in Dickson County. But what her eye took in was that her kitchen was in no shape for leaving: her bread all ready for mixing, half the flour sifted and half unsifted.

She hated to see things half done; but she had been at that when the team from town stopped to get Mr. Hale, and then the sheriff came running in to say his wife wished Mrs. Hale would come too—adding, with a grin, that he guessed she was getting scary and wanted another woman along. So she had dropped everything right where it was.

"Martha!" now came her husband's impatient voice. "Don't keep folks waiting out here in the cold."

She again opened the storm-door, and this time joined the three men and the one woman waiting for her in the big two-seated buggy.

After she had the robes tucked around her she took another look at the woman who sat beside her on the back seat. She had met Mrs. Peters the year before at the county fair, and the thing she remembered about her was that she didn't seem like a sheriff's wife. She was small and thin and didn't have a strong voice. Mrs. Gorman, sheriff's wife before Gorman went out and Peters came in, had a voice that somehow seemed to be backing up the law with every word. But if Mrs. Peters didn't look like a sheriff's wife, Peters made it up in looking like a sheriff. He was to a dot the kind of man who could get himself elected sheriff—a heavy man with a big voice, who was particularly genial with the law-abiding, as if to make it plain that he knew the difference between criminals and non-criminals. And right there it came into Mrs. Hale's mind with a stab, that this man who was so pleasant and lively with all of them was going to the Wrights' now as a sheriff.

"The country's not very pleasant this time of year," Mrs. Peters at last ventured, as if she felt they ought to be talking as well as the men.

Mrs. Hale scarcely finished her reply, for they had gone up a little hill and could see the Wright place now, and seeing it did not make her feel like talking. It looked very lonesome this cold March morning. It had always been a lonesome-looking place. It was down in a hollow, and the poplar trees around it were lonesome-looking trees. The men were looking at it and talking about what had happened. The county attorney was bending to one side of the buggy, and kept looking steadily at the place as they drew up to it.

"I'm glad you came with me," Mrs. Peters said nervously, as the two women were about to follow the men in through the kitchen door.

Even after she had her foot on the doorstep, her hand on the knob, Martha Hale had a moment of feeling she could not cross the threshold. And the reason it seemed she couldn't cross it now was simply because she hadn't crossed it before. Time and time again it had been in her mind, "I ought to go over and see Minnie Foster"—she still thought of her as Minnie Foster, though for twenty years she had been Mrs. Wright. And then there was always something to do and Minnie Foster would go from her mind. But *now* she could come.

The men went over to the stove. The women stood close together by the door. Young Henderson, the county attorney, turned around and said, "Come up to the fire, ladies."

Mrs. Peters took a step forward, then stopped. "I'm not—cold," she said.

And so the two women stood by the door, at first not even so much as looking around the kitchen.

The men talked for a minute about what a good thing it was the sheriff had sent his deputy out that morning to make a fire for them, and then Sheriff Peters stepped back from the stove, unbuttoned his outer coat, and leaned his hands on the kitchen table in a way that seemed to mark the beginning of official business. "Now, Mr. Hale," he said in a sort of semi-official voice, "before we move things about, you tell Mr. Henderson just what it was you saw when you came here yesterday morning."

The county attorney was looking around the kitchen.

"By the way," he said, "has anything been moved?" He turned to the sheriff. "Are things just as you left them yesterday?"

Peters looked from cupboard to sink; from that to a small worn rocker a little to one side of the kitchen table.

"It's just the same."

"Somebody should have been left here yesterday," said the county attorney.

"Oh—yesterday," returned the sheriff, with a little gesture as of yesterday having been more than he could bear to think of. "When I had to send Frank to Morris Center for that man who went crazy—let me tell you, I had my hands full *yesterday*. I knew you could get back from Omaha by today, George, and as long as I went over everything here myself—"

"Well, Mr. Hale," said the county attorney, in a way of letting what was past and gone go, "tell just what happened when you came here yesterday morning."

Mrs. Hale, still leaning against the door, had that sinking feeling of the mother whose child is about to speak a piece. Lewis often wandered along and got things mixed up in a story. She hoped he would tell this straight and plain, and not say unnecessary things that would just make things harder for Minnie Foster. He didn't begin at once, and she noticed that he looked queer—as if standing in that kitchen and having to tell what he had seen there yesterday morning made him almost sick.

"Yes, Mr. Hale?" the county attorney reminded.

"Harry and I had started to town with a load of potatoes," Mrs. Hale's husband began.

Harry was Mrs. Hale's oldest boy. He wasn't with them now, for the very good reason that those potatoes never got to town yesterday and he was taking them this morning, so he hadn't been home when the sheriff stopped to say he wanted Mr. Hale to come over to the Wright place and tell the county attorney his story there, where he could point it all out. With all Mrs. Hale's other emotions came the fear that maybe Harry wasn't dressed warm enough—they hadn't any of them realized how that north wind did bite.

"We come along this road," Hale was going on, with a motion of his hand to the road over which they had just come, "and as we got in sight of the house I says to Harry, 'I'm goin' to see if I can't get John Wright to take a telephone.' You see," he explained to Henderson, "unless I can get somebody to go in with me they won't come out this branch road except for a price *I* can't pay. I'd spoke to Wright about it once before; but he put me off, saying folks talked too much anyway, and all he asked was peace and quiet—guess you know about how much he talked himself. But I thought maybe if I went to the house and talked about it before his wife, and said all the womenfolks liked the telephones, and that in this lonesome stretch of road it would be a good thing —well, I said to Harry that that was what I was going to say— though I said at the same time that I didn't know as what his wife wanted made much difference to John—"

Now, there he was!—saying things he didn't need to say. Mrs. Hale tried to catch her husband's eye, but fortunately the county attorney interrupted with:

"Let's talk about that a little later, Mr. Hale. I do want to talk about that, but I'm anxious now to get along to just what happened when you got here."

When he began this time, it was very deliberately and carefully:

"I didn't see or hear anything. I knocked at the door. And still it was all quiet inside. I knew they must be up—it was past eight o'clock. So I knocked again, louder, and I thought I heard some-body say 'Come in.' I wasn't sure—I'm not sure yet. But I opened the door—this door," jerking a hand toward the door by which the two women stood, "and there, in that rocker"—pointing to it—"sat Mrs. Wright."

Everyone in the kitchen looked at the rocker. It came into Mrs. Hale's mind that that rocker didn't look in the least like Minnie Foster—the Minnie Foster of twenty years before. It was a dingy red, with wooden rungs up the back, and the middle rung was gone, and the chair sagged to one side,

"How did she—look?" the county attorney was inquiring.

"Well," said Hale, "she looked—queer."

"How do you mean—queer?"

As he asked it he took out a notebook and pencil. Mrs. Hale did not like the sight of that pencil. She kept her eye fixed on her husband, as if to keep him from saying unnecessary things that would go into that notebook and make trouble.

Hale did speak guardedly, as if the pencil had affected him too.

"Well, as if she didn't know what she was going to do next. And kind of—done up."

"How did she seem to feel about your coming?"

"Why, I don't think she minded—one way or other. She didn't pay much attention. I said, 'Ho' do, Mrs. Wright? It's cold, ain't it?' And she said, 'Is it?'—and went on pleatin' at her apron.

"Well, I was surprised. She didn't ask me to come up to the stove, or to sit down, but just set there, not even lookin' at me. And so I said: 'I want to see John.'

"And then she—laughed. I guess you would call it a laugh.

"I thought of Harry and the team outside, so I said, a little sharp, 'Can I see John?' 'No,' says she—kind of dull like. 'Ain't he home?' says I. Then she looked at me. 'Yes,' says she, 'he's home.' Then why can't I see him?' I asked her, out of patience with her now. ''Cause he's dead.' says she, just as quiet and dull—and fell to pleatin' her apron. 'Dead?' says I, like you do when you can't take in what you've heard.

"She just nodded her head, not getting a bit excited, but rockin' back and forth.

" 'Why—where is he?' says I, not knowing *what* to say.

"She just pointed upstairs—like this"—pointing to the room above.

"I got up, with the idea of going up there myself. By this time I—didn't know what to do. I walked from there to here; then I says: 'Why, what did he die of?'

" 'He died of a rope around his neck,' says she; and just went on pleatin' at her apron."

Hale stopped speaking, and stood staring at the rocker, as if he were still seeing the woman who had sat there the morning before. Nobody spoke; it was as if everyone were seeing the woman who had sat there the morning before.

"And what did you do then?" the county attorney at last broke the silence.

"I went out and called Harry. I thought I might—need help. I got Harry in, and we went upstairs." His voice fell almost to a whisper. "There he was—lying over the—"

"I think I'd rather have you go into that upstairs," the county attorney interrupted, "where you can point it all out. Just go on now with the rest of the story."

"Well, my first thought was to get that rope off. It looked—" He stopped, his face twitching.

"But Harry, he went up to him, and he said, 'No, he's dead all right, and we'd better not touch anything.' So we went downstairs.

"She was still sitting that same way. 'Has anybody been notified?' I asked. 'No,' says she, unconcerned.

" 'Who did this, Mrs. Wright?' said Harry. He said it businesslike, and she stopped pleatin' at her apron. 'I don't know,' she says. 'You don't *know?*' says Harry. 'Weren't you sleepin' in the bed with him?' 'Yes,' says she, 'but I was on the inside.' 'Somebody slipped a rope round his neck and strangled him, and you didn't wake up?' says Harry. 'I didn't wake up,' she said after him.

"We may have looked as if we didn't see how that could be, for after a minute she said, 'I sleep sound.'

"Harry was going to ask her more questions, but I said maybe that weren't our business; maybe we ought to let her tell her story first to the coroner or the sheriff. So Harry went fast as he could over to High Road—the Rivers' place, where there's a telephone."

"And what did she do when she knew you had gone for the coroner?" The attorney got his pencil in his hand all ready for writing.

"She moved from that chair to this one over here"—Hale pointed to a small chair in the corner—"and just sat there with her hands held together and looking down. I got a feeling that I ought to make some conversation, so I said I had come in to see if John wanted to put in a telephone: and at that she started to laugh, and then she stopped and looked at me—scared."

At the sound of a moving pencil the man who was telling the story looked up.

"I dunno—maybe it wasn't scared," he hastened; "I wouldn't like to say it was. Soon Harry got back, and then Dr. Lloyd came, and you, Mr. Peters, and so I guess that's all I know that you don't."

He said that last with relief, and moved a little, as if relaxing. Everyone moved a little. The county attorney walked toward the stair door.

"I guess we'll go upstairs first—then out to the barn and around there."

He paused and looked around the kitchen.

"You're convinced there was nothing important here?" he asked the sheriff. "Nothing that would—point to any motive?"

The sheriff too looked all around, as if to reconvince himself.

"Nothing here but kitchen things," he said, with a little laugh for the insignificance of kitchen things.

The county attorney was looking at the cupboard—a peculiar, ungainly structure, half closet and half cupboard, the upper part of it being built in the wall, and the lower part just the old-fashioned kitchen cupboard. As if its queerness attracted him, he got a chair and opened the upper part and looked in. After a moment he drew his hand away sticky.

"Here's a nice mess," he said resentfully.

The two women had drawn nearer, and now the sheriff's wife spoke.

"Oh—her fruit," she said, looking to Mrs. Hale for sympathetic understanding. She turned back to the county attorney and explained: "She worried about that when it turned to cold last night. She said the fire would go out and her jars might burst."

Mrs. Peters's husband broke into a laugh.

"Well, can you beat the woman! Held for murder, and worrying about her preserves!"

The young attorney set his lips.

"I guess before we're through with her she may have something more serious than preserves to worry about."

"Oh, well," said Mrs. Hale's husband, with good-natured superiority, "women are used to worrying over trifles."

The two women moved a little closer together. Neither of them spoke. The county attorney seemed suddenly to remember his manners—and think of his future.

"And yet," said he, with the gallantry of a young politician, "for all their worries, what would we do without the ladies?"

The women did not speak, did not unbend. He went to the sink and began washing his hands. He turned to wipe them on the roller towel—whirled it for a cleaner place.

"Dirty towels! Not much of a housekeeper, would you say, ladies?"

He kicked his foot against some dirty pans under the sink.

"There's a great deal of work to be done on a farm," said Mrs. Hale stiffly.

"To be sure. And yet"—with a little bow to her—"I know there are some Dickson County farmhouses that do not have such roller towels." He gave it a pull to expose its full length again.

"Those towels get dirty awful quick. Men's hands aren't always as clean as they might be."

"Ah, loyal to your sex, I see," he laughed. He stopped and gave her a keen look. "But you and Mrs. Wright were neighbors. I suppose you were friends, too."

Martha Hale shook her head.

"I've seen little enough of her of late years. I've not been in this house—it's more than a year."

"And why was that? You didn't like her?"

"I liked her well enough," she replied with spirit. "Farmers' wives have their hands full, Mr. Henderson. And then"—She looked around the kitchen.

"Yes?" he encouraged.

"It never seemed a very cheerful place," said she, more to herself than to him.

"No," he agreed; "I don't think anyone could call it cheerful. I shouldn't say she had the homemaking instinct."

"Well, I don't know as Wright had, either," she muttered.

"You mean they didn't get on very well?" he was quick to ask.

"No; I don't mean anything," she answered, with decision. As she turned a little away from him, she added: "But I don't think a place would be any the cheerfuler for John Wright's bein' in it."

"I'd like to talk to you about that a little later, Mrs. Hale," he said. "I'm anxious to get the lay of things upstairs now."

He moved toward the stair door, followed by the two men.

"I suppose anything Mrs. Peters does'll be all right?" the sheriff inquired. "She was to take in some clothes for her, you know—and a few little things. We left in such a hurry yesterday."

The county attorney looked at the two women whom they were leaving alone there among the kitchen things.

"Yes—Mrs. Peters," he said, his glance resting on the woman who was not Mrs. Peters, the big farmer woman who stood behind the sheriff's wife. "Of course Mrs. Peters is one of us," he said, in a manner of entrusting responsibility. "And keep your eye out, Mrs. Peters, for anything that might be of use. No telling; you women might come upon a clue to the motive—and that's the thing we need."

Mr. Hale rubbed his face after the fashion of a show man getting ready for a pleasantry.

"But would the women know a clue if they did come upon it?" he said; and, having delivered himself of this, he followed the others through the stair door.

The women stood motionless and silent, listening to the footsteps, first upon the stairs, then in the room above them.

Then, as if releasing herself from something strange, Mrs. Hale began to arrange the dirty pans under the sink, which the county attorney's disdainful push of the foot had deranged.

"I'd hate to have men comin' into my kitchen," she said testily—"snoopin' around and criticizin'."

"Of course it's no more than their duty," said the sheriff's wife, in her manner of timid acquiescence.

"Duty's all right," replied Mrs. Hale bluffly; "but I guess that deputy sheriff that come out to make the fire might have got a little of this on." She gave the roller towel a pull. "Wish I'd thought of that sooner! Seems mean to talk about her for not having things slicked up when she had to come away in such a hurry."

She looked around the kitchen. Certainly it was not "slicked up." Her eye was held by a bucket of sugar on a low shelf. The cover was off the wooden bucket, and beside it was a paper bag—half full.

Mrs. Hale moved toward it.

"She was putting this in here," she said to herself—slowly.

She thought of the flour in her kitchen at home—half sifted, half not sifted. She had been interrupted, and had left things half done. What had interrupted Minnie Foster? Why had that work been left half done? She made a move as if to finish it,— unfinished things always bothered her,—and then she glanced around and saw that Mrs. Peters was watching her—and she didn't want Mrs. Peters to get that feeling she had got of work begun and then—for some reason—not finished.

"It's a shame about her fruit," she said, and walked toward the cupboard that the county attorney had opened, and got on the chair, murmuring: "I wonder if it's all gone."

It was a sorry enough looking sight, but "Here's one that's all right," she said at last. She held it toward the light. "This is cherries, too." She looked again. "I declare I believe that's the only one."

With a sigh, she got down from the chair, went to the sink, and wiped off the bottle.

"She'll feel awful bad, after all her hard work in the hot weather. I remember the afternoon I put up my cherries last summer."

She set the bottle on the table, and, with another sigh, started to sit down in the rocker. But she did not sit down. Something kept her from sitting down in that chair. She straightened—stepped back, and, half turned away, stood looking at it, seeing the woman who sat there "pleatin' at her apron."

The thin voice of the sheriff's wife broke in upon her: "I must be getting those things from the front room closet." She opened the door into the other room, started in, stepped back. "You coming with me, Mrs. Hale?" she asked nervously. "You—you could help me get them."

They were soon back—the stark coldness of that shut-up room was not a thing to linger in.

"My!" said Mrs. Peters, dropping the things on the table and hurrying to the stove.

Mrs. Hale stood examining the clothes the woman who was being detained in town had said she wanted.

"Wright was close!" she exclaimed, holding up a shabby black skirt that bore the marks of much making over. "I think maybe that's why she kept so much to herself. I s'pose she felt she couldn't do her part; and then, you don't enjoy things when you feel shabby. She used to wear pretty clothes and be lively—when she was Minnie Foster, one of the town girls, singing in the choir. But that—oh, that was twenty years ago."

With a carefulness in which there was something tender, she folded the shabby clothes and piled them at one corner of the table. She looked at Mrs. Peters, and there was something in the other woman's look that irritated her.

"She don't care," she said to herself. "Much difference it makes to her whether Minnie Foster had pretty clothes when she was a girl."

Then she looked again, and she wasn't so sure; in fact, she hadn't at any time been perfectly sure about Mrs. Peters. She had that shrinking manner, and yet her eyes looked as if they could see a long way into things.

"This all you was to take in?" asked Mrs. Hale.

"No," said the sheriff's wife; "she said she wanted an apron. Funny thing to want," she ventured in her nervous little way, "for there's not much to get you dirty in jail, goodness knows. But I suppose just to make her feel more natural. If you're used to wearing an apron . . . She said they were in the bottom drawer of this cupboard. Yes—here they are. And then her little shawl that always hung on the stair door."

She took the small gray shawl from behind the door leading upstairs, and stood a minute looking at it.

Suddenly Mrs. Hale took a quick step toward the other woman. "Mrs. Peters!"

"Yes, Mrs. Hale?"

"Do you think she—did it?"

A frightened look blurred the other things in Mrs. Peters's eyes.

"Oh, I don't know," she said, in a voice that seemed to shrink away from the subject.

"Well, I don't think she did," affirmed Mrs. Hale stoutly. "Asking for an apron, and her little shawl. Worryin' about her fruit."

"Mr. Peters says—" Footsteps were heard in the room above; she stopped, looked up, then went on in a lowered voice: "Mr. Peters says—it looks bad for her. Mr. Henderson is awful sarcastic in a speech, and he's going to make fun of her saying she didn't—wake up."

For a moment Mrs. Hale had no answer. Then, "Well, I guess John Wright didn't wake up—when they was slippin' that rope under his neck," she muttered.

"No, it's *strange*," breathed Mrs. Peters. "They think it was such a—funny way to kill a man."

She began to laugh; at the sound of the laugh, abruptly stopped.

"That's just what Mr. Hale said," said Mrs. Hale, in a resolutely natural voice. "There was a gun in the house. He says that's what he can't understand."

"Mr. Henderson said, coming out, that what was needed for the case was a motive. Something to show anger—or sudden feeling."

"Well, I don't see any signs of anger around here," said Mrs. Hale. "I don't—"

She stopped. It was as if her mind tripped on something. Her eye was caught by a dish-towel in the middle of the kitchen table. Slowly she moved toward the table. One half of it was wiped clean, the other half messy. Her eyes made a slow, almost unwilling turn to the bucket of sugar and the half empty bag beside it. Things begun—and not finished.

After a moment she stepped back, and said, in that manner of releasing herself:

"Wonder how they're finding things upstairs? I hope she had it a little more red up up there. You know"—she paused, and feeling gathered—"it seems kind of *sneaking*; locking her up in town and coming out here to get her own house to turn against her!"

"But, Mrs. Hale," said the sheriff's wife, "the law is the law."

"I s'pose 'tis," answered Mrs. Hale shortly.

She turned to the stove, saying something about that fire not being much to brag of. She worked with it a minute, and when she straightened up she said aggressively:

"The law is the law—and a bad stove is a bad stove. How'd you like to cook on this?"—pointing with the poker to the broken lining. She opened the oven door and started to express her opinion of the oven; but she was swept into her own thoughts, thinking of what it would mean, year after year, to have that stove to wrestle with. The thought of Minnie Foster trying to bake in that oven—and the thought of her never going over to see Minnie Foster—

She was startled by hearing Mrs. Peters say: "A person gets discouraged—and loses heart."

The sheriff's wife had looked from the stove to the sink—to the pail of water which had been carried in from outside. The two women stood there silent, above them the footsteps of the men who were looking for evidence against the woman who had worked in that kitchen. That look of seeing into things, of seeing through a thing to something else, was in the eyes of the sheriff's wife now. When Mrs. Hale next spoke to her, it was gently:

"Better loosen up your things, Mrs. Peters. We'll not feel them when we go out."

Mrs. Peters went to the back of the room to hang up the fur tippet she was wearing. A moment later she exclaimed, "Why, she was piecing a quilt," and held up a large sewing basket piled high with quilt pieces.

Mrs. Hale spread some of the blocks on the table.

"It's log-cabin pattern," she said, putting several of them together. "Pretty, isn't it?"

They were so engaged with the quilt that they did not hear the footsteps on the stairs. Just as the stair door opened Mrs. Hale was saying:

"Do you suppose she was going to quilt it or just knot it?"

The sheriff threw up his hands.

"They wonder whether she was going to quilt it or just knot it!"

There was a laugh for the ways of women, a warming of hands over the stove, and then the county attorney said briskly:

"Well, let's go right out to the barn and get that cleared up."

"I don't see as there's anything so strange," Mrs. Hale said resentfully, after the outside door had closed on the three men—

"our taking up our time with little things while we're waiting for them to get the evidence. I don't see as it's anything to laugh about."

"Of course they've got awful important things on their minds," said the sheriff's wife apologetically.

They returned to an inspection of the blocks for the quilt. Mrs. Hale was looking at the fine, even sewing, and preoccupied with thoughts of the woman who had done that sewing, when she heard the sheriff's wife say, in a queer tone:

"Why, look at this one."

She turned to take the block held out to her.

"The sewing," said Mrs. Peters, in a troubled way. "All the rest of them have been so nice and even—but—this one. Why, it looks as if she didn't know what she was about!"

Their eyes met—something flashed to life, passed between them; then, as if with an effort, they seemed to pull away from each other. A moment Mrs. Hale sat there, her hands folded over that sewing which was so unlike all the rest of the sewing. Then she had pulled a knot and drawn the threads.

"Oh, what are you doing, Mrs. Hale?" asked the sheriff's wife, startled.

"Just pulling out a stitch or two that's not sewed very good," said Mrs. Hale mildly.

"I don't think we ought to touch things," Mrs. Peters said, a little helplessly.

"I'll just finish up this end," answered Mrs. Hale, still in that mild, matter-of-fact fashion.

She threaded a needle and started to replace bad sewing with good. For a little while she sewed in silence. Then, in that thin, timid voice, she heard:

"Mrs. Hale!"

"Yes, Mrs. Peters?"

"What do you suppose she was so—nervous about?"

"Oh, *I* don't know," said Mrs. Hale, as if dismissing a thing not important enough to spend much time on. "I don't know as she was—nervous. I sew awful queer sometimes when I'm just tired."

She cut a thread, and out of the corner of her eye looked up at Mrs. Peters. The small, lean face of the sheriff's wife seemed to have tightened up. Her eyes had that look of peering into something. But the next moment she moved, and said in her thin, indecisive way:

"Well, I must get those clothes wrapped. They may be through sooner than we think. I wonder where I could find a piece of paper—and string."

"In that cupboard, maybe," suggested Mrs. Hale, after a glance around.

One piece of the crazy sewing remained unripped. Mrs. Peters's back turned, Martha Hale now scrutinized that piece, compared it with the dainty, accurate sewing of the other blocks. The difference was startling. Holding this block made her feel queer, as if the distracted thoughts of the woman who had perhaps turned to it to try and quiet herself were communicating themselves to her.

Mrs. Peters's voice roused her.

"Here's a birdcage," she said. "Did she have a bird, Mrs. Hale?"

"Why, I don't know whether she did or not." She turned to look at the cage Mrs. Peters was holding up. "I've not been here in so long." She sighed. "There was a man round last year selling canaries cheap—but I don't know as she took one. Maybe she did. She used to sing real pretty herself."

Mrs. Peters looked around the kitchen.

"Seems kind of funny to think of a bird here." She half laughed—an attempt to put up a barrier. "But she must have had one—or why would she have a cage? I wonder what happened to it."

"I suppose maybe the cat got it," suggested Mrs. Hale, resuming her sewing.

"No, she didn't have a cat. She's got that feeling some people have about cats—being afraid of them. When they brought her to our house yesterday, my cat got in the room, and she was real upset and asked me to take it out."

"My sister Bessie was like that," laughed Mrs. Hale.

The sheriff's wife did not reply. The silence made Mrs. Hale turn around. Mrs. Peters was examining the birdcage.

"Look at this door," she said slowly. "It's broke. One hinge has been pulled apart."

Mrs. Hale came nearer.

"Looks as if some one must have been—rough with it."

Again their eyes met—startled, questioning, apprehensive. For a moment neither spoke nor stirred. Then Mrs. Hale, turning away, said brusquely:

"If they're going to find any evidence, I wish they'd be about it. I don't like this place."

"But I'm awful glad you came with me, Mrs. Hale." Mrs. Peters put the birdcage on the table and sat down. "It would be lonesome for me—sitting here alone."

"Yes, it would, wouldn't it?" agreed Mrs. Hale, a certain determined naturalness in her voice. She picked up the sewing, but now it dropped in her lap, and she murmured in a different voice: "But I tell you what I *do* wish, Mrs. Peters. I wish I had come over sometimes when she was here. I wish—I had."

"But of course you were awful busy, Mrs. Hale. Your house—and your children."

"I could've come," retorted Mrs. Hale shortly. "I stayed away because it weren't cheerful—and that's why I ought to have come. I"—she looked around—"I've never liked this place. Maybe because it's down in a hollow and you don't see the road. I don't know what it is, but it's a lonesome place, and always was. I wish I had come over to see Minnie Foster sometimes. I can see now—" She did not put it into words.

"Well, you mustn't reproach yourself," counseled Mrs. Peters. "Somehow, we just don't see how it is with other folks till—something comes up."

"Not having children makes less work," mused Mrs. Hale, after a silence, "but it makes a quiet house—and Wright out to work all day—and no company when he did come in. Did you know John Wright, Mrs. Peters?"

"Not to know him. I've seen him in town. They say he was a good man."

"Yes—good," conceded John Wright's neighbor grimly. "He didn't drink, and kept his word as well as most, I guess, and paid his debts. But he was a hard man, Mrs. Peters. Just to pass the time of day with him—" She stopped, shivered a little. "Like a raw wind that gets to the bone." Her eye fell upon the cage on the table before her, and she added, almost bitterly: "I should think she would've wanted a bird!"

Suddenly she leaned forward, looking intently at the cage. "But what do you s'pose went wrong with it?"

"I don't know," returned Mrs. Peters; "unless it got sick and died."

But after she said it she reached over and swung the broken door. Both women watched it as if somehow held by it.

"You didn't know—her?" Mrs. Hale asked, a gentler note in her voice.

"Not till they brought her yesterday," said the sheriff's wife.

"She—come to think of it, she was kind of like a bird herself. Real sweet and pretty, but kind of timid and—fluttery. How—she—did—change."

That held her for a long time. Finally, as if struck with a happy thought and relieved to get back to everyday things, she exclaimed:

"Tell you what, Mrs. Peters, why don't you take the quilt in with you? It might take up her mind."

"Why, I think that's a real nice idea, Mrs. Hale," agreed the sheriff's wife, as if she too were glad to come into the atmosphere of a simple kindness. "There couldn't possibly be any objection to that, could there? Now, just what will I take? I wonder if her patches are in here—and her things."

They turned to the sewing basket.

"Here's some red," said Mrs. Hale, bringing out a roll of cloth. Underneath that was a box. "Here, maybe her scissors are in here—and her things." She held it up. "What a pretty box! I'll warrant that was something she had a long time ago—when she was a girl."

She held it in her hand a moment; then, with a little sigh, opened it.

Instantly her hand went to her nose.

"Why—!"

Mrs. Peters drew nearer—then turned away.

"There's something wrapped up in this piece of silk," faltered Mrs. Hale.

"This isn't her scissors," said Mrs. Peters in a shrinking voice.

Her hand not steady, Mrs. Hale raised the piece of silk. "Oh, Mrs. Peters!" she cried. "It's—"

Mrs. Peters bent closer.

"It's the bird," she whispered.

"But, Mrs. Peters!" cried Mrs. Hale. "*Look* at it! Its neck—look at its neck! It's all—other side *to*."

She held the box away from her.

The sheriff's wife again bent closer.

"Somebody wrung its neck," said she, in a voice that was slow and deep.

And then again the eyes of the two women met—this time clung together in a look of dawning comprehension, of growing horror. Mrs. Peters looked from the dead bird to the broken door of the cage. Again their eyes met. And just then there was a sound at the outside door.

Mrs. Hale slipped the box under the quilt pieces in the basket, and sank into the chair before it. Mrs. Peters stood holding to the table. The county attorney and the sheriff came in from outside.

"Well, ladies," said the county attorney, as one turning from serious things to little pleasantries, "have you decided whether she was going to quilt it or knot it?"

"We think," began the sheriff's wife in a flurried voice, "that she was going to—knot it."

He was too preoccupied to notice the change that came in her voice on that last.

"Well, that's very interesting, I'm sure," he said tolerantly. He caught sight of the birdcage. "Has the bird flown?"

"We think the cat got it," said Mrs. Hale in a voice curiously even.

He was walking up and down, as if thinking something out.

"Is there a cat?" he asked absently.

Mrs. Hale shot a look up at the sheriff's wife.

"Well, not *now*," said Mrs. Peters. "They're superstitious, you know; they leave."

She sank into her chair.

The county attorney did not heed her. "No sign at all of any one having come in from the outside," he said to Peters, in the manner of continuing an interrupted conversation. "Their own rope. Now let's go upstairs again and go over it, piece by piece. It would have to have been some one who knew just the—"

The stair door closed behind them and their voices were lost.

The two women sat motionless, not looking at each other, but as if peering into something and at the same time holding back. When they spoke now it was as if they were afraid of what they were saying, but as if they could not help saying it.

"She liked the bird," said Martha Hale, low and slowly. "She was going to bury it in that pretty box."

"When I was a girl," said Mrs. Peters, under her breath, "my kitten—there was a boy took a hatchet, and before my eyes— before I could get there—" She covered her face an instant. "If they hadn't held me back I would have"—she caught herself, looked upstairs where footsteps were heard, and finished weakly—"hurt him."

Then they sat without speaking or moving.

"I wonder how it would seem," Mrs. Hale at last began, as if feeling her way over strange ground—"never to have had any children around?" Her eyes made a slow sweep of the kitchen, as if seeing what that kitchen had meant through all the years. "No, Wright wouldn't like the bird," she said after that—"a thing that sang. She used to sing. He killed that too." Her voice tightened.

Mrs. Peters moved uneasily.

"Of course we don't know who killed the bird."

"I knew John Wright," was Mrs. Hale's answer.

"It was an awful thing was done in this house that night, Mrs. Hale," said the sheriff's wife. "Killing a man while he slept—slipping a thing round his neck that choked the life out of him."

Mrs. Hale's hand went out to the birdcage.

"His neck. Choked the life out of him."

"We don't *know* who killed him," whispered Mrs. Peters wildly. "We don't *know*."

Mrs. Hale had not moved. "If there had been years and years of—nothing, then a bird to sing to you, it would be awful—still—after the bird was still."

It was as if something within her not herself had spoken, and it found in Mrs. Peters something she did not know as herself.

"I know what stillness is," she said, in a queer, monotonous voice. "When we homesteaded in Dakota, and my first baby died—after he was two years old—and me with no other then—"

Mrs. Hale stirred.

"How soon do you suppose they'll be through looking for evidence?"

"I know what stillness is," repeated Mrs. Peters, in just that same way. Then she too pulled back. "The law has got to punish crime, Mrs. Hale," she said in her tight little way.

"I wish you'd seen Minnie Foster," was the answer, "when she wore a white dress with blue ribbons, and stood up there in the choir and sang."

The picture of that girl, the fact that she had lived neighbor to that girl for twenty years, and had let her die for lack of life, was suddenly more than she could bear.

"Oh, I *wish* I'd come over here once in a while!" she cried. "That was a crime! That was a crime! Who's going to punish that?"

"We mustn't take on," said Mrs. Peters, with a frightened look toward the stairs.

"I might 'a' *known* she needed help! I tell you, it's *queer*, Mrs. Peters. We live close together, and we live far apart. We all go through the same things—it's all just a different kind of the same thing! If it weren't—why do you and I *understand?* Why do we *know*—what we know this minute?"

She dashed her hand across her eyes. Then, seeing the jar of fruit on the table, she reached for it and choked out:

"If I was you I wouldn't *tell* her her fruit was gone! Tell her it *ain't.* Tell her it's all right—all of it. Here—take this in to prove it to her! She—she may never know whether it was broke or not."

She turned away.

Mrs. Peters reached out for the bottle of fruit as if she were glad to take it—as if touching a familiar thing, having something to do, could keep her from something else. She got up, looked about for something to wrap the fruit in, took a petticoat from the pile of clothes she had brought from the front room, and nervously started winding that round the bottle.

"My!" she began in a high, false voice, "it's a good thing the men couldn't hear us! Getting all stirred up over a little thing like a—dead canary." She hurried over that. "As if that could have anything to do with—with—my, wouldn't they *laugh?*"

Footsteps were heard on the stairs.

"Maybe they would," muttered Mrs. Hale—"maybe they wouldn't."

"No, Peters," said the county attorney incisively: "it's all perfectly clear, except the reason for doing it. But you know juries when it comes to women. If there was some definite thing— something to show. Something to make a story about. A thing that would connect up with this clumsy way of doing it."

In a covert way Mrs. Hale looked at Mrs. Peters. Mrs. Peters was looking at her. Quickly they looked away from each other. The outer door opened and Mr. Hale came in.

"I've got the team round now," he said. "Pretty cold out there."

"I'm going to stay here awhile by myself," the county attorney suddenly announced. "You can send Frank out for me, can't you?" he asked the sheriff. "I want to go over everything. I'm not satisfied we can't do better."

Again, for one brief moment, the two women's eyes found one another.

The sheriff came up to the table.

"Did you want to see what Mrs. Peters was going to take in?"

The county attorney picked up the apron. He laughed.

"Oh, I guess they're not very dangerous things the ladies have picked out."

Mrs. Hale's hand was on the sewing basket in which the box was concealed. She felt that she ought to take her hand off the basket. She did not seem able to. He picked up one of the quilt blocks which she had piled on to cover the box. Her eyes felt like fire. She had a feeling that if he took up the basket she would snatch it from him.

But he did not take it up. With another little laugh, he turned away, saying:

"No; Mrs. Peters doesn't need supervising. For that matter, a sheriff's wife is married to the law. Ever think of it that way, Mrs. Peters?"

Mrs. Peters was standing beside the table. Mrs. Hale shot a look up at her; but she could not see her face. Mrs. Peters had turned away. When she spoke, her voice was muffled.

"Not—just that way," she said.

"Married to the law!" chuckled Mrs. Peters's husband. He moved toward the door into the front room, and said to the county attorney:

"I just want you to come in here a minute, George. We ought to take a look at these windows."

"Oh—windows," said the county attorney scoffingly.

"We'll be right out, Mr. Hale," said the sheriff to the farmer, who was still waiting by the door.

Hale went to look after the horses. The sheriff followed the county attorney into the other room. Again—for one moment—the two women were alone in that kitchen.

Martha Hale sprang up, her hands tight together, looking at that other woman, with whom it rested. At first she could not see her eyes, for the sheriff's wife had not turned back since she turned away at that suggestion of being married to the law. But now Mrs. Hale made her turn back. Her eyes made her turn back. Slowly, unwillingly, Mrs. Peters turned her head until her eyes met the eyes of the other woman. There was a moment when they held each other in a steady, burning look in which there was no evasion nor flinching. Then Martha Hale's eyes pointed the way to the basket in which was hidden the thing that would make certain the conviction of the other woman—that woman who was not there and yet who had been there with them all through the hour.

For a moment Mrs. Peters did not move. And then she did it. With a rush forward, she threw back the quilt pieces, got the box, tried to put in in her handbag. It was too big. Desperately she opened it, started to take the bird out. But there she broke—she could not touch the bird. She stood helpless, foolish.

There was a sound of a knob turning in the inner door. Martha Hale snatched the box from the sheriff's wife, and got it in the pocket of her big coat just as the sheriff and the county attorney came back into the kitchen.

"Well, Henry," said the county attorney facetiously, "at least we found out that she was not going to quilt it. She was going to—what is it you call it, ladies?"

Mrs. Hale's hand was against the pocket of her coat.

"We call it—knot it, Mr. Henderson."

The Man Who Knew How

DOROTHY L. SAYERS

Dorothy Leigh Sayers (1893–1957) is one of the most remarkable and influential figures in crime fiction history. Born in Oxford and a graduate of Somerville College, Oxford, she was a language teacher, publisher's reader, and advertising copywriter before becoming a full-time writer. In *Whose Body?* (1923), she introduced one of the most famous gentleman detectives in literature, Lord Peter Wimsey, a somewhat Wodehousian character, affected in speech and manner with pronounced "silly ass" tendencies, who would become a much deeper and more fully developed figure as his career went on. In *Strong Poison* (1930), Wimsey met novelist Harriet Vane, whom he would save from a charge of murder, then (in reckless disregard of the rules against romance in Golden Age detective novels) woo through several novels, including the academic classic *Gaudy Night* (1935), and finally wed in *Busman's Honeymoon* (1937), the final detective novel completed by Sayers. (The fragmentary *Thrones, Dominations* would be completed with remarkable fidelity many years later by Jill Paton Walsh and published under their joint byline in 1998.)

Sayers, who became a feminist icon in the 1970s, in part because of the independence she personified in her own life and in part because of her creation of Harriet Vane, has been the subject of more biographical works and critical analyses than any Golden Age of Detection figure save Agatha Christie, and certainly few equaled her in her devotion to the games-playing elements of the detective story. However, she left detective fiction in the latter part of her life in favor of other literary pursuits, including some highly regarded religious plays and a translation of Dante.

Though Dorothy L. Sayers wrote a number of short stories about Lord Peter Wimsey, her best shorter works tend to be those without a series detective. In "The Man Who Knew How," Sayers is able to comment wittily on her detective fiction speciality while developing a situation that could as easily have taken the title of another of her best short stories: "Suspicion." "The Man Who Knew How" is the sort of crime story ideally suited to radio adaptation, as it was in a memorable *Suspense* broadcast starring Charles Laughton as Pender, with Hans Conreid in the title role.

For the twentieth time since the train had left Carlisle, Pender glanced up from *Murder at the Manse* and caught the eye of the man opposite.

He frowned a little. It was irritating to be watched so closely, and always with that faint, sardonic smile. It was still more irritating to allow oneself to be so much disturbed by the smile and the scrutiny. Pender wrenched himself back to his book with a determination to concentrate upon the problem of the minister murdered in the library.

But the story was of the academic kind that crowds all its exciting incidents into the first chapter, and proceeds thereafter by a long series of deductions to a scientific solution in the last. Twice Pender had to turn back to verify points that he had missed in reading. Then he became aware that he was not thinking about the murdered minister at all—he was becoming more and more actively conscious of the other man's face. A queer face, Pender thought.

There was nothing especially remarkable about the features in themselves; it was their expression that daunted Pender. It was a secret face, the face of one who knew a great deal to other people's disadvantage. The mouth was a little crooked and tightly tucked in at the corners, as though savoring a hidden amusement. The eyes, behind a pair of rimless pince-nez, glittered curiously; but that was possibly due to the light reflected in the glasses. Pender wondered what the man's profession might be. He was dressed in a dark lounge suit, a raincoat and a shabby soft hat; his age was perhaps about forty.

Pender coughed unneccessarily and settled back into his

corner, raising the detective story high before his face, barrier-fashion. This was worse than useless. He gained the impression that the man saw through the maneuver and was secretly entertained by it. He wanted to fidget, but felt obscurely that his doing so would in some way constitute a victory for the other man. In his self-consciousness he held himself so rigid that attention to his book became a sheer physical impossibility.

There was no stop now before Rugby, and it was unlikely that any passenger would enter from the corridor to break up this disagreeable *solitude à deux*. Pender could, of course, go out into the corridor and not return, but that would be an acknowledgment of defeat. Pender lowered *Murder at the Manse* and caught the man's eye again.

"Getting tired of it?" asked the man.

"Night journeys are always a bit tedious," replied Pender, half relieved and half reluctant. "Would you like a book?"

He took *The Paper-Clip Clue* from his briefcase and held it out hopefully. The other man glanced at the title and shook his head.

"Thanks very much," he said, "but I never read detective stories. They're so—inadequate, don't you think so?"

"They are rather lacking in characterization and human interest, certainly," said Pender, "but on a railway journey—"

"I don't mean that," said the other man. "I am not concerned with humanity. But all these murderers are so incompetent—they bore me."

"Oh, I don't know," replied Pender. "At any rate they are usually a good deal more imaginative and ingenious than murderers in real life."

"Than the murderers who are found out in real life, yes," admitted the other man.

"Even some of those did pretty well before they got pinched," objected Pender. "Crippen, for instance; he need never have been caught if he hadn't lost his head and run off to America. George Joseph Smith did away with at least two brides quite successfully before fate and the *News of the World* intervened."

"Yes," said the other man, "but look at the clumsiness of it all; the elaboration, the lies, the paraphernalia. Absolutely unnecessary."

"Oh come!" said Pender. "You can't expect committing a murder and getting away with it to be as simple as shelling peas."

"Ah!" said the other man. "You think that, do you?"

Pender waited for him to elaborate this remark, but nothing came of it. The man leaned back and smiled in his secret way at the roof of the carriage; he appeared to think the conversation not worth going on with. Pender found himself noticing his companion's hands. They were white and surprisingly long in the fingers. He watched them gently tapping upon their owner's knee—then resolutely turned a page—then put the book down once more and said:

"Well, if it's so easy, how would *you* set about committing a murder?"

"I?" repeated the man. The light on his glasses made his eyes quite blank to Pender, but his voice sounded gently amused. "That's different; *I* should not have to think twice about it."

"Why not?"

"Because I happen to know how to do it."

"Do you indeed?" muttered Pender, rebelliously.

"Oh yes; there's nothing to it."

"How can you be sure? You haven't tried, I suppose?"

"It isn't a case of trying," said the man. "There's nothing uncertain about my method. That's just the beauty of it."

"It's easy to say that," retorted Pender, "but what *is* this wonderful method?"

"You can't expect me to tell you that, can you?" said the other man, bringing his eyes back to rest on Pender's. "It might not be safe. You look harmless enough, but who could look more harmless than Crippen? Nobody is fit to be trusted with *absolute* control over other people's lives."

"Bosh!" exclaimed Pender. "I shouldn't think of murdering anybody."

31

"Oh yes you would," said the other man, "if you really believed it was safe. So would anybody. Why are all these tremendous artificial barriers built up around murder by the Church and the law? Just because it's everybody's crime and just as natural as breathing."

"But that's ridiculous!" cried Pender, warmly.

"You think so, do you? That's what most people would say. But I wouldn't trust 'em. Not with sulphate of thanatol to be bought for two pence at any chemist's."

"Sulphate of what?" asked Pender sharply.

"Ah! you think I'm giving something away. Well, it's a mixture of that and one or two other things—all equally ordinary and cheap. For nine pence you could make up enough to poison the entire Cabinet. Though of course one wouldn't polish off the whole lot at once; it might look funny if they all died simultaneously in their baths."

"Why in their baths?"

"That's the way it would take them. It's the action of the hot water that brings on the effect of the stuff, you see. Any time from a few hours to a few days after administration. It's quite a simple chemical reaction and it couldn't possibly be detected by analysis. It would just look like heart failure."

Pender eyed him uneasily. He did not like the smile; it was not only derisive, it was smug, it was almost gloating, triumphant! He could not quite put the right name to it.

"You know," pursued the man, pulling a pipe from his pocket and beginning to fill it, "it is very odd how often one seems to read of people being found dead in their baths. It must be a very common accident. Quite temptingly so. After all, there is a fascination about murder. The thing grows upon one—that is, I imagine it would, you know."

"Very likely," said Pender.

"I'm sure of it. No, I wouldn't trust anybody with that formula—not even a virtuous young man like yourself."

The long white fingers tamped the tobacco firmly into the bowl and struck a match.

"But how about you?" said Pender, irritated. (Nobody cares to be called a virtuous young man.) "If nobody is fit to be trusted—"

"I'm not, eh?" replied the man. "Well, that's true, but it can't be helped now, can it? I know the thing and I can't unknow it again. It's unfortunate, but there it is. At any rate you have the comfort of knowing that nothing disagreeable is likely to happen to *me*. Dear me! Rugby already. I get out here. I have a little bit of business to do at Rugby."

He rose and shook himself, buttoned his raincoat about him, and pulled the shabby hat more firmly down about his enigmatic glasses. The train slowed down and stopped. With a brief good night and a crooked smile the man stepped onto the platform. Pender watched him stride quickly away into the drizzle beyond the radius of the gas light.

"Dotty or something," said Pender, oddly relieved. "Thank goodness, I seem to be going to have the compartment to myself."

He returned to *Murder at the Manse*, but his attention still kept wandering from the book he held in his hand.

"What was the name of that stuff the fellow talked about? Sulphate of what?"

For the life of him he could not remember.

It was on the following afternoon that Pender saw the news item. He had bought the *Standard* to read at lunch, and the word "Bath" caught his eye; otherwise he would probably have missed the paragraph altogether, for it was only a short one.

WEALTHY MANUFACTURER DIES IN BATH
WIFE'S TRAGIC DISCOVERY

A distressing discovery was made early this morning by Mrs. John Brittlesea, wife of the well-known head of Brittlesea's Engineering Works at Rugby. Finding that her husband, whom she had seen alive and well less than an hour previously, did not come down in time for his breakfast, she searched for him in the bathroom, where the engineer was found lying dead in his bath; life having been extinct, according to the medical men, for half an hour. The cause of the death is pronounced to be heart failure. The deceased manufacturer . . .

"That's an odd coincidence," said Pender. "At Rugby. I should think my unknown friend would be interested—if he is still there, doing his bit of business. I wonder what his business is, by the way."

It is a very curious thing how, when once your attention is attracted to any particular set of circumstances, that set of circumstances seems to haunt you. You get appendicitis: immediately the newspapers are filled with paragraphs about statesmen suffering from appendicitis and victims dying of it; you learn that all your acquaintances have had it, or know friends who have had it and either died of it, or recovered from it with more surprising and spectacular rapidity than yourself; you cannot open a popular magazine without seeing its cure mentioned as one of the triumphs of modern surgery, or dip into a scientific treatise without coming across a comparison of the vermiform appendix in men and monkeys. Probably these references to appendicitis are equally frequent at all times, but you only notice them when your mind is attuned to the subject. At any rate, it was in this way that Pender accounted to himself for the extraordinary frequency with which people seemed to die in their baths at this period.

The thing pursued him at every turn. Always the same sequence of events: the hot bath, the discovery of the corpse, the inquest. Always the same medical opinion: heart failure following immersion in too hot water. It began to seem to Pender that it was scarcely safe to enter a hot bath at all. He took to making his own bath cooler and cooler each day, until it almost ceased to be enjoyable.

He skimmed his paper each morning for headlines about baths

before settling down to read the news; and was at once relieved and vaguely disappointed if a week passed without a hot-bath tragedy.

One of the sudden deaths that occurred in this way was that of a young and beautiful woman whose husband, an analytical chemist, had tried without success to divorce her a few months previously. The coroner displayed a tendency to suspect foul play, and put the husband through a severe cross-examination. There seemed, however, to be no getting behind the doctor's evidence. Pender, brooding over the improbable possible, wished, as he did every day of the week, that he could remember the name of that drug the man in the train had mentioned.

Then came the excitement in Pender's own neighborhood. An old Mr. Skimmings, who lived alone with a housekeeper in a street just around the corner, was found dead in his bathroom. His heart had never been strong. The housekeeper told the milkman that she had always expected something of the sort to happen, for the old gentleman would always take his bath so hot. Pender went to the inquest.

The housekeeper gave her evidence. Mr. Skimmings had been the kindest of employers, and she was heartbroken at losing him. No, she had not been aware that Mr. Skimmings had left her a large sum of money, but it was just like his goodness of heart. The verdict of course was accidental death.

Pender, that evening, went out for his usual stroll with the dog. Some feeling of curiosity moved him to go around past the late Mr. Skimmings's house. As he loitered by, glancing up at the blank windows, the garden gate opened and a man came out. In the light of a street lamp, Pender recognized him at once.

"Hullo!" he said.

"Oh, it's you, is it?" said the man. "Viewing the site of the tragedy, eh? What do *you* think about it all?"

"Oh, nothing very much," said Pender. "I didn't know him. Odd, our meeting again like this."

"Yes, isn't it? You live near here, I suppose."

"Yes," said Pender; and then wished he hadn't. "Do you live in these parts too?"

"Me?" said the man. "Oh no. I was only here on a little matter of business."

"Last time we met," said Pender, "you had business at Rugby." They had fallen into step together, and were walking slowly down to the turning Pender had to take in order to reach his house.

"So I had," agreed the other man. "My business takes me all over the country. I never know where I may be wanted next, you see."

"It was while you were at Rugby that old Brittlesea was found dead in his bath, wasn't it?" remarked Pender carelessly.

"Yes. Funny thing, coincidence." The man glanced up at him sideways through his glittering glasses. "Left all his money to his wife, didn't he? She's a rich woman now. Good-looking girl—a lot younger than he was."

They were passing Pender's gate. "Come in and have a drink," said Pender, and again immediately regretted the impulse.

The man accepted, and they went into Pender's bachelor study.

"Remarkable lot of these bath deaths lately," observed Pender as he squirted soda into the tumblers.

"You think it's remarkable?" said the man, with his irritating trick of querying everything that was said to him. "Well, I don't know. Perhaps it is. But it's always a fairly common accident."

"I suppose I've been taking more notice on account of that conversation we had in the train." Pender laughed, a little self-consciously. "It just makes me wonder—you know how one does—whether anybody else had happened to hit on that drug you mentioned—what was its name?"

The man ignored the question.

"Oh, I shouldn't think so," he said. "I fancy I'm the only person who knows about that. I only stumbled on the thing by accident myself when I was looking for something else. I don't imagine it could have been discovered simultaneously in so many parts of the country. But all these verdicts just show, don't they, what a safe way it would be of getting rid of a person."

"You're a chemist, then?" asked Pender, catching at the one phrase which seemed to promise information.

"Oh, I'm a bit of everything. Sort of general utility man. I do a good bit of studying on my own, too. You've got one or two interesting books here, I see."

Pender was flattered. For a man in his position—he had been in a bank until he came into that little bit of money—he felt that he had improved his mind to some purpose, and he knew that his collection of modern first editions would be worth money some day. He went over to the glass-fronted bookcase and pulled out a volume or two to show his visitor.

The man displayed intelligence, and presently joined him in front of the shelves.

"These, I take it, represent your personal tastes?" He took down a volume of Henry James and glanced at the fly-leaf. "That your name? E. Pender?"

Pender admitted that it was. "You have the advantage of me," he added.

"Oh! I am one of the great Smith clan," said the other with a laugh, "and work for my bread. You seem to be very nicely fixed here."

Pender explained about the clerkship and the legacy.

"Very nice, isn't it?" said Smith. "Not married? No. You're one of the lucky ones. Not likely to be needing any sulphate of . . . any useful drugs in the near future. And you never will, if you stick to what you've got and keep off women and speculation."

He smiled up sideways at Pender. Now that his hat was off, Pender saw that he had a quantity of closely curled gray hair, which made him look older than he had appeared in the railway carriage.

"No, I shan't be coming to you for assistance yet a while," said Pender, laughing. "Besides, how should I find you if I wanted you?"

"You wouldn't have to," said Smith. "*I* should find *you*. There's never any difficulty about that." He grinned, oddly. "Well, I'd better be getting on. Thank you for your hospitality. I don't expect we shall meet again—but we may, of course. Things work out so queerly, don't they?"

When he had gone, Pender returned to his own armchair. He took up his glass of whiskey, which stood there nearly full. "Funny!" he said to himself. "I don't remember pouring that out. I suppose I got interested and did it mechanically." He emptied his glass slowly, thinking about Smith.

What in the world was Smith doing at Skimmings's house?

An odd business altogether. If Skimmings's housekeeper had known about that money . . . But she had not known, and if she had, how could she have found out about Smith and his sulphate of . . . the word had been on the tip of his tongue, then.

"You would not need to find me. *I* should find *you*." What had the man meant by that? But this was ridiculous. Smith was not the devil, presumably. But if he really had this secret—if he liked to put a price upon it—nonsense.

"Business at Rugby—a little bit of business at Skimmings's house." Oh, absurd!

"Nobody is fit to be trusted. *Absolute* power over another man's life . . . it grows on you. That is, I imagine it would."

Lunacy! And, if there was anything in it, the man was mad to tell Pender about it. If Pender chose to speak he could get the fellow hanged. The very existence of Pender would be dangerous.

That whiskey!

More and more, thinking it over, Pender became persuaded that he had never poured it out. Smith must have done it while his back was turned. Why that sudden display of interest in the bookshelves? It had had no connection with anything that had gone before. Now Pender came to think of it, it had been a very stiff whiskey. Was it imagination, or had there been something about the flavor of it?

A cold sweat broke out on Pender's forehead.

A quarter of an hour later, after a powerful dose of mustard and water, Pender was downstairs again, very cold and shivering, huddling over the fire. He had had a narrow escape—if he had escaped. He did not know how the stuff worked, but he would not take a hot bath again for some days. One never knew.

Whether the mustard and water had done the trick in time, or whether the hot bath was an essential part of the treatment, at any rate Pender's life was saved for the time being. But he was still uneasy. He kept the front door on the chain and warned his servant to let no strangers into the house.

He ordered two more morning papers and the *News of the World* on Sundays, and kept a careful watch upon their columns. Deaths in baths became an obsession with him. He neglected his first editions and took to attending inquests.

Three weeks later he found himself at Lincoln. A man had died of heart failure in a Turkish bath—a fat man, of sedentary habits. The jury added a rider to their verdict of accidental death to the effect that the management should exercise a stricter supervision over the bathers and should never permit them to be left unattended in the hot room.

As Pender emerged from the hall he saw ahead of him a shabby hat that seemed familiar. He plunged after it, and caught Mr. Smith about to step into a taxi.

"Smith," he cried, gasping a little. He clutched him fiercely by the shoulder.

"What, you again?" said Smith. "Taking notes of the case, eh? *Can I do anything for you?*"

"You devil!" said Pender. "You're mixed up in this! You tried to kill me the other day."

"Did I? Why should I do that?"

"You'll swing for this," shouted Pender menacingly.

A policeman pushed his way through the gathering crowd.

"Here!" said he. "What's all this about?"

Smith touched his forehead significantly.

"It's all right, Officer," said he. "The gentleman seems to think I'm here for no good. Here's my card. The coroner knows me. But he attacked me. You'd better keep an eye on him."

"That's right," said a bystander.

"This man tried to kill me," said Pender.

The policeman nodded.

"Don't you worry about that, sir," he said. "You think better of it. The 'eat in there has upset you a bit. All right, *all* right."

"But I want to charge him," said Pender.

"I wouldn't do that if I was you," said the policeman.

"I tell you," said Pender, "that this man Smith has been trying to poison me. He's a murderer. He's poisoned scores of people."

The policeman winked at Smith.

"Best be off, sir," he said. "I'll settle this. Now, my lad"—he held Pender firmly by the arms—"just you keep cool and take it quiet. That gentleman's name ain't Smith nor nothing like it. You've got a bit mixed up like."

"Well, what is his name?" demanded Pender.

"Never mind," replied the constable. "You leave him alone, or you'll be getting yourself into trouble."

The taxi had driven away. Pender glanced around at the circle of amused faces and gave in.

"All right, Officer," he said. "I won't give you any trouble. I'll come round with you to the police station and tell you about it."

"What do you think o' that one?" asked the inspector of the sergeant when Pender had stumbled out of the station.

"Up the pole an' 'alfway round the flag, if you ask me," replied his subordinate. "Got one o' them ideez fix what they talk about."

"H'm!" replied the inspector. "Well, we've got his name and address. Better make a note of 'em. He might turn up again. Poisoning people so as they die in their baths, eh? That's a pretty good 'un. Wonderful how these barmy ones thinks it all out, isn't it?"

*

The spring that year was a bad one—cold and foggy. It was March when Pender went down to an inquest at Deptford, but a thick blanket of mist was hanging over the river as though it were November. The cold ate into your bones. As he sat in the dingy little court, peering through the yellow twilight of gas and fog, he could scarcely see the witnesses as they came to the table. Everybody in the place seemed to be coughing. Pender was coughing too. His bones ached, and he felt as though he were about due for a bout of influenza.

Straining his eyes, he thought he recognized a face on the other side of the room, but the smarting fog which penetrated every crack stung and blinded him. He felt in his overcoat pocket, and his hand closed comfortably on something thick and heavy. Ever since that day in Lincoln he had gone about armed for protection. Not a revolver—he was no hand with firearms. A sandbag was much better. He had bought one from an old man wheeling a pushcart. It was meant for keeping out draughts from the door—a good, old-fashioned affair.

The inevitable verdict was returned. The spectators began to push their way out. Pender had to hurry now, not to lose sight of his man. He elbowed his way along, muttering apologies. At the door he almost touched the man, but a stout woman intervened. He plunged past her, and she gave a little squeak of indignation. The man in front turned his head, and the light over the door glinted on his glasses.

Pender pulled his hat over his eyes and followed. His shoes had crêpe rubber soles and made no sound on the pavement. The man went on, jogging quietly up one street and down another, and never looking back. The fog was so thick that Pender was forced to keep within a few yards of him. Where was he going? Into the lighted streets? Home by bus or tram? No. He turned off to the left, down a narrow street.

The fog was thicker here. Pender could no longer see his quarry, but he heard the footsteps going on before him at the same even pace. It seemed to him that they were two alone in the world—

pursued and pursuer, slayer and avenger. The street began to slope more rapidly. They must be coming out somewhere near the river.

Suddenly the dim shapes of the houses fell away on either side. There was an open space, with a lamp vaguely visible in the middle. The footsteps paused. Pender, silently hurrying after, saw the man standing close beneath the lamp, apparently consulting something in a notebook.

Four steps, and Pender was upon him. He drew the sandbag from his pocket.

The man looked up.

"I've got you this time," said Pender, and struck with all his force.

Pender was quite right. He did get influenza. It was a week before he was out and about again. The weather had changed, and the air was fresh and sweet. In spite of the weakness left by the malady he felt as though a heavy weight had been lifted from his shoulders. He tottered down to a favorite bookshop of his in the Strand, and picked up a D. H. Lawrence "first" at a price which he knew to be a bargain. Encouraged by this, he turned into a small chophouse chiefly frequented by newspaper men, and ordered a grilled cutlet and a half-tankard of bitter.

Two journalists were seated by the next table.

"Going to poor old Buckley's funeral?" asked one.

"Yes," said the other. "Poor devil! Fancy his getting bashed on the head like that. He must have been on his way down to interview the widow of that fellow who died in a bath. It's a rough district. Probably one of Jimmy the Card's crowd had it in for him. He was a great crime-reporter—they won't get another like Bill Buckley in a hurry."

"He was a decent sort, too. Great old sport. No end of a practical joker. Remember his great stunt sulphate of thanatol?"

Pender started. *That* was the word that had eluded him for so many months. A curious dizziness came over him.

". . . looking at you as sober as a judge," the journalist was saying. "No such stuff, of course, but he used to work off that wheeze on poor boobs in railway carriages to see how they'd take it. Would you believe that one chap actually offered him—"

"Hullo!" interrupted his friend. "That bloke over there has fainted. I thought he was looking a bit white."

I Can Find My Way Out

NGAIO MARSH

Ngaio (pronounced ny'-o) Marsh (1895–1982) was born and lived most of her life in New Zealand, though she followed the anti-regional custom of the time in setting the majority of her detective novels in England, which she first visited in 1928. Through most of her more lucrative career as a novelist, she had a parallel existence in her first love, the theater, as actress, producer, director, designer, educator, and playwright. For thirty years, beginning in 1941, she spent part of each year directing and touring plays with the Student Drama Society of Canterbury University College in Christchurch, New Zealand. (Following theatrical tradition, Marsh's official birth date for many years, 1899, shaved four years off her actual age.)

Marsh's first novel, *A Man Lay Dead* (1934), had a stage background as did several of its successors, including her final book, *Light Thickens* (1982). In a more subtle expression of her theatrical enthusiasm, most of her murders take place in the course of some sort of performance. Ironically, according to biographer Margaret Lewis writing in *St. James Guide to Crime & Mystery Writers* (fourth edition, 1996), Marsh was unable to duplicate the success of Agatha Christie in adapting her novels to the stage, because she "lost her sense of theatre and sought to preserve the general shape of the novels, with all the interviews, questions, and answers."

Marsh was unusual at a time of gentleman amateur detectives in giving center stage to a policeman—but to be truthful, Roderick Alleyn of Scotland Yard had more in common in personal and professional style with Dorothy L. Sayers's Lord Peter Wimsey and Margery Allingham's Albert Campion than he did with a real law officer. Alleyn also had in common with Wimsey and Campion eventual marriage, in his case to Agatha Troy, a character who resembled Marsh herself and enjoyed the career of a successful painter Marsh had envisioned for herself early in her life.

Marsh had a remarkably consistent career as a writer of detective fiction. The puzzle was at the center of her work from the beginning, and she was a master of reader deception. If her writing and characterization became richer, the essential pattern of crime, investigation, and solution never changed. Remarkably, her last novels, published when she was in her mid-eighties, showed no perceptible decline in quality from their predecessors, in fact were among her best works, a statement that unfortunately can't be made of such long-running writers as Agatha Christie and Erle Stanley Gardner.

One of the author's rare short stories, "I Can Find My Way Out" is a Roderick Alleyn novel in miniature, appropriately featuring Marsh's patented backstage setting.

At half-past six on the night in question, Anthony Gill, unable to eat, keep still, think, speak, or act coherently, walked from his rooms to the Jupiter Theatre. He knew that there would be nobody backstage, that there was nothing for him to do in the theater, that he ought to stay quietly in his rooms and presently dress, dine, and arrive at, say, a quarter to eight. But it was as if something shoved him into his clothes, thrust him into the street and compelled him to hurry through the West End to the Jupiter. His mind was overlaid with a thin film of inertia. Odd lines from the play occurred to him, but without any particular significance. He found himself busily reiterating a completely irrelevant sentence: "She has a way of laughing that would make a man's heart turn over."

Piccadilly, Shaftesbury Avenue. "Here I go," he thought, turning into Hawke Street, "towards my play. It's one hour and twenty-nine minutes away. A step a second. It's rushing towards me. Tony's first play. Poor young Tony Gill. Never mind. Try again."

The Jupiter. Neon lights: I CAN FIND MY WAY OUT—*by Anthony Gill*. And in the entrance the bills and photographs. *Coralie Bourne with H. J. Bannington, Barry George and Canning Cumberland*.

Canning Cumberland. The film across his mind split and there was the Thing itself and he would have to think about it. How bad would Canning Cumberland be if he came down drunk? Brilliantly bad, they said. He would bring out all the tricks. Clever actor stuff, scoring off everybody, making a fool of the dramatic balance. "In Mr. Canning Cumberland's hands indifferent dialogue and unconvincing situations seemed almost real." What can you do with a drunken actor?

He stood in the entrance feeling his heart pound and his insides deflate and sicken.

Because, of course, it was a bad play. He was at this moment and for the first time really convinced of it. It was terrible. Only one virtue in it and that was not his doing. It had been suggested to him by Coralie Bourne: "I don't think the play you have sent me will do as it is but it has occurred to me—" It was a brilliant idea. He had rewritten the play round it and almost immediately and quite innocently he had begun to think of it as his own although he had said shyly to Coralie Bourne: "You should appear as joint author." She had quickly, overemphatically, refused. "It was nothing at all," she said. "If you're to become a dramatist you will learn to get ideas from everywhere. A single situation is nothing. Think of Shakespeare," she added lightly. "Entire plots! Don't be silly." She had said later, and still with the same hurried, nervous air: "Don't go talking to everyone about it. They will think there is more, instead of less, than meets the eye in my small suggestion. Please promise." He promised, thinking he'd made an error in taste when he suggested that Coralie Bourne, so famous an actress, should appear as joint author with an unknown youth. And how right she was, he thought, because, of course, it's going to be a ghastly flop. She'll be sorry she consented to play in it.

Standing in front of the theater he contemplated nightmare possibilities. What did audiences do when a first play flopped? Did they clap a little, enough to let the curtain rise and quickly fall again on a discomforted group of players? How scanty must the applause be for them to let him off his own appearance? And they were to go on to the Chelsea Arts Ball. A hideous prospect. Thinking he would give anything in the world if he could stop his play, he turned into the foyer. There were lights in the offices and he paused, irresolute, before a board of photographs. Among them, much smaller than the leading players, was Dendra Gay with the eyes looking straight into his. *She had a way of laughing that would make a man's heart turn over.* "Well," he thought, "so I'm in love with her." He turned away from the photograph. A man came out of the office. "Mr. Gill? Telegrams for you."

Anthony took them and as he went out he heard the man call after him: "Very good luck for tonight, sir."

There were queues of people waiting in the side street for the early doors.

At six thirty Coralie Bourne dialed Canning Cumberland's number and waited.

She heard his voice. "It's me," she said.

"O, God! darling, I've been thinking about you." He spoke rapidly, too loudly. "Coral, I've been thinking about Ben. You oughtn't to have given that situation to the boy."

"We've been over it a dozen times, Cann. Why not give it to Tony? Ben will never know." She waited and then said nervously, "Ben's gone, Cann. We'll never see him again."

"I've got a 'Thing' about it. After all, he's your husband."

"No, Cann, no."

"Suppose he turns up. It'd be like him to turn up."

"He won't turn up."

She heard him laugh. "I'm sick of all this," she thought suddenly. "I've had it once too often. I can't stand any more . . . Cann," she said into the telephone. But he had hung up.

At twenty to seven, Barry George looked at himself in his bathroom mirror. "I've got a better appearance," he thought, "than Cann Cumberland. My head's a good shape, my eyes are bigger, and my jawline's cleaner. I never let a show down. I don't drink. I'm a better actor." He turned his head a little, slewing his eyes to watch the effect. "In the big scene," he thought, "I'm the star. He's the feed. That's the way it's been produced and that's what the author wants. I ought to get the notices."

Past notices came up in his memory. He saw the print, the size of the paragraphs; a long paragraph about Canning Cumberland, a line tacked on the end of it. "Is it unkind to add that Mr. Barry George trotted in the wake of Mr. Cumberland's virtuosity with an air of breathless dependability?" And again: "It is a little hard on Mr. Barry George that he should be obliged to act as foil to this brilliant performance." Worst of all: "Mr. Barry George succeeded in looking tolerably unlike a stooge, an achievement that evidently exhausted his resources."

"Monstrous!" he said loudly to his own image, watching the fine glow of indignation in the eyes. Alcohol, he told himself, did two things to Cann Cumberland. He raised his finger. Nice, expressive hand. An actor's hand. Alcohol destroyed Cumberland's artistic integrity. It also invested him with devilish cunning. Drunk, he would burst the seams of a play, destroy its balance, ruin its form, and himself emerge blazing with a showmanship that the audience mistook for genius. "While I," he said aloud, "merely pay my author the compliment of faithful interpretation. Psha!"

He returned to his bedroom, completed his dressing and pulled his hat to the right angle. Once more he thrust his face close to the mirror and looked searchingly at its image. "By God!" he told himself, "he's done it once too often, old boy. Tonight we'll even the score, won't we? By God, we will."

Partly satisfied, and partly ashamed, for the scene, after all, had smacked a little of ham, he took his stick in one hand and a case holding his costume for the Arts Ball in the other, and went down to the theatre.

At ten minutes to seven, H. J. Bannington passed through the gallery queue on his way to the stage door alley, raising his hat and saying: "Thanks so much," to the gratified ladies who let him through. He heard them murmur his name. He walked briskly along the alley, greeted the stage-doorkeeper, passed under a dingy lamp, through an entry and so to the stage. Only working lights were up. The walls of an interior set rose dimly into shadow. Bob Reynolds, the stage manager, came out through the prompt-entrance. "Hello, old boy," he said, "I've changed the dressing rooms. You're third on the right: they've moved your things in. Suit you?"

"Better, at least, than a black hole the size of a WC but without its appointments," H.J. said acidly. "I suppose the great Mr. Cumberland still has the star-room?"

"Well, yes, old boy."

"And who pray, is next to him? In the room with the other gas fire?"

"We've put Barry George there, old boy. You know what he's like."

"Only too well, old boy, and the public, I fear, is beginning to find out." H.J. turned into the dressing-room passage. The stage manager returned to the set where he encountered his assistant. "What's biting *him?*" asked the assistant. "He wanted a dressing room with a fire." "Only natural," said the ASM nastily. "He started life reading gas meters."

On the right and left of the passage, nearest the stage end, were two doors, each with its star in tarnished paint. The door on the left was open. H.J. looked in and was greeted with the smell of greasepaint, powder, wet-white, and flowers. A gas fire droned comfortably. Coralie Bourne's dresser was spreading out towels. "Good evening, Katie, my jewel," said H.J. "La Belle not down yet?" "We're on our way," she said.

H.J. hummed stylishly: "*Bella filia del amore*," and returned to the passage. The star-room on the right was closed but he could hear Cumberland's dresser moving about inside. He went on to the next door, paused, read the card, "MR. BARRY GEORGE," warbled a high derisive note, turned in at the third door, and switched on the light.

Definitely not a second lead's room. No fire. A wash basin, however, and opposite mirrors. A stack of telegrams had been placed on the dressing table. Still singing he reached for them, disclosing a number of bills that had been tactfully laid underneath and a letter, addressed in a flamboyant script.

His voice might have been mechanically produced and arbitrarily switched off, so abruptly did his song end in the middle of a roulade. He let the telegrams fall on the table, took up the letter and tore it open. His face, wretchedly pale, was reflected and endlessly rereflected in the mirrors.

At nine o'clock the telephone rang. Roderick Alleyn answered it. "This is Sloane 84405. No, you're on the wrong number. *No.*" He hung up and returned to his wife and guest. "That's the fifth time in two hours."

"Do let's ask for a new number."

"We might get next door to something worse."

The telephone rang again. "This is not 84406," Alleyn warned it. "No, I cannot take three large trunks to Victoria Station. No, I am not the Instant All Night Delivery. No."

"They're 84406," Mrs. Alleyn explained to Lord Michael Lamprey. "I suppose it's just faulty dialing, but you can't imagine how angry everyone gets. Why do you want to be a policeman?"

"It's a dull hard job, you know—" Alleyn began.

"Oh," Lord Mike said, stretching his legs and looking critically at his shoes, "I don't for a moment imagine I'll leap immediately into false whiskers and plainclothes. No, no. But I'm revoltingly healthy, sir. Strong as a horse. And I don't think I'm as stupid as you might feel inclined to imagine—"

The telephone rang.

"I say, do let me answer it," Mike suggested and did so.

"Hullo?" he said winningly. He listened, smiling at his hostess. "I'm afraid—," he began. "Here, wait a bit— Yes, but—" His expression became blank and complacent. "May I," he said presently, "repeat your order, sir? Can't be too sure, can we? Call at 11 Harrow Gardens, Sloane Square, for one suitcase to be delivered immediately at the Jupiter Theatre to Mr. Anthony Gill. Very good, sir. Thank you, sir. Collect. Quite."

He replaced the receiver and beamed at the Alleyns.

"What the devil have you been up to?" Alleyn said.

"He just simply wouldn't listen to reason. I tried to tell him."

"But it may be urgent," Mrs. Alleyn ejaculated.

"It couldn't be more urgent, really. It's a suitcase for Tony Gill at the Jupiter."

"Well, then—"

"I was at Eton with the chap," said Mike reminiscently. "He's four years older than I am so of course he was madly important while I was less than the dust. This'll larn him."

"I think you'd better put that order through at once," said Alleyn firmly.

"I rather thought of executing it myself, do you know, sir. It'd be a frightfully neat way of gate-crashing the show, wouldn't it? I did try to get a ticket but the house was sold out."

"If you're going to deliver this case you'd better get a bend on."

"It's clearly an occasion for dressing up though, isn't it? I say," said Mike modestly, "would you think it most frightful cheek if I—well I'd promise to come back and return everything. I mean—"

"Are you suggesting that my clothes look more like a vanman's than yours?"

"I thought you'd have things—"

"For Heaven's sake, Rory," said Mrs. Alleyn, "dress him up and let him go. The great thing is to get that wretched man's suitcase to him."

"I know," said Mike earnestly. "It's most frightfully sweet of you. That's how I feel about it."

Alleyn took him away and shoved him into an old and begrimed raincoat, a cloth cap, and a muffler. "You wouldn't deceive a village idiot in a total eclipse," he said, "but out you go."

He watched Mike drive away and returned to his wife.

"What'll happen?" she asked.

"Knowing Mike, I should say he will end up in the front stalls and go on to supper with the leading lady. She, by the way, is Coralie Bourne. Very lovely and twenty years his senior so he'll probably fall in love with her." Alleyn reached for his tobacco jar and paused. "I wonder what's happened to her husband," he said.

"Who was he?"

"An extraordinary chap. Benjamin Vlasnoff. Violent temper. Looked like a bandit. Wrote two very good plays and got run in three times for common assault. She tried to divorce him but it didn't go through. I think he afterwards lit off to Russia." Alleyn yawned. "I believe she had a hell of a time with him," he said.

"All Night Delivery," said Mike in a hoarse voice, touching his cap. "Suitcase. One." "Here you are," said the woman who had answered the door. "Carry it carefully, now, it's not locked and the catch springs out."

"Thanks," said Mike. "Much obliged. Chilly, ain't it?"

He took the suitcase out to the car.

It was a fresh spring night. Sloane Square was threaded with mist and all the lamps had halos round them. It was the kind of night when individual sounds separate themselves from the conglomerate voice of London; hollow sirens spoke imperatively down on the river and a bugle rang out over in Chelsea Barracks; a night, Mike thought, for adventure.

He opened the rear door of the car and heaved the case in. The catch flew open, the lid dropped back and the contents fell out. "Damn!" said Mike and switched on the inside light.

Lying on the floor of the car was a false beard.

It was flaming red and bushy and was mounted on a chin-piece. With it was incorporated a stiffened moustache. There were wire hooks to attach the whole thing behind the ears. Mike laid it carefully on the seat. Next he picked up a wide black hat, then a vast overcoat with a fur collar, finally a pair of black gloves.

Mike whistled meditatively and thrust his hands into the pockets of Alleyn's mackintosh. His right-hand fingers closed on a card. He pulled it out. "Chief Detective-Inspector Alleyn," he read, "CID. New Scotland Yard."

"Honestly," thought Mike exultantly, "this is a gift."

Ten minutes later a car pulled into the curb at the nearest parking place to the Jupiter Theatre. From it emerged a figure carrying a suitcase. It strode rapidly along Hawke Street and turned into the stage-door alley. As it passed under the dirty lamp it paused, and thus murkily lit, resembled an illustration from some Edwardian spy story. The face was completely shadowed, a black cavern from which there projected a square of scarlet beard, which was the only note of color.

The doorkeeper who was taking the air with a member of stage staff, moved forward, peering at the stranger.

"Was you wanting something?"

"I'm taking this case in for Mr. Gill."

"He's in front. You can leave it with me."

"I'm so sorry," said the voice behind the beard, "but I promised I'd leave it backstage myself."

"So you will be leaving it. Sorry, sir, but no one's admitted be'ind without a card."

"A card? Very well. Here is a card."

He held it out in his black-gloved hand. The stage-doorkeeper, unwillingly removing his gaze from the beard, took the card and examined it under the light. "Coo!" he said, "what's up, governor?"

"No matter. Say nothing of this."

The figure waved its hand and passed through the door. "'Ere!" said the doorkeeper excitedly to the stagehand, "take a slant at this. That's a plainclothes flattie, that was."

"*Plain*clothes!" said the stagehand. "Them!"

"'E's disguised," said the doorkeeper. "That's what it is. 'E's disguised 'isself."

"'E's bloody well lorst 'isself be'ind them whiskers if you arst me."

Out on the stage someone was saying in a pitched and beautifully articulate voice: "*I've always loathed the view from these windows. However if that's the sort of thing you admire. Turn off the lights, damn you. Look at it.*"

"Watch it, now, watch it," whispered a voice so close to Mike that he jumped. "OK," said a second voice somewhere above his head. The lights on the set turned blue. "Kill that working light." "Working light gone."

Curtains in the set were wrenched aside and a window flung open. An actor appeared, leaning out quite close to Mike, seeming to look into his face and saying very distinctly: "God: it's frightful!" Mike backed away towards a passage, lit only from an open door. A great volume of sound broke out beyond the stage. "House lights," said the sharp voice. Mike turned into the passage. As he did so, someone came through the door. He found himself face to face with Coralie Bourne, beautifully dressed and heavily painted.

For a moment she stood quite still; then she made a curious gesture with her right hand, gave a small breathy sound and fell forward at his feet.

Anthony was tearing his program into long strips and dropping them on the floor of the OP box. On his right hand, above and below, was the audience; sometimes laughing, sometimes still, sometimes as one corporate being, raising its hands and striking them together. As now; when down on the stage, Canning Cumberland, using a strange voice, and inspired by some inward devil, flung back the window and said: "God: it's frightful!"

"Wrong! Wrong!" Anthony cried inwardly, hating Cumberland, hating Barry George because he let one speech of three words override him, hating the audience because they liked it. The curtain descended with a long sigh on the second act and a sound like heavy rain filled the theatre, swelled prodigiously and continued after the house lights welled up.

"They seem," said a voice behind him, "to be liking your play."

It was Gosset, who owned the Jupiter and had backed the show. Anthony turned on him stammering: "He's destroying it. It should be the other man's scene. He's stealing."

"My boy," said Gosset, "he's an actor."

"He's drunk. It's intolerable."

He felt Gosset's hand on his shoulder.

"People are watching us. You're on show. This is a big thing for you; a first play, and going enormously. Come and have a drink, old boy. I want to introduce you—"

Anthony got up and Gosset, with his arm across his shoulders, flashing smiles, patting him, led him to the back of the box.

"I'm sorry," Anthony said, "I can't. Please let me off. I'm going backstage."

"Much better not, old son." The hand tightened on his shoulder. "Listen, old son—" But Anthony had freed himself and slipped through the pass-door from the box to the stage.

At the foot of the breakneck stairs Dendra Gay stood waiting. "I thought you'd come," she said.

Anthony said: "He's drunk. He's murdering the play."

"It's only one scene, Tony. He finishes early in the next act. It's going colossally."

"But don't you understand—"

"I do. You *know* I do. But you're a success, Tony darling! You can hear it and smell it and feel it in your bones."

"Dendra—" he said uncertainly.

Someone came up and shook his hand and went on shaking it. Flats were being laced together with a slap of rope on canvas. A chandelier ascended into darkness. "Lights," said the stage manager, and the set was flooded with them. A distant voice began chanting. "Last act, please. Last act."

"Miss Bourne all right?" the stage manager suddenly demanded.

"She'll be all right. She's not on for ten minutes," said a woman's voice.

"What's the matter with Miss Bourne?" Anthony asked.

"Tony, I must go and so must you. Tony, it's going to be grand. *Please* think so. *Please.*"

"Dendra—," Tony began, but she had gone.

Beyond the curtain, horns and flutes announced the last act.

"Clear please."

The stagehands came off.

"House lights."

"House lights gone."

"Stand by."

And while Anthony still hesitated in the OP corner, the curtain rose. Canning Cumberland and H. J. Bannington opened the last act.

As Mike knelt by Coralie Bourne he heard someone enter the passage behind him. He turned and saw, silhouetted against the lighted stage, the actor who had looked at him through a window in the set. The silhouette seemed to repeat the gesture Coralie Bourne had used, and to flatten itself against the wall.

A woman in an apron came out of the open door.

"I say—here!" Mike said.

Three things happened almost simultaneously. The woman cried out and knelt beside him. The man disappeared through a door on the right.

The woman, holding Coralie Bourne in her arms, said violently: "Why have you come back?" Then the passage lights came on. Mike said: "Look here, I'm most frightfully sorry," and took off the broad black hat. The dresser gaped at him, Coralie Bourne made a crescendo sound in her throat and opened her eyes. "Katie?" she said.

"It's all right, my lamb. It's not him, dear. You're all right." The dresser jerked her head at Mike: "Get out of it," she said.

"Yes, of course, I'm most frightfully—" He backed out of the passage, colliding with a youth who said: "Five minutes, please." The dresser called out: "Tell them she's not well. Tell them to hold the curtain."

"No," said Coralie Bourne strongly. "I'm all right, Katie. Don't say anything. Katie, what was it?"

They disappeared into the room on the left.

Mike stood in the shadow of a stack of scenic flats by the entry into the passage. There was great activity on the stage. He caught a glimpse of Anthony Gill on the far side talking to a girl. The call-boy was speaking to the stage manager who now shouted into space: "Miss Bourne all right?" The dresser came into the passage and called: "She'll be all right. She's not on for ten minutes." The youth began chanting: "Last act, please." The stage manager gave a series of orders. A man with an eyeglass and a florid beard came from farther down the passage and stood outside the set, bracing his figure and giving little tweaks to his clothes. There was a sound of horns and flutes. Canning Cumberland emerged from the room on the right and on his way to the stage, passed close to Mike, leaving a strong smell of alcohol behind him. The curtain rose.

Behind his shelter, Mike stealthily removed his beard and stuffed it into the pocket of his overcoat.

A group of stagehands stood nearby. One of them said in a hoarse whisper: "'E's squiffy." "Garn, 'e's going good." "So 'e may be going good. And for why? *Becos* 'e's squiffy."

Ten minutes passed. Mike thought: "This affair has definitely not gone according to plan." He listened. Some kind of tension seemed to be building up on the stage. Canning Cumberland's voice rose on a loud but blurred note. A door in the set opened. "Don't bother to come," Cumberland said. "Good-bye. I can find my way out." The door slammed. Cumberland was standing near Mike. Then, very close, there was a loud explosion. The scenic flats vibrated, Mike's flesh leapt on his bones, and Cumberland went into his dressing room. Mike heard the key turn in the door. The smell of alcohol mingled with the smell of gunpowder. A stagehand moved to a trestle table and laid a pistol on it. The actor with the eyeglass made an exit. He spoke for a moment to the stage manager, passed Mike, and disappeared in the passage.

Smells. There were all sorts of smells. Subconsciously, still listening to the play, he began to sort them out. Glue. Canvas. Greasepaint. The call-boy tapped on doors. "Mr. George, please." "Miss Bourne, please." They came out, Coralie Bourne with her dresser. Mike heard her turn a door handle and say something. An indistinguishable voice answered her. Then she and her dresser passed him. The others spoke to her and she nodded and then seemed to withdraw into herself, waiting with her head bent, ready to make her entrance. Presently she drew back, walked swiftly to the door in the set, flung it open, and swept on, followed a minute later by Barry George.

Smells. Dust, stale paint, cloth. Gas. Increasingly, the smell of gas.

The group of stagehands moved away behind the set to the side of the stage. Mike edged out of cover. He could see the prompt-corner. The stage manager stood there with folded arms, watching the action. Behind him were grouped the players who were not on. Two dressers stood apart, watching. The light from the set caught their faces. Coralie Bourne's voice sent phrases flying like birds into the auditorium.

Mike began peering at the floor. Had he kicked some gas fitting adrift? The call-boy passed him, stared at him over his shoulder and went down the passage, tapping. "Five minutes to the curtain, please. Five minutes." The actor with the elderly makeup followed the call-boy out. "God, what a stink of gas," he whispered. "Chronic, ain't it?" said the call-boy. They stared at Mike and then crossed to the waiting group. The man said something to the stage manager who tipped his head up, sniffing. He made an impatient gesture and turned back to the prompt-box, reaching over the prompter's head. A bell rang somewhere up in the flies and Mike saw a stagehand climb to the curtain platform.

The little group near the prompt-corner was agitated. They looked back towards the passage entrance. The call-boy nodded and came running back. He knocked on the first door on the right. "*Mr. Cumberland! Mr. Cumberland!* You're on for the call." He rattled the door handle. "*Mr. Cumberland! You're on.*"

Mike ran into the passage. The call-boy coughed retchingly and jerked his hand at the door. "Gas!" he said. "Gas!"

"Break it in."

"I'll get Mr. Reynolds."

He was gone. It was a narrow passage. From halfway across

the opposite room Mike took a run, head down, shoulder forward, at the door. It gave a little and a sickening increase in the smell caught him in the lungs. A vast storm of noise had broken out and as he took another run he thought: "It's hailing outside."

"Just a minute if *you* please, sir."

It was a stagehand. He'd got a hammer and screwdriver. He wedged the point of the screwdriver between the lock and the doorpost, drove it home and wrenched. The screws squeaked, the wood splintered and gas poured into the passage. "No winders," coughed the stagehand.

Mike wound Alleyn's scarf over his mouth and nose. Half-forgotten instructions from antigas drill occurred to him. The room looked queer but he could see the man slumped down in the chair quite clearly. He stooped low and ran in.

He was knocking against things as he backed out, lugging the dead weight. His arms tingled. A high insistent voice hummed in his brain. He floated a short distance and came to earth on a concrete floor among several pairs of legs. A long way off, someone said loudly: "I can only thank you for being so kind to what I know, too well, is a very imperfect play." Then the sound of hail began again. There was a heavenly stream of clear air flowing into his mouth and nostrils. "I could eat it," he thought and sat up.

The telephone rang. "Suppose," Mrs. Alleyn suggested, "that this time you ignore it."

"It might be the Yard," Alleyn said, and answered it.

"Is that Chief Detective-Inspector Alleyn's flat? I'm speaking from the Jupiter Theatre. I've rung up to say that the Chief Inspector is here and that he's had a slight mishap. He's all right, but I think it might be as well for someone to drive him home. No need to worry."

"What sort of mishap?" Alleyn asked.

"Er—well—er, he's been a bit gassed."

"*Gassed!* All right. Thanks, I'll come."

"*What* a bore for you, darling," said Mrs. Alleyn. "What sort of case is it? Suicide?"

"Masquerading within the meaning of the act, by the sound of it. Mike's in trouble."

"What trouble, for Heaven's sake?"

"Got himself gassed. He's all right. Good night, darling. Don't wait up."

When he reached the theatre, the front of the house was in darkness. He made his way down the side alley to the stage-door where he was held up.

"Yard," he said, and produced his official card.

"'Ere," said the stage-doorkeeper. "'ow many more of you?"

"The man inside was working for me," said Alleyn and walked in. The doorkeeper followed, protesting.

To the right of the entrance was a large scenic dock from which the double doors had been rolled back. Here Mike was sitting in an armchair, very white about the lips. Three men and two women, all with painted faces, stood near him and behind them a group of stagehands with Reynolds, the stage manager, and, apart from these, three men in evening dress. The men looked woodenly shocked. The women had been weeping.

"I'm most frightfully sorry, sir," Mike said. "I've tried to explain. This," he added generally, "is Inspector Alleyn."

"I can't understand all this," said the oldest of the men in evening dress irritably. He turned on the doorkeeper. "You said—"

"I seen 'is card—"

"I know," said Mike, "but you see—"

"This is Lord Michael Lamprey," Alleyn said. "A recruit to the Police Department. What's happened here?"

"Doctor Rankin, would you—?"

The second of the men in evening dress came forward. "All right, Gosset. It's a bad business, Inspector. I've just been saying the police would have to be informed. If you'll come with me—"

Alleyn followed him through a door onto the stage proper. It was dimly lit. A trestle table had been set up in the center and on it, covered with a sheet, was an unmistakable shape. The smell of gas, strong everywhere, hung heavily about the table.

"Who is it?"

"Canning Cumberland. He'd locked the door of his dressing room. There's a gas fire. Your young friend dragged him out, very pluckily, but it was no go. I was in front. Gosset, the manager, had asked me to supper. It's a perfectly clear case of suicide as you'll see."

"I'd better look at the room. Anybody been in?"

"God, no. It was a job to clear it. They turned the gas off at the main. There's no window. They had to open the double doors at the back of the stage and a small outside door at the end of the passage. It may be possible to get in now."

He led the way to the dressing-room passage. "Pretty thick, still," he said. "It's the first room on the right. They burst the lock. You'd better keep down near the floor."

The powerful lights over the mirror were on and the room still had its look of occupation. The gas fire was against the left-hand wall, Alleyn squatted down by it. The tap was still turned on, its face lying parallel with the floor. The top of the heater, the tap itself, and the carpet near it, were covered with a creamish powder. On the end of the dressing-table shelf nearest to the stove was a box of this powder. Farther along the shelf, grease-paints were set out in a row beneath the mirror. Then came a wash basin and in front of this an overturned chair. Alleyn could see the track of heels, across the pile of the carpet, to the door immediately opposite. Beside the wash basin was a quart bottle of whiskey, three-parts empty, and a tumbler. Alleyn had had about enough and returned to the passage.

"Perfectly clear," the hovering doctor said again, "isn't it?"

"I'll see the other rooms, I think."

The one next to Cumberland's was like his in reverse, but smaller. The heater was back to back with Cumberland's. The dressing-shelf was set out with much the same assortment of greasepaints. The tap of this heater, too, was turned on. It was of precisely the same make as the other and Alleyn, less embarrassed here by fumes, was able to make a longer examination. It was a common enough type of gas fire. The lead-in was from a pipe through a flexible metallic tube with a rubber connection. There were two taps, one in the pipe and one at the junction of the tube with the heater itself. Alleyn disconnected the tube and examined the connection. It was perfectly sound, a close fit and stained red at the end. Alleyn noticed a wiry thread of some reddish stuff resembling packing that still clung to it. The nozzle and tap were brass, the tap pulling over when it was turned on, to lie in a parallel plane with the floor. No powder had been scattered about here.

He glanced round the room, returned to the door and read the card: MR. BARRY GEORGE.

The doctor followed him into the rooms opposite these, on the left-hand side of the passage. They were a repetition in design of the two he had already seen but were hung with women's clothes and had a more elaborate assortment of greasepaint and cosmetics.

There was a mass of flowers in the star-room. Alleyn read the cards. One in particular caught his eye: "From Anthony Gill to say a most inadequate 'thank you' for the great idea." A vase of red roses stood before the mirror: "To your greatest triumph, Coralie darling. C.C." In Miss Gay's room there were only two bouquets, one from the management and one "from Anthony, with love."

Again in each room he pulled off the lead-in to the heater and looked at the connection.

"All right, aren't they?" said the doctor.

"Quite all right. Tight fit. Good solid gray rubber."

"Well, then—"

Next on the left was an unused room, and opposite it, "Mr. H. J. Bannington." Neither of these rooms had gas fires. Mr. Bannington's dressing-table was littered with the usual array of greasepaint, the materials for his beard, a number of telegrams and letters, and several bills.

"About the body," the doctor began.

"We'll get a mortuary van from the Yard."

"But—Surely in a case of suicide—"

"I don't think this is suicide."

"But, good God!—D'you mean there's been an accident?"

"No accident," said Alleyn.

At midnight, the dressing-room lights in the Jupiter Theatre were brilliant, and men were busy there with the tools of their trade. A constable stood at the stage-door and a van waited in the yard. The front of the house was dimly lit and there, among the shrouded stalls, sat Coralie Bourne, Basil Gosset, H. J. Bannington, Dendra Gay, Anthony Gill, Reynolds, Katie the dresser, and the call-boy. A constable sat behind them and another stood by the doors into the foyer. They stared across the backs of seats at the fire curtain. Spirals of smoke rose from their cigarettes and about their feet were discarded programs. "Basil Gosset presents *I Can Find My Way Out* by Anthony Gill."

In the manager's office Alleyn said: "You're sure of your facts, Mike?"

"Yes, sir. Honestly. I was right up against the entrance into the passage. They didn't see me because I was in the shadow. It was very dark offstage."

"You'll have to swear to it."

"I know."

"Good. All right, Thompson. Miss Gay and Mr. Gosset may go home. Ask Miss Bourne to come in."

When Sergeant Thompson had gone Mike said: "I haven't had a chance to say I know I've made a perfect fool of myself. Using your card and everything."

"Irresponsible gaiety doesn't go down very well in the service, Mike. You behaved like a clown."

"I *am* a fool," said Mike wretchedly.

The red beard was lying in front of Alleyn on Gosset's desk. He picked it up and held it out. "Put it on," he said.

"She might do another faint."

"I think not. Now the hat: yes—yes, I see. Come in."

Sergeant Thompson showed Coralie Bourne in and then sat at the end of the desk with his notebook.

Tears had traced their course through the powder on her face, carrying black cosmetic with them and leaving the greasepaint shining like snail-tracks. She stood near the doorway looking dully at Michael. "Is he back in England?" she said. "Did he tell you to do this?" She made an impatient movement. "Do take it off," she said, "it's a very bad beard. If Cann had only looked—" Her lips trembled. "Who told you to do it?"

"Nobody," Mike stammered, pocketing the beard. "I mean—as a matter of fact, Tony Gill—"

"*Tony?* But *he* didn't know. Tony wouldn't do it. Unless—"

"Unless?" Alleyn said.

She said frowning: "Tony didn't want Cann to play the part that way. He was furious."

"He says it was his dress for the Chelsea Arts Ball," Mike mumbled. "I brought it here. I just thought I'd put it on—it was idiotic, I know—for fun. I'd no idea you and Mr. Cumberland would mind."

"Ask Mr. Gill to come in," Alleyn said.

Anthony was white and seemed bewildered and helpless. "I've told Mike," he said. "It was my dress for the ball. They sent it round from the costume-hiring place this afternoon but I forgot it. Dendra reminded me and rang up the Delivery people—or Mike, as it turns out—in the interval."

"Why," Alleyn asked, "did you choose that particular disguise?"

"I didn't. I didn't know what to wear and I was too rattled to think. They said they were hiring things for themselves and would get something for me. They said we'd all be characters out of a Russian melodrama."

"Who said this?"

"Well—well, it was Barry George, actually."

"*Barry*," Coralie Bourne said. "*It was Barry.*"

"I don't understand," Anthony said. "Why should a fancy dress upset everybody?"

"It happened," Alleyn said, "to be a replica of the dress usually worn by Miss Bourne's husband who also had a red beard. That was it, wasn't it, Miss Bourne? I remember seeing him—"

"Oh, yes," she said, "you would. He was known to the police." Suddenly she broke down completely. She was in an armchair near the desk but out of the range of its shaded lamp. She twisted and writhed, beating her hand against the padded arm of the chair. Sergeant Thompson sat with his head bent and his hand over his notes. Mike, after an agonized glance at Alleyn, turned his back. Anthony Gill leant over her: "Don't," he said violently. "Don't! For God's sake, stop."

She twisted away from him and gripping the edge of the desk, began to speak to Alleyn; little by little gaining mastery of herself. "I want to tell you. I want you to understand. Listen." Her husband had been fantastically cruel, she said. "It was a kind of slavery." But when she sued for divorce he brought evidence of adultery with Cumberland. They had thought he knew nothing. "There was an abominable scene. He told us he was going away. He said he'd keep track of us and if I tried again for divorce, he'd come home. He was very friendly with Barry in those days." He had left behind him the first draft of a play he had meant to write for her and Cumberland. It had a wonderful scene for them. "And now you will never have it," he had said, "because there is no other playwright who could make this play for you but I." He was, she said, a melodramatic man but he was never ridiculous. He returned to the Ukraine where he was born and they had heard no more of him. In a little while she would have been able to presume death. But years of waiting did not agree with Canning Cumberland. He drank consistently and at his worst used to imagine her husband was about to return. "He was really terrified of Ben," she said. "He seemed like a creature in a nightmare."

Anthony Gill said: "This play—was it—?"

"Yes. There was an extraordinary similarity between your play and his. I saw at once that Ben's central scene would enormously strengthen your piece. Cann didn't want me to give it to you. Barry knew. He said: 'Why not?' He wanted Cann's part and was furious when he didn't get it. So you see, when he suggested you should dress and make-up like Ben—" She turned to Alleyn. "You see?"

"What did Cumberland do when he saw you?" Alleyn asked Mike.

"He made a queer movement with his hands as if—well, as if he expected me to go for him. Then he just bolted into his room."

"He thought Ben had come back," she said.

"Were you alone at any time after you fainted?" Alleyn asked.

"I? No. No, I wasn't. Katie took me into my dressing room and stayed with me until I went on for the last scene."

"One other question. Can you, by any chance, remember if the heater in your room behaved at all oddly?"

She looked wearily at him. "Yes, it did give a sort of plop, I think. It made me jump. I was nervy."

"You went straight from your room to the stage?"

"Yes. With Katie. I wanted to go to Cann. I tried the door when we came out. It was locked. He said: 'Don't come in.' I said: 'It's all right. It wasn't Ben,' and went on to the stage."

"I heard Miss Bourne," Mike said.

"He must have made up his mind by then. He was terribly drunk when he played his last scene." She pushed her hair back from her forehead. "May I go?" she asked Alleyn.

"I've sent for a taxi. Mr. Gill, will you see if it's there? In the meantime, Miss Bourne, would you like to wait in the foyer?"

"May I take Katie home with me?"

"Certainly. Thompson will find her. Is there anyone else we can get?"

"No, thank you. Just old Katie."

Alleyn opened the door for her and watched her walk into the foyer. "Check up with the dresser, Thompson," he murmured, "and get Mr. H. J. Bannington."

He saw Coralie Bourne sit on the lower step of the dress-circle stairway and lean her head against the wall. Nearby, on a gilt easel, a huge photograph of Canning Cumberland smiled handsomely at her.

H. J. Bannington looked pretty ghastly. He had rubbed his hand across his face and smeared his makeup. Florid red paint from his lips had stained the crêpe hair that had been gummed on and shaped into a beard. His monocle was still in his left eye and gave him an extraordinarily rakish look. "See here," he complained, "I've about *had* this party. When do we go home?"

Alleyn uttered placatory phrases and got him to sit down. He checked over H.J.'s movements after Cumberland left the stage and found that his account tallied with Mike's. He asked if H.J. had visited any of the other dressing rooms and was told acidly that H.J. knew his place in the company. "I remained in my unheated and squalid kennel, thank you very much."

"Do you know if Mr. Barry George followed your example?"

"Couldn't say, old boy. He didn't come near *me*."

"Have you any theories at all about this unhappy business, Mr. Bannington?"

"Do you mean, why did Cann do it? Well, speak no ill of the dead, but I'd have thought it was pretty obvious he was morbid-drunk. Tight as an owl when we finished the second act. Ask the great Mr. Barry George. Cann took the big scene away from Barry with both hands and left him looking pathetic. All wrong artistically, but that's how Cann was in his cups." H.J.'s wicked little eyes narrowed. "The great Mr. George," he said, "must be feeling very unpleasant by now. You might say he'd got a suicide on his mind, mightn't you? Or don't you know about that?"

"It was not suicide."

The glass dropped from H.J.'s eye. "God!" he said. "God, I told Bob Reynolds! I told him the whole plant wanted overhauling."

"The gas plant, you mean?"

"Certainly. I was in the gas business years ago. Might say I'm in it still with a difference, ha-ha!"

"Ha-ha!" Alleyn agreed politely. He leaned forward. "Look here," he said: "We can't dig up a gas man at this time of night and may very likely need an expert opinion. You can help us."

"Well, old boy, I was rather pining for a spot of shut-eye. But, of course—"

"I shan't keep you very long."

"God, I hope not!" said H.J. earnestly.

Barry George had been made up pale for the last act. Colorless lips and shadows under his cheekbones and eyes had skillfully underlined his character as a repatriated but broken prisoner-of-war. Now, in the glare of the office lamp, he looked like a grossly exaggerated figure of mourning. He began at once to tell Alleyn how grieved and horrified he was. Everybody, he said, had their faults, and poor old Cann was no exception but wasn't it terrible to think what could happen to a man who let himself go down-hill? He, Barry George, was abnormally sensitive and he didn't think he'd ever really get over the awful shock this had been to him. What, he wondered, could be at the bottom of it? Why had poor old Cann decided to end it all?

"Miss Bourne's theory—" Alleyn began. Mr. George laughed. "Coralie?" he said. "So she's got a theory! Oh, well. Never mind."

"Her theory is this. Cumberland saw a man whom he mistook for her husband and, having a morbid dread of his return, drank the greater part of a bottle of whiskey and gassed himself. The clothes and beard that deceived him had, I understand, been ordered by you for Mr. Anthony Gill."

This statement produced startling results. Barry George broke into a spate of expostulation and apology. There had been no thought in his mind of resurrecting poor old Ben, who was no doubt dead but had been, mind you, in many ways one of the best. They were all to go to the Ball as exaggerated characters from melodrama. "Not for the world—" He gesticulated and protested. A line of sweat broke out along the margin of his hair. "I don't know what you're getting at," he shouted. "What are you suggesting?"

"I'm suggesting, among other things, that Cumberland was murdered."

"You're mad! He'd locked himself in. They had to break down the door. There's no window. You're crazy!"

"Don't," Alleyn said wearily, "let us have any nonsense about sealed rooms. Now, Mr. George, you knew Benjamin Vlasnoff pretty well. Are you going to tell us that when you suggested Mr. Gill should wear a coat with a fur collar, a black sombrero, black gloves, and a red beard, it never occurred to you that his appearance might be a shock to Miss Bourne and to Cumberland?"

"I wasn't the only one," he blustered. "H.J. knew. And if it had scared him off, *she* wouldn't have been so sorry. She'd had about enough of him. Anyway if this is murder, the costume's got nothing to do with it."

"That," Alleyn said, getting up, "is what we hope to find out."

In Barry George's room, Detective-Sergeant Bailey, a fingerprint expert, stood by the gas heater. Sergeant Gibson, a police photographer, and a uniformed constable were near the door. In the center of the room stood Barry George, looking from one man to another and picking at his lips.

"I don't know why he wants me to watch all this," he said. "I'm exhausted. I'm emotionally used up. What's he doing? Where is he?"

Alleyn was next door in Cumberland's dressing room, with H.J., Mike, and Sergeant Thompson. It was pretty clear now of fumes and the gas fire was burning comfortably. Sergeant Thompson sprawled in the armchair near the heater, his head sunk and his eyes shut.

"This is the theory, Mr. Bannington," Alleyn said. "You and Cumberland have made your final exits; Miss Bourne and Mr.

George and Miss Gay are all on the stage. Lord Michael is standing just outside the entrance to the passage. The dressers and stage-staff are watching the play from the side. Cumberland has locked himself in this room. There he is, dead drunk and sound asleep. The gas fire is burning, full pressure. Earlier in the evening he powdered himself and a thick layer of the powder lies undisturbed on the tap. Now."

He tapped on the wall.

The fire blew out with a sharp explosion. This was followed by the hiss of escaping gas. Alleyn turned the taps off. "You see," he said, "I've left an excellent print on the powdered surface. Now, come next door."

Next door, Barry George appealed to him stammering: "But I didn't know. I don't know anything about it. I don't *know*."

"Just show Mr. Bannington, will you, Bailey?"

Bailey knelt down. The lead-in was disconnected from the tap on the heater. He turned on the tap in the pipe and blew down the tube.

"An air lock, you see. It works perfectly."

H.J. was staring at Barry George. "But I don't know about gas, H.J. H.J., tell them—"

"One moment." Alleyn removed the towels that had been spread over the dressing-shelf, revealing a sheet of clean paper on which lay the rubber push-on connection.

"Will you take this lens, Bannington, and look at it. You'll see that it's stained a florid red. It's a very slight stain but it's unmistakably greasepaint. And just above the stain you'll see a wiry hair. Rather like some sort of packing material, but it's not that. It's crêpe hair, isn't it?"

The lens wavered above the paper.

"Let me hold it for you," Alleyn said. He put his hand over H.J.'s shoulder and, with a swift movement, plucked a tuft from his false moustache and dropped it on the paper. "Identical, you see. Ginger. It seems to be stuck to the connection with spirit gum."

The lens fell. H.J. twisted round, faced Alleyn for a second, and then struck him full in the face. He was a small man but it took three of them to hold him.

"In a way, sir, it's handy when they have a smack at you," said Detective-Sergeant Thompson half an hour later. "You can pull them in nice and straightforward without any 'will you come to the station and make a statement' business."

"Quite," said Alleyn, nursing his jaw.

Mike said: "He must have gone to the room after Barry George and Miss Bourne were called."

"That's it. He had to be quick. The call-boy would be round in a minute and he had to be back in his own room."

"But look here—what about motive?"

"That, my good Mike, is precisely why, at half-past one in the morning, we're still in this miserable theatre. You're getting a view of the duller aspect of homicide. Want to go home?"

"No. Give me another job."

"Very well. About ten feet from the prompt-entrance, there's a sort of garbage tin. Go through it."

At seventeen minutes to two, when the dressing rooms and passage had been combed clean and Alleyn had called a spell, Mike came to him with filthy hands. "*Eureka*," he said, "I hope."

They all went into Bannington's room. Alleyn spread out on the dressing-table the fragments of paper that Mike had given him.

"They'd been pushed down to the bottom of the tin," Mike said.

Alleyn moved the fragments about. Thompson whistled through his teeth. Bailey and Gibson mumbled together.

"There you are," Alleyn said at last.

They collected round him. The letter that H. J. Bannington had opened at this same table six hours and forty-five minutes earlier, was pieced together like a jigsaw puzzle.

"Dear H.J.

Having seen the monthly statement of my account, I called at my bank this morning and was shown a check that is undoubtedly a forgery. Your histrionic versatility, my dear H.J., is only equalled by your audacity as a calligraphist. But fame has its disadvantages. The teller recognized you. I propose to take action."

"Unsigned," said Bailey.

"Look at the card on the red roses in Miss Bourne's room, signed C.C. It's a very distinctive hand." Alleyn turned to Mike. "Do you still want to be a policeman?"

"Yes."

"Lord help you. Come and talk to me at the office tomorrow."

"Thank you, sir."

They went out, leaving a constable on duty. It was a cold morning. Mike looked up at the facade of the Jupiter. He could just make out the shape of the neon sign: I CAN FIND MY WAY OUT *by Anthony Gill.*

The Summer People

SHIRLEY JACKSON

Shirley Hardie Jackson (1916–65) was a prolific novelist and short-story writer, but her name is most readily associated with a single story, "The Lottery" (1948). Born in San Francisco, she grew up in Burlingame, California, and attended University of Rochester and Syracuse University. Her first major publication was the short story "My Life with R. H. Macy," published in *The New Republic* in 1941. Her first novel, *The Road Through the Wall*, was published in 1948, the same year "The Lottery" appeared in *The New Yorker* to considerable controversy. According to Jackson's essay "Biography of a Story" (1960), no one (including her agent and the editor who bought it) liked "The Lottery"; *New Yorker* editor in chief Harold Ross did not understand it; and it was the subject of torrents of disturbed reader mail. Jackson has been pegged as a specialist in horror and the supernatural because of her famous story but was actually far more versatile, her work including children's books and lighthearted domestic humor in her autobiographies *Life Among the Savages* (1953) and *Raising Demons* (1957).

Jackson's celebrated touch for understated horror developed quite early; see, for example, her very short story, "Janice" (1938), about a college student's devastatingly casual description of her suicide attempt. According to her husband Stanley Edgar Hyman's introduction to the posthumous collection *Come Along with Me* (1968), it was this story, written while she was a sophomore at Syracuse, that led to their first meeting.

"The Summer People" is a subtle tale, troublingly unresolved, with a sense of gathering menace assaulting the everyday. Is it an allegory, a horror story, a crime story? Are the Allisons dying or is some human agency terrorizing them? It makes a detective of the reader but doesn't necessarily verify the reader's conclusions.

The Allisons' country cottage, seven miles from the nearest town, was set prettily on a hill; from three sides it looked down on soft trees and grass that seldom, even at midsummer, lay still and dry. On the fourth side was the lake, which touched against the wooden pier the Allisons had to keep repairing, and which looked equally well from the Allisons' front porch, their side porch, or any spot on the wooden staircase leading from the porch down to the water. Although the Allisons loved their summer cottage, looked forward to arriving in the early summer and hated to leave in the fall, they had not troubled themselves to put in any improvements, regarding the cottage itself and the lake as improvement enough for the life left to them. The cottage had no heat, no running water except the precarious supply from the backyard pump, and no electricity. For seventeen summers, Janet Allison had cooked on a kerosene stove, heating all their water; Robert Allison had brought buckets full of water daily from the pump and read his paper by kerosene light in the evenings and they had both, sanitary city people, become stolid and matter-of-fact about their backhouse. In the first two years they had gone through all the standard vaudeville and magazine jokes about backhouses and by now, when they no longer had frequent guests to impress, they had subsided to a comfortable security which made the backhouse, as well as the pump and the kerosene, an indefinable asset to their summer life.

In themselves, the Allisons were ordinary people. Mrs. Allison was fifty-eight years old and Mr. Allison sixty; they had seen their children outgrow the summer cottage and go on to families of their own and seashore resorts; their friends were either dead or settled in comfortable year-round houses, their nieces and nephews vague. In the winter they told one another they could stand their New York apartment while waiting for the summer; in the summer they told one another that the winter was well worthwhile, waiting to get to the country.

Since they were old enough not to be ashamed of regular habits, the Allisons invariably left their summer cottage the Tuesday after Labor Day, and were as invariably sorry when the months of September and early October turned out to be pleasant and almost insufferably barren in the city; each year they recognized that there was nothing to bring them back to New York, but it was not until this year that they overcame their traditional inertia enough to decide to stay at the cottage after Labor Day.

"There isn't really anything to take us back to the city," Mrs. Allison told her husband seriously, as though it were a new idea, and he told her, as though neither of them had ever considered it, "We might as well enjoy the country as long as possible."

Consequently, with much pleasure and a slight feeling of adventure, Mrs. Allison went into their village the day after Labor Day and told those natives with whom she had dealings, with a pretty air of breaking away from tradition, that she and her husband had decided to stay at least a month longer at their cottage.

"It isn't as though we had anything to take us back to the city," she said to Mr. Babcock, her grocer. "We might as well enjoy the country while we can."

"Nobody ever stayed at the lake past Labor Day before," Mr. Babcock said. He was putting Mrs. Allison's groceries into a large cardboard carton, and he stopped for a minute to look reflectively into a bag of cookies. "Nobody," he added.

"But the city!" Mrs. Allison always spoke of the city to Mr. Babcock as though it were Mr. Babcock's dream to go there. "It's so hot—you've really no idea. We're always sorry when we leave."

"Hate to leave," Mr. Babcock said. One of the most irritating native tricks Mrs. Allison had noticed was that of taking a trivial statement and rephrasing it downward, into an even more trite statement. "I'd hate to leave myself," Mr. Babcock said, after deliberation, and both he and Mrs. Allison smiled. "But I never heard of anyone ever staying out at the lake after Labor Day before."

"Well, we're going to give it a try," Mrs. Allison said, and Mr. Babcock replied gravely, "Never know till you try."

Physically, Mrs. Allison decided, as she always did when leaving the grocery after one of her inconclusive conversations with Mr. Babcock, physically, Mr. Babcock could model for a statue of Daniel Webster, but mentally . . . it was horrible to think into what old New England Yankee stock had degenerated. She said as much to Mr. Allison when she got into the car, and he said, "It's generations of inbreeding. That and the bad land."

Since this was their big trip into town, which they made only once every two weeks to buy things they could not have delivered, they spent all day at it, stopping to have a sandwich in the newspaper and soda shop, and leaving packages heaped in the back of the car. Although Mrs. Allison was able to order groceries delivered regularly, she was never able to form any accurate idea of Mr. Babcock's current stock by telephone, and her lists of odds and ends that might be procured was always supplemented, almost beyond their need, by the new and fresh local vegetables Mr. Babcock was selling temporarily, or the packaged candy which had just come in. This trip Mrs. Allison was tempted, too, by the set of glass baking dishes that had found themselves completely by chance in the hardware and clothing and general store, and which had seemingly been waiting there for no one but Mrs. Allison, since the country people, with their instinctive distrust of anything that did not look as permanent as trees and rocks and sky, had only recently begun to experiment in aluminum baking dishes instead of ironware, and had, apparently within the memory of local inhabitants, discarded stoneware in favor of iron.

Mrs. Allison had the glass baking dishes carefully wrapped, to endure the uncomfortable ride home over the rocky road that led up to the Allisons' cottage, and while Mr. Charley Walpole, who, with his younger brother Albert, ran the hardware-clothing-general store (the store itself was called Johnson's, because it stood on the site of the old Johnson cabin, burned fifty years before Charley Walpole was born), laboriously unfolded newspapers to wrap around the dishes, Mrs. Allison said, informally, "Course, I *could* have waited and gotten those dishes in New York, but we're not going back so soon this year."

"Heard you was staying on," Mr. Charley Walpole said. His old fingers fumbled maddeningly with the thin sheets of newspaper, carefully trying to isolate only one sheet at a time, and he did not look up at Mrs. Allison as he went on, "Don't know about staying on up there to the lake. Not after Labor Day."

"Well, you know," Mrs. Allison said, quite as though he deserved an explanation, "it just seemed to us that we've been hurrying back to New York every year, and there just wasn't any need for it. You know what the city's like in the fall." And she smiled confidingly up at Mr. Charley Walpole.

Rhythmically he wound string around the package. He's giving me a piece long enough to save, Mrs. Allison thought, and she looked away quickly to avoid giving any sign of impatience. "I feel sort of like we belong here, more," she said. "Staying on after everyone else has left." To prove this, she smiled brightly across the store at a woman with a familiar face, who might have been the woman who sold berries to the Allisons one year, or the woman who occasionally helped in the grocery and was probably Mr. Babcock's aunt.

"Well," Mr. Charley Walpole said. He shoved the package a little across the counter, to show that it was finished and that for a sale well made, a package well wrapped, he was willing to accept pay. "Well," he said again. "Never been summer people before, at the lake after Labor Day."

Mrs. Allison gave him a five-dollar bill, and he made change methodically, giving great weight even to the pennies. "Never after Labor Day," he said, and nodded at Mrs. Allison, and went soberly along the store to deal with two women who were looking at cotton housedresses.

As Mrs. Allison passed on her way out she heard one of the women say acutely, "Why is one of them dresses one dollar and thirty-nine cents and this one here is only ninety-eight?"

"They're great people," Mrs. Allison told her husband as they went together down the sidewalk after meeting at the door of the hardware store. "They're so solid, and so reasonable, and so *honest*."

"Makes you feel good, knowing there are still towns like this," Mr. Allison said.

"You know, in New York," Mrs. Allison said, "I might have paid a few cents less for these dishes, but there wouldn't have been anything sort of *personal* in the transaction."

"Staying on to the lake?" Mrs. Martin, in the newspaper and sandwich shop, asked the Allisons. "Heard you was staying on."

"Thought we'd take advantage of the lovely weather this year," Mr. Allison said.

Mrs. Martin was a comparative newcomer to the town; she had married into the newspaper and sandwich shop from a neighboring farm, and had stayed on after her husband's death. She served bottled soft drinks, and fried egg and onion sandwiches on thick bread, which she made on her own stove at the back of the store. Occasionally when Mrs. Martin served a sandwich it would carry with it the rich fragrance of the stew or the pork chops cooking alongside for Mrs. Martin's dinner.

"I don't guess anyone's ever stayed out there so long before," Mrs. Martin said. "Not after Labor Day, anyway."

"I guess Labor Day is when they usually leave," Mr. Hall, the Allisons' nearest neighbor, told them later, in front of Mr. Babcock's store, where the Allisons were getting into their car to go home. "Surprised you're staying on."

"It seemed a shame to go so soon," Mrs. Allison said. Mr. Hall lived three miles away; he supplied the Allisons with butter and eggs, and occasionally, from the top of their hill, the Allisons could see the lights in his house in the early evening before the Halls went to bed.

"They usually leave Labor Day," Mr. Hall said.

The ride home was long and rough; it was beginning to get dark, and Mr. Allison had to drive very carefully over the dirt road by the lake. Mrs. Allison lay back against the seat, pleasantly relaxed after a day of what seemed whirlwind shopping compared with their day-to-day existence; the new glass baking dishes lurked agreeably in her mind, and the half bushel of red eating apples, and the package of colored thumbtacks with which she was going to put up new shelf edging in the kitchen. "Good to get home," she said softly as they came in sight of their cottage, silhouetted above them against the sky.

"Glad we decided to stay on," Mr. Allison agreed.

Mrs. Allison spent the next morning lovingly washing her baking dishes, although in his innocence Charley Walpole had neglected to notice the chip in the edge of one; she decided, wastefully, to use some of the red eating apples in a pie for dinner, and, while the pie was in the oven and Mr. Allison was down getting the mail, she sat out on the little lawn the Allisons had made at the top of the hill, and watched the changing lights on the lake, alternating gray and blue as clouds moved quickly across the sun.

Mr. Allison came back a little out of sorts; it always irritated him to walk the mile to the mailbox on the state road and come back with nothing, even though he assumed that the walk was good for his health. This morning there was nothing but a circular from a New York department store, and their New York paper, which arrived erratically by mail from one to four days later than it should, so that some days the Allisons might have three papers and frequently none. Mrs. Allison, although she shared with her husband the annoyance of not having mail when they so anticipated it, pored affectionately over the department store circular, and made a mental note to drop in at the store when she finally went back to New York, and check on the sale of wool blankets;

it was hard to find good ones in pretty colors nowadays. She debated saving the circular to remind herself, but after thinking about getting up and getting into the cottage to put it away safely somewhere, she dropped it into the grass beside her chair and lay back, her eyes half closed.

"Looks like we might have some rain," Mr. Allison said, squinting at the sky.

"Good for the crops," Mrs. Allison said laconically, and they both laughed.

The kerosene man came the next morning while Mr. Allison was down getting the mail; they were getting low on kerosene and Mrs. Allison greeted the man warmly; he sold kerosene and ice, and, during the summer, hauled garbage away for the summer people. A garbage man was only necessary for improvident city folk; country people had no garbage.

"I'm glad to see you," Mrs. Allison told him. "We were getting pretty low."

The kerosene man, whose name Mrs. Allison had never learned, used a hose attachment to fill the twenty-gallon tank which supplied light and heat and cooking facilities for the Allisons; but today, instead of swinging down from his truck and unhooking the hose from where it coiled affectionately around the cab of the truck, the man stared uncomfortably at Mrs. Allison, his truck motor still going.

"Thought you folks'd be leaving," he said.

"We're staying on another month," Mrs. Allison said brightly. "The weather was so nice, and it seemed like—"

"That's what they told me," the man said. "Can't give you no oil, though."

"What do you mean?" Mrs. Allison raised her eyebrows. "We're just going to keep on with our regular—"

"After Labor Day," the man said. "I don't get so much oil myself after Labor Day."

Mrs. Allison reminded herself, as she had frequently to do when in disagreement with her neighbors, that city manners were no good with country people; you could not expect to overrule a country employee as you could a city worker, and Mrs. Allison smiled engagingly as she said, "But can't you get extra oil, at least while we stay?"

"You see," the man said. He tapped his finger exasperatingly against the car wheel as he spoke. "You see," he said slowly, "I order this oil. I order it down from maybe fifty, fifty-five miles away. I order back in June, how much I'll need for the summer. Then I order again . . . oh, about November. Round about now it's starting to get pretty short." As though the subject were closed, he stopped tapping his finger and tightened his hands on the wheel in preparation for departure.

"But can't you give us *some?*" Mrs. Allison said. "Isn't there anyone else?"

"Don't know as you could get oil anywheres else right now," the man said consideringly. "*I* can't give you none." Before Mrs. Allison could speak, the truck began to move; then it stopped for a minute and he looked at her through the back window of the cab. "Ice?" he called. "I could let you have some ice."

Mrs. Allison shook her head; they were not terribly low on ice, and she was angry. She ran a few steps to catch up with the truck, calling, "Will you try to get us some? Next week?"

"Don't see's I can," the man said. "After Labor Day, it's harder." The truck drove away, and Mrs. Allison, only comforted by the thought that she could probably get kerosene from Mr. Babcock or, at worst, the Halls, watched it go with anger. "Next summer," she told herself, "just let *him* trying coming around next summer!"

There was no mail again, only the paper, which seemed to be coming doggedly on time, and Mr. Allison was openly cross when he returned. When Mrs. Allison told him about the kerosene man he was not particularly impressed.

"Probably keeping it all for a high price during the winter," he commented. "What's happened to Anne and Jerry, do you think?"

Anne and Jerry were their son and daughter, both married, one living in Chicago, one in the far west; their dutiful weekly letters were late; so late, in fact, that Mr. Allison's annoyance at the lack of mail was able to settle on a legitimate grievance. "Ought to realize how we wait for their letters," he said. "Thoughtless, selfish children. Ought to know better."

"Well, dear," Mrs. Allison said placatingly. Anger at Anne and Jerry would not relieve her emotions toward the kerosene man. After a few minutes she said, "Wishing won't bring the mail, dear. I'm going to go call Mr. Babcock and tell him to send up some kerosene with my order."

"At least a postcard," Mr. Allison said as she left.

As with most of the cottage's inconveniences, the Allisons no longer noticed the phone particularly, but yielded to its eccentricities without conscious complaint. It was a wall phone, of a type still seen in only few communities; in order to get the operator, Mrs. Allison had first to turn the side-crank and ring once. Usually it took two or three tries to force the operator to answer, and Mrs. Allison, making any kind of telephone call, approached the phone with resignation and a sort of desperate patience. She had to crank the phone three times this morning before the operator answered, and then it was still longer before Mr. Babcock picked up the receiver at his phone in the corner of the grocery behind the meat table. He said "Store?" with the rising inflection that seemed to indicate suspicion of anyone who tried to communicate with him by means of this unreliable instrument.

"This is Mrs. Allison, Mr. Babcock. I thought I'd give you my order a day early because I wanted to be sure and get some—"

"What say, Mrs. Allison?"

Mrs. Allison raised her voice a little; she saw Mr. Allison, out on the lawn, turn in his chair and regard her sympathetically. "I said, Mr. Babcock, I thought I'd call in my order early so you could send me—"

"Mrs. Allison?" Mr. Babcock said. "You'll come and pick it up?"

"Pick it up?" In her surprise Mrs. Allison let her voice drop back to its normal tone and Mr. Babcock said loudly, "What's that, Mrs. Allison?"

"I thought I'd have you send it out as usual," Mrs. Allison said.

"Well, Mrs. Allison," Mr. Babcock said, and there was a pause while Mrs. Allison waited, staring past the phone over her husband's head out into the sky. "Mrs. Allison," Mr. Babcock went on finally, "I'll tell you, my boy's been working for me went back to school yesterday, and now I got no one to deliver. I only got a boy delivering summers, you see."

"I thought you *always* delivered," Mrs. Allison said.

"Not after Labor Day, Mrs. Allison," Mr. Babcock said firmly, "you never been here after Labor Day before, so's you wouldn't know, of course."

"Well," Mrs. Allison said helplessly. Far inside her mind she was saying, over and over, can't use city manners on country folk, no use getting mad.

"Are you *sure?*" she asked finally. "Couldn't you just send out an order today, Mr. Babcock?"

"Matter of fact," Mr. Babcock said, "I guess I couldn't, Mrs. Allison. It wouldn't hardly pay, delivering, with no one else out at the lake."

"What about Mr. Hall?" Mrs. Allison asked suddenly, "the people who live about three miles away from us out here? Mr. Hall could bring it out when he comes."

"Hall?" Mr. Babcock said. "John Hall? They've gone to visit her folks upstate, Mrs. Allison."

"But they bring all our butter and eggs," Mrs. Allison said, appalled.

"Left yesterday," Mr. Babcock said. "Probably didn't think you folks would stay on up there."

"But I told Mr. Hall . . ." Mrs. Allison started to say, and then stopped. "I'll send Mr. Allison in after some groceries tomorrow," she said.

"You got all you need till then," Mr. Babcock said, satisfied; it was not a question, but a confirmation.

After she hung up, Mrs. Allison went slowly out to sit again in her chair next to her husband. "He won't deliver," she said.

"You'll have to go in tomorrow. We've got just enough kerosene to last till you get back."

"He should have told us sooner," Mr. Allison said.

It was not possible to remain troubled long in the face of the day; the country had never seemed more inviting, and the lake moved quietly below them, among the trees, with the almost incredible softness of a summer picture. Mrs. Allison sighed deeply, in the pleasure of possessing for themselves that sight of the lake, with the distant green hills beyond, the gentleness of the small wind through the trees.

The weather continued fair; the next morning Mr. Allison, duly armed with a list of groceries, with "kerosene" in large letters at the top, went down the path to the garage, and Mrs. Allison began another pie in her new baking dishes. She had mixed the crust and was starting to pare the apples when Mr. Allison came rapidly up the path and flung open the screen door into the kitchen.

"Damn car won't start," he announced, with the end-of-the-tether voice of a man who depends on a car as he depends on his right arm.

"What's wrong with it?" Mrs. Allison demanded, stopping with the paring knife in one hand and an apple in the other. "It was all right on Tuesday."

"Well," Mr. Allison said between his teeth, "it's not all right on Friday."

"Can you fix it?" Mrs. Allison asked.

"No," Mr. Allison said, "I can not. Got to call someone, I guess."

"Who?" Mrs. Allison asked.

"Man runs the filling station, I guess." Mr. Allison moved purposefully toward the phone. "He fixed it last summer one time."

A little apprehensive, Mrs. Allison went on paring apples absentmindedly, while she listened to Mr. Allison with the phone, ringing, waiting, ringing, waiting, finally giving the number to the operator, then waiting again and giving the number again, giving the number a third time, and then slamming down the receiver.

"No one there," he announced as he came into the kitchen.

"He's probably gone out for a minute," Mrs. Allison said nervously; she was not quite sure what made her so nervous, unless it was the probability of her husband's losing his temper completely. "He's there alone, I imagine, so if he goes out there's no one to answer the phone."

"That must be it," Mr. Allison said with heavy irony. He slumped into one of the kitchen chairs and watched Mrs. Allison paring apples. After a minute, Mrs. Allison said soothingly, "Why don't you go down and get the mail and then call him again?"

Mr. Allison debated and then said, "Guess I might as well." He rose heavily and when he got to the kitchen door he turned and said, "But if there's no mail—" and leaving an awful silence behind him, he went off down the path.

Mrs. Allison hurried with her pie. Twice she went to the window to glance at the sky to see if there were clouds coming up. The room seemed unexpectedly dark, and she herself felt in the state of tension that precedes a thunderstorm, but both times when she looked the sky was clear and serene, smiling indifferently down on the Allisons' summer cottage as well as on the rest of the world. When Mrs. Allison, her pie ready for the oven, went a third time to look outside, she saw her husband coming up the path; he seemed more cheerful, and when he saw her, he waved eagerly and held a letter in the air.

"From Jerry," he called as soon as he was close enough for her to hear him, "at last—a letter!" Mrs. Allison noticed with concern that he was no longer able to get up the gentle slope of the path without breathing heavily; but then he was in the doorway, holding out the letter. "I saved it till I got here," he said.

Mrs. Allison looked with an eagerness that surprised her on the familiar handwriting of her son; she could not imagine why the letter excited her so, except that it was the first they had received in so long, it would be a pleasant, dutiful letter, full of the doings of Alice and the children, reporting progress with his job, commenting on the recent weather in Chicago, closing with love from all; both Mr. and Mrs. Allison could, if they wished, recite a pattern letter from either of their children.

Mr. Allison slit the letter open with great deliberation, and then he spread it out on the kitchen table and they leaned down and read it together.

"*Dear Mother and Dad,*" it began, in Jerry's familiar, rather childish handwriting, "*Am glad this goes to the lake as usual, we always thought you came back too soon and ought to stay up there as long as you could. Alice says that now that you're not as young as you used to be and have no demands on your time, fewer friends, etc., in the city, you ought to get what fun you can while you can. Since you two are both happy up there, it's a good idea for you to stay.*"

Uneasily Mrs. Allison glanced sideways at her husband; he was reading intently, and she reached out and picked up the empty envelope, not knowing exactly what she wanted from it. It was addressed quite as usual, in Jerry's handwriting, and was post-marked Chicago. Of course it's postmarked Chicago, she thought quickly, why would they want to postmark it anywhere else? When she looked back down at the letter, her husband had turned the page, and she read on with him: "*—and of course if they get measles, etc., now, they will be better off later. Alice is well, of course, me too. Been playing a lot of bridge lately with some people you don't know, named Carruthers. Nice young couple, about our age. Well, will close now as I guess it bores you to hear about things so far away. Tell Dad old Dickson, in our Chicago office, died. He used to ask about Dad a lot. Have a good time up at the lake, and don't bother about hurrying back. Love from all of us, Jerry.*"

"Funny," Mr. Allison commented.

"It doesn't sound like Jerry," Mrs. Allison said in a small voice. "He never wrote anything like . . ." she stopped.

"Like what?" Mr. Allison demanded. "Never wrote anything like what?"

Mrs. Allison turned the letter over, frowning. It was impossible to find any sentence, any word, even, that did not sound like Jerry's regular letters. Perhaps it was only that the letter was so late, or the unusual number of dirty fingerprints on the envelope.

"I don't *know*," she said impatiently.

"Going to try that phone call again," Mr. Allison said.

Mrs. Allison read the letter twice more, trying to find a phrase that sounded wrong. Then Mr. Allison came back and said, very quietly, "Phone's dead."

"What?" Mrs. Allison said, dropping the letter.

"Phone's dead," Mr. Allison said.

The rest of the day went quickly; after a lunch of crackers and milk, the Allisons went to sit outside on the lawn, but their afternoon was cut short by the gradually increasing storm clouds that came up over the lake to the cottage, so that it was as dark as evening by four o'clock. The storm delayed, however, as though in loving anticipation of the moment it would break over the summer cottage, and there was an occasional flash of lightning, but no rain. In the evening Mr. and Mrs. Allison, sitting close together inside their cottage, turned on the battery radio they had brought with them from New York. There were no lamps lighted in the cottage, and the only light came from the lightning outside and the small square glow from the dial of the radio.

The slight framework of the cottage was not strong enough to withstand the city noises, the music and the voices, from the radio, and the Allisons could hear them far off echoing across the lake, the saxophones in the New York dance band wailing over the water, the flat voice of the girl vocalist going inexorably out into the clean country air. Even the announcer, speaking glowingly of the virtues of razor blades, was no more than an inhuman voice sounding out from the Allisons' cottage and echoing back, as though the lake and the hills and the trees were returning it unwanted.

During one pause between commercials, Mrs. Allison turned and smiled weakly at her husband. "I wonder if we're supposed to . . . *do* anything," she said.

"No," Mr. Allison said consideringly. "I don't think so. Just wait."

Mrs. Allison caught her breath quickly, and Mr. Allison said, under the trivial melody of the dance band beginning again, "The car had been tampered with, you know. Even I could see that."

Mrs. Allison hesitated a minute and then said very softly, "I suppose the phone wires were cut."

"I imagine so," Mr. Allison said.

After a while, the dance music stopped and they listened attentively to a news broadcast, the announcer's rich voice telling them breathlessly of a marriage in Hollywood, the latest baseball scores, the estimated rise in food prices during the coming week. He spoke to them, in the summer cottage, quite as though they still deserved to hear news of a world that no longer reached them except through the fallible batteries on the radio, which were already beginning to fade, almost as though they still belonged, however tenuously, to the rest of the world.

Mrs. Allison glanced out the window at the smooth surface of the lake, the black masses of the trees, and the waiting storm, and said conversationally, "I feel better about that letter of Jerry's."

"I knew when I saw the light down at the Hall place last night," Mr. Allison said.

The wind, coming up suddenly over the lake, swept around the summer cottage and slapped hard at the windows. Mr. and Mrs. Allison involuntarily moved closer together, and with the first sudden crash of thunder, Mr. Allison reached out and took his wife's hand. And then, while the lightning flashed outside, and the radio faded and sputtered, the two old people huddled together in their summer cottage and waited.

St. Patrick's Day in the Morning

CHARLOTTE ARMSTRONG

Charlotte Armstrong (1905–69) is one of a lustrous group of writers who give the lie to the revisionist history claim that American women mystery writers of the fifties and sixties were downtrodden and unappreciated victims of hardboiled masculine dominance. The Mystery Writers of America awarded her an Edgar for *A Dram of Poison* (1956), and her two 1967 titles, *The Gift Shop* and *Lemon in the Basket*, were best-novel nominees in the same year. At the height of her reputation, not even Cornell Woolrich was more celebrated as a purveyor of pure suspense.

After a couple of unsuccessful (albeit New York–produced) plays and three relatively conventional detective novels featuring a character named MacDougall Duff, the Michigan-born Armstrong made a major impact and stirred controversy among fans and critics with *The Unsuspected* (1946). Howard Haycraft, traditionalist author of the standard history *Murder for Pleasure* (1941), admired the novel's strengths but insisted it would have been even better had Armstrong concealed the identity of the villain in standard whodunnit fashion rather than letting the reader in on the secret. The novel was filmed in 1947, with a script by Armstrong, and she followed it with *The Chocolate Cobweb* (1948), *Mischief* (1950), *The Black-Eyed Stranger* (1951), and many more novels through the posthumously published *The Protégé* (1970).

Armstrong was as effective at short-story as novel length. "St. Patrick's Day in the Morning" demonstrates both her creation of reader anxiety and her strong sense of human interdependence and responsibility—plus the problems it can cause. It also shows her affinity to Woolrich in its unusual variant on one of his favorite situations (the lady vanishes) and to the theater—the main character is a playwright, and the story is easy to imagine as a play.

Very carefully, in a state of fearful pleasure, he put all the pieces of paper in order. One copy of the manuscript he put into an envelope and addressed it. The other copies he put into an empty suitcase. Then he called an airline and was lucky. A seat for New York in the morning. Morning? What morning? St. Patrick's Day in the morning.

He had been out of this world. But now he stretched, breathed, blinked, and put out feelers for what is known as reality.

See now. He was Mitchel Brown, playwright (God willing), and he had finished the job of revision he had come home to Los Angeles to do. Wowee! Finished!

The hour was a quarter after one in the morning and therefore already the seventeenth of March. The place was his ground-floor apartment, and it was a mess: smoky, dirty, disorderly . . . Oh, well, first things had come first. His back was aching, his eyes were burning, his head was light. He would have to clean up, eat, sleep, bathe, shave, dress, pack. But first . . .

He slammed a row of airmail stamps on the envelope and went out. The street was dark and deserted. A few cars sat lumpishly along the curbs. The manuscript thumped down into the mailbox—safe in the bosom of the Postal Service. Now, even if he, the plane, and the other copies perished . . .

Mitch laughed at himself and turned the corner, feeling suddenly let down, depressed, and forlorn.

The Parakeet Bar and Grill, he noted gratefully, was still open. He walked the one block and went in. The Bar ran all the way along one wall and the Grill, consisting of eight booths, ran all the way along the other. The narrow room was dim and felt empty. Mitch groped for a stool.

"Hi, Toby. Business slow?"

"Hi, Mr. Brown." The bartender seemed glad to see him. He was a small man with a crest of dark hair, a blue chin, and a blue tinge to the whites of his eyes. "This late on a weeknight, I'm never crowded."

"The kitchen's gone home, eh?" Mitch said. The kitchen was not the heart of this establishment.

"That's right, Mr. Brown. You want any food, you better go elsewhere."

"A drink will do me," said Mitch with a sigh. "*I* can go home and scramble yet another egg."

Toby turned to his bottles. When he turned back with Mitch's usual, he said in an anxious whine, "Fact is, I got to close up pretty soon and I don't know what to do."

"What do you mean, what to do?"

"Look at her." Toby's gaze passed over Mitch's left shoulder.

Mitch glanced behind him and was startled to see there was a woman sitting in one of the booths. Or perhaps one could say lying, since her fair hatless head was down on the red-checked tablecloth. Mitch turned again and wagged inquiring eyebrows.

"Out like a light," said Toby in a hoarse whisper. "Listen, I don't want to call the cops. Thing like that, not so good for the place. But I got a kid sick and my wife is all wore out and I wanted to get home."

"You try black coffee?"

"Sure, I tried." Toby's shoulders despaired.

"How'd she get this way?"

"Not here," said Toby quickly. "Don't see how. So help me, a coupla drinks hit her like that. Trouble is, she's not a bum. You can see that. So what should I do?"

"Put her in a taxi," said Mitch blithely. "Just ship her where she belongs. Why not? She'll have something on her for identity."

"I don't want to mess around with her pocketbook," Toby said fearfully.

"Hm. Well, let's see . . ." Mitch got off the stool. His drink had gone down and bounced lightly and he was feeling cheerful and friendly toward all the world. Furthermore, he felt *very* intelligent and he understood that he had been born to understand everybody.

Toby came too, and they lifted the woman's torso.

Her face was slack in drunken sleep; but even so it was not an ugly face. It was not young; neither was it old. Her clothing was expensive. No, she wasn't a tramp.

Then she opened her eyes and said in a refined voice, "I beg your pardon."

She was not exactly conscious; still this was encouraging. The two men got her to her feet. With their support she could stand. In fact, she could walk. Mitch ran his left arm through the handle of her expensive-looking handbag. The two of them walked her to the door.

"The air maybe?" said the bartender hopefully.

"Right," said Mitch. "Listen, there's a cab stand next to the movie theater. By the time we walk her over there . . ."

Toby said shrilly. "I got to lock up. I got to take care of the place."

"Go ahead," said Mitch, standing in the sweet night air with the strange woman heavy in his arms, "I've got her."

He heard the lock click behind him as he set off on the sidewalk, the woman putting one foot ahead of the other willingly enough. Musing on the peculiar and surprising qualities of "reality," Mitch had guided her halfway along the block before he recognized the fact that the bartender had taken him literally and was not coming along at all.

Oh, well. Mitch was not annoyed. On the contrary, he felt filled with compassion for all human beings. This woman was human and, therefore, frail. He was glad to try to help her to some place of her own.

The neighborhood business section was deserted. They were moving in an empty world. When Mitch had struggled all the way to the next corner, he could see ahead that there were no cabs near the theater. At this time of night the theater was dead and dark, as he should have known. He guessed he hadn't quite been meshed with the gears of ordinary time.

Anyhow, he couldn't turn her over to a handy cab driver. Nor to the police, since there were no policemen around either. There was nothing but pavement, those few lumps of metal left at the curb for the night, and no traffic.

Mitch wouldn't have hailed a motorist anyway. Most motorists were suspicious and afraid. So he did the only thing he could— he kept walking.

He guided her automatic steps around the corner and down the street, for surely, he thought, if he kept her walking she would begin to be conscious and he could then ask her what *she* wanted him to do about her. This he felt was the right thing. Perhaps he could get out his own car . . .

But the air was not having the desired effect. She began to stumble. Her weight slumped against him. Mitch found he was almost carrying her. Then he discovered that he was standing, holding her upright with both arms, directly in front of his own building. Obviously, the only thing to do was take her inside, where he could investigate her identity and telephone for a taxi.

The apartment had not tidied itself up during his absence. He let her weight go and she sagged down on his sofa. He guided her blond head to a pillow. There she lay, out like a light, a perfect stranger. To straighten the body and make it look more comfortable, he lifted the lower part of the legs. One of her shoes— beautiful shoes in a fine green leather, with a high spike heel and a small brass buckle—one of them came off.

Mitch took hold of the other shoe and also removed it. Full of cosmic thoughts about females and heels, he put her shoes on his desk and slipped her handbag off her arm. It was the same fine green leather.

It did feel sneaky to be rifling the property of a strange woman. Still, it had to be done.

Her name, on the driver's license, was Natalie Maxwell. Her address was in Santa Barbara. Mitch whistled. That knocked over his scheme of sending her home in a cab, since her home was a hundred miles away. Then he found a letter addressed to Mrs. Julius Maxwell and Mitch whistled again. So she was married!

Furthermore, she was married to somebody whose name was familiar. Julius Maxwell. All that came to Mitch's musing memory was an aroma of money. She probably wasn't broke, then. He peered into her wallet and saw a few bills. Not many. So he riffled her checkbook and whistled for the third time. Well! No penniless waif, this one.

Mitch ran his hand through his hair and considered his predicament. Here he was, harboring a wealthy matron from Santa Barbara who had passed out from liquor. What was he going to do with her?

There was nothing in the bag to tell him where she was staying locally. The letter was woman's chatter from someone in San Francisco.

So what to do?

Well, he might phone the police and dump her on them. This he could not quite imagine. Or, he could phone the residence of Julius Maxwell, in Santa Barbara, and if her husband were there, ask for instructions; or, if he were not there, surely Mitch could ask somebody where Mrs. Maxwell was staying in Los Angeles, and dump her *there*. All this went through his mind and was rejected.

Why cause another human being humiliation and trouble? He didn't think she was ill. Just stinko. Sooner or later the fumes would wear away and she would come to herself. Meantime, she was perfectly safe, right where she was. Heaven knew he had no evil thoughts.

Also, he—Mitchel Brown, playwright, artist, apostle of compassion—*he* was no bourgeois to conform, cravenly fearing for his reputation if he were to do what is "not done." Was he, being what he was, to put this human being into a jam with the Law, or even with her own husband? When this human being, for some human reason, had simply imbibed a little too much alcohol? He couldn't do it.

Okay. He had been dragooned by his mood and by the perfidious desertion of Toby the bartender into acting the Samaritan. Why not be the *good* Samaritan, then? Give her a break.

This pleased him. It felt lucky to him. Give her a break. God knows we all need them, he thought piously.

So Mitch scribbled a note. *Dear Mrs. Maxwell: Use my phone if you like. Or be my guest, as long as you need to be.*

He signed it, went into his bedroom, got a light blanket, and spread it over her. She was snoring faintly. He studied her face a moment more. He put the note on the rug under her shoes where she would be sure to see it. Then he went into his bedroom, closed the door, and went to bed.

Mitchel Brown woke up on St. Patrick's Day, early in the morning, absolutely ravenous. He had forgotten to eat anything. Now he remembered. New York! Catch plane! Pack!

He started for his kitchen and at the bedroom door remembered the lady. So he turned and put a robe on before emerging.

He needn't have bothered. She was gone. Her shoes were gone. Her bag was gone. His note was gone. In fact, there was no trace of her at all.

He did *not* wonder whether he had been dreaming. So she had come to and fled. Hm, without even a "Thank you"? Oh, well, panic, he supposed. Ah, human frailty! Mitch shrugged. But he had things to do and not enough time to do them in.

He went into a spell of demon housekeeping, threw everything perishable out of his refrigerator, everything dirty into the laundry bag, everything wearable into his suitcase. He caught the plane by a whisker.

Once on it he began to suffer. He reread his manuscript in his mind's eye and squirmed with doubt. He tried to nap and could not, and then, suddenly, he could . . . and then he was in New York and God was willing and his producer was still hot and eager . . .

Six weeks later Mitchel Brown, playwright, got off the plane in Los Angeles. He had a play on Broadway. The verdict was *comme ci, comme ça.* Time, box office, word of mouth . . . personally he could bear no more. He wasn't licked, but he knew he would be unless he got home and got to work on something else and that, soon.

He had been out of this world all this time, for when one has a play in rehearsal, earthquake, major catastrophe, declaration of war mean nothing. Nothing whatever.

He got to his apartment about five a.m. and kicked aside the pile of newspapers he had forgotten to stop. The place smelled stale and wasn't really clean, but no matter. He opened all the windows, mixed himself a highball, and sat down with the last paper on the heap to catch up with the way the Western world had wagged since he had left it. International affairs he had glanced over, the last week in the East. Local affairs, of course, were completely unknown to him.

The latest murder, hm . . . Los Angeles papers are always hopeful that a murder is going to turn out to be a big one, so any and every murder gets off with a bang. This one didn't look promising. A mere brawl, he judged. Would die down in a couple of days.

He skimmed the second page where all the older murders were followed up. He had missed two or three. Some woman knifed by an ex-husband. Some man shot in his own hall. Run-of-the-mill. Mitch yawned. He would get out his car, go somewhere for a decent meal, he decided. Tomorrow, back to the salt mines.

At 6:30 p.m. he walked into his favorite restaurant, ordered a drink, settled to contemplate the menu.

She came in quietly about ten minutes later and sat down by herself at a table directly across from Mitch. The first thing he noted, with the tail of his eye, was her shoes. He had seen them before. Yes, and held them—held them in his hands.

His eyes traveled higher and there was Mrs. Julius Maxwell. (Natalie was her given name, he remembered.) It was not only Mrs. Julius Maxwell in the flesh, but Mrs. Julius Maxwell *in the very same clothing she had worn before!* The same green suit, the same pale blouse, and no hat. She was a lady, well groomed, prosperous, pretty, and poised—and now perfectly sober.

Mitch kept his head cocked and his eyes on her, waiting for her to feel his stare and respond to it. Her eyes came to his in a moment, but they were cool and empty of recognition.

Well, of course, he thought. How would she know me? She never *saw* me. He glanced away, feeling amused, then glanced back. Natalie Maxwell was ordering. She sat back, relaxed, and her gaze slipped past him again, returned briefly to note his interest, then went away, indicating none on her part.

Mitch could not help feeling that this was not fair. He got up and crossed to her. "How do you do, Mrs. Maxwell?" he said pleasantly. "I am glad you are feeling better."

"I beg your pardon?" she said. He remembered that he had heard her say this, and only this, once before.

"I'm Mitchel Brown." He waited, smiling down at her.

"I don't believe . . ." she murmured in genteel puzzlement. She had a nice straight nose and, although she was looking up at him, she seemed to be looking down that nose.

"I'm sure you remember the name," Mitch said. "It was the sixteenth of March. No, it was Saint Patrick's Day in the morning, actually."

"I don't quite . . ."

Was she stupid or what? Mitch said, with a bit of a sting in the tone, "Did you have much of a hangover?"

"I'm very *sorry,*" she said with a little exasperated laugh, "but I really don't know what you are talking about."

"Oh, come now, Natalie," said Mitch, beginning to feel miffed, "it was my apartment."

"What?" she said.

"My apartment that you passed out in—here in Los Angeles."

"I am afraid you are making a mistake," she said distantly.

Mitch did not think so.

"Aren't you Mrs. Julius Maxwell?"

"Yes, I am."

"From Santa Barbara?"

"Why, yes, I am." She was frowning a little.

"Then the apartment you woke up in, on Saint Patrick's Day in the morning, was *my* apartment," said Mitch huffily, "and why the amnesia?"

"What is this?" said a male voice.

Mitch swivelled his head and knew at once that here was Mr. Julius Maxwell. He saw a medium-sized, taut-muscled, middle-aged man with a thatch of salt-and-pepper hair and fierce black eyes under heavy black brows. Everything about this man blazoned aggression and possession. He reeked of push and power, of *I* and *Mine.*

Mitchel Brown, playwright, artist, and apostle of compassion, drew his own forces together, as if he folded in some wings.

"Julius," said the blond woman, "this man knows my name. He keeps talking about Saint Patrick's Day in the morning."

"Oh, he does?" said her husband.

"He says I was in his apartment, here in Los Angeles."

To Mitch Brown came a notion that would explain all this. Obviously, Natalie's husband had never found out where Natalie had been that night. So Natalie had to pretend she didn't know Mitch, because *she* knew, as he did not, that Julius Maxwell was nearby and would appear. But something in the woman's manner did not quite fit this theory. She didn't seem to be concerned enough. She looked straight ahead and her bewilderment was perfunctory.

Still, he thought he should be gallant. "I must have made a mistake" he said. "But the resemblance is remarkable. Perhaps you have a double, ma'am?"

He thought this was handsome of him and that it gave her a way out.

"A double?" said Julius Maxwell nastily. "Who uses my wife's *name?*"

Well, of course, if the man was going to be intelligent about it, that tore it. "Sorry," said Mitch lightly.

"Sit down and tell me about it," said Maxwell commandingly. "Mr. . . . er . . . ?"

"Brown," said Mitch shortly. He was of a mind to turn on his heel and go away. But he glanced at Natalie. She had opened her handbag and found her compact. This stuck him as either offensively nonchalant or pathetically trusting. Or what? Curiosity rose in Mitch—and he sat down.

"Why, I happened into a bar where a lady had had too much to drink," he said, as if this were nothing unusual. "I volunteered to put her in a taxi but there was no taxi. I wound up leaving her passed out on my sofa. In the morning she was gone. That's all there is to the story."

"This was on Saint Patrick's Day?" said Maxwell intently.

"In the small hours. In the morning."

"Then the lady was not my wife. My wife was with me in Santa Barbara at our home that night."

"With you?" said Mitch carefully, feeling a bit of shock.

"Certainly." Maxwell's tone was belligerent.

Mitch was beginning to wonder. The woman had powdered her nose and sat looking as if she couldn't care less. "Not simply in the same building," Mitch inquired, "as you may have assumed?"

"Not simply in the same building," said Julius Maxwell, "and no assumption. She was *with* me, *speaking* to me, *touching* me, if you like." His black eyes were hostile.

Oh, ho, thought Mitch, then you are a liar, too. Now what *is* all this? He did not care for this Maxwell at all.

"Perhaps I have mistaken her for another lady," he said smoothly. "But isn't it strange that she is wearing exactly the same clothes now that she was wearing on Saint Patrick's Day?"

(Try that one on for size, Mitch thought smugly.)

Julius said ominously, "Do you know who I am?"

"I have heard your name," said Mitch.

"You know that I am an influential man?"

"Oh, yes," said Mitch pleasantly. "In fact, I can smell the money from here."

"How much do you want to forget that you saw my wife in Los Angeles that night?"

Mitch's brows went up.

"On Saint Patrick's Day in the morning," added Julius sneeringly.

Mitch felt his feathers ruffling, his temper flaring. "Why? What is it worth?" he said.

They locked gazes. It was ridiculous. Mitch felt as if he had strayed into a Class B movie. Then Maxwell rose from the table. "Excuse me." He lashed Mitch with a sharp look which seemed to be saying, "Stay," as if Mitch were a dog. Then he strode off.

Mitch, alone with the blond woman, said to her quickly, "What do you want me to do or say?"

He was looking at her hand, long-fingered, pink-nailed, limp on the table. It did not clench. It did not even move. "I don't understand," she said in a mechanical way.

"Okay," said Mitch disgustedly. "I came here for dinner and I see no profit in this discussion, so please excuse me."

He got up, crossed over to his own table, and ordered his meal.

Julius Maxwell returned in a few moments and stood looking at Mitch with a triumphant light in his eyes. Mitch waved the wand of reason over the very human activity of his own glands. It was necessary for Mitch's self-respect that he dine here, as he had planned to do, and that he remain unperturbed by these strange people.

His steak had come when a man walked into the room and up to Maxwell's table. There was an exchange of words. Julius rose. Both men came over to Mitch.

Julius said, "This is the fellow, Lieutenant."

Mitch found that the stranger was slipping into the seat beside him and Julius was slipping in beside him on his other hand. He rejected a feeling of being trapped. "What's all this?" he inquired mildly, patting his lips with his napkin.

"Name's Prince," said the stranger. "Los Angeles Police Department. Mr. Maxwell tells me you are saying something about Mrs. Maxwell's being here in town on the night of the sixteenth of March and the morning of the seventeenth?"

Mitch sipped from his water glass, watchful and wary.

Julius Maxwell said, "This man was trying to blackmail me with a crazy story."

"I was *what!*" Mitch exploded.

The police lieutenant, or whoever he was, had a long lean face, slightly crooked at the bottom, and he had very tired eyelids. He said, "Your story figured to destroy her alibi?"

"Her alibi for *what?*" Mitch leaned back.

"Oh, come off that, Brown," said Julius Maxwell, "or whatever your name is. You knew my wife from having seen her picture in the newspaper."

Mitch's brain was racing. "I haven't seen the papers for six weeks," he said aggressively.

Julius Maxwell's black eyes were bright with that triumphant shine. "Now that," he said flatly, "is impossible."

"Oh, is it?" said Mitch rather gently. His role of apostle of compassion was fast fading out. Mitch was now a human clashing with another human and he knew he had to look out for himself. He could feel his wings retracting into his spine. "Alibi for what?" he insisted, looking at the policeman intently.

The policeman sighed. "You want it from me? Okay. On the sixteenth of last March, late in the evening," he droned, "a man named Joseph Carlisle was shot to death in his own front hall." (Mitch, ears pricked up, remembered the paragraph he had seen just tonight.) "Lived in a canyon, Hollywood Hills," the lieutenant continued. "Winding road, lonely spot. Looked like somebody rang his bell, he answered, they talked in the hall. It was his own gun that he kept in a table there. Whoever shot him closed the front door, which locked it, and threw the gun in the shrubbery. Then beat it. Wasn't seen—by anybody."

"And what has this got to do with Mrs. Maxwell?" Mitch asked.

"Mrs. Maxwell used to be married to this Carlisle," said the policeman. "We had to check her out. She has this alibi."

"I see," said Mitch.

"Mrs. Maxwell," said Julius through his teeth, "was with me in our home in Santa Barbara that evening and all that night."

Mitch saw. He saw that either Maxwell was trying to save his wife from the embarrassment of suspicion or . . . that compassion was a fine thing but it can get a well-meaning person into trouble. And a few drinks might hit a murderess very hard and very fast. Mitch *knew*, that whatever else Maxwell said, he was lying in his teeth about this alibi. Because the woman, still sitting across this restaurant, was the very same woman whom Mitch Brown had taken in, had given a break.

But nobody was giving Mitch Brown any break. And why all this nonsense about blackmail? Mitch, with his wings folded tight away, said to the lieutenant, "Suppose I tell you my story." And he did so, coldly, briefly.

Afterward, Maxwell laughed. "You believe that? You believe that he would take a drunken woman home with him—and close the door?"

In his breast Mitch Brown felt the smolder of dislike burst into a flame of hatred.

"No, no," said Maxwell. "What must have happened was this. He spotted my wife here. Oh, he'd read the papers—don't you believe that he hadn't. He knew she had been married to Joe Carlisle. So, spur of the moment, he tried out his little lie. Might be some profit in it—who knows? Listen to this: when I asked him how much he wanted to keep this story to himself, he asked *me* how much it was worth."

Mitch chewed his lip. "You've got a bad ear for dialogue," he said. "That is not exactly what I said. Nor is it the sense of what I said."

"Oh, oh," said Maxwell, smiling.

The lieutenant was pursing noncommittal lips.

Mitch spoke to him. "Who else gives Mrs. Maxwell her alibi?"

"Servants," said the lieutenant gloomily.

"Servants?" said Mitch brightly.

"It's only natural," the lieutenant said, even more gloomily.

"Right," said Mitch Brown. "You mean it is probable that when a man and his wife are at home together only the servants will see them there. But it isn't so probable that a stranger will take in a drunken woman, and leave her to heaven . . . simply because he feels like giving a human being a break. So this is a study in probability, is it?"

The lieutenant's mouth moved and Mitch said quickly, "But you want the facts, eh? Okay. The only thing for us to do is go and talk to the bartender."

"That seems to be it," said the lieutenant promptly. "Right."

Maxwell said, "Right. Wait for us."

He rose and went to fetch his wife. Mitch stood beside the lieutenant. "Fingerprints?" he murmured. The Lieutenant shrugged. Under those weary eyelids, Mitch judged, the eyes were human. "She has a car? Was the car out?" The lieutenant shrugged again. "Who else would shoot this Carlisle? Any enemies?"

"Who hasn't?" the lieutenant said. "We better check with this bartender."

The four of them went in the lieutenant's car. The Parakeet Bar and Grill was doing well this evening. It looked brighter and more prosperous. Toby the bartender was there. "Hi, Mr. Brown," he said. "Long time no see."

"I've been back East. Tell this man, Toby, what happened around one thirty on the morning of March seventeenth."

"Huh?" said Toby. The flesh of his cheeks seemed to go flatter. His eye went duller. Suddenly Mitch knew what was going to happen.

"You see this man or this lady in here between one, two o'clock in the morning last March seventeenth?" said the lieutenant and added, "I'm Lieutenant Prince, LAPD."

"No, sir," said Toby. "I know Mr. Brown, of course. He comes in now and again, see? Lives around here. A writer, he is. But I don't remember I ever seen this lady before."

"What about Brown? Was he in here that night or that morning?"

"I don't think so," said Toby. "That's the night, now that I think back—yeah, my kid was sick and I shut the place up earlier than usual. Ask my wife," said Toby the bartender with the fixed righteous gaze of the liar.

Lieutenant Prince turned his long face, his sad eyelids, on Mitch Brown.

Mitch Brown was grinning. "Oh, no!" he said. "Not the old Paris Exposition gag!" He leaned on the bar and emitted silent laughter.

"What are you talking about?" Lieutenant Prince said sourly. "You give me corroboration for this story you're telling. Who can tell me about it? Who saw you and this lady that night?"

"Nobody. Nobody," said Mitch genially. "The streets were empty. Nobody was around. Well! I wouldn't have believed it! The old Paris Exposition gag!"

The lieutenant made an exasperated sound.

Mitch said gaily, "Don't you remember that one? There's this girl and her mother. They go to a Paris hotel. Separate rooms. Girl wakes up in the morning, no mother. Nobody ever saw any mother. No mother's name on the register. No room's got the mother's number. Wait. No—that wasn't it. There *was* a room, but the wallpaper was different."

Julius Maxwell said, "A writer"—as if that explained everything.

"Why don't we all sit down," said Mitch cheerfully, "and tell each other stories?"

His suggestion was accepted. Natalie Maxwell slipped into a booth first; she was blond, expensive, protected . . . and numb. (Is she doped up with tranquilizers or what? Mitch wondered.) Her husband sat on her right and the policeman sat on her left.

Mitch slid in the other side of the Law and faced his adversary.

Mitch Brown's mood was by no means as jaunty as his words had implied. He didn't like the idea of being the victim of the old Paris Exposition gag. But he was not rattled or panicky. On the contrary, his mind began to reconnoiter the enemy. Julius Maxwell, flamboyantly successful—Mitch savored the flavor of the man's reputation. The buccaneer type, ruthless and bold. Julius Maxwell—with money like a club in his hand. Going to make a fool out of Mitchel Brown. Also, there was the little matter of justice. Or mercy.

Mitch felt his wings begin to rustle again.

He said to the woman, gently, "Would you care for something? A highball?"

"I don't drink," said Natalie primly. Her lashes came down. Her tongue touched her lips.

Mitch Brown ran his tongue over his upper lip, very thoughtfully.

Julius Maxwell's energy was barely contained in this place. "Never mind the refreshments," he said. "Get to it. This young man, whoever he is, spotted my wife and knew her from the publicity. He knows I am a rich man. So he thought he'd try a big lie. For the sake of the nuisance value, he thought I'd pay *something*. Well, an opportunist," said Julius with a nasty smile, "I can understand."

"I doubt if you understand *me*," said Mitch quietly. "I'm sure you don't realize how old hat that Paris Exposition story is."

"What has any Paris Exposition got to do with it?" snapped Julius. "Now look here, Lieutenant Prince. Can I prosecute this man?"

"You can't prove extortion," said the lieutenant gloomily. "You should have let him take the money, with witnesses."

"He couldn't do that," said Mitch, "because he knows the thought of money never crossed my mind."

The lieutenant's eyes closed all the way in great weariness. They opened again and it was apparent that he believed nothing and nobody, yet. "Want to get this straight. Now you say, Mr. Maxwell—"

Julius said, "I say that my wife was at home that evening and all night, as the servants also say, and as the authorities know. So this man is a liar. Who can say why? It is plain that he can't bring anyone or anything to corroborate this yarn he is telling. The bartender denies it. And, if you ask me, the most ridiculous thing he says is his claim that he hasn't read the newspapers for six weeks. Shows you the fantastic kind of mind he's got."

The lieutenant, without comment, turned to Mitch. "And you say—"

"I say," said Mitch, "that I have been in New York City since the seventeenth of March, attending rehearsals of my play and its opening night."

"A playwriter," said Julius.

"A play*wright*," corrected Mitch. "I guess you don't know what that is. For one thing, it is a person committed to trying to understand human beings. Oddly enough, even you." Mitch leaned over the table. "You are the bold buccaneer, so I've heard. You've pirated money out of the world and now you think money can buy whatever you want. Suppose *I* tell *your* story?"

Julius Maxwell now had a faint sneering smile, but Mitch noted that Natalie had her eyes open. Perhaps her ears were open too. Mitch plunged on.

"Your wife drove down here and shot her ex," he said brutally. (Natalie did not even wince.) "Well, now . . ." Mitch's imagination began to function, from long practice. "I suppose that Natalie felt bad enough, upset enough, maybe even sorry enough, to need a drink and to take too many drinks until she forgot her troubles." Natalie was looking at him. "But when she woke up in my apartment she ran—ran to her car which she must have had. Ran home. Ah, well, what else could she do?" Mitch mused aloud. "She had done this awful thing. Somebody would have to help her."

(Was Natalie holding her breath?)

"Who would help her?" Mitch said sharply. "*You* would, Maxwell. Why? I'll tell you why. You are not the type to want any wife of yours and the accent is on *yours*—to die in a gas chamber for murder. She'd done something stupid. You bawled her out, I imagine, for the stupidity of it. But you told her not to worry. She was yours, so you would fix it. Money can buy anything. She must do exactly as you say, and then she could forget it." Mitch hesitated. "Did you think she *could* forget it?" he murmured.

Nobody moved or spoke, so Mitch went on. "Well, you got to work. You bribed the servants. Bribed Toby, here. And you checked all around and discovered that there was only one other person who could reveal that she really had no alibi. That was a playwright. Oh, you checked on me too. Sure you did. You knew very well where I was and what I was doing. You found out the day and the hour I was due back in Los Angeles."

Lieutenant Prince snorted. "Sounds nuts," he broke in. "You say he's been bribing everybody? Why didn't he bribe *you*?"

Mitch turned a glazed eye on him. "Trouble was, I *hadn't* read the papers. I didn't know that I knew. So how could he bribe me? He put me down for an idiot," said Mitch. "For what sane person doesn't read the paper for six weeks? And then he thought of a way."

Mitch addressed himself to Maxwell. "You had some hireling watching my apartment. And you and Natalie were ready and waiting, and quite nearby." Mitch sensed the policeman's shrug coming and he added quickly, "Otherwise, how come the very first day I'm in town I run into Natalie, and Natalie in exactly the same clothes?"

"Who says they're the same," said Maxwell smoothly, "except you?"

"She came into the restaurant," said Mitch, "alone."

"Since I had a phone call to make . . ."

"Alone," Mitch persisted, ignoring the interruption, "and why? To encourage me to come over and speak to her. That's why the same clothes—to make sure I'd recognize her again. After she pulls the blank on me, Maxwell moves in. You, knowing how deep you've bribed your defenses behind you, press me into the position of looking like an opportunist—possibly like an extortionist. 'Brown's a writer,' you say to yourself. Which is 'a nut,' in your book. 'Nobody is going to believe a word *he* says.' You'll discredit me. You'll rig a little scene. You'll call a real policeman for a witness."

"Why?" croaked the lieutenant.

Mitch was startled. "Why what?"

"Why cook all this up and call *me*?"

"Simple," Mitch said. "What if I had finally read the papers and recognized her name? What if *I* had come to *you*? What am I then? A good citizen. Isn't that so? This way, he's made it look as if I came to *them*. Making me look like an opportunist. And he's the good citizen who called you in."

Air came out of the lieutenant, signifying nothing.

"What a wacky scheme!" Mitch said it first. (Damn it, it *was* wacky. It wasn't going to sound probable.) "How unrealistic you are!" he taunted desperately.

Maxwell sat there smugly. "You've got the imagination, all right," he said with a wry smile. "Wild one."

Then the policeman surprised them both. "Wait a minute, Brown. You're saying that Maxwell *knows* his wife is the killer. That he's acting as accessory after the fact? You *mean* to say that?"

Mitch hesitated.

Maxwell said, "He hasn't thought it out. Listen, he is just spinning a yarn, Lieutenant. He was challenged to do it. He's proving that he's clever. And that he is—for fiction. Call it a good try."

Mitch saw his way pointed out for him.

"Or, possibly," said Maxwell after a moment, "he was only trying to pick up a good-looking woman." Maxwell showed his teeth in a smile.

Mitch understood—he was being shown how to save face. It was very seductive. Not only that, he was aware that if he went along, the power, the money, the influence here, there, and everywhere, would work to Mitchel Brown's commercial advantage.

So he said slowly, "I *know* that he is a liar. I *believe* that he is an accessory after the fact. Yes, that's what I mean to say."

Julius Maxwell's face darkened, "Prove it," he snapped. "Because if you just *tell* it, I will have legal recourse, and I will have your skin. I don't sit still to be called a liar."

Mitch looked up and said with an air of pure detached curiosity, "What ever made you think that *I* would?"

"Look, give me *something*," said the lieutenant with sudden anger, "give me something to go on."

Maxwell said contemptuously, "He can't. It's all moonshine."

Mitch was scrambling for something that would help him. "I never thought of a car," he murmured. "But I should have guessed from the shoes she wears, that she hadn't walked here. I don't suppose she has walked much since she married so much money."

Mitch knew that Maxwell was swelling up with rage, or simulated rage. But he thought that Natalie was listening. It came to him, with conviction, that in spite of everything she *was* a human being.

So he looked at her and said, "Why did you leave this Joe Carlisle, I wonder? What kind of man was he? Did you quarrel? Did you hate him? How did he still have the power to hurt you that much?"

She looked at him, lips parted, eyes bright, startled. Her husband was on the point of getting up and hitting someone, and Mitch knew whom.

Lieutenant Prince said, "Sit down, Maxwell." He said to Mitch, "And you, hold on to your tongue. Don't analyze me any characters. Or emote me any motives. She's got an alibi unless you can break it, and evidence is what the law requires."

"But what about *my* motive for lying?" Mitch demanded. "Money? That's ridiculous!" He stopped, staring. Natalie Maxwell had opened her bag, taken out a lipstick. Murder, prison . . . she paints her mouth. Slander, blackmail . . . she paints her mouth. How probable was that?

"Give me proof," the lieutenant said angrily.

"In a minute," Mitch said, as his heart bounced upward. He leaned back. "Let me pursue the theme of money. I imagine Natalie's got whatever money can buy. Her living is paid for. She has charge accounts."

Maxwell said, "Let's go. He's rambling now."

The lieutenant began to push at Mitch's thigh, nudging him out of the booth.

"Know what I *can* prove?" Mitch said.

"What?" said the lieutenant.

"That I was working in my apartment all that day and into the night on the sixteenth, seventeenth of March. Those walls are cardboard and I am a nuisance—well known in the building."

"So you were working," said the policeman. "What of it?"

"I wasn't in Santa Barbara," said Mitch cheerfully. He reached over and plucked up Natalie's handbag, the green one that matched the shoes.

"Now just a minute," Maxwell growled.

"See if her checkbook is in there," said Mitch, pushing the bag at the Lieutenant. "It's a fat one. Her name's printed on it, and all that: I don't think she has much occasion to write checks. It may be the same one."

The lieutenant had his hands on the bag, but he looked un-enlightened.

"Look at it. It's evidence," Mitch said.

The lieutenant's hands moved and Maxwell said, "I'm not sure you have the right . . ." But the policeman's weary lids came up, only briefly, and Maxwell was silent.

The lieutenant took out a checkbook. "It's fat," he said. "Starts February twenty-first. What of it?"

Mitch Brown leaned his head on the red leatherette and kept his eyes high. "Nobody on earth . . . unless Natalie remembers, which I doubt . . . but nobody *else* on earth can know what the

115

balance on her check stubs was on Saint Patrick's Day in the morning. Even her bank couldn't know. *But what if I know?* How could I? Because *I looked*, while she was snoring on my sofa and I had to find out who she was and how I could help her and whether she needed any money."

The lieutenant's hand riffled the stubs. "Well?"

"Shall I name it for you? To the penny?" Mitch was sweating. "Four thousand six hundred and fourteen dollars, and sixty-one cents," he said slowly and carefully.

"Right," snapped the lieutenant and his eyes came up, wide-open and baleful on Julius Maxwell.

But Mitch Brown was not heeding and felt no triumph. "Natalie," he said, "I'm sorry. I wanted to give you a break. I didn't know what the trouble was. I wish you could have told me."

Her newly reddened lips were trembling.

"Not so I could buy off the consequences," Mitch said. "I'd have called the police. But I *would* have listened."

Natalie put her blond head down on the red-checked table-cloth where it had once rested before. "I didn't mean to do it," she sobbed. "But he kept at me, Joe did. Until I couldn't take any more."

Julius Maxwell, who had been thinking about evidence, said too late, "Shut up!"

The lieutenant went for the phone.

Mitch sat there, quiet now. The woman was weeping. Maxwell said in a cold, severe way, "Natalie, if you . . ." He drew away from contamination. He was going to pretend ignorance.

But she cried out, "*You* shut up! *You* shut up! I've told you and told you and you never even tried to understand. You said, give Joe a thousand dollars. He'd go away. You said that's all he wanted. You wouldn't even listen to what I was going through, and Joe talking, talking, about our baby that was dead . . . starved, Joe said, because she had no mother. *My* baby," she shrieked, "that *you* wouldn't have, because she wasn't yours."

Now her pink-painted fingernails clawed at her scalp and the rings on her fingers were tangled in her hair. "I'm sorry," she wept. "I never meant to make the gun go off. I just wanted to stop him. I just couldn't take any more. He was killing me . . . driving me crazy . . . and money wouldn't stop him."

Mitch's heart was heavy for her. "Didn't you know what *matters?*" he barked at Maxwell. "Did you think it was mink, diamonds—that stuff?"

"The child died," said Julius Maxwell, "of natural causes."

"*Yes*, he thought it was mink," screamed Natalie. "And oh, my God . . . it *was!* I know that now. So he said he would fix it—but he can't fix what I know, and I hope to die."

Then she lay silent, as if already dead, across the red-checked tablecloth.

Julius Maxwell's face was losing color, as the policeman came back and murmured, "Have to wait." But the lieutenant was uneasy. "Say, Brown," he said, "you can remember a row of six figures for six weeks? You a mathematical genius or something? You got what they call a photographic memory?"

Mitch felt his brain stir. He said lightly, "It stuck in my mind. First place, it repeats. You see that? Four six one, four six one. To me that's an awful lot of money."

"To me too," the lieutenant said. "Everybody in here heard what she said, I guess."

"Sure, heard her confess and implicate him as the accessory. Take a look at Toby, for instance. *He's* had it. There's going to be plenty of evidence."

The lieutenant looked down upon the ruin of the Maxwells. "Guess so," he said tightly.

Later that night Mitch Brown was sitting up to a strange bar. He said to the strange bartender, "Say, you ever know that the seventeenth of March is *not* Saint Patrick's birthday?"

"What d'ya know?" the bartender murmured politely.

"Nope. It's the day he died," said Mitch. "I write, see? So I read. Bits of information like that stick in my mind. I've got no memory for figures and yet . . . Know the year Saint Patrick died? It was the year 461."

"That so?" said the bartender.

"You take four sixty-one twice and put the decimal in the right place. Of course that's not very *believable*," Mitch said, "although it really happened—on Saint Patrick's Day in the morning. How come I knew—me a person who doesn't always read the newspaper—the year Saint Patrick died? Well, a fellow doesn't want to be made a fool of, does he? And probable is probable and improbable is improbable—but it's all we've got to go on sometimes. But I'll tell *you* something," Mitch pounded the bar. "Money couldn't have bought it."

The bartender said soothingly, "I guess not, Mac."

The Purple Is Everything

DOROTHY SALISBURY DAVIS

Dorothy Salisbury Davis (b. 1916), born in Chicago and a graduate of Barat College, is clearly a person for the long haul. Her marriage to actor Harry Davis lasted from 1946 until his death in 1993, and she continues to contribute to a field of writing she entered more than half a century ago with the novel *The Judas Cat* (1949), most recently with a new story in the anthology *Murder Among Friends* (2000). Davis is, by her own account, an odd fit in the crime-fiction genre. She has bemoaned her inability to create a memorable series character, though Julie Hayes of her last few novels makes the grade, and she has a distaste for violence and murder. (One of the anthologies she edited for the Mystery Writers of America is called *Crime Without Murder* [1970].) However, her expressed enthusiasm for villains over heroes helps to explain her success in the field. Among her best-known books are the regional classic *The Clay Hand* (1950), the Roman Catholic–themed *A Gentle Murderer* (1951), and the 1969 bestseller *Where the Dark Streets Go*.

In introducing her collection *Tales for a Stormy Night* (1984), Davis credits her late friend and fellow mystery writer Margaret Manners with giving her the method for stealing a painting used in the Edgar-nominated "The Purple Is Everything." "I even remember the spot," Davis wrote, "Sixth Avenue and Twenty-fourth Street, a few paces, in those days, from Guffanti's Restaurant." Though it is unquestionably a crime story, it has its author's moral concerns at its heart and it is of a quality that might as well have been published in *The New Yorker* as *Ellery Queen's Mystery Magazine*.

You are likely to say, reading about Mary Gardner, that you knew her, or that you once knew someone like her. And well you may have, for while her kind is not legion it endures and sometimes against great popular odds.

You will see Mary Gardner—or someone like her—at the symphony, in the art galleries, at the theatre, always well-dressed if not quite fashionable, sometimes alone, sometimes in the company of other women all of whom have an aura, not of sameness, but of mutuality. Each of them has made—well, if not a good life for herself, at least the best possible life it was in her power to make.

Mary Gardner was living at the time in a large East Coast city. In her late thirties, she was a tall lean woman, unmarried, quietly feminine, gentle, even a little hesitant in manner but definite in her tastes. Mary was a designer in a well-known wallpaper house. Her salary allowed her to buy good clothes, to live alone in a pleasant apartment within walking distance of her work, and to go regularly to the theater and the Philharmonic. As often as she went to the successful plays, she attended little theater and the experimental stage. She was not among those who believed that a play had to say something. She was interested in "the submerged values." This taste prevailed also in her approach to the visual arts—a boon surely in the wallpaper business whose customers for the most part prefer their walls to be seen but not heard.

In those days Mary was in the habit of going during her lunch hour—or sometimes when she needed to get away from the drawing board—to the Institute of Modern Art which was less than a city block from her office. She had fallen in love with a small, early Monet titled *Trees Near L'Havre,* and when in love Mary was a person of searching devotion. Almost daily she discovered new voices in the woodland scene, trees and sky reflected in a shimmering pool—with more depths in the sky, she felt, than in the water.

The more she thought about this observation the more convinced she became that the gallery had hung the picture upside down. She evolved a theory about the signature: it was hastily done by the artist, she decided, long after he had finished the painting and perhaps at a time when the light of day was fading. She would have spoken to a museum authority about it—if she had known a museum authority.

Mary received permission from the Institute to sketch within its halls and often stood before the Monet for an hour, sketchbook in hand. By putting a few strokes on paper she felt herself conspicuously inconspicuous among the transient viewers and the guards. She would not for anything have presumed to copy the painting and she was fiercely resentful of the occasional art student who did.

So deep was Mary in her contemplation of Claude Monet's wooded scene that on the morning of the famous museum fire, when she first smelled the smoke, she thought it came from inside the picture itself. She was instantly furious, and by an old association she indicted a whole genre of people—the careless American tourist in a foreign land. She was not so far away from reality, however, that she did not realize almost at once there was actually a fire in the building.

Voices cried out alarms in the corridors and men suddenly were running. Guards dragged limp hoses along the floor and dropped them—where they lay like great withered snakes over which people leaped as in some tribal rite. Blue smoke layered the ceiling and then began to fall in angled swatches—like theatrical scrims gone awry. In the far distance fire sirens wailed.

Mary Gardner watched, rooted and muted, as men and women, visitors like herself, hastened past bearing framed pictures in their arms; and in one case two men carried between them a huge Chagall night scene in which the little creatures seemed to be jumping on and off the canvas, having an uproarious time in transit. A woman took the Rouault from the wall beside the Monet and hurried with it after the bearers of the Chagall.

Still Mary hesitated. That duty should compel her to touch where conscience had so long forbidden it—this conflict increased her confusion. Another thrust of smoke into the room made the issue plainly the picture's survival, if not indeed her own. In desperate haste she tried to lift the Monet from the wall, but it would not yield.

She strove, pulling with her full strength—such strength that when the wire broke, she was catapulted backward and fell over the viewer's bench, crashing her head into the painting. Since the canvas was mounted on board, the only misfortune—aside from her bruised head which mattered not at all—was that the picture had jarred loose from its frame. By then Mary cared little for the frame. She caught up the painting, hugged it to her, and groped her way to the gallery door.

She reached the smoke-bogged corridor at the instant the water pressure brought the hoses violently to life. Jets of water spurted from every connection. Mary shielded the picture with her body until she could edge it within the raincoat she had worn against the morning drizzle.

She hurried along the corridor, the last apparently of the volunteer rescuers. The guards were sealing off the wing of the building, closing the fire prevention door. They showed little patience with her protests, shunting her down the stairs. By the time she reached the lobby the police had cordoned off civilians. Imperious as well as impervious, a policeman escorted her into the crowd, and in the crowd, having no use of her arms—they were still locked around the picture—she was shoved and jostled toward the door and there pitilessly jettisoned into the street. On the sidewalk she had no hope at all finding anyone in that surging, gaping mob on whom she could safely bestow her art treasure.

People screamed and shouted that they could see the flames. Mary did not look back. She hastened homeward, walking proud and fierce, thinking that the city was after all a jungle. She hugged the picture to her, her raincoat its only shield but her life a ready forfeit for its safety.

It had been in her mind to telephone the Institute office at once. But in her own apartment, the painting propped up against cushions on the sofa, she reasoned that until the fire was extinguished she had no hope of talking with anyone there. She called her own office and pleaded a sudden illness—something she had eaten at lunch though she had not had a bite since breakfast.

The walls of her apartment were hung with what she called her "potpourri": costume prints and color lithographs—all, she had been proud to say, limited editions or artists' prints. She had sometimes thought of buying paintings, but plainly she could not afford her own tastes. On impulse now, she took down an Italian lithograph and removed the glass and mat from the wooden frame. The Monet fit quite well. And to her particular delight she could now hang it right side up. As though with a will of its own, the painting claimed the place on her wall most favored by the light of day.

There is no way of describing Mary's pleasure in the company she kept that afternoon. She would not have taken her eyes from the picture at all except for the joy that was renewed at each returning. Reluctantly she turned on the radio at five o'clock so that she might learn more of the fire at the Institute. It had been extensive and destructive—an entire wing of the building was gutted.

She listened with the remote and somewhat smug solicitude that one bestows on other people's tragedies to the enumeration of the paintings which had been destroyed. The mention of *Trees Near L'Havre* startled her. A full moment later she realized the explicit meaning of the announcer's words. She turned off the radio and sat a long time in the flood of silence.

Then she said aloud tentatively, "You are a thief, Mary Gardner," and after a bit repeated, "Oh, yes. You are a thief." But she did not mind at all. Nothing so portentous had ever been said about her before, even by herself.

She ate her dinner from a tray before the painting, having with it a bottle of French wine. Many times that night she went from her bed to the living-room door until she seemed to have slept between so many wakenings. At last she did sleep.

But the first light of morning fell on Mary's conscience as early as upon the painting. After one brief visit to the living room she made her plans with the care of a religious novice well aware of the devil's constancy. She dressed more severely than was her fashion, needing herringbone for backbone—the ridiculous phrase kept running through her mind at breakfast. In final appraisal of herself in the hall mirror she thought she looked like the headmistress of an English girls' school, which she supposed satisfactory to the task before her.

Just before she left the apartment, she spent one last moment alone with the Monet. Afterward, wherever, however the Institute chose to hang it, she might hope to feel that a little part of it was forever hers.

On the street she bought a newspaper and confirmed the listing of *Trees Near L'Havre.* Although that wing of the Institute had been destroyed, many of its paintings had been carried to safety by way of the second-floor corridor.

Part of the street in front of the Institute was still cordoned off when she reached it, congesting the flow of morning traffic. The police on duty were no less brusque than those whom Mary had encountered the day before. She was seized by the impulse to postpone her mission—an almost irresistible temptation, especially when she was barred from entering the museum unless she could show a pass such as had been issued to all authorized personnel.

"Of course I'm not authorized," she exclaimed. "If I were I shouldn't be out here."

The policeman directed her to the sergeant in charge. He was at the moment disputing with the fire insurance representative as to how much of the street could be used for the salvage operation. "The business of this street is business," the sergeant said, "and that's my business."

Mary waited until the insurance man stalked into the building. He did not need a pass, she noticed. "Excuse me, officer, I have a painting—"

"Lady . . ." He drew the long breath of patience. "Yes, ma'am?"

"Yesterday during the fire a painting was supposedly destroyed—a lovely, small Monet called—"

"Was there now?" the sergeant interrupted. Lovely small Monets really touched him.

Mary was becoming flustered in spite of herself. "It's listed in this morning's paper as having been destroyed. But it wasn't. I have it at home."

The policeman looked at her for the first time with a certain compassion. "On your living-room wall, no doubt," he said with deep knowingness.

"Yes, as a matter of fact."

He took her gently but firmly by the arm. "I tell you what you do. You go along to police headquarters on Fifty-seventh Street. You know where that is, don't you? Just tell them all about it like a good girl." He propelled her into the crowd and there released her. Then he raised his voice: "Keep moving! You'll see it all on the television."

Mary had no intention of going to police headquarters where, she presumed, men concerned with armed robbery, mayhem, and worse were even less likely to understand the subtlety of her problem. She went to her office and throughout the morning tried periodically to reach the museum curator's office by telephone. On each of her calls either the switchboard was tied up or his line was busy for longer than she could wait.

Finally she hit on the idea of asking for the Institute's Public Relations Department, and to someone there, obviously distracted—Mary could hear parts of three conversations going on at the same time—she explained how during the fire she had saved Monet's *Trees Near L'Havre.*

"Near where, madam?" the voice asked.

"L'Havre." Mary spelled it. "By Monet," she added.

"Is that two words or one?" the voice asked.

"Please transfer me to the curator's office," Mary said and ran her fingers up and down the lapel of her herringbone suit.

Mary thought it a wise precaution to meet the Institute's representative in the apartment lobby where she first asked to see his credentials. He identified himself as the man to whom she had given her name and address on the phone. Mary signaled for the elevator and thought about his identification: Robert Attlebury III. She had seen his name on the museum roster; Curator of . . . she could not remember.

He looked every inch the curator, standing erect and remote while the elevator bore them slowly upward. A curator perhaps, but she would not have called him a connoisseur. One with his face and disposition would always taste and spit out, she thought. She could imagine his scorn of things he found distasteful, and instinctively she knew herself to be distasteful to him.

Not that it really mattered what he felt about her. She was nobody. But how must the young unknown artist feel standing with his work before such superciliousness? Or had he a different mien and manner for people of his own kind? In that case she would have given a great deal for the commonest of his courtesies.

"Everything seems so extraordinary—in retrospect," Mary said to break the silence of their seemingly endless ascent.

"How fortunate for you," he said, and Mary thought, perhaps it was.

When they reached the door of her apartment, she paused before turning the key. "Shouldn't you have brought a guard—or someone?"

He looked down on her as from Olympus. "I am someone."

Mary resolved to say nothing more. She opened the door and left it open. He preceded her and moved across the foyer into the living room and stood before the Monet. His rude directness oddly comforted her: he did, after all, care about painting. She ought not to judge men, she thought, from her limited experience of them.

He gazed at the Monet for a few moments, then he tilted his head ever so slightly from one side to the other. Mary's heart began to beat erratically. For months she had wanted to discuss with someone who really knew about such things her theory of what was reflection and what was reality in *Trees Near L'Havre*. But now that her chance was at hand she could not find the words.

Still, she had to say something—something . . . casual. "The frame is mine," she said, "but for the picture's protection you may take it. I can get it the next time I'm at the museum."

Surprisingly, he laughed. "It may be the better part at that," he said.

"I beg your pardon?"

He actually looked at her. "Your story is ingenious, madam, but then it was warranted by the occasion."

"I simply do not understand what you are saying," Mary said.

"I have seen better copies than this one," he said. "It's too bad your ingenuity isn't matched by a better imitation."

Mary was too stunned to speak. He was about to go. "But . . . it's signed," Mary blurted out, and feebly tried to direct his attention to the name in the upper corner.

"Which makes it forgery, doesn't it?" he said almost solicitously.

His preciseness, his imperturbability in the light of the horrendous thing he was saying, etched detail into the nightmare.

"That's not my problem!" Mary cried, giving voice to words she did not mean, saying what amounted to a betrayal of the painting she so loved.

"Oh, but it is. Indeed it is, and I may say a serious problem if I were to pursue it."

"Please do pursue it!" Mary cried.

Again he smiled, just a little. "That is not the Institute's way of dealing with these things."

"You do not *like* Monet," Mary challenged desperately, for he had started toward the door.

"That's rather beside the point, isn't it?"

"You don't *know* Monet. You can't! Not possibly!"

"How could I dislike him if I didn't know him? Let me tell you something about Monet." He turned back to the picture and trailed a finger over one vivid area. "In Monet the purple is everything."

"The purple?" Mary said.

"You're beginning to see it yourself now, aren't you?" His tone verged on the pedagogic.

Mary closed her eyes and said, "I only know how this painting came to be here."

"I infinitely prefer not to be made your confidant in that matter," he said. "Now I have rather more important matters to take care of." And again he started toward the door.

Mary hastened to block his escape. "It doesn't matter what you think of Monet, or of me, or of anything. You've got to take that painting back to the museum."

"And be made a laughingstock when the hoax is discovered?" He set an arm as stiff as a brass rail between them and moved out of the apartment.

Mary followed him to the elevator, now quite beside herself. "I shall go to the newspapers!" she cried.

"I think you might regret it."

"Now I know. I understand!" Mary saw the elevator door open. "You were glad to think the Monet had been destroyed in the fire."

"Savage!" he said.

Then the door closed between them.

In time Mary persuaded—and it wasn't easy—certain experts, even an art critic, to come and examine "her" Monet. It was a more expensive undertaking than she could afford—all of them seemed to expect refreshments, including expensive liquors. Her friends fell in with "Mary's hoax," as they came to call her story, and she was much admired in an ever-widening and increasingly esoteric circle for her unwavering account of how she had come into possession of a "genuine Monet." Despite the virtue of simplicity, a trait since childhood, she found herself using words in symbolic combinations—the language of the company she now kept—and people far wiser than she would say of her: "How perceptive!" or "What insight!"—and then pour themselves another drink.

One day her employer, the great man himself, who prior to her "acquisition" had not known whether she lived in propriety or in sin, arrived at her apartment at cocktail time bringing with him a famous art historian.

The expert smiled happily over his second Scotch while Mary told again the story of the fire at the Institute and how she had simply walked home with the painting because she could not find anyone to whom to give it. While she talked, his knowing eyes wandered from her face to the painting, to his glass, to the painting, and back to her face again.

"Oh, I could believe it," he said when she had finished. "It's the sort of mad adventure that actually could happen." He set his glass down carefully where she could see that it was empty. "I suppose you know that there has never been an officially complete catalogue of Monet's work?"

"No," she said, and refilled his glass.

"It's so, unfortunately. And the sad truth is that quite a number of museums today are hanging paintings under his name that are really unauthenticated."

"And mine?" Mary said, lifting a chin she tried vainly to keep from quivering.

Her guest smiled. "*Must* you know?"

For a time after that Mary tried to avoid looking at the Monet. It was not that she liked it less, but that now she somehow liked herself less in its company. What had happened, she realized, was that, like the experts, she now saw not the painting, but herself.

This was an extraordinary bit of self-discovery for one who

had never had to deal severely with her own psyche. Till now, so far as Mary was concerned, the chief function of a mirror had been to determine the angle of a hat. But the discovery of the flaw does not in itself effect a cure; often it aggravates the condition. So with Mary.

She spent less and less time at home, and it was to be said for some of her new-found friends that they thought it only fair to reciprocate for having enjoyed the hospitality of so enigmatically clever a hostess. How often had she as a girl been counseled by parent and teacher to get out more, to see more people. Well, Mary was at last getting out more. And in the homes of people who had felt free to comment on her home and its possessions, she too felt free to comment. The more odd her comment—the nastier, she would once have said of it—the more popular she became. Oh, yes. Mary was seeing more people, lots more people.

In fact, her insurance agent—who was in the habit of just dropping in to make his quarterly collection—had to get up early one Saturday morning to make sure he caught her at home.

It was a clear, sharp day, and the hour at which the Monet was most luminous. The man sat staring at it, fascinated. Mary was amused, remembering how hurt he always was that his clients failed to hang his company calendar in prominence. While she was gone from the room to get her checkbook, he got up and touched the surface of the painting.

"Ever think of taking out insurance on that picture?" he asked when she returned. "Do you mind if I ask how much it's worth?"

"It cost me . . . a great deal," Mary said, and was at once annoyed with both him and herself.

"I tell you what," the agent said. "I have a friend who appraises these objects of art for some of the big galleries, you know? Do you mind if I bring him round and see what he thinks it's worth?"

"No, I don't mind," Mary said in utter resignation.

And so the appraiser came and looked carefully at the painting. He hedged about putting a value on it. He wasn't the last word on these nineteenth-century Impressionists and he wanted to think it over. But that afternoon he returned just as Mary was about to go out, and with him came a bearded gentleman who spoke not once to Mary or to the appraiser, but chatted constantly with himself while he scrutinized the painting. Then with a "tsk, tsk, tsk," he took the painting from the wall, examined the back, and rehung it—but reversing it, top to bottom.

Mary felt the old flutter interrupt her heartbeat, but it passed quickly.

Even walking out of her house the bearded gentleman did not speak to her; she might have been invisible. It was the appraiser who murmured his thanks but not a word of explanation. Since the expert had not drunk her whiskey Mary supposed the amenities were not required of him.

She was prepared to forget him as she had the others—it was easy now to forget them all; but when she came home to change between matinee and cocktails, another visitor was waiting. She noticed him in the lobby and realized, seeing the doorman say a word to him just as the elevator door closed off her view, that his business was with her. The next trip of the elevator brought him to her door.

"I've come about the painting, Miss Gardner," he said, and offered his card. She had opened the door only as far as the latch chain permitted. He was representative of the Continental Assurance Company, Limited.

She slipped off the latch chain.

Courteous and formal behind his double-breasted suit, he waited for Mary to seat herself. He sat down neatly opposite her, facing the painting, for she sat beneath it, erect, and she hoped, formidable.

"Lovely," he said, gazing at the Monet. Then he wrenched his eyes from it. "But I'm not an expert," he added and gently cleared his throat. He was chagrined, she thought, to have allowed himself even so brief a luxury of the heart.

"But is it authenticated?" She said it much as she would once have thought but not said, Fie on you!

"Sufficient to my company's requirements," he said. "But don't misunderstand—we are not proposing to make any inquiries. We are always satisfied in such delicate negotiations just to have the painting back."

Mary did not misunderstand, but she certainly did not understand either.

He took from his inside pocket a piece of paper which he placed on the coffee table and with the tapering fingers of an artist—or a banker—or a pickpocket—he gently maneuvered it to where Mary could see that he was proffering a certified check.

He did not look at her and therefore missed the spasm she felt contorting her mouth. "The day of the fire," she thought, but the words never passed her lips.

She took up the check in her hand: $20,000.

"May I use your phone, Miss Gardner?"

Mary nodded and went into the kitchen where she again looked at the check. It was a great deal of money, she thought wryly, to be offered in compensation for a few months' care of a friend.

She heard her visitor's voice as he spoke into the telephone—an expert now, to judge by his tone. A few minutes later she heard the front door close. When she went back into the living room both her visitor and the Monet were gone . . .

Some time later Mary attended the opening of the new wing of the Institute. She recognized a number of people she had not known before and whom, she supposed, she was not likely to know much longer.

They had hung the Monet upside down again.

Mary thought of it after she got home, and as though two rights must surely right a possible wrong, she turned the check upside down while she burned it over the kitchen sink.

Money to Burn

MARGERY ALLINGHAM

Margery Allingham (1904–66) was a writing prodigy whose first novel, the swashbuckler *Blackkerchief Dick* (1923), was published by major American and British firms when she was still a teenager. The London-born author, who came from a literary family, served an apprenticeship as a prolific writer of formula magazine fiction before becoming one of the key figures of the Golden Age of Detection between the two World Wars. Her first mystery novel, *The White Cottage Mystery* (1928), anticipated a least-suspected-person device later used by Ellery Queen and Agatha Christie, and her second, *The Crime at Black Dudley* (1929), introduced the inconspicuous and self-effacing Albert Campion, one of the most celebrated gentleman detectives of his time and, with a hint of royal blood in his veins, probably the highest born. Like that other aristocratic sleuth, Dorothy L. Sayers's Lord Peter Wimsey, Campion gradually developed from a semi-comic "silly ass" caricature to a fully realized character.

Of the celebrated Golden Age detective-story writers, some (like Agatha Christie and Ngaio Marsh) stuck to the pure who-dunnit formula for decades thereafter; others (like Sayers and Anthony Berkeley) left the field for other sorts of writing or retired altogether; and a few (like the Ellery Queen team) stayed with the basic format but deepened their exploration of character and theme. Allingham, whose understanding of human foibles and keen social observations were always manifest, belongs to that third group. While Mr. Campion continued to appear through most of her writing career, her post-war novels laid less stress on the formal puzzle, and in some of them Campion was relegated to a secondary role. (Campion received name-in-the-title billing only after his creator's death in two novels written by her husband and sometime collaborator, Philip Youngman Carter.) Of Allingham's early novels, *Death of a Ghost* (1934) and *The Fashion in Shrouds* (1938) are often cited as highlights; of the post-war group, *The Tiger in the Smoke* (1952), with its unflinching examination of pure evil, is considered a crime classic.

It is appropriate that Allingham, with her insights into the puzzles of human character, should be represented by "Money to Burn," a 1957 non-Campion tale which represents that rarest of detective story subtypes: the pure whydunnit.

D id you ever see a man set light to money? Real money: using it as a spill to light a cigarette, just to show off? I have. And that's why, when you used the word "psychologist" just now, a little fish leaped in my stomach and my throat felt suddenly tight. Perhaps you think I'm too squeamish. I wonder.

I was born in this street. When I was a girl I went to school just round the corner and later on, after I'd served my apprenticeship in the big dress houses here and in France, I took over the lease of this old house and turned it into the smart little gown shop you see now. It was when I came back to go into business for myself that I saw the change in Louise.

When we went to school together she was something of a beauty, with streaming yellow hair and the cockney child's ferocious, knowing grin. All the kids used to tease her because she was better-looking than we were. The street was just the same then as it is now. Adelaide Street, Soho: shabby and untidy, and yet romantic, with every other doorway in its straggling length leading to a restaurant of some sort. You can eat in every language of the world here. Some places are as expensive as the Ritz and others are as cheap as Louise's papa's Le Coq au Vin, with its one dining room and its single palm in the whitewashed tub outside.

Louise had an infant sister and a father who could hardly speak English but who looked at one with proud foreign eyes from under arched brows. I was hardly aware that she had a mother until a day when that gray woman emerged from the cellar under the restaurant to put her foot down and Louise, instead of coming with me into the enchantment of the workshops, had to go down into the kitchens of Le Coq au Vin.

For a long time we used to exchange birthday cards, and then even that contact dropped; but somehow I never forgot Louise and when I came back to the street I was glad to see the name Frosné still under the sign of Le Coq au Vin. The place looked much brighter than I remembered it and appeared to be doing fair business. Certainly it no longer suffered so much by comparison with the expensive Glass Mountain which Adelbert kept opposite. There is no restaurant bearing that name in this street now, nor is there a restaurateur called Adelbert, but diners-out of a few years ago may remember him—if not for his food, at least for his conceit and the two rolls of white fat which were his eyelids.

I went in to see Louise as soon as I had a moment to spare. It was a shock, for I hardly recognized her; but she knew me at once and came out from behind the cashier's desk to give me a welcome which was pathetic. It was like seeing thin ice cracking all over her face—as if by taking her unawares I'd torn aside a barrier.

I heard all the news in the first ten minutes. Both the old people were dead. The mother had gone first but the old man had not followed her for some years after, and in the meantime Louise had carried everything including his vagaries on her shoulders. But she did not complain. Things were a bit easier now. Violetta, the little sister, had a young man who was proving his worth by working there for a pittance, learning the business.

It was a success story of a sort, but I thought Louise had paid pretty dearly for it. She was a year younger than I was, yet she looked as if life had already burned out over her, leaving her hard and polished like a bone in the sun. The gold had gone out of her hair and even her thick lashes looked bleached and tow-colored. There was something else there, too: something hunted which I did not understand at all.

I soon fell into the habit of going in to have supper with her once a week and at these little meals she used to talk. It was evident that she never opened her lips on any personal matter to anyone else; but for some reason she trusted me. Even so it took me months to find out what was the matter with her. When it came out, it was obvious.

Le Coq au Vin had a debt hanging over it. In Mama Frosné's time the family had never owed a penny, but in the year or so between her death and his own, Papa Frosné had somehow contrived not only to borrow the best part of four thousand pounds from Adelbert of the Glass Mountain but to lose every cent of it in half a dozen senile little schemes.

Louise was paying it back in five-hundred-pound installments. As she first told me about it, I happened to glance into her eyes and in them I saw one sort of hell. It has always seemed to me that there are people who can stand Debt in the same way that some men can stand Drink. It may undermine their constitutions but it does not make them openly shabby. Yet to the others, Debt does something unspeakable. The Devil was certainly having his money's worth out of Louise.

I did not argue with her, of course. It was not my place. I sat there registering sympathy until she surprised me by saying suddenly:

"It's not so much the work and the worry, nor even the skimping, that I really hate so much. It's the awful ceremony when I have to pay him. I dread that."

"You're too sensitive," I told her. "Once you have the money in the bank, you can put a check in an envelope, send it to him, and then forget about it, can't you?"

She glanced at me with an odd expression in her eyes; they were almost lead-colored between the bleached lashes.

"You don't know Adelbert," she said. "He's a queer bit of work. I have to pay him in cash and he likes to make a regular little performance of it. He comes here by appointment, has a drink, and likes to have Violetta as a witness by way of audience. If I don't show I'm a bit upset, he goes right on talking until I do. Calls himself a psychologist—says he knows everything I'm thinking."

"That's not what I'd call him," I said. I was disgusted. I hate that sort of thing.

Louise hesitated. "I have watched him burn most of the money just for the effect," she admitted. "There, in front of me."

I felt my eyebrows rising up into my hair. "You can't mean it!" I exclaimed. "The man's not right in the head."

She sighed and I looked at her sharply.

"Why, he's twenty years older than you are, Louise," I began. "Surely there wasn't ever anything between you? You know . . . anything like *that?*"

"No. No, there wasn't, Ellie, honestly." I believed her—she was quite frank about it and obviously as puzzled as I was. "He did speak to Papa once about me when I was a kid. Asked for me formally, you know, as they still did round here at that time. I never heard what the old man said but he never minced words, did he? All I can remember is that I was kept downstairs out of sight for a bit and after that Mama treated me as if I'd been up to something; but I hadn't even spoken to the man—he wasn't a person a young girl *would* notice, was he? That was years ago, though. I suppose Adelbert could have remembered it all that time—but it's not reasonable, is it?"

"That's the one thing it certainly isn't," I told her. "Next time *I'll* be the witness."

"Adelbert would enjoy that," Louise said grimly. "I don't know that I won't hold you to it. You ought to see him!"

We let the subject drop, but I couldn't get it out of my mind. I could see them both from behind the curtains in my shop window and it seemed that whenever I looked out, there was the tight-lipped silent woman, scraping every farthing, and there was the fat man watching her from his doorway across the street, a secret satisfaction on his sallow face.

In the end it got on my nerves and when that happens I have to talk—I can't help it.

There was no one in the street I dared to gossip with, but I did mention the tale to a customer. She was a woman named

Mrs. Marten whom I'd particularly liked ever since she'd come in to inquire after the first dress I ever put in my shop window. I made most of her clothes and she had recommended me to one or two ladies in the district where she lived, which was up at Hampstead, nice and far away from Soho. I was fitting her one day when she happened to say something about men and the things they'll stoop to if their pride has been hurt, and before I'd realized what I was doing I'd come out with the story Louise had told me. I didn't mention names, of course, but I may have conveyed that it was all taking place in this street. Mrs. Marten was a nice, gentle little soul with a sweet face, and she was shocked.

"But how awful," she kept saying, "how perfectly awful! To burn the money in front of her after she's worked so hard for it. He must be quite insane. And dangerous."

"Oh, well," I said hastily, "it's his money by the time he does that, and I don't suppose he destroys much of it. Only enough to upset my friend." I was sorry I'd spoken. I hadn't expected Mrs. Marten to be quite so horrified. "It just shows you how other people live." I finished and hoped she'd drop the subject. She didn't, however. The idea seemed to fascinate her even more than it had me. I couldn't get her to leave it alone and she chattered about it all throughout the fitting. Then, just as she was putting on her hat to leave, she suddenly said, "Miss Kaye, I've just had a thought. My brother-in-law is Assistant Commissioner at Scotland Yard. He might be able to think of some way of stopping that dreadful man from torturing that poor little woman you told me about. Shall I mention it to him?"

"Oh, no! Please don't!" I exclaimed. "She'd never forgive me. There's nothing the police could do to help her. I do hope you'll forgive me for saying so, Madam, but I do hope you won't do anything of the sort."

She seemed rather hurt, but she gave me her word. I had no faith in it, naturally. Once a woman has considered talking about a thing, it's as good as done. I was quite upset for a day or two because the last thing I wanted was to get involved; but nothing happened and I'd just started to breathe easily again when I had to go down to Vaughan's, the big wholesale trimmings house at the back of Regent's Street. I was coming out with my parcels when a man came up to me. I knew he was a detective: he was the type, with a very short haircut, a brown raincoat, and that look of being in a settled job and yet not in anything particular. He asked me to come along to his office and I couldn't refuse. I realized he'd been following me until I was far enough away from Adelaide Street where no one would have noticed him approach me.

He took me to his superior who was quite a nice old boy in his way—on nobody's side but his own, as is the way with the police; but I got the impression that he was on the level, which is more than some people are. He introduced himself as Detective Inspector Cumberland, made me sit down, and sent out for a cup of tea for me. Then he asked me about Louise.

I got into a panic because when you're in business in Adelaide Street, you're in business, and the last thing you can afford to do is get into trouble with your neighbors. I denied everything, of course, insisting that I hardly knew the woman.

Cumberland wouldn't have that. I must say he knew how to handle me. He kept me going over and over my own affairs until I was thankful to speak about anything else. In the end I gave way because, after all, nobody was doing anything criminal as far as I could see. I told him all I knew, letting him draw it out bit by bit, and when I'd finished he laughed at me, peering at me with little bright eyes under brows which were as thick as silver fox fur.

"Well," he said, "there's nothing so terrible in all that, is there?"

"No," I said sulkily. He made me feel like a fool.

He sighed and leaned back in his chair.

"You run away and forget this little interview," he told me. "But just so that you don't start imagining things, let me point out something to you. The police are in business too, in a way.

In their own business, that is, and when an officer in my position gets an inquiry from higher up he's got to investigate it, hasn't he? He may well think that the crime of destroying currency—"defacing the coin of the realm," we call it—is not very serious compared with some of the things he's got to deal with; but all the same if he's asked about it he's got to make some sort of move and send in some sort of report. Then it can all be . . . er . . . filed and forgotten, can't it?"

"Yes," I agreed, very relieved. "Yes, I suppose it can."

They showed me out and that seemed to be the end of it. I'd had my lesson though, and I never opened my lips again on the subject to anybody. It quite put me off Louise and for a time I avoided her. I made excuses and didn't go in to eat with her. However, I could still see her through the window—see her sitting at the cashier's desk; and I could still see Adelbert peering at her from his doorway.

For a month or two everything went on quietly. Then I heard that Violetta's boy had got tired of the restaurant business and had taken a job up North. He had given the girl the chance of marrying and going with him, and they'd gone almost without saying goodbye. I was sorry for Louise, being left alone that way; so I had to go and see her.

She was taking it very well—actually she was pretty lucky, for she had got a new waiter almost at once and her number one girl in the kitchen had stood by her and they managed very well. Louise was very lonely though, so I drifted back into the habit of going in there for a meal once a week. I paid, of course, but she used to come and have hers with me.

I kept her off the subject of Adelbert, but one day near the midsummer's quarter day she referred to him outright and asked me straight if I remembered my promise to be witness on the next payday. Since Violetta was gone, she'd mentioned me to Adelbert, and he'd seemed pleased.

Well, I couldn't get out of it without hurting her feelings and since nothing seemed to turn on it I agreed. I don't pretend I wasn't curious: it was a love affair without, so far as I could see, any love at all.

The time for payment was fixed for half an hour after closing time on Midsummer's Day, and when I slipped down the street to the corner the blinds of Le Coq au Vin were closed and the door shut. The new waiter was taking a breath of air on the basement steps and he let me in through the kitchens. I went up the dark service stairs and found the two of them already sitting there, waiting for me.

The dining room was dark except for a single shaded bulb over the alcove table where they sat and I had a good look at them as I came down the room. They made an extraordinary pair.

I don't know if you've seen one of those fat little Chinese gods whom people keep on their mantel shelves to bring them luck? They are all supposed to be laughing but some only pretend and the folds of their china faces are stiff and merciless for all the upward lines. Adelbert reminded me of one of those. He always wore a black dinner jacket for work, but it was very thin and very loose. It came into my mind that when he took it off it must have hung like a gown. He was sitting swathed in it, looking squat and flabby against the white paneling of the wall.

Louise, on the other hand, in her black dress and tight woolen cardigan, was as spare and hard as a withered branch. Just for an instant I realized how furious she must make him. There was nothing yielding or shrinking about her. She wasn't giving any more than she was forced to—not an inch. I never saw anything so unbending in my life. She stood up to him all the time.

There was a bottle of Dubonnet on the table and they each had a small glass. When I appeared, Louise poured one for me.

The whole performance was very formal. Although they'd both lived in London all their lives, the French blood in both of them was very apparent. They each shook hands with me and Adelbert kicked the chair out for me if he only made a pretense of rising.

Louise had the big bank envelope in her black bag which she nursed as if it was a pet, and as soon as I'd taken a sip of my drink she produced the envelope and pushed it across the table to the man.

"Five hundred," she said. "The receipt is in there, already made out. Perhaps you'd sign it, please."

There was not a word out of place, you see, but you could have cut the atmosphere with a knife. She hated him and he was getting his due and nothing else.

He sat looking at her for a moment with a steady, fishy gaze; he seemed to be waiting for something—just a flicker of regret or resentment, I suppose. But he got nothing, and presently he took the envelope between his sausage fingers and thumbed it open. The five crisp green packages fell out on the white table-cloth. I looked at them with interest, as one does at money. It wasn't a fortune, of course; but to people like myself and Louise, who have to earn every cent the hard way, it was a tidy sum that represented hours of toil and scheming and self-privation.

I didn't like the way the man's fingers played over it and the sneaking spark of sympathy I'd begun to feel for him died abruptly. I knew then that if he'd had his way and married her when she was little more than a child all those years ago, he would have treated her abominably. He was a cruel beast; it took him that way.

I glanced at Louise and saw that she was unmoved. She just sat there with her hands folded, waiting for her receipt.

Adelbert began to count the money. I've always admired the way tellers in banks handle notes, but the way Adelbert did it opened my eyes. He went through them the way a gambler goes through a pack of cards—as if each individual note were alive and part of his hand. He loved the stuff, you could see it.

"All correct," he said at last, and put the bundles in his inside pocket. Then he signed the receipt and handed it to her. Louise took it and put it in her bag. I assumed that was the end of it and wondered what all the fuss was about. I raised my glass to Louise, who acknowledged it, and was getting up when Adelbert stopped me.

"Wait," he said. "We must have a cigarette and perhaps another little glass—if Louise can afford it."

He smiled but she didn't. She poured him another glass and sat there stolidly waiting for him to drink it. He was in no hurry. Presently he took the money out again and laid a fat hand over it as he passed his cigarette case round. I took a cigarette, Louise didn't. There was one of those metal match stands on the table and he bent forward. I moved too, expecting him to give me a light; but he laughed and drew back.

"This gives it a better flavor," he said, and, peeling off one note from the top wad, he lit it and offered me the flame. I had guessed what was coming, so I didn't show my surprise. If Louise could keep a poker face, so could I. I watched the banknote burn out, and then he took another and lit that.

Having failed to move us, he started to talk. He spoke quite normally about the restaurant business—how hard times were and what a lot of work it meant getting up at dawn to go to the market with the chef and how customers liked to keep one up late at night, talking and dawdling as if there was never going to be a tomorrow. It was all directed at Louise, rubbing it in, holding her nose down to exactly what he was doing. But she remained perfectly impassive, her eyes dark like lead, her mouth hard.

When that failed, he got more personal. He said he remembered us both when we were girls and how work and worry had changed us. I was nettled, but not too upset, for it soon became quite obvious that he did not remember me at all. With Louise it was different: he remembered her—every detail—and with something added.

"Your hair was like gold," he said, "and your eyes were blue as glass and you had a little soft wide mouth which was so gay. Where is it now, eh? Here." He patted the money, the old brute. "All here, Louise. I am a psychologist, I see these things. And what is it worth to me? Nothing. Exactly nothing."

He was turning me cold. I stared at him fascinated and saw him suddenly take up a whole package of money and fluff it out until it looked like a lettuce. Louise neither blinked nor spoke. She sat looking at him as if he was nothing, a passerby in the street. No one at all. I'd turned my head to glance at her and missed seeing him strike another match—so when he lit the crisp leaves it took me completely off guard.

"Look out!" I said involuntarily. "Mind what you're doing!"

He laughed like a wicked child, triumphant and delighted. "What about you, Louise? What do you say?"

She continued to look bored and they sat there facing one another squarely. Meantime, of course, the money was blazing.

The whole thing meant nothing to me; perhaps that is why it was my control which snapped.

Anyway, I knocked the cash out of his hand. With a sudden movement I sent the whole hundred notes flying out of his grasp. All over the place they went—on the floor, the table, everywhere. The room was alight with blazing banknotes.

He went after them like a lunatic—you wouldn't have thought a man that fat could have moved so fast.

It was the one that laddered my stocking which gave the game away. A spark burned the nylon and as I felt it, I looked down and snatched the charred note, holding it up to the light. We all saw the flaw in it at the same moment. The ink had run and there was a great streak through the middle, like the veining in a marble slab.

There was a long silence and the first sound came not from us but from the service door. It opened and the new waiter, looking quite different now that he'd changed his coat for one with a policeman's badge on it, came down the room followed by Inspector Cumberland.

They went up to Adelbert and the younger, heavier man put a hand on his shoulder. Cumberland ignored everything but the money. He stamped out the smoldering flames and gathered up the remains and the four untouched wads on the table. Then he smiled briefly.

"Got you, Adelbert. With it on you. We've been wondering

who was passing slush in this street and when it came to our ears that someone was burning cash we thought we ought to look into it."

I was still only half comprehending and I held out the note we'd been staring at.

"There's something wrong with this one," I said stupidly.

He took it from me and grunted.

"There's something wrong with all these, my dear. Miss Frosné's money is safe in his pocket where you saw him put it. These are some of the gang's failures. Every maker of counterfeit money has them—as a rule they never leave the printing room. This one in particular is a shocker. I wonder he risked it even for burning. You didn't like wasting it, I suppose, Adelbert. What a careful soul you are."

"How did you find out?" Louise looked from them to me.

Cumberland saved me.

"A policeman, too, Madam," he said, laughing, "can be a psychologist."

A Nice Place to Stay

NEDRA TYRE

Nedra (pronounced NEE-dra) Tyre (1912–90), a native of Georgia, was the author of a half-dozen mystery novels between 1952 and 1971 and about forty short stories for *Ellery Queen's Mystery Magazine* and other publications. A specialist in small-town Southern backgrounds, she won critical acclaim in her lifetime but, in part because of her small output, is largely overlooked in most reference sources on the genre. Her first and best-known novel, the Atlanta-based *Mouse in Eternity* (1952), drew on her own background as a social worker and anticipated the later trend toward regionalism in American mysteries.

Tyre was living in Richmond, Virginia, when she told *Contemporary Authors* (volume 104, 1982), "I've worked in offices, been a social worker, library assistant, clerk in a book department, done copy in an advertising agency, and taught sociology. I've done everything and it seems to me I've never made even minimum wage. Life is real and life is earnest, but most of all, it's ridiculous. Now I am a staff writer in an agency that gives financial assistance to desperately poor children in twenty-five countries.

"For the last four years I have been totally deaf. It's amazingly interesting to be deaf, although it's awkward socially. Politically I am what would be called a liberal and religiously I am a protestant with a small p. Almost everything defeats me and everything amazes me."

Tyre's social work background as well as the world view expressed above informs "A Nice Place to Stay," with its deep understanding of the psychology of poverty.

All my life I've wanted a nice place to stay. I don't mean anything grand, just a small room with the walls freshly painted and a few neat pieces of furniture and a window to catch the sun so that two or three pot plants could grow. That's what I've always dreamed of. I didn't yearn for love or money or nice clothes, though I was a pretty enough girl and pretty clothes would have made me prettier—not that I mean to brag.

Things fell on my shoulders when I was fifteen. That was when Mama took sick, and keeping house and looking after Papa and my two older brothers—and of course nursing Mama—became my responsibility. Not long after that Papa lost the farm and we moved to town. I don't like to think of the house we lived in near the C & R railroad tracks, though I guess we were lucky to have a roof over our heads—it was the worst days of the Depression and a lot of people didn't even have a roof, even one that leaked, plink, plonk; in a heavy rain there weren't enough pots and pans and vegetable bowls to set around to catch all the water.

Mama was the sick one but it was Papa who died first—living in town didn't suit him. By then my brothers had married and Mama and I moved into two back rooms that looked onto an alley and everybody's garbage cans and dump heaps. My brothers pitched in and gave me enough every month for Mama's and my barest expenses even though their wives grumbled and complained.

I tried to make Mama comfortable. I catered to her every whim and fancy. I loved her. All the same I had another reason to keep her alive as long as possible. While she breathed I knew I had a place to stay. I was terrified of what would happen to me when Mama died. I had no high school diploma and no experience at outside work and I knew my sisters-in-law wouldn't take me in or let my brothers support me once Mama was gone.

Then Mama drew her last breath with a smile of thanks on her face for what I had done.

Sure enough, Norine and Thelma, my brothers' wives, put their feet down. I was on my own from then on. So that scared feeling of wondering where I could lay my head took over in my mind and never left me.

I had some respite when Mr. Williams, a widower twenty-four years older than me, asked me to marry him. I took my vows seriously. I meant to cherish him and I did. But that house we lived in! Those walls couldn't have been dirtier if they'd been smeared with soot and the plumbing was stubborn as a mule. My left foot stayed sore from having to kick the pipe underneath the kitchen sink to get the water to run through.

Then Mr. Williams got sick and had to give up his shoe repair shop that he ran all by himself. He had a small savings account and a few of those twenty-five-dollar government bonds and drew some disability insurance until the policy ran out in something like six months.

I did everything I could to make him comfortable and keep him cheerful. Though I did all the laundry I gave him clean sheets and clean pajamas every third day and I think it was by my will power alone that I made a begonia bloom in that dark back room Mr. Williams stayed in. I even pestered his two daughters and told them they ought to send their father some get-well cards and they did once or twice. Every now and then when there were a few pennies extra I'd buy cards and scrawl signatures nobody could have read and mailed them to Mr. Williams to make him think some of his former customers were remembering him and wishing him well.

Of course when Mr. Williams died his daughters were johnny-on-the-spot to see that they got their share of the little bit that tumbledown house brought. I didn't begrudge them—I'm not one to argue with human nature.

I hate to think about all those hardships I had after Mr. Williams died. The worst of it was finding somewhere to sleep; it all boiled down to having a place to stay. Because somehow you can manage not to starve. There are garbage cans to dip into—you'd be surprised how wasteful some people are and how much good food they throw away. Or if it was right after the garbage trucks had made their collections and the cans were empty I'd go into a supermarket and pick, say, at the cherries pretending I was selecting some to buy. I didn't slip their best ones into my mouth. I'd take either those so ripe that they should have been thrown away or those that weren't ripe enough and shouldn't have been put out for people to buy. I might snitch a withered cabbage leaf or a few pieces of watercress or a few of those small round tomatoes about the size of hickory nuts—I never can remember their right name. I wouldn't make a pig of myself, just eat enough to ease my hunger. So I managed. As I say, you don't have to starve.

The only work I could get hardly ever paid me anything beyond room and board. I wasn't a practical nurse, though I knew how to take care of sick folks, and the people hiring me would say that since I didn't have the training and qualifications I couldn't expect much. All they really wanted was for someone to spend the night with Aunt Myrtle or Cousin Kate or Mama or Daddy; no actual duties were demanded of me, they said, and they really didn't think my help was worth anything except meals and a place to sleep. The arrangements were pretty makeshift. Half the time I wouldn't have a place to keep my things, not that I had any clothes to speak of, and sometimes I'd sleep on a cot in the hall outside the patient's room or on some sort of contrived bed in the patient's room.

I cherished every one of those sick people, just as I had cherished Mama and Mr. Williams. I didn't want them to die. I did everything I knew to let them know I was interested in their welfare—first for their sakes, and then for mine, so I wouldn't have to go out and find another place to stay.

Well, now, I've made out my case for the defense, a term I never thought I'd have to use personally, so now I'll make out the case for the prosecution.

I stole.

I don't like to say it, but I was a thief.

I'm not light-fingered. I didn't want a thing that belonged to anybody else. But there came a time when I felt forced to steal. I had to have some things. My shoes fell apart. I needed some stockings and underclothes. And when I'd ask a son or a daughter or a cousin or a niece for a little money for those necessities they acted as if I was trying to blackmail them. They reminded me that I wasn't qualified as a practical nurse, that I might even get into trouble with the authorities if they found I was palming myself off as a practical nurse—which I wasn't and they knew it. Anyway, they said that their terms were only bed and board.

So I began to take things—small things that had been pushed into the backs of drawers or stored high on shelves in boxes— things that hadn't been used or worn for years and probably would never be used again. I made my biggest haul at Mrs. Bick's where there was an attic full of trunks stuffed with clothes and doodads from the twenties all the way back to the nineties— uniforms, ostrich fans, Spanish shawls, beaded bags. I sneaked out a few of these at a time and every so often sold them to a place called Way Out, Hippie Clothiers.

I tried to work out the exact amount I got for selling something. Not, I know, that you can make up for theft. But, say, I got a dollar for a feather boa belonging to Mrs. Bick: well, then I'd come back and work at a job that the cleaning woman kept putting off, like waxing the hall upstairs or polishing the andirons or getting the linen closet in order.

All the same I *was* stealing—not everywhere I stayed, not even in most places, but when I had to I stole. I admit it.

But I didn't steal that silver box.

I was as innocent as a baby where that box was concerned. So when that policeman came toward me grabbing at the box I stepped aside, and maybe I even gave him the push that sent him to his death. He had no business acting like that when that box was mine, whatever Mrs. Crowe's niece argued.

Fifty thousand nieces couldn't have made it not mine.

Anyway, the policeman was dead and though I hadn't wanted him dead I certainly hadn't wished him well. And then I got to thinking: well, I didn't steal Mrs. Crowe's box but I had stolen other things and it was the mills of God grinding exceeding fine, as I once heard a preacher say, and I was being made to pay for the transgressions that had caught up with me.

Surely I can make a little more sense out of what happened than that, though I never was exactly clear in my own mind about everything that happened.

Mrs. Crowe was the most appreciative person I ever worked for. She was bedridden and could barely move. I don't think the registered nurse on daytime duty considered it part of her job to massage Mrs. Crowe. So at night I would massage her, and that pleased and soothed her. She thanked me for every small thing I did—when I fluffed her pillow, when I'd put a few drops of perfume on her earlobes, when I'd straighten the wrinkled bedcovers.

I had a little joke. I'd pretend I could tell fortunes and I'd take Mrs. Crowe's hand and tell her she was going to have a wonderful day but she must beware of a handsome blond stranger—or some such foolishness that would make her laugh. She didn't sleep well and it seemed to give her pleasure to talk to me most of the night about her childhood or her dead husband.

She kept getting weaker and weaker and two nights before she died she said she wished she could do something for me but that when she became an invalid she had signed over everything to her niece. Anyway, Mrs. Crowe hoped I'd take her silver box. I thanked her. It pleased me that she liked me well enough to give me the box. I didn't have any real use for it. It would have made a nice trinket box, but I didn't have any trinkets. The box seemed to be Mrs. Crowe's fondest possession. She kept it on the table beside her and her eyes lighted up every time she looked at it. She might have been a little girl first seeing a brand-new baby doll early on a Christmas morning.

So when Mrs. Crowe died and the niece on whom I set eyes for the first time dismissed me, I gathered up what little I had and took the box and left. I didn't go to Mrs. Crowe's funeral. The paper said it was private and I wasn't invited. Anyway, I wouldn't have had anything suitable to wear.

I still had a few dollars left over from those things I'd sold to the hippie place called Way Out, so I paid a week's rent for a room that was the worst I'd ever stayed in.

It was freezing cold and no heat came up to the third floor where I was. In that room with falling plaster and buckling floorboards and darting roaches, I sat wearing every stitch I owned, with a sleazy blanket and a faded quilt draped around me waiting for the heat to rise, when in swept Mrs. Crowe's niece in a fur coat and a fur hat and shiny leather boots up to her knees. Her face was beet red from anger when she started telling me that she had traced me through a private detective and I was to give her back the heirloom I had stolen.

Her statement made me forget the precious little bit I knew of the English language. I couldn't say a word, and she kept on screaming that if I returned the box immediately no criminal charge would be made against me. Then I got back my voice and I said that box was mine and that Mrs. Crowe had wanted me to have it, and she asked if I had any proof or if there were any witnesses to the gift, and I told her that when I was given a present I said thank you, that I didn't ask for proof and witnesses, and that nothing could make me part with Mrs. Crowe's box.

The niece stood there breathing hard, in and out, almost counting her breaths like somebody doing an exercise to get control of herself.

"You'll see," she yelled, and then she left.

The room was colder than ever and my teeth chattered.

Not long afterward I heard heavy steps clumping up the stairway. I realized that the niece had carried out her threat and that the police were after me.

I was panic-stricken. I chased around the room like a rat with a cat after it: Then I thought that if the police searched my room and couldn't find the box it might give me time to decide what to do. I grabbed the box out of the top dresser drawer and scurried down the back hall. I snatched the back door open. I think what I intended to do was run down the back steps and hide the box somewhere, underneath a bush or maybe in a garbage can.

Those back steps were steep and rose almost straight up for three stories and they were flimsy and covered with ice.

I started down. My right foot slipped. The handrail saved me. I clung to it with one hand and to the silver box with the other hand and picked and chose my way across the patches of ice.

When I was midway I heard my name shrieked. I looked around to see a big man leaping down the steps after me. I never saw such anger on a person's face. Then he was directly behind me and reached out to snatch the box.

I swerved to escape his grasp and he cursed me. Maybe I pushed him. I'm not sure—not really.

Anyway, he slipped and fell down and down and down, and then after all that falling he was absolutely still. The bottom step was beneath his head like a pillow and the rest of his body was spreadeagled on the brick walk.

The almost like a pet that wants to follow its master, the silver box jumped from my hand and bounced down the steps to land beside the man's left ear.

My brain was numb. I felt paralyzed. Then I screamed.

Tenants from that house and the houses next door and across the alley pushed windows open and flung doors open to see what the commotion was about, and then some of them began to run toward the back yard. The policeman who was the dead man's partner—I guess you'd call him that—ordered them to keep away.

After a while more police came and they took the dead man's body and drove me to the station where I was locked up.

From the very beginning I didn't take to that young lawyer they assigned to me. There wasn't anything exactly that I could put my finger on. I just felt uneasy with him. His last name was Stanton. He had a first name of course, but he didn't tell me what it was; he said he wanted me to call him Bat like all his friends did.

He was always smiling and reassuring me when there wasn't anything to smile or be reassured about, and he ought to have known it all along instead of filling me with false hope.

All I could think was that I was thankful Mama and Papa and Mr. Williams were dead and that my shame wouldn't bring shame on them.

"It's going to be all right," the lawyer kept saying right up to the end, and then he claimed to be indignant when I was found guilty of resisting arrest and of manslaughter and theft or robbery—there was the biggest hullabaloo as to whether I was guilty of theft or robbery. Not that I was guilty of either, at least in this particular instance, but no one would believe me.

You would have thought it was the lawyer being sentenced instead of me, the way he carried on. He called it a terrible miscarriage of justice and said we might as well be back in the eighteenth century when they hanged children.

Well, that was an exaggeration, if ever there was one; nobody was being hanged and nobody was a child. That policeman had died and I had had a part in it. Maybe I had pushed him. I couldn't be sure. In my heart I really hadn't meant him any harm. I was just scared. But he was dead all the same. And as far as stealing went, I hadn't stolen the box but I had stolen other things more than once.

And then it happened. It was a miracle. All my life I'd dreamed of a nice room of my own, a comfortable place to stay. And that's exactly what I got.

The room was on the small side but it had everything I needed in it, even a wash basin with hot and cold running water, and the walls were freshly painted, and they let me choose whether I wanted a wing chair with a chintz slipcover or a modern Danish armchair. I even got to decide what color bedspread I preferred. The window looked out on a beautiful lawn edged with shrubbery, and the matron said I'd be allowed to go to the greenhouse and select some pot plants to keep in my room. The next day I picked out a white gloxinia and some russet chrysanthemums.

I didn't mind the bars at the windows at all. Why, this day and age some of the finest mansions have barred windows to keep burglars out.

The meals—I simply couldn't believe there was such delicious food in the world. The woman who supervised their preparation had embezzled the funds of one of the largest catering companies in the state after working herself up from assistant cook to treasurer.

The other inmates were very friendly and most of them had led the most interesting lives. Some of the ladies occasionally used words that you usually see written only on fences or printed on sidewalks before the cement dries, but when they were scolded they apologized. Every now and then somebody would get angry with someone and there would be a little scratching or hair pulling, but it never got too bad. There was a choir—I can't sing but I love music—and they gave a concert every Tuesday morning at chapel, and Thursday night was movie night. There wasn't any admission charge. All you did was go in and sit down anywhere you pleased.

We all had a special job and I was assigned to the infirmary. The doctor and nurse both complimented me. The doctor said that I should have gone into professional nursing, that I gave confidence to the patients and helped them get well. I don't know about that but I've had years of practice with sick people and I like to help anybody who feels bad.

I was so happy that sometimes I couldn't sleep at night. I'd get up and click on the light and look at the furniture and the walls. It was hard to believe I had such a pleasant place to stay. I'd remember supper that night, how I'd gone back to the steam table for a second helping of asparagus with lemon and herb sauce, and I compared my plenty with those terrible times when I had slunk into supermarkets and nibbled overripe fruit and raw vegetables to ease my hunger.

Then one day here came that lawyer, not even at regular visiting hours, bouncing around congratulating me that my appeal had been upheld, or whatever the term was, and that I was as free as a bird to leave right that minute.

He told the matron she could send my belongings later and he dragged me out front where TV cameras and newspaper reporters were waiting.

As soon as the cameras began whirring and the photographers began to aim, the lawyer kissed me on the cheek and pinned a flower on me. He made a speech saying that a terrible miscarriage of justice had been rectified. He had located people who testified that Mrs. Crowe had given me the box—she had told the gardener and the cleaning woman. They hadn't wanted to testify because they didn't want to get mixed up with the police, but the lawyer had persuaded them in the cause of justice and humanity to come forward and make statements.

The lawyer had also looked into the personnel record of the dead policeman and had learned that he had been judged emotionally unfit for his job, and the psychiatrist had warned the Chief of Police that something awful might happen either to the man himself or to a suspect unless he was relieved of his duties.

All the time the lawyer was talking into the microphones he had latched onto me like I was a three-year-old that might run away, and I just stood and stared. Then when he had finished his speech about me the reporters told him that like his grandfather and his uncle he was sure to end up as governor but at a much earlier age.

At that the lawyer gave a big grin in front of the camera and waved good-bye and pushed me into his car.

I was terrified. The nice place I'd found to stay in wasn't mine any longer. My old nightmare was back—wondering how I could manage to eat and how much stealing I'd have to do to live from one day to the next.

The cameras and reporters had followed us.

A photographer asked me to turn down the car window beside me, and I overheard two men way in the back of the crowd talking. My ears are sharp. Papa always said I could hear thunder three states away. Above the congratulations and bubbly talk around me I heard one of those men in back say, "This is a bit too much, don't you think? Our Bat is showing himself the champion of the Senior Citizen now. He's already copped the teenyboppers and the under thirties using methods that ought to have disbarred him. He should have made the gardener and cleaning woman testify at the beginning, and from the first he should have checked into the policeman's history. There ought never to have been a case at all, much less a conviction. But Bat wouldn't have got any publicity that way. He had to do it in his own devious, spectacular fashion." The other man just kept nodding and saying after every sentence, "You're damned right."

Then we drove off and I didn't dare look behind me because I was so heartbroken over what I was leaving.

The lawyer took me to his office. He said he hoped I wouldn't mind a little excitement for the next few days. He had mapped out some public appearances for me. The next morning I was to be on an early television show. There was nothing to be worried about. He would be right beside me to help me just as he had helped me throughout my trouble. All that I had to say on the TV program was that I owed my freedom to him.

I guess I looked startled or bewildered because he hurried on to say that I hadn't been able to pay him a fee but that now I was able to pay him back—not in money but in letting the public know about how he was the champion of the underdog.

I said I had been told that the court furnished lawyers free of charge to people who couldn't pay, and he said that was right, but his point was that I could repay him now by telling people all that he had done for me. Then he said the main thing was to talk over our next appearance on TV. He wanted to coach me in what I was going to say, but first he would go into his partner's office and tell him to take all the incoming calls and handle the rest of his appointments.

When the door closed after him I thought that he was right. I did owe my freedom to him. He was to blame for it. The smart alec. The upstart. Who asked him to butt in and snatch me out of my pretty room and the work I loved and all that delicious food?

It was the first time in my life I knew what it meant to despise someone.

I hated him.

Before, when I was convicted of manslaughter, there was a lot of talk about malice aforethought and premeditated crime.

There wouldn't be any argument this time.

I hadn't wanted any harm to come to that policeman. But I did mean harm to come to this lawyer.

I grabbed up a letter opener from his desk and ran my finger along the blade and felt how sharp it was. I waited behind the door and when he walked through I gathered all my strength and stabbed him. Again and again and again.

Now I'm back where I want to be—in a nice place to stay.

Clever and Quick

CHRISTIANNA BRAND

Many aficionados of pure, fair-play detection would echo the great critic Anthony Boucher in nominating the trio of John Dickson Carr, Ellery Queen, and Agatha Christie as their big three. But there were other writers who, if not quite as prolific, could equal those three in their devotion to and talent for devious puzzle plotting. One of these was the creator of Inspector Cockrill, Christianna Brand (1907–88). Born Mary Christianna Milne of British parents in Malaya, Brand lived in India during her childhood. Like many writers, she held a variety of jobs in her early life, including governess, model, and dancer. Her experience working as a salesperson in a fashion house inspired her first novel, *Death in High Heels* (1941). Brand showed she could construct puzzles with the best of them in novels like *Green for Danger* (1944), memorably filmed with Alistair Sim, and *Tour de Force* (1955). By her own account, she was equally scrupulous about polishing her style and deploying her clues, seeking to bamboozle the reader while observing absolute fair play. At various times in her career, she departed from pure detection to produce a speculation on the *Marie Celeste* mystery (*The Honey Harlot* [1978]), children's books (*Danger Unlimited* [1948] and a three-book series beginning with *Nurse Matilda* [1964]), a fact-crime account (*Heaven Knows Who* [1960]), and pseudonymous mainstream novels, but crime fiction remained her main interest.

A beloved figure at mystery conventions late in her life, she is remembered in the field for her personality as much as for her writing. In introducing her short-story collection *Buffet for Unwelcome Guests* (1983), Robert E. Briney recalls her speaking style: "The topics and anecdotes varied, though some of them had to be reprised by popular demand. (The story of Dorothy L. Sayers and the blood in the stairwell has become a word-of-mouth classic.) But the audience reaction was always the same. Listeners were delighted by the sharp verbal portraits; they listened intently whenever a serious note was introduced; they anticipated exactly as much of a story's trend as they were intended to, and responded with appreciative chagrin when the punchline turned out to be other than what they had been induced to expect. In fact, they reacted much as readers of Christianna Brand's fiction have been doing for some forty years."

In the short-story form, Brand specialized less in pure detection than in the twist-upon-twist double-or-triple-cross crime story of which "Clever and Quick" is a prime example.

You had to keep up appearances; so the apartment was very showy, everything phony right down to the massive brass fender in front of the electric fire. But keeping up appearances was one thing and keeping up the payments was another; and with the theater as it was these days, both of them had been "resting" for a long, long time. So the fact was that they really ought to let Trudi go.

Trudi was the au pair girl and for different reasons neither one wanted her to go.

They were having a row about it now, standing in front of the fireplace. They had a row on an average of once an hour these days—nag, nag, bloody nag. Colette was driving Raymond out of his mind. And now this thing about Trudi. If he secretly (somehow) made up Trudi's pay? He suggested, "Try offering her a bit less for the work."

"*You* try offering her a bit less—for the pleasure," said Colette. It touched him as ever on the raw. "Are you suggesting—?"

"Raymond, that girl thinks of nothing but money and you know it."

Yes, he knew it, and with the knowledge his heart grew chill. If a time came when he could no longer give Trudi presents— He was mad about her—a little sharp-eyed, shrew-faced mittel-European—and yet here he was, caught, crazy for her, helpless in the grip of her greedy little claws. He, Raymond Gray, who all his life had been, on stage and off, irresistible to women, now caught in the toils of a woman himself. If I were slipping a bit, he said to himself, if my profile were going, if my hair and my teeth weren't so perfect as once they were—but he was wearing marvelously well. Why, even that drooling old monster in the opposite apartment—

She was not a monster, though she was a big woman and, having once been something of an athlete, now found all the fine muscle running to flabby white fat. But drooling? She was disgusting, she thought, out of her mind—a fat, ugly, aging widow, sitting here drooling over a has-been matinee idol not much more than half my age.

But, as he was caught and helpless, so was she—caught and helpless, sitting there like a silly schoolgirl, yearning only to pop out to her balcony and see if, through his window, she could catch a glimpse of him. From her room she could not see into his; the apartments were not in fact opposite each other but across a corner, at the same level.

But she dared not venture forth. The plane trees in the street just below were in full pollination and if she so much as poked out her nose, her allergy would blow up sky high. And even just passing in the corridor, going up and down the elevator, he mustn't see her with streaming red eyes and nose.

She spent a good deal of time in the corridors and the elevator. "Oh, Raymond," she would cry, "fancy running into you again!" She had long ago scraped up an acquaintance and it was Raymond, Colette, and Rosa between them now. They were not unwilling—her place was rich in champagne cocktails and dry martinis, with lots of caviar on little triangles of toast. She was loaded.

Colette said so now "Can't you wangle something out of the old bitch over there? She's loaded, and if you'd so much as kiss her hand she'd chop it off and give it to you, diamond rings and all."

Her hand was like a frog's back, all speckled with the greeny-brown patches of aging skin. "All the same, I'll tell you something," he said. "If you were out of the way, damn nagging so-and-so that you are, she'd make me a ruddy millionaire, I swear she would."

"Yes and where would your precious Trudi be then? Because," said Colette nastily, "I don't think dear Rosa would put up with very much of *that* little load of fancy tripe."

"Don't you call Trudi names!" he shouted.

"I'll call her what she is. I'm entitled to that much, surely?"

She had a vile mind, a vile mind and a foul mouth to express what was in it. It flashed across him in a moment of hazy light, red-streaked, that once he had loved her—never dreaming that behind the façade lay this creature of venom and dirt, never dreaming that one day he would stand here with upraised hand, would lunge forward and strike out at her, would have it in his mind to silence her forever.

But his hand did not touch her. She stepped back and away from him, tripped over the rug on the polished floor before the fireplace, fell heavily, almost violently throwing herself back and out of his reach. A brief shriek, arms flailing, a sickening scrunch as the base of her skull hit the rounded knob of the heavy brass fender. And suddenly—stillness.

He knew she was dead.

Trudi stood in the doorway, then moved forward to him slowly. She said, "Is all right. I saw. You did not touch her." And she fumbled for the English word. "Was—accident?" She came close beside him, staring down. "But she is dead," she said.

She was dead. He had not touched her, it had been an accident. But she was dead—and he was free.

It took him a little while to accept that Trudi was not going to tie up her life with an out-of-work, has-been actor, free or not free. "But, darrleeng, you know that your money is all gone, soon I must anyway leave. Mrs. Gray she has told me so." And since Mrs. Gray was lying there dead on the floor and could not contradict, she improvised a hurried tally of the debts already owing to her. "And this I must have, Raymond, soon I go home if I have no more a job here."

To be free—to be free to marry her and now to lose her! He pleaded, "Don't you love me at all?"

"But of course! Only how can we marry, darrleeng, if you have no money to live? So this money I must have, to go home."

"You can't go yet, anyway. You'll have to stand by me about— her." He had almost forgotten the poor dead thing lying there, ungainly, at their feet. "You'll have to give evidence for me."

She shrugged. "Of course. Was accident. But then I go home."

"Leaving me here like this? Trudi, I have no wife now, no money—"

The little shrug again, so endearing to his infatuated heart, half comic, half rueful; the wag of the pretty little head toward the window across the corner. "As to wife, as to money—over there, plenty both."

He said quickly, "Then I should be rich. So you and I—?"

But she said, as a few minutes earlier Colette had said, "I don't think Mrs. Rosa Fox puts up with nonsense. I think she suddenly pulls the moneybags—tight."

Did the idea come to him all in a flash as it seemed at the time?—or was there an interval while he thought?—while he stood over his wife's dead body and carefully, deliberately, thought it all through to the end? All he knew afterward was that suddenly he had Trudi by the arm, was talking to her urgently, pulling her to kneel down beside as, very delicately, he scraped from the round brass knob of the fender a fleck of the blood so rapidly congealing there, smearing it over the round brass knob of the poker, the knob identical in size, covering the smears with his own hand. And finally he threw the poker back into the fireplace.

"Now, Trudi, slip out, don't let anyone see you. Buy something somewhere. Come back right away and this time let the porter see you."

He did not look back, as he scrambled to his feet, at the still sprawled body—he had not even that moment to spend on the past. The future was now ahead of him. Only, he prayed, as he furtively slid out into the corridor, let Rosa be in! And let her be alone!

She was in and alone. She was always in and alone these days, flopped in an armchair, dreaming like an adolescent girl of her hopeless, her helpless, love. "A woman of my age," she thought, "sitting here mooning over another woman's husband." But she'd been quite a gal in her day and widowed a long, long time. Now she said, "Raymond—how lovely!" And at once, "But what's the matter, my dear? Are you ill?"

"Rosa," he said, "You must help me!" And he fell on his knees before her, grabbing at her skirt with shuddering hands—really, with all that talent it was quite extraordinary that he couldn't get more work! He threw a hoarse quaver into his voice. "I've killed her," he said.

She stepped back and away from him. "Killed her?"

"Colette. I've killed her. She went on and on. She said horrible things about—about you, Rosa. She thinks you—she always said that you—Rosa, I know you've liked me—"

"I love you," she said simply; but she took a deep, deep breath while the future spread out before her—as earlier his own had opened out to him. His wife was dead and he was free.

He pretended amazement at her answer—amazement and gratitude; but he was too clever to claim immediately a return of her feeling. He came at last to the point. "Then, even more, Rosa, may I dare to ask you what I was going to. I am throwing myself on your mercy, just praying that out of friendship you will help me. And now, if you really mean that you—"

And he went with her to the sofa and sat there gripping her hands and poured it all out to her. "She was being so vile. She had—well, she's dead, but Colette had a filthy mind, Rosa. She'd been going on like this for weeks and suddenly I couldn't stand it any more. I saw red. I—I picked up the poker. I didn't mean to harm her—honestly, I swear it—just to frighten her. But when I came to myself again—" And he prayed, "Oh, my God, please try to understand!"

"You did this because she was saying foul things about *me?*"

"You've always been so nice to us, Rosa; it just made me sick, her talking like that, sneering and jeering." And he poured it all out again, living through the scene, only substituting her name for Trudi's. Her big plain face went first white, then scarlet, then white again. She held tightly to his hand. "What do you want me to do?"

"Rosa, I thought very quickly—I do think quickly when I'm in a spot. It seems awful now, her lying there dead and me just thinking of myself, trying to fight my way out of it. But that's what I did. And then I knelt down and—well, there are two brass knobs on the fender exactly like the one on the poker and I—I moved her head so that it looked as though she'd hit it against one of the fender knobs, and then I cleaned all the—the blood and stuff off the poker—"

She was a clever woman—quick and clever. The body might have slowed down, the body that once had been so strong and under control, but the mind was still clever and quick. "An accident," she said.

"Yes, but—people knew we were always quarreling. Trudi must have known it, of course. They could say I'd pushed her, given her a shove." He gave her a sick look that was not too difficult to assume. "At the least—manslaughter," he said.

Clever and quick. "You want me to say that I *saw* what happened? That you didn't hit her?"

"My God," he said, "you're marvelous! Yes. You could say you saw it all through the window, saw me standing there talking to her, say frankly that we seemed to be arguing, make it look as though you're not too much on my side, just a casual neighbor. And then—there's a rug there, you know it, very silky and slippery—you skidded on it once yourself, remember? Perfectly possible for her to have taken a backward step, slipped and fallen backward; and of course that would be all you'd know—you can't see down to the floor of our room, even from your balcony."

"But I'd have to say I was out *on* the balcony. I can't see your window from in here."

He had thought that out too. "Your balcony's only overlooked by two flats, and all those people will have been out; I know them. No one could say that you *weren't* there."

"All right," she said.

"You'll do it for me?"

"Of course. But what about that girl, that little trollop, whatever her name is—the au pair?"

He could hardly keep the stiffness from his voice but he controled himself. "Out shopping, thank God!" And thank God, also, that Rosa couldn't in fact have been on the balcony, looking in, seeing Trudi there in the room with him. He knew all about the allergy, and one glance at her face confirmed it—Rosa hadn't been out.

"Well, go back now. You must call a doctor quick. And say nothing about me. Just tell your story, don't seem even to think of bringing me into it. They'll be round here soon enough, asking if I saw anything. Now, time's passing, you really must go."

He started for the door but suddenly he paused. "Rosa!" He had assumed a look of shame but over the shame a flush of exultancy. "Rosa, it's awful to have even thought of it, but suddenly it's come to me. A trial for murder! You know how things are in the theatrical business, you know how things have been with me lately. But if I were suddenly in the news! Accused of murder—standing there at the Old Bailey, headlines in all the papers, a *cause célèbre!* And then—the dramatic intervention, the witness who'd seen it all, the last-minute evidence." He stood before her, half shame-faced, half pleading. "Rosa?"

"Why didn't I give evidence before? They'd never even have charged you if I'd spoken at once."

"Well, that's the point. I *must* get myself arrested and tried. You'd have to say you hadn't realized, you didn't want to get mixed up in it. But then of course the moment you heard I was accused—"

"Even so you wouldn't get further than the first hearing, whatever it's called. No publicity in that."

"You couldn't—just be abroad for a little while, out of touch?"

She opened her mouth to say that none of it mattered, he'd never need to work again. But she held her peace. He was an actor, actors needed to work, they had to express themselves. "Leave it all to me. I'll handle it," she said.

The earlier headlines were not too bad though hardly sensational and then came the long dull period before the trial opened. However, at last—the day. Himself in the dock, very pale, very handsome. The police in the witness box. "Accused stated—" A flipped-over page in a notebook. "Accused stated, 'Oh, my God, this is awful, I must have hit out at her, I must have had a blackout, she was nag nag nag at me the whole bloody time because I wasn't getting work, but I never meant to harm her, I swear I did not.'"

And the forensic evidence. "On the head of the poker I found a small smear of blood." The smear had been consistent with the blood of the dead woman, with having come there at the time of her death. Tests showed that the accused had handled the poker after the blood came there. Yes, consistent with his having attempted to remove marks of blood with the palm of his hand, missing the one small smear. The blade of the poker appeared to have been wiped—it showed no fingerprints.

In reply to defense counsel: yes, it was true that the blade of a poker would not be much handled in the ordinary way and the wiping might well have been simply the previous routine cleaning. The doctor testified that the woman had been dead between half an hour and an hour when he saw her.

Trudi in the box for the defense: shrewd and cool. Had arrived back from the shoppings to find Mr. Gray on his knees beside the body; had had almost to lift him to his feet. Yes, he might very well have touched the poker with his hand, made bloody by his examination of the wound; his arms were all over the place as she hauled him up. She had tried to get him calm; wanted to call a doctor but did not know the number of him, and Mr. Gray seemed so dazed she could get no sense from him. And anyway, what was the hurry, said Trudi with one of her shrugs. Anybody could see that Madame was dead.

And so at last to Rosa Fox. She had with extraordinary dedication deliberately shed all aids to such doubtful charms as she possessed—stripped off the jewelry, dressed herself drably, sacrificed the cosmetics which ordinarily, to some extent at least, disguised the ravages of her age. Not for one moment could anyone suspect that here stood a woman with whom the prisoner could ever have had the slightest rapport.

Into the agreed routine. The casual acquaintance, the occasional drink together. The question of the police directly after the—accident. Agreed she had previously insisted she had seen nothing. She had been unwell, under great private tensions, wanted only to get abroad to a health spa where she had been ever since. She hadn't wished to become involved. Never dreamed, of course, that there could possibly be any charge against Mr. Gray, knowing as she did with absolute certainly that the thing had been entirely an accident. Because in fact she had actually seen it happen.

"From my balcony you can look straight into their room. I glanced over and saw them standing there. They seemed to be having an argument. He said something angry, she jerked away from him as though he had raised his hand against her—"

"Mrs. Fox, had he anything in his hand?"

"In his hand? Oh, the poker you mean? No, nothing, no poker or anything. And anyway, he never raised his hand."

"He never raised his hand? You can swear to that?"

The Judge from the Bench said solemnly, "Mr. Tree, she *is* swearing to that. She is swearing to everything she says. She is under oath."

"Well, I could see it all quite clearly and I certainly can swear—well, I mean I am absolutely sure he never raised his hand at all. He said something. She stepped back and then she seemed to trip and topple over backwards. I thought to myself. "Oh, she's skidded on that rug of theirs!" I know that rug—very treacherous it is on the parquet floor. I nearly slipped on it once myself.

Well, and then I went back into my room and thought no more about it."

"It didn't occur to you that she might have injured herself?"

"I thought she might have banged her head or something but of course no more than that. As I say, I'd slipped there myself and been none the worse for it." And she made a little face and admitted that if the lady had collected a couple of bruises it would have been no more than she deserved. "I think she nagged him. But of course I didn't know them well."

Headlines, yes. But not much really and often not even on the center pages, let alone the front page. But there was a big picture of him planned for Sunday, with an interview—celebrating, a glass of champagne raised to the neighbor whose testimony had confirmed his innocence. Not perhaps in the best of taste, the picture taken right there in front of the fireplace where his wife had died. But it wasn't a best-of-taste newspaper and one settled for what one could get.

And the reporters withdrew; and at last they were alone in his apartment.

She held out her hands to him. "Well, Raymond?"

She looked about a hundred years old standing there before him, the sagging face devoid of its makeup, the ugly dull dress, the droopy hairdo, the mottled hands without their customary diamond flash. She revolted him.

"Well, Rosa, you did a beautiful job."

She did not hear the chill in his voice, or did not believe it. She said softly, "And one day soon—shall I collect my reward?"

"Reward?" he said.

"After all, my darling, I have perjured myself for you."

"Yes, so you have, haven't you?" he said.

Now the unpowdered skin took on a strange ashen color, and her eyes grew frightened and sick. "Raymond, what do you mean?"

"I mean that you perjured yourself, as you say; and you know, perhaps, what happens to perjurers?"

A clever woman, quick and clever. But still she insisted, "I don't understand."

"I need money, Rosa," he said.

"Money? But if we were married—"

He moved aside so that she looked over his shoulder and into the mirror above the fireplace.

He said, "You? And I? *Married?*"

She looked long, long at her pitiful reflection. She said at last, "Is this blackmail?"

"Wasn't it blackmail when you thought that by saving me from prison you could force me to marry you?"

"Yes," she said. "I think perhaps it was." And she thought to herself that now she was beaten at her own game. "If you give me away," she said, "you'll have to admit you murdered her."

"In fact I didn't murder her. I can say it happened almost exactly as you said in court."

"Very well then," she said swiftly, "I can change my story. Who can prove that I didn't see you murder her?"

"*I* can prove that you didn't see it. You couldn't have been out on your balcony. The plane trees were pollinating and anyone will confirm to the police what happens if you so much as open a window when the pollen's flying about. But when they first saw you, you showed no traces of any allergic reaction. I know, because I'd just seen you myself.

"Besides, they couldn't touch me. I've been 'put in peril,' as they say—*autre fois acquit* is the legal name for it. Once acquitted I can't be tried again for the same crime. I could shout from the housetops that I'd killed her and still be safe."

"And live with that reputation?"

"Well, of course I *wouldn't* say I'd been guilty—which anyway, as I keep telling you, I wasn't. I'd still claim it had been an accident. But *you* would be in the soup."

"I see." She pondered it long and carefully, still staring, but unseeingly now, at her sad reflection in the glass. "You thought all this out from the very first, didn't you? In detail, from the very first?"

"Quite a nice little bit of opportunism," he suggested, proud of it.

"All that about the publicity? The blood deliberately smeared on the poker? Yes, I see. You had to give them something, you had to get yourself accused and charged, you had to be tried and acquitted before it was safe to accuse me. Two purposes to my perjury: first to supply the evidence that would set you free and second to make me vulnerable to blackmail." She said almost curiously, almost as though she were humbled for him rather than for herself, "Did you never even like me?"

"I didn't mind you," he said indifferently. "But as for marrying you—I think I'm a trifle more particular than that." And he picked up her handbag, helped himself to the thick wad of banknotes there, stuffed them loosely into his wallet, tucked the wallet away. "Just a very, very small beginning, my dear," he said.

"I won't even ask how much you're demanding. You'll be back again and again and again of course, won't you? But by way of a start—?"

"Make it ten thousand," he said. "You can get that much quickly." He smiled at her with cruel and ugly triumph. "And I need it quickly—for my honeymoon," he said.

Clever and quick. Clever not even to have to ask the name, to have summed it all up in one bright intuitive flash. And quick. The poker with its round brass knob lay there on the fender. She snatched it up—and struck.

Trudi burst open the door, darted forward from her listening post, slowed, then came smoothly the rest of the way and knelt beside him. For what seemed a long, long time they both stared down as only a few short months ago Raymond Gray himself had looked down at the dead body of his wife. It was his turn now.

Rosa's fat white arms retained something, it seemed, of their once splendid muscle; long-ago anatomical training had suggested the most susceptible spot. The heavy ball of the poker had smashed to a cobweb of fractures Raymond's delicate temple bone.

Trudi moved. With a small sick grimace she shifted Raymond's head a little way, so that the wound lay crushed against the round brass knob of the fender.

"That rug!" she said, getting up to her feet again. "Always so dangerous! Fancy, a second time, just the same like the poor wife!" She grinned with brutal complacence into the heavy white face with its look of dead despair. "So lucky that this time *I* was present, to see that it all was again just a terrible accident."

Raymond's jacket had fallen open. She stooped and with fastidious fingers picked out the wad of notes and stuffed them into her apron pocket.

"Just a verry, verrry small beginning," she quoted and took the poker out of Rosa's inert hand. "Go back to your flat, Madame. Collapse upon your bed. I see to everything, then I make telephone to the doctor." The Trudi shrug. "This time I know the number of him."

Rosa went back to her own apartment. She did not, however, collapse upon her bed.

"Police?" she said, holding the telephone receiver in a steady hand. She gave Raymond Gray's address. "You'd better get over there quick. I've just seen from my balcony the au pair girl going for him with a poker. And this time—no question of an accident."

She listened with a satisfied smile to a sharp voice cracking out orders. The voice returned to her. "Well, I wouldn't know about that—I can't see to the floor of the room. The girl disappeared from sight for a bit and when she got up she was stuffing money into her apron pocket. You'll find it, I daresay, hidden somewhere in her room. An affair going on, you know, even before the poor wife died; and now I suppose he was refusing to marry her."

Country Lovers

NADINE GORDIMER

Nobel Prize winner Nadine Gordimer (b. 1923) was born in the gold mining region of South Africa, the daughter of a jeweler. Receiving her early education at a convent, she graduated from University of the Witwatersrand in Johannesburg. Like many writers, she was solitary as a child, out of school from the age of eleven to sixteen because of an apparently imaginary heart ailment, her only companions her mother and her adult friends, with no contact with other children. First published at the age of fifteen, she eventually contributed short stories to such major U.S. markets as *The New Yorker, Harper's,* and *Mademoiselle.* Her first story collection, *The Soft Voice of the Serpent and Other Stories,* appeared in 1952, her first novel, *The Lying Days,* in 1955. Her views on racial equality and her celebration of human variety, which eventually led to outspoken opposition to her country's apartheid policies, she credited to her reading rather than any example from her apolitical parents. She listed as one of her favorite writers J. D. Salinger, another specialist in depicting the societal outsider.

Gordimer wrote critically of the South African regime in both fiction and non-fiction. One of her novels, *Burger's Daughter* (1979), was briefly banned in her home country. A *Time* magazine reviewer of her second novel, *A World of Strangers* (1958), as quoted in *Current Biography* (1959 yearbook), wrote that Gordimer "not only tells the truth about her countrymen, but she tells it so well that she has become at once their goad and their best writer." Surely, her conscientious opposition, along with that of other South African writers and thinkers, was a factor in the eventual end of apartheid.

Generally, Gordimer is not regarded even tangentially as a writer of crime fiction, but "Country Lovers," a painfully real story that reflects her concern about her country's policies while confronting some basic truths about racism, certainly qualifies for the category.

The farm children play together when they are small; but once the white children go away to school they soon don't play together any more, even in the holidays. Although most of the black children get some sort of schooling, they drop every year further behind the grades passed by the white children; the childish vocabulary, the child's exploration of the adventurous possibilities of dam, koppies, mealie lands and veld—there comes a time when the white children have surpassed these with the vocabulary of boarding-schools and the possibilities of inter-school sports matches and the kind of adventures seen at the cinema. This usefully coincides with the age of twelve or thirteen; so that by the time early adolescence is reached, the black children are making, along with the bodily changes common to all, an easy transition to adult forms of address, beginning to call their old playmates *missus* and *baasie*—little master.

The trouble was Paulus Eysendyck did not seem to realize that Thebedi was now simply one of the crowd of farm children down at the kraal, recognizable in his sisters' old clothes. The first Christmas holidays after he had gone to boarding-school he brought home for Thebedi a painted box he had made in his woodwork class. He had to give it to her secretly because he had nothing for the other children at the kraal. And she gave him, before he went back to school, a bracelet she had made of thin brass wire and the grey-and-white beans of the castor-oil crop his father cultivated. (When they used to play together, she was the one who had taught Paulus how to make clay oxen for their toy spans.) There was a craze, even in the *platteland* towns like the one where he was at school, for boys to wear elephant-hair and other bracelets beside their watch-straps; his was admired, friends asked him to get similar ones for them. He said the natives made them on his father's farm and he would try.

When he was fifteen, six feet tall, and tramping round at school dances with the girls from the "sister" school in the same town; when he had learnt how to tease and flirt and fondle quite intimately these girls who were the daughters of prosperous farmers like his father; when he had even met one who, at a wedding he had attended with his parents on a nearby farm, had let him do with her in a locked storeroom what people did when they made love—when he was as far from his childhood as all this, he still brought home from a shop in town a red plastic belt and gilt hoop earrings for the black girl, Thebedi. She told her father the missus had given these to her as a reward for some work she had done—it was true she sometimes was called to help out in the farmhouse. She told the girls in the kraal that she had a sweetheart nobody knew about, far away, away on another farm, and they giggled, and teased, and admired her. There was a boy in the kraal called Njabulo who said he wished he could have bought her a belt and earrings.

When the farmer's son was home for the holidays she wandered far from the kraal and her companions. He went for walks alone. They had not arranged this; it was an urge each followed independently. He knew it was she, from a long way off. She knew that his dog would not bark at her. Down at the dried-up riverbed where five or six years ago the children had caught a leguaan one great day—a creature that combined ideally the size and ferocious aspect of the crocodile with the harmlessness of the lizard—they squatted side by side on the earth bank. He told her traveler's tales: about school, about the punishments at school, particularly, exaggerating both their nature and his indifference to them. He told her about the town of Middleburg, which she had never seen. She had nothing to tell but she prompted with many questions, like any good listener. While he talked he twisted and tugged at the roots of white stinkwood and Cape willow trees that looped out of the eroded earth around them. It had always been a good spot for children's games, down there hidden by the mesh of old, ant-eaten trees held in place by vigorous ones, wild asparagus bushing up between the trunks, and here and there prickly-pear cactus sunken-skinned and bristly, like an old man's face, keeping alive sapless until the next rainy season. She punctured the dry hide of a prickly-pear again and again with a sharp stick while she listened. She laughed a lot at what he told her, sometimes dropping her face on her knees, sharing amusement with the cool shady earth beneath her bare feet. She put on her pair of shoes—white sandals, thickly Blanco-ed against the farm dust—when he was on the farm, but these were taken off and laid aside, at the river-bed.

One summer afternoon when there was water flowing there and it was very hot she waded in as they used to do when they were children, her dress bunched modestly and tucked into the legs of her pants. The schoolgirls he went swimming with at dams or pools on neighboring farms wore bikinis but the sight of their dazzling bellies and thighs in the sunlight had never made him feel what he felt now, when the girl came up the bank and sat beside him, the drops of water beading off her dark legs the only points of light in the earth-smelling, deep shade. They were not afraid of one another, they had known one another always; he did with her what he had done that time in the store-room at the wedding, and this time it was so lovely, so lovely, he was surprised . . . and she was surprised by it, too—he could see in her dark face that was part of the shade, with her big dark eyes, shiny as soft water, watching him attentively: as she had when they used to huddle over their teams of mud oxen, as she had when he told her about detention weekends at school.

They went to the river-bed often through those summer holidays. They met just before the light went, as it does quite quickly, and each returned home with the dark—she to her mother's hut, he to the farmhouse—in time for the evening meal. He did not tell her about school or town any more. She did not ask questions any longer. He told her, each time, when they would meet again. Once or twice it was very early in the morning; the lowing of the cows being driven to graze came to them where they lay, dividing them with unspoken recognition of the sound read in their two pairs of eyes, opening so close to each other.

He was a popular boy at school. He was in the second, then the first soccer team. The head girl of the "sister" school was said to have a crush on him; he didn't particularly like her, but there was a pretty blonde who put up her long hair into a kind of doughnut with a black ribbon round it, whom he took to see films when the schoolboys and girls had a free Saturday afternoon. He had been driving tractors and other farm vehicles since he was ten years old, and as soon as he was eighteen he got a driver's license and in the holidays, this last year of his school life, he took neighbors' daughters to dances and to the drive-in cinema that had just opened twenty kilometers from the farm. His sisters were married, by then; his parents often left him in charge of the farm over the weekend while they visited the young wives and grandchildren.

When Thebedi saw the farmer and his wife drive away on a Saturday afternoon, the boot of their Mercedes filled with fresh-killed poultry and vegetables from the garden that it was part of her father's work to tend, she knew that she must come not to the river-bed but up to the house. The house was an old one, thick-walled, dark against the heat. The kitchen was its lively thoroughfare, with servants, food supplies, begging cats and dogs, pots boiling over, washing being damped for ironing, and the big deep-freeze the missus had ordered from town, bearing a crocheted mat and a vase of plastic irises. But the dining-room with the bulging-legged heavy table was shut up in its rich, old smell of soup and tomato sauce. The sitting-room curtains were drawn and the TV set silent. The door of the parents' bedroom was locked and the empty rooms where the girls had slept had sheets of plastic spread over the beds. It was in one of these that she and the farmer's son stayed together whole nights—almost:

she had to get away before the house servants, who knew her, came in at dawn. There was a risk someone would discover her or traces of her presence if he took her to his own bedroom, although she had looked into it many times when she was helping out in the house and knew well, there, the row of silver cups he had won at school.

When she was eighteen and the farmer's son nineteen and working with his father on the farm before entering a veterinary college, the young man Njabulo asked her father for her. Njabulo's parents met with hers and the money he was to pay in place of the cows it is customary to give a prospective bride's parents was settled upon. He had no cows to offer; he was a laborer on the Eysendyck farm, like her father. A bright youngster; old Eysendyck had taught him bricklaying and was using him for odd jobs in construction, around the place. She did not tell the farmer's son that her parents had arranged for her to marry. She did not tell him, either, before he left for his first term at the veterinary college, that she thought she was going to have a baby. Two months after her marriage to Njabulo, she gave birth to a daughter. There was no disgrace in that; among her people it is customary for a young man to make sure, before marriage, that the chosen girl is not barren, and Njabulo had made love to her then. But the infant was very light and did not quickly grow darker as most African babies do. Already at birth there was on its head a quantity of straight, fine floss, like that which carries the seeds of certain weeds in the veld. The unfocused eyes it opened were grey flecked with yellow. Njabulo was the matt, opaque coffee-grounds color that had always been called black; the color of Thebedi's legs on which beaded water looked oyster-shell blue, the same color as Thebedi's face, where the black eyes, with their interested gaze and clear whites, were so dominant.

Njabulo made no complaint. Out of his farm laborer's earnings he bought from the Indian store a cellophane-windowed pack containing a pink plastic bath, six napkins, a card of safety pins, a knitted jacket, cap and bootees, a dress, and a tin of Johnson's Baby Powder, for Thebedi's baby.

When it was two weeks old Paulus Eysendyck arrived home from the veterinary college for the holidays. He drank a glass of fresh, still-warm milk in the childhood familiarity of his mother's kitchen and heard her discussing with the old house-servant where they could get a reliable substitute to help out now that the girl Thebedi had had a baby. For the first time since he was a small boy he came right into the kraal. It was eleven o'clock in the morning. The men were at work in the lands. He looked about him, urgently; the women turned away, each not wanting to be the one approached to point out where Thebedi lived. Thebedi appeared, coming slowly from the hut Njabulo had built in white man's style, with a tin chimney, and a proper window with glass panes set in straight as walls made of unfired bricks would allow. She greeted him with hands brought together and a token movement representing the respectful bob with which she was accustomed to acknowledge she was in the presence of his father or mother. He lowered his head under the doorway of her home and went in. He said, "I want to see. Show me."

She had taken the bundle off her back before she came out into the light to face him. She moved between the iron bedstead made up with Njabulo's checked blankets and the small wooden table where the pink plastic bath stood among food and kitchen pots, and picked up the bundle from the snugly-blanketed grocer's box where it lay. The infant was asleep; she revealed the closed, pale, plump tiny face, with a bubble of spit at the corner of the mouth, the spidery pink hands stirring. She took off the woolen cap and the straight fine hair flew up after it in static electricity, showing gilded strands here and there. He said nothing. She was watching him as she had done when they were little, and the gang of children had trodden down a crop in their games or transgressed in some other way for which he, as the farmer's son, the white one among them, must intercede with the farmer. She disturbed the sleeping face by scratching or tickling gently at a cheek with one finger, and slowly the eyes opened, saw nothing, were still asleep, and then, awake, no longer narrowed, looked out at them, grey with yellowish flecks, his own hazel eyes.

He struggled for a moment with a grimace of tears, anger and self-pity. She could not put out her hand to him. He said, "You haven't been near the house with it?"

She shook her head.

"Never?"

Again she shook her head.

"Don't take it out. Stay inside. Can't you take it away somewhere? You must give it to someone—"

She moved to the door with him.

He said, "I'll see what I will do. I don't know." And then he said: "I feel like killing myself."

Her eyes began to glow, to thicken with tears. For a moment there was the feeling between them that used to come when they were alone down at the river-bed.

He walked out.

Two days later, when his mother and father had left the farm for the day, he appeared again. The women were away on the lands, weeding, as they were employed to do as casual labor in summer; only the very old remained, propped up on the ground outside the huts in the flies and the sun. Thebedi did not ask him in. The child had not been well; it had diarrhea. He asked where its food was. She said, "The milk comes from me." He went into Njabulo's house, where the child lay; she did not follow but stayed outside the door and watched without seeing an old crone who had lost her mind, talking to herself, talking to the fowls who ignored her.

She thought she heard small grunts from the hut, the kind of infant grunt that indicates a full stomach, a deep sleep. After a time, long or short she did not know, he came out and walked away with plodding stride (his father's gait) out of sight, toward his father's house.

The baby was not fed during the night and although she kept

telling Njabulo it was sleeping, he saw for himself in the morning that it was dead. He comforted her with words and caresses. She did not cry but simply sat, staring at the door. Her hands were cold as dead chickens' feet to his touch.

Njabulo buried the little baby where farm workers were buried, in the place in the veld the farmer had given them. Some of the mounds had been left to weather away unmarked, others were covered with stones and a few had fallen wooden crosses. He was going to make a cross but before it was finished the police came and dug up the grave and took away the dead baby: someone—one of the other laborers? their women?—had reported that the baby was almost white, that, strong and healthy, it had died suddenly after a visit by the farmer's son. Pathological tests on the infant corpse showed intestinal damage not always consistent with death by natural causes.

Thebadi went for the first time to the country town where Paulus had been to school, to give evidence at the preparatory examination into the charge of murder brought against him. She cried hysterically in the witness box, saying yes, yes (the gilt hoop earrings swung in her ears), she saw the accused pouring liquid into the baby's mouth. She said he had threatened to shoot her if she told anyone.

More than a year went by before, in that same town, the case was brought to trial. She came to court with a newborn baby on her back. She wore gilt hoop earrings; she was calm, she said she had not seen what the white man did in the house.

Paulus Eysendyck said he had visited the hut but had not poisoned the child.

The defense did not contest that there had been a love relationship between the accused and the girl, or that intercourse had taken place, but submitted there was no proof that the child was the accused's.

The judge told the accused there was strong suspicion against him but not enough proof that he had committed the crime. The court could not accept the girl's evidence because it was clear she had committed perjury either at this trial or at the preparatory examination. There was the suggestion in the mind of the court that she might be an accomplice in the crime; but, again, insufficient proof.

The judge commended the honorable behavior of the husband (sitting in court in a brown-and-yellow-quartered golf cap bought for Sundays) who had not rejected his wife and had "even provided clothes for the unfortunate infant out of his slender means."

The verdict on the accused was "not guilty."

The young white man refused to accept the congratulations of press and public and left the court with his mother's raincoat shielding his face from photographers. His father said to the press, "I will try and carry on as best I can to hold up my head in the district."

Interviewed by the Sunday papers, who spelled her name in a variety of ways, the black girl, speaking in her own language, was quoted beneath her photograph: "It was a thing of our childhood, we don't see each other any more."

The Irony of Hate

RUTH RENDELL

When lists are made fifty or a hundred years hence of the best writers of our time, regardless of genre, Ruth Rendell (b. 1930), despite her career-long identification with crime and detective fiction, may well rank high. She was born Ruth Barbara Grasemann in London, the daughter of two teachers who both found a creative outlet in painting. After leaving school at eighteen, she eschewed university for a brief career as a newspaper reporter in Essex. After marrying fellow reporter Donald Rendell and producing a son, she quit journalism for full-time motherhood and self-education through voracious reading.

Rendell's first novel *From Doon with Death* (1964), introducing her odd-couple police team of Reg Wexford and Mike Burden, is solidly traditional, the trickiness of its plot inviting the inevitable Agatha Christie comparison. Rendell would never abandon this devotion to fair-play plotting as her novels increased in psychological and thematic depth. Her second novel, *To Fear a Painted Devil* (1965), is non-series, and throughout her career she has mixed the Wexford and Burden books, immensely popular with readers, with often dark-hued crime novels that have achieved even greater critical acclaim. Writing in the Scribner Writers Series volume *Mystery and Suspense Writers* (1998), B. J. Rahn describes these non-series books as "centered in the consciousness of the main character—whether villain or victim—whose feelings of alienation, anxiety, fear, hatred, and anguish are experienced firsthand by the reader." Rendell, who was called Ruth by her father and Barbara by her mother, answers to both and now writes as both, having adopted the pseudonym Barbara Vine with *A Dark-Adapted Eye* (1986). According to

Rahn, the Vine novels "plumb the depths of the human psyche more in the manner of Henry James than Patricia Highsmith or Alfred Hitchcock . . . The novels are distinguished by subtle manipulation of the narrative viewpoint and complex patterning, which often produce startling ironic surprises."

Along with her prolific book-or-two-per-year output, Rendell has also kept busy as a short-story writer. Her first collection, *The Fallen Curtain and Other Stories* (1976) has been followed by at least six more, including *Piranha to Scurfy and Other Stories* (2000). "The Irony of Hate," revealing who did what in the very first sentence, demonstrates Rendell's psychological insight as well as her ability to surprise the reader.

I murdered Brenda Goring for what I suppose is the most unusual of motives. She came between me and my wife. By that I don't mean to say that there was anything abnormal in their relationship. They were merely close friends, though "merely" is hardly the word to use in connection with a relationship which alienates and excludes a once-loved husband. I murdered her to get my wife to myself once more, but instead I have parted us perhaps for ever, and I await with dread, with impotent panic, with the most awful helplessness I have ever known, the coming trial.

By setting down the facts—and the irony, the awful irony that runs through them like a sharp glittering thread—I may come to see things more clearly. I may find some way to convince those inexorable powers that be of how it really was; to make Defending Counsel believe me and not raise his eyebrows and shake his head; to ensure, at any rate, that if Laura and I must be separated she will know as she sees me taken from the court to my long imprisonment, that the truth is known and justice done.

Alone here with nothing else to do, with nothing to wait for but that trial, I could write reams about the character, the appearance, the neuroses, of Brenda Goring. I could write the great hate novel of all time. In this context, though, much of it would be irrelevant, and I shall be as brief as I can.

Some character in Shakespeare says of a woman, "Would I had never seen her!" And the reply is: "Then you would have left unseen a very wonderful piece of work." Well, would indeed I had never seen Brenda. As for her being a wonderful piece of work, I suppose I would agree with that too. Once she had had a husband. To be rid of her for ever, no doubt, he paid her enormous alimony and had settled on her a lump sum with which she bought the cottage up the lane from our house. On our village she made the impact one would expect of such a newcomer. Wonderful she was, an amazing refreshment to all those retired couples and cautious weekenders, with her clothes, her long blond hair, her sports car, her talents, and her jet-set past. For a while, that is. Until she got too much for them to take.

From the first she fastened on to Laura. Understandable in a way, since my wife was the only woman in the locality who was of comparable age, who lived there all the time and who had no job. But surely—or so I thought at first—she would never have singled out Laura if she had had a wider choice. To me my wife is lovely, all I could ever want, the only woman I have ever really cared for, but I know that to others she appears shy, colorless, a simple and quiet little housewife. What, then, had she to offer to that extrovert, that bright bejeweled butterfly? She gave me the beginning of the answer herself.

"Haven't you noticed the way people are starting to shun her darling? The Goldsmiths didn't ask her to their party last week and Mary Williamson refuses to have her on the fête committee."

"I can't say I'm surprised," I said. "The way she talks and the things she talks about."

"You mean her love affairs and all that sort of thing? But, darling, she's lived in the sort of society where that's quite normal. It's natural for her to talk like that, it's just that she's open and honest."

"She's not living in that sort of society now," I said, "and she'll have to adapt if she wants to be accepted. Did you notice Isabel Goldsmith's face when Brenda told that story about going off for a weekend with some chap she'd picked up in a bar? I tried to stop her going on about all the men her husband named in his divorce action, but I couldn't. And then she's always saying, 'When I was living with so-and-so' and 'That was the time of my affair with what's-his-name.' Elderly people find that a bit upsetting, you know."

"Well, we're not elderly," said Laura, "and I hope we can be a bit more broad-minded. You do like her, don't you?"

I was always very gentle with my wife. The daughter of clever domineering parents who belittled her, she grew up with an ineradicable sense of her own inferiority. She is a born victim, an inviter of bullying, and therefore I have tried never to bully her, never even to cross her. So all I said was that Brenda was all right and that I was glad, since I was out all day, that she had found a friend and companion of her own age.

And if Brenda had befriended and companioned her only during the day, I daresay I shouldn't have objected. I should have got used to the knowledge that Laura was listening, day in and day out, to stories of a world she had never known, to hearing illicit sex and duplicity glorified, and I should have been safe in the conviction that she was incorruptible. But I had to put up with Brenda myself in the evenings when I got home from my long commuting. There she would be, lounging on our sofa, in her silk trousers or long skirt and high boots, chain-smoking. Or she would arrive with a bottle of wine just as we had sat down to dinner and involve us in one of those favorite debates of hers on the lines of "Is marriage a dying institution?" or "Are parents necessary?" And to illustrate some specious point of hers she would come out with some personal experience of the kind that had so upset our elderly friends.

Of course I was not obliged to stay with them. Ours is quite a big house, and I could go off into the dining room or the room Laura called my study. But all I wanted was what I had once had, to be alone in the evenings with my wife. And it was even worse when we were summoned to coffee or drinks with Brenda, there in her lavishly furnished, over-ornate cottage to be shown the latest thing she had made—she was always embroidering and weaving and potting and messing about with watercolors— and shown too the gifts she had received at some time or another from Mark and Larry and Paul and all the dozens of other men there had been in her life. When I refused to go Laura would become nervous and depressed, then pathetically elated if, after a couple of blissful Brenda-less evenings, I suggested for the sake of pleasing her that I supposed we might as well drop in on old Brenda.

What sustained me was the certainty that sooner or later any woman so apparently popular with the opposite sex would find herself a boyfriend and have less or no time for my wife. I couldn't understand why this hadn't happened already and I said so to Laura.

"She does see her men friends when she goes up to London," said my wife.

"She never has any of them down here," I said, and that evening when Brenda was treating us to a highly colored account of some painter she knew called Laszlo who was terribly attractive and who adored her, I said I'd like to meet him and why didn't she invite him down for the weekend?

Brenda flashed her long green-painted fingernails about and gave Laura a conspiratorial woman-to-woman look. "And what would all the old fuddy-duddies have to say about that, I wonder?"

"Surely you can rise above all that sort of thing, Brenda," I said.

"Of course I can. Give them something to talk about. I'm quite well aware it's only sour grapes. I'd have Laszlo here like a shot, only he wouldn't come. He hates the country, he'd be bored stiff."

Apparently Richard and Jonathan and Stephen also hated the country or would be bored or couldn't spare the time. It was much better for Brenda to go up and see them in town, and I noticed that after my probing about Laszlo, Brenda seemed to go to London more often and that the tales of her escapades after these visits became more and more sensational. I think I am quite a perceptive man and soon there began to form in my mind an idea so fantastic that for a while I refused to admit it even to myself. But I put it to the test. Instead of just listening to Brenda and throwing in the occasional rather sour rejoinder, I started asking her questions. I took her up on names and dates. "I thought you said you met Mark in America?" I would say, or "But surely you didn't have that holiday with Richard until after your divorce?" I tied her up in knots without her realizing it, and the idea began to seem not so fantastic after all. The final test came at Christmas.

I had noticed that Brenda was a very different woman when she was alone with me than when Laura was with us. If, for example, Laura was out in the kitchen making coffee or, as sometimes happened at the weekends, Brenda dropped in when Laura was out, she was rather cool and shy with me. Gone then were the flamboyant gestures and the provocative remarks, and Brenda would chat about village matters as mundanely as Isabel Goldsmith. Not quite the behavior one would expect from a self-styled Messalina alone with a young and reasonably personable man. It struck me then that in the days when Brenda had been invited to village parties, and now when she still met neighbors at our parties, she never once attempted a flirtation. Were all the men too old for her to bother with? Was a slim, handsome man of going on fifty too ancient to be considered fair game for a woman who would never see thirty again? Of course they were all married, but so were her Paul and her Stephen, and, if she were to be believed, she had had no compunction about taking them away from their wives.

If she were to be believed. That was the crux of it. Not one of them wanted to spend Christmas with her. No London lover invited her to a party or offered to take her away. She would be with us, of course, for Christmas lunch, for the whole of the day, and at our Boxing Day gathering of friends and relatives. I had hung a bunch of mistletoe in our hall, and on Christmas morning I admitted her to the house myself, Laura being busy in the kitchen.

"Merry Christmas," I said. "Give us a kiss, Brenda," and I took her in my arms under that mistletoe and kissed her on the mouth.

She stiffened. I swear a shudder ran through her. She was as awkward, as apprehensive, as repelled as a sheltered twelve-year-old. And then I knew. Married she may have been—and it was not hard now to guess the cause of her divorce—but she had never had a lover or enjoyed an embrace or even been alone with a man longer than she could help. She was frigid. A good-looking, vivacious, healthy girl, she nevertheless had that particular disability. She was as cold as a nun. But because she couldn't bear the humiliation of admitting it, she had created for herself a fantasy life, a fantasy past, in which she queened it as a fantasy nymphomaniac.

At first I thought it a huge joke and I couldn't wait to tell Laura. But I wasn't alone with her till two in the morning and then she was asleep when I came to bed. I didn't sleep much. My elation dwindled as I realized I hadn't any real proof and that if I told Laura what I'd been up to, probing and questioning and testing, she would only be bitterly hurt and resentful. How could I tell her I'd kissed her best friend and got an icy response? That, in her absence, I'd tried flirting with her best friend and been repulsed? And then, as I thought about it, I understood what I really had discovered, that Brenda hated men, that no man would ever come and take her away or marry her and live here with her and absorb all her time. For ever she would stay here alone, living a stone's throw from us, in and out of our house daily, she and Laura growing old together.

I could have moved house, of course. I could have taken Laura away. From her friends? From the house and the countryside she loved? And what guarantee would I have had that Brenda wouldn't have moved too to be near us still? For I knew now what Brenda saw in my wife, a gullible innocent, a trusting ever-lastingly credulous audience whose own inexperience kept her from seeing the holes and discrepancies in those farragos of nonsense and whose pathetic determination to be worldly prevented her from showing distaste. As the dawn came and I looked with love and sorrow at Laura sleeping beside me, I knew what I must do, the only thing I could do. At the season of peace and goodwill, I decided to kill Brenda Goring for my own and Laura's good and peace.

Easier decided than done. I was buoyed up and strengthened by knowing that in everyone's eyes I would have no motive. Our neighbors thought us wonderfully charitable and tolerant to put up with Brenda at all. I resolved to be positively nice to her instead of just negatively easygoing, and as the New Year came in I took to dropping in on Brenda on my way back from the post or the village shop, and if I got home from work to find Laura alone I asked where Brenda was and suggested we should phone her at once and ask her to dinner or for a drink. This pleased Laura enormously.

"I always felt you didn't really like Brenda, darling," she said, "and it made me feel rather guilty. It's marvelous that you're beginning to see how nice she really is."

What I was actually beginning to see was how I could kill her and get away with it, for something happened which seemed to deliver her into my hands. On the outskirts of the village, in an isolated cottage, lived an elderly unmarried woman called Peggy Daley, and during the last week of January the cottage was broken into and Peggy stabbed to death with her own kitchen knife. The work of some psychopath, the police seemed to believe, for nothing had been stolen or damaged. When it appeared likely that they weren't going to find the killer. I began thinking of how I could kill Brenda in the same way so that the killing could look like the work of the same perpetrator. Just as I was working this out Laura went down with a flu bug she caught from Mary Williamson.

Brenda, of course, came in to nurse her, cooked my dinner for me and cleaned the house. Because everyone believed that Peggy Daley's murderer was still stalking the village, I walked Brenda home at night, even though her cottage was only a few yards up the lane or narrow path that skirted the end of our garden. It was pitch dark there as we had all strenuously opposed the installation of street lighting, and it brought me an ironical amusement to notice how Brenda flinched and recoiled when on these occasions I made her take my arm. I always made a point of going into the house with her and putting all the lights on. When Laura began to get better and all she wanted in the evenings was to sleep I sometimes went earlier to Brenda's, had a nightcap with her, and once, on leaving, I gave her a comradely kiss on the doorstep to show any observing neighbor what friends we were and how much I appreciated all Brenda's kindness to my sick wife.

Then I got the flu myself. At first this seemed to upset my plans, for I couldn't afford to delay too long. Already people were beginning to be less apprehensive about our marauding murderer and were getting back to their old habits of leaving their back doors unlocked. But then I saw how I could turn my illness to my advantage. On the Monday, when I had been confined to bed for three days and that ministering angel Brenda was fussing about me nearly as much as my own wife was, Laura remarked that she wouldn't go across to the Goldsmiths that evening as she had promised because it seemed wrong to leave me. Instead, if I was better by then, she would go on the Wednesday, her purpose being to help Isabel cut out a dress. Brenda, of course, might have offered to stay with me instead, and I think Laura was a little surprised that she didn't. I knew the reason and had a little quiet laugh to myself about it. It was one thing for Brenda to flaunt about, regaling us with stories of all the men she had nursed in the past, quite another to find herself alone with a not very sick man in that man's bedroom.

So I had to be sick enough to provide myself with an alibi but not sick enough to keep Laura at home. On the Wednesday morning I was feeling a good deal better. Dr. Lawson looked in on his way back from his rounds in the afternoon and pronounced, after a thorough examination, that I still had phlegm on my chest. While he was in the bathroom washing his hands and doing something with his stethoscope, I held the thermometer he had stuck in my mouth against the radiator at the back of the bed. This worked better than I had hoped, worked, in fact, almost too well. The mercury went up to a hundred and three, and I played up to it by saying in a feeble voice that I felt dizzy and kept alternating between the sweats and the shivers.

"Keep him in bed," Dr. Lawson said, "and give him plenty of warm drinks. I doubt if he could get up if he tried."

I said rather shamefacedly that I had tried and I couldn't and that my legs felt like jelly. Immediately Laura said she wouldn't go out that night, and I blessed Lawson when he told her not to be silly. All I needed was rest and to be allowed to sleep. After a good deal of fussing and self-reproach and promises not to be gone more than two hours at the most, she finally went off at seven.

As soon as the car had departed, I got up. Brenda's house could be seen from my bedroom window, and I saw that she had lights on but no porch light. The night was dark, moonless and starless. I put trousers and a sweater on over my pajamas and made my way downstairs.

By the time I was halfway down I knew that I needn't have pretended to be ill or bothered with the thermometer ploy. I *was* ill. I was shivering and swaying, great waves of dizziness kept coming over me, and I had to hang on to the banisters for support. That wasn't the only thing that had gone wrong. I had intended, when the deed was done and I was back home again, to cut up my coat and gloves with Laura's electric scissors and burn the pieces on our living room fire. But I couldn't find the scissors and I realized Laura must have taken them with her to her dressmaking session. Worse than that, there was no fire alight. Our central heating was very efficient and we only had an open fire for the pleasure and coziness of it, but Laura hadn't troubled to light one while I was upstairs ill. At that moment I nearly gave up. But it was then or never. I would never again have such circumstances and such an alibi. Either kill her now, I thought, or live in an odious *ménage à trois* for the rest of my life.

We kept the raincoats and gloves we used for gardening in a cupboard in the kitchen by the back door. Laura had left only the hall light on, and I didn't think it would be wise to switch on any more. In the semi-darkness I fumbled about in the cupboard for my raincoat, found it and put it on. It seemed tight on me, my body was so stiff and sweaty, but I managed to button it up, and then I put on the gloves. I took with me one of our kitchen knives and let myself out by the back door. It wasn't a frosty night, but raw and cold and damp.

I went down the garden, up the lane and into the garden of Brenda's cottage. I had to feel my way round the side of the house, for there was no light there at all. But the kitchen light was on and the back door unlocked. I tapped and let myself in without waiting to be asked. Brenda, in full evening rig, glittery sweater, gilt necklace, long skirt, was cooking her solitary supper. And then, for the first time ever, when it didn't matter any more, when it was too late, I felt pity for her. There she was, a handsome, rich, gifted woman with the reputation of a seductress, but in reality as destitute of people who really cared for her as poor old Peggy Daley had been; there she was, dressed for a party, heating up tinned spaghetti in a cottage kitchen at the back of beyond.

She turned round, looking apprehensive, but only, I think, because she was always afraid when we were alone that I would try to make love to her.

"What are you doing out of bed?" she said, and then, "Why are you wearing those clothes?"

I didn't answer her. I stabbed her in the chest again and again. She made no sound but a little choking moan and she crumpled up on the floor. Although I had known how it would be, had hoped for it, the shock was so great and I had already been feeling so swimmy and strange, that all I wanted was to throw myself down too and close my eyes and sleep. That was impossible. I turned off the cooker. I checked that there was no blood on my trousers and my shoes, though of course there was plenty on the raincoat, and then I staggered out, switching off the light behind me.

I don't know how I found my way back, it was so dark and by then I was lightheaded and my heart was drumming. I just had the presence of mind to strip off the raincoat and the gloves and push them into our garden incinerator. In the morning I would have to get up enough strength to burn them before Brenda's body was found. The knife I washed and put back in the drawer.

Laura came back about five minutes after I had got myself to bed. She had been gone less than half an hour. I turned over and managed to raise myself up to ask her why she was back so soon. It seemed to me that she had a strange distraught look about her.

"What's the matter?" I mumbled. "Were you worried about me?"

"No," she said, "no," but she didn't come up close to me or put her hand on my forehead. "It was—Isabel Goldsmith told me something—I was upset—I . . . It's no use talking about it now, you're too ill." She said in a sharper tone than I had ever heard her use, "Can I get you anything?"

"I just want to sleep," I said.

"I shall sleep in the spare room. Good night."

That was reasonable enough, but we had never slept apart before during the whole of our marriage, and she could hardly have been afraid of catching the flu, having only just got over it herself. But I was in no state to worry about that, and I fell into the troubled nightmare-ridden sleep of fever. I remember one of those dreams. It was of Laura finding Brenda's body herself, a not unlikely eventuality.

However, she didn't find it. Brenda's cleaner did. I knew what must have happened because I saw the police car arrive from my window. An hour or so later Laura came in to tell me the news which she had got from Jack Williamson.

"It must have been the same man who killed Peggy," she said.

I felt better already. Things were going well. "My poor darling," I said, "you must feel terrible, you were such close friends."

She said nothing. She straightened my bedclothes and left the room. I knew I should have to get up and burn the contents of the incinerator, but I couldn't get up. I put my feet out and reached for the floor, but it was as if the floor came up to meet me and threw me back again. I wasn't over-worried. The police would think what Laura thought, what everyone must think.

That afternoon they came, a chief inspector and a sergeant. Laura brought them up to our bedroom and they talked to us together. The chief inspector said he understood we were close friends of the dead woman, wanted to know when we had last seen her and what we had been doing on the previous evening. Then he asked if we had any idea at all as to who had killed her.

"That maniac who murdered the other woman, of course," said Laura.

"I can see you don't read the papers," he said.

Usually we did. It was my habit to read a morning paper in the office and to bring an evening paper home with me. But I had been at home ill. It turned out that a man had been arrested on the previous morning for the murder of Peggy Daley. The shock made me flinch and I'm sure I turned pale. But the policemen didn't seem to notice. They thanked us for our co-operation, apologized for disturbing a sick man, and left. When they had gone I asked Laura what Isabel had said to upset her the night before. She came up to me and put her arms round me.

"It doesn't matter now," she said. "Poor Brenda's dead and it was a horrible way to die, but—well, I must be very wicked—but I'm not sorry. Don't look at me like that, darling. I love you and I know you love me, and we must forget her and be as we used to be. You know what I mean."

I didn't, but I was glad whatever it was had blown over. I had enough on my plate without a coldness between me and my wife. Even though Laura was beside me that night, I hardly slept for worrying about the stuff in that incinerator. In the morning I put up the best show I could of being much better. I dressed and announced, in spite of Laura's expostulations, that I was going into the garden. The police were there already, searching all our gardens, actually digging up Brenda's.

They left me alone that day and the next, but they came in once and interviewed Laura on her own. I asked her what they had said, but she passed it off quite lightly. I supposed she didn't think I was well enough to be told they had been enquiring about my movements and my attitude towards Brenda.

"Just a lot of routine questions, darling," she said, but I was sure she was afraid for me, and a barrier of her fear for me and mine for myself came up between us. It seems incredible but that Sunday we hardly spoke to each other and when we did Brenda's name wasn't mentioned. In the evening we sat in silence my arm round Laura, her head on my shoulder, waiting, waiting . . .

The morning brought the police with a search warrant. They asked Laura to go into the living room and me to wait in the study. I knew then that it was only a matter of time. They would find the knife, and of course they would find Brenda's blood on it. I had been feeling so ill when I cleaned it that now I could no longer remember whether I had scrubbed it or simply rinsed it under the tap.

After a long while the chief inspector came in alone.

"You told us you were a close friend of Miss Goring's."

"I was friendly with her," I said, trying to keep my voice steady. "She was my wife's friend."

He took no notice of this. "You didn't tell us you were on intimate terms with her, that you were, in point of fact, having a sexual relationship with her."

Nothing he could have said would have astounded me more.

"That's absolute rubbish!"

"Is it? We have it on sound authority."

"What authority?" I said. "Or is that the sort of thing you're not allowed to say?"

"I see no harm in telling you," he said easily. "Miss Goring herself informed two women friends of hers in London of the fact. She told one of your neighbors she met at a party in your house. You were seen to spend evenings alone with Miss Goring while your wife was ill, and we have a witness who saw you kissing her good night."

Now I knew what it was that Isabel Goldsmith had told Laura which had so distressed her. The irony of it, the irony . . . Why hadn't I, knowing Brenda's reputation and knowing Brenda's fantasies, suspected what construction would be put on my assumed friendship with her? Here was motive, the lack of which I had relied on as my last resort. Men do kill their mistresses, from jealousy, from frustration, from fear of discovery.

But surely I could turn Brenda's fantasies to my own use?

"She had dozens of men friends, lovers, whatever you like to call them. Any of them could have killed her."

"On the contrary," said the chief inspector, "apart from her ex-husband who is in Australia, we have been able to discover no man in her life but yourself."

I cried out desperately, "I didn't kill her! I swear I didn't."

He looked surprised. "Oh, we know that." For the first time he called me sir. "We know that, sir. No one is accusing you of anything. We have Dr. Lawson's word for it that you were physically incapable of leaving your bed that night, and the raincoat and gloves we found in your incinerator are not your property."

Fumbling in the dark, swaying, the sleeves of the raincoat too short, the shoulders too tight . . . "Why are you wearing those clothes?" she had asked before I stabbed her.

"I want you to try and keep calm, sir," he said very gently. But I have never been calm since. I have confessed again and again, I have written statements, I have expostulated, raved, gone over with them every detail of what I did that night, I have wept.

Then I said nothing. I could only stare at him. "I came in here to you, sir," he said, "simply to confirm a fact of which we were already certain, and to ask you if you would care to accompany your wife to the police station where she will be charged with the murder of Miss Brenda Goring."

Sweet Baby Jenny

JOYCE HARRINGTON

Joyce Harrington, a former actress who follows theatrical tradition in keeping her exact age a secret, started strong as a writer of crime fiction. Her very first short story, "The Purple Shroud" (*Ellery Queen's Mystery Magazine*, September 1972), won the Edgar award. Edward D. Hoch, writing in *St. James Guide to Crime & Mystery Writers* (fourth edition, 1996) called the story "a quiet tale of a summer art instructor and the wife he has betrayed, building into a murder story of understated terror. Harrington's second story, "The Plastic Jungle," is even better—a macabre tale of a girl and her mother living in today's plastic society."

Born in Jersey City, New Jersey, Harrington was trained for theater at the Pasadena Playhouse. She told *EQMM* she had held many jobs for many employers "from a doorknob factory to the U.S. Army Quartermaster Corps'; she later had a successful career in advertising and public relations.

Harrington has written three remarkably varied and well-received novels—*No One Knows My Name* (1980), a theatrical whodunnit; *Family Reunion* (1982), a variant on the modern gothic; and *Dreemz of the Night* (1987), with a rarely-exploited background of graffiti as art—but she remains best known as a short-story writer. Though her stories have not been collected to date, she is a master of the crime short who bears comparison with Roald Dahl and Stanley Ellin. One of her attributes is the ability to write in a variety of styles, including the rural dialect narrative of "Sweet Baby Jenny."

I never had a mother, leastways not one that I can remember. I must have had one sometime, 'cause as far as I can tell I didn't hatch out from no egg. And even chicks get to snuggle up under the hen for a little space before she kicks them out of the nest. But I didn't have no hen to snuggle up to, or to peck me upside the head if I did something wrong.

Not that I would ever do anything wrong. Leastways not if I knowed it was wrong. There are lots of things that go on that are pure puzzlement to me, and I can't tell the right from the wrong of it. For instance, I recollect when Ace—that's my biggest big brother and the one who taken care of us all after Pop went away—I recollect when he used to work driving a beer truck round to all the stores in town and the root cellar used to be full of six-packs all the time. I said to him one day, "Ace, how come if you got the cellar full of beer, I can't have the cellar full of Coke-Cola? I don't like beer." Guess I was about nine or ten years old at the time and never could get my fill of Coke-Cola.

Well, Ace, he just laughed and said, "Sweet Baby Jenny"—that's what they all called me even after I was well growed up—"Sweet Baby Jenny, if I drove a Coke-Cola truck you could float away to heaven on an ocean of it. Now, just drink your beer and learn to like it."

I wasn't ever dumb, even though I didn't do so good in school, so it didn't take much figuring to catch onto the fact that Ace was delivering almost as much beer to the root cellar as he was to Big Jumbo's Superette down on Main Street. So it didn't seem fair when I got caught in the five-and-dime with a lipstick in my pocket for him to come barreling down and given me hellfire and damnation in front of that suet-faced manager. I just stood there looking at him with pig-stickers in my eyes until we got out to the truck and I said to him, "What's the difference between one teensy-weensy lipstick and a cellar full of beer?"

He says to me, grinning, "Is that a riddle?"

And I says, "No, I would surely like to know."

And he says, "The difference, Sweet Baby Jenny, is that you got caught."

Now I ask you.

It was different, though, when he got caught. Then he cussed and swore and kicked the porch till it like to fallen off the house all the while the boys from the beer company was hauling that beer up from the root cellar and stowing it back on the truck. When they drove away, I says to him, sweet as molasses, "Ace, honey, why you carrying on so?"

And he says, "Dammit, Jenny, they taken away my beer. I don't give a hoot about the job, it was a jackass job anyway, but I worked hard for that beer and they didn't ought to taken it away."

"But, Ace," I says, hanging onto his hand and swinging it like a jumping rope, "ain't it true you stolen that beer and you got caught and you had to give it back just like I did with that lipstick?"

Well, he flung me away from him till I fetched up against the old washing machine that was resting in the yard waiting for somebody to fix it, and he yelled, "I ain't stolen anything and don't you ever say I did! That beer was what they call a fringe benefit, only they didn't know they was givin' it. They don't even pay me enough to keep you in pigtail ribbons and have beer money besides. I only taken what I deserve."

Well, he was right on one score. I didn't have anything you could rightfully call a hair ribbon, and I kept my braids tied up with the strings off of Deucy's old Bull Durham pouches.

Deucy, you maybe guessed, is my second-biggest big brother and a shiftless lazy skunk even though some people think he's handsome and should be a movie star. Ace's name in the family Bible is Arthur, and Deucy is written down as Dennis. Then there's Earl, Wesley, and Pembrook. And then there's me, Jennet Maybelle. That's the last name on the birth page. Over on the death side the last name written in is Flora Janine Taggert. It's written in black spiky letters like the pen was stabbing at the page, and the date is just about a month or so after my name was written on the birth page. I know that's my mother, although no one ever told me. And no one ever told me how she died. As for Pop, there ain't no page in the Bible for people who just up and go away.

Deucy plays guitar and sings and thinks he's Conway Twitty. Says he's gonna go to Nashville and come back driving a leop-ardskin Cadillac. I'd surely like to see that, though I don't guess I ever will. That Deucy's too lazy to get up off the porch swing to fetch himself a drink of water. It's always, "Sweet Baby Jenny, get me this and get me that." Only thing he's not too lazy for is to boost himself up to the supper table.

That don't keep the girls from flocking round, bringing him presents and smirking like the pig that et the baby's diaper. They all hope and pray that they're gonna be the one to go to Nashville with him and ride back in that Cadillac. And he don't trouble to relieve their minds on the subject. You ought to hear that porch swing creak in the dark of night. They are just so dumb.

Now, Earl and Wesley, they try. They ain't too good-looking, though they do have the Taggert black hair and the Taggert nose. I remember Pop saying he was part Cherokee and all his sons showed it. But while Ace and Deucy came out looking like Indian chiefs, Earl is crosseyed and Wesley broke his nose falling out of a buckeye tree and lost most of his hair to the scarlet fever. So they try. They are always going into business together.

Once they went into the egg business and we had the whole place full of chickens running around. They said they would sell their eggs cheaper than anyone around and make a fortune and we'd all go off to California and live in a big hotel with a swim-ming pool and waiters bringing hamburgers every time we snapped our fingers. Well, people bought the eggs all right, but what Earl and Wesley kind of forgot about was that 200 chickens eat up a lot of chicken feed and they never could figure out how to get ahead of the bill at the feed store. I could have told them how to do it was raise the price of the eggs and make them out to be something special so everyone would feel they had to have Taggert's Country-Fresh eggs no matter what they cost. But Earl and Wesley just shoved me aside and said, "Sweet Baby Jenny, you are just a girl and don't understand bidness. Now go on out and feed them chickens and gather up them eggs and let's have some of your good old peach cobbler for supper. Being in bidness sure does make a man hungry."

Well, pretty soon the feed store cut off their credit and there wasn't nothing left to feed the chickens, so we had to eat as many of them as we could before they all starved to death and that was the end of the egg business. Earl and Wesley, being both tender-hearted and brought down by gloom, couldn't bring themselves to kill a single chicken. I like to wrung my arm off wringing those chicken necks. I used to like fried chicken, but I don't any more.

Pembrook, he's the smart one. He don't steal, sing, or go into business. He's off at the state college studying how to be a lawyer. He's the only one used to talk to me and I miss him. I was always planning to ask him what happened to our mother, how she died, and why Pop ran off like he did. But I just never got up the nerve.

Pembrook writes me letters a couple times a month, telling what it's like up there at the college. It sure sounds fine. He's always going on at me how I should go back to school and finish up and come to the college and learn how to *be* somebody. Well, I'd kind of like that, but who'd look after the boys? Reason why I didn't do so good in school was I never had no time for studying, what with looking after the boys like I was their mother instead of Sweet Baby Jenny like they call me. Only Pembrook never called me that.

Another thing I always meant to ask Pembrook and never did is how come I come out looking like a canary in a cuckoo-bird's nest. Pembrook looks more or less just like the other boys, though he keeps his black hair real clean and he wears big eyeglasses on top of his sharp Taggert nose. His eyes are dark brown like theirs, and he weathers up nice and tan in the summer sun. But in summer my freckles just get more so while the part in between the freckles gets red. And my hair, which is mud-yellow most of the time, gets brighter and brighter and kinks up in tight little curls unless I keep it braided up. And never mind my eyes. They're not a bit like the boys'. Greeny-blue or bluey-green depending on the weather. As for my nose, it couldn't be less Taggert if it was a pump handle. Small and turned-up and ugly.

Could be I taken after my mother, though I don't know that for a fact 'cause I never set eyes on her nor saw any picture of her.

Pembrook says I'm pretty but that's just because he likes me. Pembrook says I look a lot like Miss Claudia Carpenter who is regarded as the prettiest girl in two counties, but I never saw her to make the comparison. She's the daughter of the town's one and only bank president. She's a year or so older than me, and she don't stick around much. Got sent away to school and always taking trips here and there. Can't be much fun, never being home in your own home place. Pembrook told me our mother used to help out at the Carpenter household, at parties and such or when their regular maid got sick. Maybe I could get such a job and put aside a little money, just in case I ever decide to do what Pembrook says.

One thing I do remember about Pop before he went away. He used to tell me stories. He used to sit himself down in his big maroon armchair and he would sit me down on his lap and he would say, "Now, listen. This here's a story about a bad little girl." The stories were always different but they were all about a girl named Bad Penny. She was ugly and mean and spiteful and nobody liked her. She was always making trouble and in the end she always got punished. Sometimes she got et up by the pigs and sometimes she got drowned in the creek. Once she got cut up in little bits by the disc harrow. And another time she fell into the granary and suffocated in the wheat. But she always came back, as mean and nasty as ever, and that's why she was called Bad Penny. After the story Pop would take me up to my room and put me to bed.

I liked the stories, even though they scared me some. I knew pigs didn't eat little girls, but I was always pretty careful around the pigpen. We don't keep pigs any more, but we had a few then and I used to carry the slops out to them.

Well, things got so bad after Ace robbed the gas station down at the crossroads and got recognized by Junior Mulligan who just happened to be having his pickup truck filled up with gas at the time and never did like Ace since the time they two went hunting together and Ace claimed it was *his* deer and knocked Junior into Dead Man's Gully and broken his leg. So off Junior went to the police and they come and drug Ace out of the Red Rooster Café where he was treating everyone to beer and hard-boiled eggs.

It was sad and lonesome around the place without Ace to stir things up, and quiet with Deucy's guitar in hock and him not able to sing a blessed note through mourning for it. Earl and Wesley tried selling insurance round about, but nobody we knew could buy any and the folks we didn't know wouldn't. So it was up to me.

I harked back to my idea of going as a maid like Pembrook had told me our mother had done. I didn't mind working in someone else's house, though Deucy said it was undignified and not befitting a Taggert. Far as I could see, Deucy thought any kind of work was undignified except maybe wearing out the porch swing. So one morning I washed my whole body including my hair, and cut my toenails so I could put shoes on, and got out one of our mother's dresses from the wardrobe in the attic, and made ready to go see Mrs. Carpenter. The dress fit me right well, though it was a little long and looked a bit peculiar with my high-top lace-up sneakers but that was all I had, so it would have to do.

I walked into town, fanning the skirt of the dress around me and blowing down the front of it from time to time so the sweat would not make stains on the green-and-white polkadots. I got to the Carpenter house before the sun got halfway up the sky, about the time Deucy would be rolling out of bed and yelling his head off for coffee. This was one morning he'd just have to find his own breakfast. I stood for a while with my hand on the iron gate looking up at the house. It was a big one, shining white like a wedding cake, and there must have been about two dozen windows on the front of it alone. It set back from the street on what looked like an acre of the greenest grass I ever saw sloping up to a row of prickly bushes that trimmed the porch.

I'd seen it before, times Ace used to take me riding in the beer truck and tell me how all he needed was to rob the bank and then we'd be living in this part of town alongside the rich folks. But I never really took a good close look, 'cause I thought he was joking. Now I looked until I got to shaking and wondering if I ought to march right up to the front door or sneak around to the back. I stood there so long I felt like my feet had taken root to the pavement, and if I could only get loose I'd run home and stay there forever.

But then I thought about how there was less than a half a pound of coffee left and just enough flour for one more batch of biscuits, and I pulled open that iron gate and set my face toward the big front door. It felt like an hour that I was walking up that path with my feet feeling like big old river rafts and my hair jumping out of the braids that I'd combed and plaited so neat. But I got up on the porch and put my finger on the door-bell and heard it ding-donging away inside. I waited. But the door stayed closed.

It was a pretty door, painted white like the rest of the house, and I studied every panel of it and the big brass doorknob and the letter box beside it while I waited. I wondered if I should ring the bell again. Maybe no one was home. Maybe I'd come all this way for nothing. They probably wouldn't want me to be their maid even if they were home. The green-and-white dress was sagging down around my shinbones and my sneakers were covered with road dust. Maybe I'd just go home and wait until I got a better idea.

I turned away and started down the porch steps, and then I heard the door open behind me and a sharp voice like a bluejay's said, "Yes?"

I looked back and saw a tall skinny woman staring at me with a frown betwixt her eyes that made me shiver in spite of the heat. "Miz Carpenter?" I said.

"Yes, I'm Mrs. Carpenter," she said. "Who are you? What do you want? I'm very busy."

My throat got choked and I couldn't swallow, so when I said, "I come to be your maid," I thought maybe she couldn't hear me, 'cause I couldn't hear me myself.

"What?" she said. "Speak up. What's this about a maid?"

"I come to be it," I said. "If you'll have me."

"Well, sakes alive!" she said, showing all her yellow teeth. "If you aren't the answer to a prayer! Where did you spring from, and who told you to come here? Well, never mind all that. Come in the house and let's get started. You look strong. I just hope you're willing."

"Yes, ma'am," I said, and quick as a wink she drug me through the house and into the kitchen and right up to the sink where there was more dishes than I'd ever seen in my life and all of them dirty.

"Just start right in," she said. "The dishwasher's right there. I'll be back in a few minutes."

Now I'd seen dishwashing machines in the Sears Roebuck wish book, but I'd never been right up close to one. I knew what *it* was supposed to do. I just wasn't too sure what *I* was supposed to do. And I didn't trust anything very much except my own two hands. So I started getting those dishes as clean as I could before I put them in the machine, just in case we had a misunderstanding. They were the prettiest dishes I ever did see, even when they was all crusted with dried-up gravy.

Mrs. Carpenter came back in a few minutes carrying a pair of black shoes and a white dress. She plopped herself down on a kitchen chair and smiled at me. "What's your name, child?"

"Jennet Maybelle."

She didn't let me get the Taggert part in, but went right on talking.

"Well, I'll call you Jenny. That Marcelline quit on me last night right in the middle of a dinner party, and I was just about to start calling around when you walked in the door. I'll pay you five dollars a day plus meals and uniform, but you have to pay for anything you break, so be careful with those dishes. Each plate cost twenty dollars."

I put down the plate I was holding and tried to think what it could be made of. It didn't look to be solid gold. Our plates at home were old and cracked and been around as long as I could remember. I didn't know what they cost. When one got broke we just threw it down in the creek bed behind the house along with all the other trash.

Mrs. Carpenter was still talking. "Now you can't be wearing those sneakers around the house, so I brought you an old pair of Claudia's shoes. Maybe they'll fit. And this uniform might be a little big for you, you're a skinny little thing, but we can cinch it in with a belt."

I didn't think much of her calling me skinny when she so closely resembled a beanpole herself. But I didn't say anything. The shoes looked nice with just a little bit of a high heel and shiny black, and the uniform dress was starched and clean.

She stopped talking for a minute and started looking me over real close. Then, "Haven't I seen you somewhere before? I could swear your face is familiar. Where do you come from?"

I pointed in the direction of home and said, "Out Clinch Valley Road." I was going to tell her how my mother had once worked as a maid for her, but she didn't give me a chance. She jumped up, left the shoes on the floor and the dress on the chair, and shook her head.

"I don't know anyone out that way. You can change your clothes in the maid's room back there." She waved her hand at a door on the other side of the kitchen. "And when you finish the dishes you'll find me upstairs. I'll show you how to do the bedrooms."

The day wore on. I didn't break any dishes and figured out on my own which button to push to start the machine. It sure gave me a start when it began churning and spattering behind its closed door, and I prayed it wouldn't go breaking any of those twenty-dollar plates and blaming it on me. Mrs. Carpenter showed me all over that house and told me what I was to do. At noon, she showed me what to make for lunch. We both ate the same thing, cold roast beef left over from the night before and some potato salad, but she ate hers in the dining room and I ate mine in the kitchen.

I drank two glasses of ice-cold milk and could have drunk some more, but I didn't want to seem greedy. In the afternoon she set me to washing windows. It wasn't hard work, I worked harder at home, and it was a treat to be looking out at the roses in the back and all that green grass in the front while I polished those windows till they looked like they weren't there at all.

Along about four o'clock she hauled me back to the kitchen and told me what Mr. Carpenter wanted for his dinner. "He's very partial to fried chicken, but nobody seems able to make it to his satisfaction. I know I can't. And he has the most outrageous sweet tooth. I don't eat dessert myself, but he won't leave the table without it."

Well. I set to work cooking up my specialties. I'd had lots of experience with chicken, and my peach cobbler was just about perfect, if I say so myself. Mrs. Carpenter left the kitchen to take a nap after telling me that Mr. Carpenter expected to sit down to his meal at 6:30 sharp.

At 6:30 sharp I brought in a platter of fried chicken and Mr. Carpenter whipped his napkin into his lap and dug in. He didn't even look at me, but I looked at him. He was a freckly sandy man with gold-rimmed glasses and a tight collar. He still had all his hair, but it was fading out to a kind of pinkish yellowish fuzz. His eyes were blue, or maybe green, it was hard to tell behind his glasses, and his nose turned up at the end like a hoe blade.

I'd fixed up a mess of greens to go with the chicken and he dug into those, too, dribbling the pot liquor down his chin and swabbing it away with his fine napkin. Mrs. Carpenter pecked at her food and watched to see how he was liking his.

When I brought in the peach cobbler he leaned back in his chair and sighed. "That's the best meal I've had in years, Marcelline."

"This isn't Marcelline," said Mrs. Carpenter. "Marcelline quit last night. This is Jenny."

He looked at me then. First through his glasses and then without his glasses. And then he polished his glasses on his napkin and put them back on and tried again. "Ah, ha!" he said. "Jenny. Well. Very nice." And he got up from the table and left the room without even tasting my peach cobbler.

Mrs. Carpenter was after him like a shot. "Paul! Paul!" she hollered. "What about your dessert?"

It didn't matter to me. Peach cobbler is best while it's hot, but it's just as good the next day. I carried it back out to the kitchen, finished cleaning up, and got back into my going-home clothes. I did hope that Mrs. Carpenter would pay me my five dollars so I would have something to show to Deucy and Earl and Wesley, so I hung around for a bit.

But it wasn't Mrs. Carpenter who came into the kitchen. It was him. He stood in the doorway, pulling at his ear and looking at me as if he wished me off the face of the earth. Then he sloped into the kitchen and came right up to me where I was standing with my back against the refrigerator and took my chin in his hand. He held my face up so I had to look at him unless I closed my eyes, which I did for half a minute, but I opened them again because I was beginning to get scared. Then he put his hand on my shoulder and took the collar of my dress between his fingers and felt of it softly. At last he spoke.

"You're a Taggert, aren't you, girl?"

"Yes, I am. I'm Jennet Maybelle Taggert." I spoke up proudly because I'd learned in the little bit of time I'd spent in school that lots of folks thought Taggerts was trash and the only way to deal with that was not to be ashamed.

Then he said something I didn't understand. "Am I never to be rid of Taggerts? Will Taggerts hound me to my grave?"

"You look pretty healthy to me," I said, adding "sir" so he wouldn't think I was being pert.

He didn't say anything to that, but took his wallet out of his pocket and opened it up. I thought he was going to pay me my five dollars, so I got ready to say thank you and good night, but he pulled out a photograph and handed it to me.

"Who do you think that is?" he asked me.

Well, I looked but I didn't know who it was. The photograph was in colour and it showed a girl about my age with yellow curling hair and a big smile. She was wearing a real pretty dress, all blue and ruffly, like she was going to a party or a dance. I handed the picture back to him.

"She's real pretty, but I don't know who she is."

"She's my daughter, Claudia."

I didn't know what else to say, so I said again, "She's real pretty."

"No, she's not," he said. "She's a spoiled brat. She thinks she's the most beautiful female creature that ever trod the earth. But she's useless, vain, and unlovable. And it's all my fault."

I didn't know why he was telling me all this, but it was making me fidgety and anyway I had to get home to get supper for the boys. They'd be pretty upset that I was so late. "Well," I said, "I guess I'll be getting along."

"Don't go." He grabbed my arm and hauled me over to where there was a mirror hanging on the wall and made me stand in front of it. "Look there," he said. "Who do you see?"

"Well, that's just me." I tried to pull away from him, but he held on tight.

"That's a pretty young woman," he said. "That's what a young woman is supposed to be, decent and clean and modest. I wish you were my daughter, Jenny Taggert, instead of that hellion who won't stay home where she belongs and behaves so no man in his right mind would marry her. How would you like that? Would you like to live here and be my girl?"

Well, I felt my neck getting hot, 'cause Ace had told me that when a man starts paying compliments there's only one thing he's after, and I'd sure heard enough of Deucy speaking sugar words to his ladies on the porch swing.

"Excuse me, Mr. Carpenter," I said, "but I got to be gettin' home and would you please pay me my five dollars so I can carry home some supper to those boys?" I know that was bold, but he was making me nervous and it just came out that way.

He let go of me and pulled out his wallet again. "Is that what Clemmie's paying you? Five dollars? Well, it's not enough. Here and here and here."

The bills came leaping out of his wallet and he stuffed them into my hands. When I looked, I saw I had three ten-dollar bills. Not only that, he started hauling out the leftover chicken that I had put away and shoving it into a paper sack.

"Take the peach cobbler, too," he said, "and anything else you'd like. Take it all."

"Now I can't do that. What would Miz Carpenter say?"

"I'll tell her I ate it for a midnight snack." He laughed then, but it wasn't a happy-sounding laugh. It sounded like something was breaking inside him.

"Thank you, sir," I said, and skedaddled out the back door before he could think up some new craziness that would get me into trouble.

His voice came after me. "You'll come back tomorrow, won't you?"

"Sure thing," I called back. But I wasn't so sure I would.

All the way home I pondered on Mr. Carpenter and his strange ways. But I just plain couldn't figure it out. All I could think was that having so much money had addled his mind and I thanked God that we was poor and couldn't afford to be crazy.

I put it all out of my mind, though, when I reached the dirt road that led up to our place. The moon was just clearing the top of the big old lilac bush at the edge of the property, and its kindly light smoothened away some of the ugliness you could see in daylight. The house looked welcoming with lights shining from its windows, and there in the dooryard was Pembrook's dinky little car. I ran up the porch and busted into the house, shouting his name.

They was all gathered in the kitchen and I could see from their dark Taggert faces that I had interrupted an argument. But I didn't care. I set the Carpenter food down on the table and said, "Here's supper, boys. Dig in." Deucy and Earl and Wesley did just that, not even bothering with plates but snatching up that chicken in their fingers.

Then I sat down and took off my left sneaker and pulled out the money. "There and there and there," I said, as I counted the bills out on the table. Deucy's eyes bugged out, and Earl and Wesley shouted, "Whoopee!" as best they could with their mouths full of drumstick meat.

Pembrook looked miserable.

"Where'd you get all that, Jenny?" he asked.

"I went as a maid," I told him.

"Where did you go as a maid?"

"To Miz Carpenter."

"And she gave you all that?"

I was about to lie and say she did, but I was never very good at lying. It makes my nose run. "No. He did."

"You're not to go there any more," said Pembrook.

Well, I'd just about decided that for myself, but I wasn't about to have Pembrook, much as I dearly love him, telling me what not to do. "I will if I want to," I said. "And when did you get home, and how long you staying for?"

"Forever, if I have to, to keep you out of trouble."

"That's pretty nice trouble," piped up Deucy. "Thirty dollars for a day's work and all this food. You ought to have some, Pem."

"Shut up, you idiot!"

I had never seen Pembrook so angry. Taggert blood boils easy, but until this minute Pembrook had always managed to keep his temper under control. He turned back to me, his eyes glittering and mean, like a chicken hawk about to pounce.

"You are not to go back to the Carpenter house, not ever again. You are to put it right out of your mind. And tomorrow I am going to mail that money back. And that's the end of it."

I only said one thing. "Why?"

"Never mind why."

Well, that did it. I had worked hard for that money. Whether it was five dollars or thirty dollars, it was mine. The first money I had ever earned. And Pembrook had no right to take it away from me. I had done nothing wrong, as far as I could see, and it wasn't fair for him to punish me. I reared back in my chair, looked him square in the eye, and opened my mouth.

"Pembrook Taggert, in case you hadn't noticed, I am no longer Sweet Baby Jenny. I am a woman growed and able to make up my own mind about things. You can't stand there and give me orders and tell me to never mind why. I took it from Pop and I took it from Ace and I been taking it from these three, while you've been off at your college learning your way out of this mess. I ain't gonna take it no more."

The hard bitterness faded from his eyes and he took my two hands in his.

"You're right, Jenny," he said. "There are things you ought to know. Come out to the porch swing and I'll tell you."

"Don't make it a long story," Deucy called after us. "Ardith Potter's comin' over tonight and we got things to discuss."

But it was a long story that Pembrook told me. One that went back through the years to the time before I was born. All the boys knew it, but Pop had sworn them on the Bible never to tell me. It accounted for all the things I'd wondered about and never had the gumption to ask. If I had asked, they wouldn't have told me, although Pembrook said he was mighty tempted from time to time because it was my life and I had a right to know.

He told me that Pop wasn't my true father, that Mr. Carpenter was. He told me that about a month after I was born, our mother had told Pop the truth and packed her bag and said she was running off with Mr. Carpenter to have a better life than scratching around on a poor old dirt farm. He told me that Pop had choked the life out of her right there in the bedroom with me looking on with my blind baby eyes from the cradle beside the bed. And then Pop had gone to Mr. Carpenter and told him the whole thing and got him to hush it up because the scandal wouldn't have done anybody any good. They gave out that our mother had died of childbirth fever.

The tears were rolling down my face, but I managed to ask, "How could you keep on living here, after he did that?"

"Well," said Pembrook, "Ace was the oldest and he wasn't but twelve. We had nowhere else to go. And he was our father."

"What happened then?" I asked. "Why did Pop run off?"

"He didn't," said Pembrook. "He lies buried under Mr. Carpenter's rose garden."

He went on to tell me how the years went by and Pop took up drinking and the farm went even further downhill until it was just a wasteland. Then one day Pop got it into his head that Mr. Carpenter ought to be paying money to take care of his child, meaning me. He went up to the Carpenter house, full of liquor and hate, and demanded a thousand dollars. Pembrook and Ace tagged along behind and listened outside the window of a room that was full of books and a big desk and a hunting rifle on the wall over the fireplace.

"I seen that room," I told him. "Miz Carpenter calls it his study."

Pembrook nodded. "That's where Pop got it."

He said how he and Ace heard them arguing in the room, and Mr. Carpenter shouted that it was blackmail and he wouldn't stand for it, and then there was a lot of scuffling around, with Pop shouting that he would kill Mr. Carpenter for ruining his life. And finally there was a shot. Just the one shot, but it was enough. They peeked over the window sill and saw Pop lying on the rug bleeding his life out, and Mr. Carpenter standing there like a statue with the rifle in his hands.

They were about to run away home, but Mr. Carpenter saw them and made them come into the house and help him carry Pop out to the rose garden. The three of them dug up the roses and put Pop in the ground and planted the roses back on top of him. Then Mr. Carpenter told them to get on home and keep their mouths shut or he'd have the marshal come and chuck us all off the farm and into reform school.

And they did, until this minute.

"I guess," said Pembrook, "I guess that's why Ace is so wild, but that's not the way to fix it up. That's why I'm studying to be a lawyer. One of these days I'll know how to take care of Mr. Carpenter legally and make it stick. So that's why I don't want you going back there, Jenny. You're likely to spoil my plan, and it isn't good for him to be reminded that you exist. I need to get him off guard when I'm ready."

I wiped my eyes and blew my nose and said, "Thank you, Pembrook, for telling me. Now I understand."

"And you won't go back."

"I'm going to bed."

And I did. But I didn't sleep. I lay there pondering over the things that Pembrook had told me, trying to find the right and the wrong of it. Our mother was maybe wrong for pleasuring herself with Mr. Carpenter, but if she hadn't I wouldn't be here. Pop was wrong for taking life away from our mother, but she gave him cause in his eyes. Mr. Carpenter was wrong for shooting Pop, but the Taggert blood was up and Pop probably attacked him first. Hardest of all to think about was me being Mr. Carpenter's daughter. If it was true and he knew it, how could he have let me live all these hard years as Sweet Baby Jenny Taggert while that other girl, that Claudia, had everything her heart desired and then some?

Just before dawn I decided what to do. The boys, even Pembrook, were all sound asleep. I got up quiet as a mouse and dressed in our mother's green-and-white polkadot dress and my high-top sneakers and snuck out to the barn. The barn used to be a busy place, but it was still and empty that morning. No more cows to bellow for me to come and milk them, no horses to gaze sad-eyed after an apple or a carrot. Way in the back, behind the piles of rotten harness, in a dark corner draped over with cobwebs, I found what I was looking for.

It was a can of stuff that Pop used to put down to kill the rats that infested the barn and ate their way through the winter fodder. There wasn't much left in the can, and what there was looked dry and caked. Maybe it was so old it wouldn't even work any more. But I scooped some out with a teaspoon and put it into one of Deucy's Bull Durham pouches and set off down the road.

I kept up a good pace because I wanted to get there before Mr. Carpenter went off to the bank, and before the boys woke up and came after me in Pembrook's car. The morning was fresh and cool, and I didn't sweat one bit.

When I got to the Carpenter house, the milkman was just driving away. I went around to the back, picked up the two quarts of milk, and knocked at the back door. Mrs. Carpenter opened up. She looked sleepy-eyed but pleased to see me.

"Why, Jenny," she said, "you're here bright and early. Come in. Come in."

"Yes, ma'am," I said. "I came to make breakfast."

"Well, that's wonderful. Mr. Carpenter is shaving. He'll be down in a few minutes. He likes two four-minute eggs, I never can get them right, two slices of toast, and lots of strong black coffee. And now that you're here, I think I'll go back to bed and get a little more beauty sleep." She giggled like a silly girl, waved at me, and pranced out.

I put the milk away and started in making the coffee. There was an electric coffee pot, but my coffee is good because I make it the old-fashioned way. I boiled up some water and when it was bubbling away, I threw in the ground coffee, lots of it, to make it nice and strong. Then I turned the fire down to keep it hot while it brewed, and I cracked an egg so I could have an eggshell to throw in to make it clear. And I emptied out the stuff that was in the tobacco pouch right into the pot.

When I heard his footsteps on the stairs I put on another pot to boil up water for his eggs. He came into the kitchen smiling and smelling sweet.

"Well, Jenny," he said. "You came back. I'm glad, because you and I are going to get along just fine. You'll be happy here. I'll see to that."

I got out a cup and saucer.

"I been hearing things, Mr. Carpenter," I said. "Things I never dreamed of."

He frowned. "What things have you been hearing, Jenny?"

I poured coffee into the cup.

"I hear that you're my daddy."

He sank down into a kitchen chair. "Yes," he said, "that's true enough."

I put the cup and saucer on the counter to let it cool off a bit so it wouldn't be too hot for him to take a nice big swallow.

"I hear that you shot our Pop and buried him in your rose garden. They're mighty pretty roses you got out there."

He held his head in his two hands. "They swore never to tell you. Those boys swore."

"Pembrook told me because he's afraid I'll come to some harm in your house." I set the cup and saucer on the table in front of him.

"Oh, Jenny, sweet baby Jenny, I would never harm you. If anything, I'd like to make up for all those years I tried to put you out of my mind. I'd like you to come and live here and be my daughter and let me give you all the things you should have had."

"Don't call me that. I'm not a baby any more."

"No, you're not. You're a fine lovely woman, just like your

mother was. God, how I loved that woman! She was the only wonderful thing that ever happened in my whole life. I wanted to take her away with me. We were all set to go. We could have gone to some other town or to a big city where no one knew us. We'd have taken you along. And we'd have been happy. Instead, she died."

"Pop killed her. Because of you."

"You know that, too." He sighed. "Yes. He killed her and I killed him, and I've been living out my days in an agony of remorse. There's no one I can talk to. Clemmie doesn't know any of this. Sometimes I wish I were dead."

"Drink your coffee."

The water for his eggs was boiling. Gently I rolled the two eggs into the pot and stuck two slices of bread into the toaster. He left the table and came to where I was working.

"Jenny." He put his hands on my shoulders and turned me around to face him. "What can I do to make it up to you? I'll do anything in my power, and believe me that's a lot. You name it. It's yours."

I thought a minute. Would it be right or wrong to take from this man? I was having my usual trouble figuring out the difference between the two. Would it be right or wrong to let him drink the coffee?

Then I said, "Could you put Pembrook through law school?"

"Consider it done."

"And Earl and Wesley, can you find jobs for them? They're good workers, only down on their luck."

"Tell them to come to the bank."

"And what about Deucy? Would you get him a new guitar and a ticket to Nashville? He sings real fine."

"Not only that. I know Johnny Cash personally. We'll work something out."

"Now this one's hard. Can you get Ace out of jail and set him on a straight path?"

"The warden is Clemmie's cousin. And I own a ranch in

Wyoming. He can go there and work off his wildness. But what about you, Jenny. What can I do for you?"

I shrugged. "Oh, I guess I'll just live here for a while. I can help Mrs. Carpenter and sort of keep an eye on things."

He hugged me and planted a big kiss on my cheek. "That's my girl," he said. "That's what I was hoping you'd say. You'll never regret it. Mmm, that coffee smells good."

He was heading back to the table and his coffee cup. But I got there first and swiped it out from under his nose.

"That's coffee's cold," I said. "Come to think of it, the whole batch is bitter. I tasted it before you came down. I'll make some fresh."

I poured all the coffee down the drain and dished him up his eggs and toast. We drank the fresh coffee together, and he went off to his bank.

And that's the way it is now. Pembrook's way *is* better, and he's studying real hard. He'll graduate sooner now that he doesn't have to work his way through. Earl and Wesley really like being bank tellers, and Deucy has his leopardskin Cadillac and all the girls he can handle, although he says he misses the porch swing. Ace sent a photograph of himself on a horse wearing a big old cowboy hat. He looks funny but he says he's doing fine.

And me? Every day while the roses are blooming I cut some and put them in the house. Mrs. Carpenter just loves them. I'm waiting. Someday us Taggerts are gonna dig up that rose garden.

Wild Mustard

MARCIA MULLER

Marcia Muller (b. 1944) is one of the most celebrated and versatile writers of crime fiction to debut in the last quarter of the twentieth century. Born in Detroit and educated at the University of Michigan, she lives in Northern California, the setting for most of her fiction. Though it caused barely a ripple at the time of its publication, Muller's *Edwin of the Iron Shoes* (1977) is now accorded primacy in one of the major trends of recent decades: the female private-eye novel. All previous efforts in this line demand an asterisk: characters like Carter Brown's Mavis Seidlitz, Henry Kane's Marla Trent, and G. G. Fickling's Honey West were male wish-fulfillment fantasies not to be taken seriously; Fran Huston's Nicole Sweet in *The Rich Get It All* (1973) was an attempt at a more realistic character but was actually the work of a man (Ron S. Miller) using an androgynous pseudonym; and the first of the wave of female-by-female private eyes, Maxine O'Callaghan's Delilah West, appeared in print in a 1974 short story but not in a novel until 1980.

Sharon McCone did not return for a second case until *Ask the Cards a Question* (1982), the same year her two most famous female p.i. colleagues, Sue Grafton's Kinsey Millhone and Sara Paretsky's V. I. Warshawski, made their debuts, but has averaged about a book a year since. McCone differs from most earlier private eyes in other ways than gender: she is not the traditional loner but part of an organization, the All Souls Legal Cooperative, and her professional and personal relationships with her colleagues are important to her. This leads to Muller's other and more subtle distinction: she was one of the pioneers of the now-general practice of equipping the series sleuth with a large supporting cast of friends, family, and co-workers that recur from book to book. Unfortunately, few of the writers who have adopted this practice are able to do it as well as Muller does.

In 1992 she married novelist Bill Pronzini, with whom she has collaborated on three novels, beginning with *Double* (1984), in which McCone shares an investigation with Pronzini's Nameless Detective; a short-story collection, many anthologies, and the valuable reference volume *1001 Midnights: The Aficionado's Guide to Mystery and Detective Fiction* (1986). Muller has also written series about two amateur detectives, museum curator Elena Oliverez, who appeared in *The Tree of Death* (1983) and two subsequent novels, and art security consultant Joanna Stark, the first of whose three appearances was *The Cavalier in White* (1986).

Among Muller's honors is a 1993 Lifetime Achievement Award from the Private Eye Writers of America. Appropriately, "Wild Mustard," one of the earliest Sharon McCone short stories, comes from the PWA's first anthology, *The Eyes Have It* (1984).

The first time I saw the old Japanese woman, I was having brunch at the restaurant above the ruins of San Francisco's Sutro Baths. The woman squatted on the slope, halfway between its cypress-covered top and the flooded ruins of the old bathhouse. She was uprooting vegetation and stuffing it into a green plastic sack.

"I wonder what she's picking," I said to my friend Greg.

He glanced out the window, raising one dark-blond eyebrow, his homicide cop's eye assessing the scene. "Probably something edible that grows wild. She looks poor; it's a good way to save grocery money."

Indeed the woman did look like the indigent old ladies one sometimes saw in Japantown; she wore a shapeless jacket and trousers, and her feet were clad in sneakers. A gray scarf wound around her head.

"Have you ever been down there?" I asked Greg, motioning at the ruins. The once-elegant baths had been destroyed by fire. All that remained now were crumbling foundations, half submerged in water. Seagulls swam on its glossy surface and, beyond, the surf tossed against the rocks.

"No. You?"

"No. I've always meant to, but the path is steep and I never have the right shoes when I come here."

Greg smiled teasingly. "Sharon, you'd let your private eye's instinct be suppressed for lack of hiking boots?"

I shrugged. "Maybe I'm not really that interested."

"Maybe not."

Greg often teased me about my sleuthing instinct, but in reality

I suspected he was proud of my profession. An investigator for All Souls Cooperative, the legal services plan, I had dealt with a full range of cases—from murder to the mystery of a redwood hot tub that didn't hold water. A couple of the murders I'd solved had been in Greg's bailiwick, and this had given rise to both rivalry and romance.

In the months that passed, my interest in the old Japanese woman was piqued. Every Sunday that we went there—and we went there often because the restaurant was a favorite—the woman was scouring the slope, foraging for . . . what?

One Sunday in early spring, Greg and I sat in our window booth, watching the woman climb slowly down the dirt path. To complement the season, she had changed her gray headscarf for bright yellow. The slope swarmed with people, enjoying the release from the winter rains. On the far barren side where no vegetation had taken hold, an abandoned truck leaned at a precarious angle at the bottom of the cliff near the baths. People scrambled down, inspected the old truck, then went to walk on the concrete foundations or disappeared into a nearby cave.

When the waitress brought our check, I said, "I've watched long enough; let's go down there and explore."

Greg grinned, reaching in his pocket for change. "But you don't have the right shoes."

"Face it, I'll never have the right shoes. Let's go. We can ask the old woman what she's picking."

He stood up. "I'm glad you finally decided to investigate her. She might be up to something sinister."

"Don't be silly."

He ignored me. "Yeah, the private eye side of you has finally won out. Or is it your Indian blood? Tracking instinct, papoose?"

I glared at him, deciding that for that comment he deserved to pay the check. My one-eighth Shoshone ancestry—which for some reason had emerged to make me a black-haired throwback in a family of Scotch-Irish towheads—had prompted

Greg's dubbing me "papoose." It was a nickname I did not favor.

We left the restaurant and passed through the chain link fence to the path. A strong wind whipped my long hair about my head, and I stopped to tie it back. The path wound in switch-backs past huge gnarled geranium plants and through a thicket. On the other side of it, the woman squatted, pulling up what looked like weeds. When I approached she smiled at me, a gold tooth flashing.

"Hello," I said. "We've been watching you and wondered what you were picking."

"Many good things grow here. This month it is the wild mustard." She held up a spring. I took it, sniffing its pungency.

"You should try it," she added. "It is good for you."

"Maybe I will." I slipped the yellow flower through my button-hole and turned to Greg.

"Fat chance," he said. "When do you ever eat anything healthy?"

"Only when you force me."

"I have to. Otherwise it would be Hershey bars day in and day out."

"So what? I'm not in bad shape." It was true; even on this steep slope I wasn't winded.

Greg smiled, his eyes moving appreciatively over me. "No, you're not."

We continued down toward the ruins, past a sign that ad-vised us:

CAUTION!
CLIFF AND SURF AREA
EXTREMELY DANGEROUS
PEOPLE HAVE BEEN SWEPT
FROM THE ROCKS AND DROWNED

I stopped, balancing with my hand on Greg's arm, and removed my shoes. "Better footsore than swept away."

We approached the abandoned truck, following the same impulse that had drawn other climbers. Its blue paint was rusted and there had been a fire in the engine compartment. Everything, including the seats and steering wheel, had been stripped.

"Somebody even tried to take the front axle," a voice beside me said, "but the fire had fused the bolts."

I turned to face a friendly looking, sunbrowned youth of about fifteen. He wore dirty jeans and a torn T-shirt.

"Yeah," another voice added. This boy was about the same age; a wispy attempt at a moustache sprouted on his upper lip. "There's hardly anything left, and it's only been here a few weeks."

"Vandalism," Greg said.

"That's it." The first boy nodded. "People hang around here and drink. Late at night they get bored." He motioned at a group of unsavory-looking men who were sitting on the edge of the baths with a couple of six-packs.

"Destruction's a very popular sport these days." Greg watched the men for a moment with a professional eye, then touched my elbow. We skirted the ruins and went toward the cave. I stopped at its entrance and listened to the roar of the surf.

"Come on," Greg said.

I followed him inside, feet sinking into coarse sand that quickly became packed mud. The cave was really a tunnel, about eight feet high. Through crevices in the wall on the ocean side I saw spray flung high from the rolling waves at the foot of the cliff. It would be fatal to be swept down through those jagged rocks.

Greg reached the other end. I hurried as fast as my bare feet would permit and stood next to him. The precipitous drop to the sea made me clutch at his arm. Above us, rocks towered.

"I guess if you were a good climber you could go up, and then back to the road," I said.

"Maybe, but I wouldn't chance it. Like the sign says . . ."

"Right." I turned, suddenly apprehensive. At the mouth of the tunnel, two of the disreputable men stood, beer cans in hand. "Let's go, Greg."

If he noticed the edge to my voice, he didn't comment. We walked in silence through the tunnel. The men vanished. When we emerged into the sunlight, they were back with the others, opening fresh beers. The boys we had spoken with earlier were perched on the abandoned truck, and they waved at us as we started up the path.

And so, through the spring, we continued to go to our favorite restaurant on Sundays, always waiting for a window booth. The old Japanese woman exchanged her yellow headscarf for a red one. The abandoned truck remained nose down toward the baths, provoking much criticism of the Park Service. People walked their dogs on the slope. Children balanced precariously on the ruins, in spite of the warning sign. The men lolled about and drank beer. The teenaged boys came every week and often were joined by friends at the truck.

Then, one Sunday, the old woman failed to show.

"Where is she?" I asked Greg, glancing at my watch for the third time.

"Maybe she's picked everything there is to pick down there."

"Nonsense. There's always something to pick. We've watched her for almost a year. That old couple is down there walking their German Shepherd. The teenagers are here. That young couple we talked to last week is over by the tunnel. Where's the old Japanese woman?"

"She could be sick. There's a lot of flu going around. Hell, she might have died. She wasn't all that young."

The words made me lose my appetite for my chocolate cream pie. "Maybe we should check on her."

Greg sighed. "Sharon, save your sleuthing for paying clients. Don't make everything into a mystery."

Greg had often accused me of allowing what he referred to as my "woman's intuition" to rule my logic—something I hated even more than references to my "tracking instinct." I knew it was no such thing; I merely gave free rein to the hunches that every good investigator follows. It was not a subject I cared to argue at the moment, however, so I let it drop.

But the next morning—Monday—I sat in the converted closet that served as my office at All Souls, still puzzling over the woman's absence. A file on a particularly boring tenants' dispute lay open on the desk in front of me. Finally I shut it and clattered down the hall of the big brown Victorian toward the front door.

"I'll be back in a couple of hours," I told Ted, the secretary.

He nodded, his fingers never pausing as he plied his new Selectric. I gave the typewriter a resentful glance. It, to my mind, was an extravagance, and the money it was costing could have been better spent on salaries. All Souls, which charged clients on a sliding-fee scale according to their incomes, paid so low that several of the attorneys were compensated by living in free rooms on the second floor. I lived in a studio apartment in the Mission District. It seemed to get smaller every day.

Grumbling to myself, I went out to my car and headed for the restaurant above the Sutro Baths.

"The old woman who gathers wild mustard on the cliff," I said to the cashier, "was she here yesterday?"

He paused. "I think so. Yesterday was Sunday. She's always here on Sunday. I noticed her about eight, when we opened up. She always comes early and stays until about two."

But she had been gone at eleven. "Do you know her? Do you know where she lives?"

He looked curiously at me. "No, I don't."

I thanked him and went out. Feeling foolish, I stood beside the Great Highway for a moment, then started down the dirt path, toward where the wild mustard grew. Halfway there I met the two teenagers. Why weren't they in school? Dropouts, I guessed.

They started by, avoiding my eyes like kids will do. I stopped them. "Hey, you were here yesterday, right?"

The mustached one nodded.

"Did you see the old Japanese woman who picks the weeds?"

He frowned. "Don't remember her."

"When did you get here?"

"Oh, late! Really late. There was this party Saturday night."

"I don't remember seeing her either," the other one said, "but maybe she'd already gone by the time we got here."

I thanked them and headed down toward the ruins.

A little farther on, in the dense thicket through which the path wound, something caught my eye and I came to an abrupt stop. A neat pile of green plastic bags lay there, and on top of them was a pair of scuffed black shoes. Obviously she had come here on the bus, wearing her street shoes, and had only switched to sneakers for her work. Why would she leave without changing her shoes?

I hurried through the thicket toward the patch of wild mustard.

There, deep in the weeds, its color blending with their foliage, was another bag. I opened it. It was a quarter full of wilting mustard greens. She hadn't had much time to forage, not much time at all.

Seriously worried now, I rushed up to the Great Highway. From the phone booth inside the restaurant, I dialled Greg's direct line at the SFPD. Busy. I retrieved my dime and called All Souls.

"Any calls?"

Ted's typewriter rattled in the background. "No, but Hank wants to talk to you."

Hank Zahn, my boss. With a sinking heart, I remembered the conference we had had scheduled for half an hour ago. He came on the line.

"Where the hell are you?"

"Uh, in a phone booth."

"What I mean is, why aren't you here?"

"I can explain—"

"I should have known."

"What?"

"Greg warned me you'd be off investigating something."

"Greg? When did you talk to him?"

"Fifteen minutes ago. He wants you to call. It's important."

"Thanks!"

"Wait a minute—"

I hung up and dialed Greg again. He answered, sounding rushed. Without preamble, I explained what I'd found in the wild mustard patch.

"That's why I called you." His voice was unusually gentle. "We got word this morning."

"What word?" My stomach knotted.

"An identification on a body that washed up near Devil's Slide yesterday evening. Apparently she went in at low tide, or she would have been swept much farther to sea."

I was silent.

"Sharon?"

"Yes, I'm here."

"You know how it is out there. The signs warn against climbing. The current is bad."

But I'd never, in almost a year, seen the old Japanese woman near the sea. She was always up on the slope, where her weeds grew. "When was low tide, Greg?"

"Yesterday? Around eight in the morning."

Around the time the restaurant cashier had noticed her, and several hours before the teenagers had arrived. And in between? What had happened out there?

I hung up and stood at the top of the slope, pondering. What should I look for? What could I possibly find?

I didn't know, but I felt certain the old woman had not gone into the sea by accident. She had scaled those cliffs with the best of them.

I started down, noting the shoes and the bags in the thicket, marching resolutely past the wild mustard toward the abandoned truck. I walked all around it, examining its exterior and interior, but it gave me no clues. Then I started toward the tunnel in the cliff.

The area, so crowded on Sundays, was sparsely populated now. San Franciscans were going about their usual business, and visitors from the tour buses parked at nearby Cliff House were leery of climbing down here. The teenagers were the only other people in sight. They stood by the mouth of the tunnel, watching me. Something in their postures told me they were afraid. I quickened my steps.

The boys inclined their heads toward one another. Then they whirled and ran into the mouth of the tunnel.

I went after them. Again, I had the wrong shoes. I kicked them off and ran through the coarse sand. The boys were halfway down the tunnel.

One of them paused, frantically surveying a rift in the wall. I prayed he wouldn't go that way, into the boiling waves below.

He turned and ran after his companion. They disappeared at the end of the tunnel.

I hit the hard-packed dirt and increased my pace. Near the end, I slowed and approached more cautiously. At first I thought the boys had vanished, but then I looked down. They crouched on a ledge below. Their faces were scared and young, so young.

I stopped where they could see me and made a calming motion. "Come on back up," I said. "I won't hurt you."

The mustached one shook his head.

"Look, there's no place you can go. You can't swim in that surf."

Simultaneously they glanced down. They looked back at me and both shook their heads.

I took a step forward. "Whatever happened, it couldn't have—" Suddenly I felt the ground crumble. My foot slipped and I pitched forward. I fell to one knee, my arms frantically searching for a support.

"Oh, God!" the mustached boy cried. "Not you, too!" He stood up, swaying, his arms outstretched.

I kept sliding. The boy reached up and caught me by the arm. He staggered back toward the edge and we both fell to the hard rocky ground. For a moment, we both lay there panting. When I finally sat up, I saw we were inches from the sheer drop to the surf.

The boy sat up, too, his scared eyes on me. His companion was flattened against the cliff wall.

"It's okay," I said shakily.

"I thought you'd fall just like the old woman," the boy beside me said.

"It was an accident, wasn't it?"

He nodded. "We didn't mean for her to fall."

"Were you teasing her?"

"Yeah. We always did, for fun. But this time we went too far. We took her purse. She chased us."

"Through the tunnel, to here."

"Yes."

"And then she slipped."

The other boy moved away from the wall. "Honest, we didn't mean for it to happen. It was just that she was so old. She slipped."

"We watched her fall," his companion said. "We couldn't do anything."

"What did you do with the purse?"

"Threw it in after her. There were only two dollars in it. Two lousy dollars." His voice held a note of wonder. "Can you imagine, chasing us all the way down here for two bucks?"

I stood up carefully, grasping the rock for support. "Okay," I said. "Let's get out of here."

They looked at each other and then down at the surf.

"Come on. We'll talk some more. I know you didn't mean for her to die. And you saved my life."

They scrambled up, keeping their distance from me. Their faces were pale under their tans, their eyes afraid. They were so young. To them, products of the credit-card age, fighting to the death for two dollars was inconceivable. And the Japanese woman had been so old. For her, eking out a living with the wild mustard, two dollars had probably meant the difference between life and death.

I wondered if they'd ever understand.

Jemima Shore at the Sunny Grave

ANTONIA FRASER

Lady Antonia Fraser (b. 1932), the London-born daughter of Lord Longford, earned bachelor's and master's degrees in history at Lady Margaret Hall, Oxford, and served as editor of the publisher Weidenfeld and Nicolson's Kings and Queens of England series before her marriage to Hugh Fraser in 1956. Her first books were children's accounts of King Arthur and Robin Hood, followed by *Dolls* (1963) and *A History of Toys* (1966). Beginning with the hugely successful *Mary Queen of Scots* (1969), she became a best-selling author of popular British history and biography. Books on Cromwell, James I, Charles II, and the wives of Henry VIII followed. Her broad literary background also includes a translation from the French of Christian Dior's autobiography, radio and television plays, and the editorship of a number of poetry anthologies. Her first marriage having been dissolved in 1977, she married the playwright Harold Pinter in 1980.

She turned to crime fiction with *Quiet As a Nun* (1977), the first novel about Jemima Shore, one of the first and most successful sleuths to come from the world of broadcast journalism. In the final revised edition of his crime-fiction history *Bloody Murder* (1992), Julian Symons wrote that Fraser "might reasonably be called a feminist crime writer, but she could also be called a cosy one. Her writing has an evident pleasure in what she is doing that is engaging but her individual distinction is in the construction of particularly clever plots, of which *Cool Repentance* (1982) seems to me the most brilliant."

Detection with a touch of romance in an exotic background show the author and character at their best in "Jemima Shore at the Sunny Grave."

"This is your graveyard in the sun—" The tall young man standing in her path was singing the words lightly but clearly. It took Jemima Shore a moment to realize exactly what message he was intoning to the tune of the famous calypso. Then she stepped back. It was a sinister and not particularly welcoming little parody.

> "This is my island in the sun
> Where my people have toiled since time begun—"

Ever since she had arrived in the Caribbean, she seemed to have had the tune echoing in her ears. How old was it? How many years was it since the inimitable Harry Belafonte had first implanted it in everybody's consciousness? No matter. Whatever its age, the calypso was still being sung today with charm, vigour, and a certain relentlessness on Bow Island, and on the other West Indian islands she had visited in the course of her journey.

It was not the only tune to be heard, of course. The loud noise of music, she had discovered, was an inseparable part of Caribbean life, starting with the airport. The heavy, irresistible beat of the steel band, the honeyed wail of the singers, all this was happening somewhere if not everywhere all over the islands late into the night: the joyous sound of freedom, of dancing, of drinking (rum punch), and, for the tourists at any rate, the sound of holiday.

It wasn't the sound of holiday for Jemima Shore, Investigator. Or not officially so. That was all to the good, Jemima being one of those people temperamentally whose best holidays combined some work with a good deal of pleasure. She could hardly believe it when Megalith Television, her employers, had agreed to a program which took her away from freezing Britain to the sunny Caribbean in late January. This was a reversal of normal practice, by which Cy Fredericks, Jemima's boss—and the effective boss of Megalith—was generally to be found relaxing in the Caribbean in February while Jemima herself, if she got there at all, was liable to be dispatched there in the inconvenient humidity of August. And it was a fascinating project to boot. This was definitely her lucky year.

"This is my island in the sun—" But what the young man facing her had actually sung was "your *graveyard* in the sun." Hers? Or whose? Since the man was standing between Jemima and the historic grave she had come to visit, it was possible that he was being proprietorial as well as aggressive. On second thought, surely not. It was a joke, a cheerful joke on a cheerful, very sunny day. But the young man's expression was, it seemed to her, more threatening than that.

Jemima gazed back with that special sweet smile so familiar to viewers of British television. (These same viewers were also aware from past experience that Jemima, sweet as her smile might be, stood no nonsense from anyone, at least not on her program.) On closer inspection, the man was not really as young as all that. She saw someone of perhaps roughly her own age—early thirties. He was white, although so deeply tanned that she guessed he wasn't a tourist but one of the small loyal European population of Bow Island, a place fiercely proud of its recent independence from a much larger neighbor.

The stranger's height, unlike his youth, was not an illusion. He towered over Jemima and she herself was not short. He was also handsome, or would have been except for an oddly formed, rather large nose with a high bridge to it and a pronounced aquiline curve. But if the nose marred the regularity of his features, the impression left was not unattractive. He was wearing whitish cotton shorts, like more or less every male on Bow Island, black or white. His orange T-shirt bore the familiar island logo or crest: the outline of a bow in black and a black hand drawing it back. Beneath the logo was printed one of the enormous variety of local slogans—cheerful again—designed to make a play upon the island's name. This one read: THIS IS THE END OF THE SUN-BOW!

No, in that friendly T-shirt, he was surely not intending to be aggressive.

In that case, the odd thing about the whole encounter was that the stranger still stood absolutely still in Jemima's path. She could glimpse the large stone Archer Tomb just behind him, which she recognized from the postcards. For a smallish place, Bow Island was remarkably rich in historic relics. Nelson in his time had visited it with his fleet, for like its neighbors Bow Island had found itself engulfed in the Napoleonic Wars. Two hundred or so years before that, first British, then French, then British again had invaded and settled the island which had once belonged to Caribs, and before that Arawaks. Finally, into this melting pot, Africans had been brought forcibly to work the sugar plantations on which its wealth depended. All these elements in various degrees had gone to make up the people now known casually among themselves as the Bo'landers.

The Archer Tomb, the existence of which had in a sense brought Jemima across the Atlantic, belonged to the period of the second—and final—British settlement. Here was buried the most celebrated Governor in Bow Island's history, Sir Valentine Archer. Even its name commemorated his long reign. Bow Island had originally been called by the name of a saint, and while it was true the island was vaguely formed in the shape of a bow it was Governor Archer who had made the change: to signify ritually that this particular archer was in command of this particular bow.

Jemima knew that the monument, splendidly carved, would show Sir Valentine Archer with Isabella, his wife, beside him. This double stone bier was capped with a white wood structure reminiscent of a small church, done either to give the whole monument additional importance—although it must always have dominated the small churchyard by its sheer size—or to protect it from the weather. Jemima had read that there were no Archer children inscribed on the tomb, contrary to the usual seventeenth-century practice. This was because, as a local historian delicately put it, Governor Archer had been as a parent to the entire island. Or in the words of another purely local calypso:

"Across the sea came old Sir Valentine—
He came to be your daddy, and he came to be mine."

In short, no one monument could comprise the progeny of a man popularly supposed to have sired over a hundred children, legitimate and illegitimate. The legitimate line was, however, now on the point of dying out. It was to see Miss Isabella Archer, officially at least the last of her race, that Jemima had come to the Caribbean. She hoped to make a program about the old lady and her home, Archer Plantation House, alleged to be untouched in its decoration these fifty years. She wanted also to interview her generally about the changes Miss Archer had seen in her lifetime in this part of the world.

"Greg Harrison," said the man standing in Jemima's path suddenly. "And this is my sister, Coralie." A girl who had been standing unnoticed by Jemima in the shade of the arched church porch stepped rather shyly forward. She, too, was extremely brown and her blond hair, whitened almost to flax by the sun, was pulled back into a ponytail. His sister. Was there a resemblance? Coralie Harrison was wearing a similar orange T-shirt, but otherwise she was not much like her brother. She was quite short, for one thing, and her features were appealing rather than beautiful—and, perhaps fortunately, she lacked her brother's commanding nose.

"Welcome to Bow Island, Miss Shore," she began. But her brother interrupted her. He put out a hand, large, muscular, and burnt to nut color by the sun.

"I know why you're here and I don't like it," said Greg Harrison. "Stirring up forgotten things. Why don't you leave Miss Izzy to die in peace?" The contrast between his apparently friendly hand-shake and the hostile, if calmly spoken words was disconcerting.

"I'm Jemima Shore," she said, though he obviously knew that. "Am I going to be allowed to inspect the Archer Tomb? Or is it to be across your dead body?" Jemima smiled again with sweetness.

"*My* dead body!" Greg Harrison smiled back in his turn. The effect, however, was not particularly warming. "Have you come armed to the teeth, then?" Before she could answer, he began to hum the famous calypso again. Jemima imagined the words: "This is your graveyard in the sun." Then he added: "Might not be such a bad idea, that, when you start to dig up things that should be buried."

Jemima decided it was time for action. Neatly sidestepping Greg Harrison, she marched firmly toward the Archer Tomb. There lay the carved couple. She read: "Sacred to the memory of Sir Valentine Archer, first Governor of this island, and his only wife, Isabella, daughter of Randal Oxford, gentleman." She was reminded briefly of her favorite Philip Larkin poem about the Arundel Monument, beginning, "The Earl and Countess lie in stone—" and ending, "All that remains of us is love."

But that couple lay a thousand miles away in the cloistered cool of Chichester Cathedral. Here the hot tropical sun burnt down on her naked head. She found she had taken off her large straw hat as a token of respect and quickly clapped it back on again. Here, too, in contrast to the very English-looking stone church with pointed Gothic windows beyond, there were palm trees among the graves instead of yews, their slender trunks bending like giraffes' necks in the breeze. She had once roman-tically laid white roses on the Arundel Monument. It was as the memory of the gesture returned to her that she spied the heap of bright pink and orange hibiscus blossoms lying on the stone before her. A shadow fell across it.

"Tina puts them there." Greg Harrison had followed her. "Every day she can manage it. Most days. Then she tells Miss Izzy what she's done. Touching, isn't it?" But he did not make it sound as if he found it especially touching. In fact, there was so much bitterness, even malevolence, in his voice that for a moment, standing as she was in the sunny graveyard, Jemima felt quite chilled. "Or is it revolting?" he added, the malevolence now quite naked.

"Greg," murmured Coralie Harrison faintly, as if in protest.

"Tina?" Jemima said. "That's Miss Archer's—Miss Izzy's—companion. We've corresponded. For the moment I can't remember her other name."

"She's known as Tina Archer these days, I think you'll find. When she wrote to you, she probably signed the letter Tina Harrison." Harrison looked at Jemima sardonically but she had genuinely forgotten the surname of the companion—it was, after all, not a particularly uncommon one.

They were interrupted by a loud hail from the road. Jemima saw a young black man at the wheel of one of the convenient roofless minis everyone seemed to drive around Bow Island. He stood up and started to shout something.

"Greg! Cora! You coming on to—" She missed the rest of it—something about a boat and a fish. Coralie Harrison looked suddenly radiant, and for a moment even Greg Harrison actually looked properly pleased.

He waved back. "Hey, Joseph. Come and say hello to Miss Jemima Shore of BBC Television!"

"Megalith Television," Jemima interrupted, but in vain. Harrison continued:

"You heard, Joseph. She's making a program about Miss Izzy."

The man leapt gracefully out of the car and approached up the palm-lined path. Jemima saw that he, too, was extremely tall. And like the vast majority of the Bo'landers she had so far met, he had the air of being a natural athlete. Whatever the genetic mix in the past of Carib and African and other people that had produced them, the Bo'landers were certainly wonderful-looking. He kissed Coralie on both cheeks and patted her brother on the back.

"Miss Shore, meet Joseph—" but even before Greg Harrison had pronounced the surname, his mischievous expression had warned Jemima what it was likely to be "—Joseph Archer. Undoubtedly one of the ten thousand descendants of the philo-progenitive old gentleman at whose tomb you are so raptly gazing." All that remains of us is love indeed, thought Jemima irreverently as she shook Joseph Archer's hand—with all due respect to Philip Larkin, it seemed that a good deal more remained of Sir Valentine than that.

"Oh, you'll find we're all called Archer round here," murmured Joseph pleasantly. Unlike Greg Harrison, he appeared to be genuinely welcoming. "As for Sir Val-en-tine"—he pronounced it syllable by syllable like the calypso—"don't pay too much attention to the stories. Otherwise, how come we're not all living in that fine old Archer Plantation House?"

"Instead of merely my ex-wife. No, Coralie, don't protest. I could kill her for what she's doing." Again Jemima felt a chill at the extent of the violence in Greg Harrison's voice. "Come, Joseph, we'll see about that fish of yours. Come on, Coralie." He strode off, unsmiling, accompanied by Joseph, who did smile. Coralie, however, stopped to ask Jemima if there was anything she could do for her. Her manner was still shy but in her brother's absence a great deal more friendly. Jemima also had the strong impression that Coralie Harrison wanted to communicate something to her, something she did not necessarily want her brother to hear.

"I could perhaps interpret, explain—" Coralie stopped. Jemima said nothing. "Certain things," went on Coralie. "There are so many layers in a place like this. Just because it's small, an outsider doesn't always understand—"

"And I'm the outsider? Of course I am." Jemima had started

to sketch the tomb for future reference, something for which she had a minor but useful talent. She forbore to observe truthfully, if platitudinously, that an outsider could also sometimes see local matters rather more clearly than those involved—she wanted to know what else Coralie had to say. Would she explain, for example, Greg's quite blatant dislike of his former wife?

But an impatient cry from her brother now in the car beside Joseph meant that Coralie for the time being had nothing more to add. She fled down the path and Jemima was left to ponder with renewed interest on her forthcoming visit to Isabella Archer of Archer Plantation House. It was a visit which would include, she took it, a meeting with Miss Archer's companion, who, like her employer, was currently dwelling in comfort there.

Comfort! Even from a distance, later that day, the square, lowbuilt mansion had a comfortable air. More than that, it conveyed an impression of gracious and old-fashioned tranquillity. As Jemima drove her own rented Mini up the long avenue of palm trees— much taller than those in the churchyard—she could fancy she was driving back in time to the days of Governor Archer, his copious banquets, parties, and balls, all served by black slaves.

At that moment, a young woman with coffee-colored skin and short black curly hair appeared on the steps. Unlike the maids in Jemima's hotel who wore a pastiche of bygone servants' costume at dinner—brightly colored dresses to the ankle, white-muslin aprons, and turbans—this girl was wearing an up-to-the-minute scarlet halter-top and cutaway shorts revealing most of her smooth brown legs. Tina Archer: for so she introduced herself.

It did not surprise Jemima Shore one bit to discover that Tina Archer—formerly Harrison—was easy to get on with. Anyone who left the hostile and graceless Greg Harrison was already ahead in Jemima's book. But with Tina Archer chatting away at her side, so chic and even trendy in her appearance, the revelation of the interior of the house was far more of a shock to her than it would otherwise have been. There was nothing, nothing at all, of the slightest modernity about it. Dust and cobwebs were not literally there perhaps, but they were suggested in its gloom, its heavy wooden furniture—where were the light cane chairs so suitable to the climate?—and above all in its desolation. Archer Plantation House reminded her of poor Miss Havisham's time-warp home in *Great Expectations*. And still worse, there was an atmosphere of sadness hanging over the whole interior. Or perhaps it was mere loneliness, a kind of somber, sterile grandeur you felt must stretch back centuries.

All this was in violent contrast to the sunshine still brilliant in the late afternoon, the rioting bushes of brightly colored tropical flowers outside. None of it had Jemima expected. Information garnered in London had led her to form quite a different picture of Archer Plantation House, something far more like her original impression, as she drove down the avenue of palm trees, of antique mellow grace.

Just as Jemima was adapting to this surprise, she discovered the figure of Miss Archer herself to be equally astonishing. That is to say, having adjusted rapidly from free and easy Tina to the moldering, somber house, she now had to adjust with equal rapidity all over again. For the very first inspection of the old lady, known by Jemima to be at least eighty, quickly banished all thoughts of Miss Havisham. Here was no aged, abandoned bride, forlorn in the decaying wedding-dress of fifty years before. Miss Izzy Archer was wearing a coolie straw hat, apparently tied under her chin with a duster, a loose, white, man's shirt, and faded blue-jeans cut off at the knee. On her feet were a pair of what looked like child's brown sandals. From the look of her, she had either just taken a shower wearing all this or been swimming. She was dripping wet, making large pools on the rich carpet and dark, polished boards of the formal drawing room, all dark-red brocade and swagged, fringed curtains, where she had received Jemima. It was possible to see this even in the filtered light seeping through the heavy brown shutters which shut out the view of the sea.

"Oh, don't fuss so, Tina dear," exclaimed Miss Izzy impatiently—although Tina had, in fact, said nothing. "What do a few drops of water matter? Stains? What stains?" (Tina still had not spoken.) "Let the government put it right when the time comes."

Although Tina Archer continued to be silent, gazing amiably, even cheerfully, at her employer, nevertheless in some way she stiffened, froze in her polite listening attitude. Instinctively Jemima knew that she was in some way upset.

"Now don't be silly, Tina, don't take on, dear." The old lady was now shaking herself free of water like a small but stout dog. "You know what I mean. If you don't, who does—since half the time I don't know what I mean, let alone what I say. You can put it all right one day, is that better? After all, you'll have plenty of money to do it. You can afford a few new covers and carpets." So saying, Miss Izzy, taking Jemima by the hand and attended by the still-silent Tina, led the way to the farthest dark-red sofa. Looking remarkably wet from top to toe, she sat down firmly in the middle of it.

It was in this way that Jemima first realized that Archer Plantation House would not necessarily pass to the newly independent government of Bow Island on its owner's death. Miss Izzy, if she had her way, was intending to leave it all, house and fortune, to Tina. Among other things, this meant that Jemima was no longer making a program about a house destined shortly to be a national museum—which was very much part of the arrangement that had brought her to the island and had, incidentally, secured the friendly cooperation of that same new government. Was all this new? How new? Did the new government know? If the will had been signed, they must know.

"I've signed the will this morning, dear," Miss Archer pronounced triumphantly, with an uncanny ability to answer unspoken questions. "I went swimming to celebrate. I always celebrate things with a good swim—so much more healthy than rum or champagne. Although there's still plenty of *that* in the cellar."

She paused. "So there you are, aren't you, dear? Or there you will be. Here you will be. Thompson says there'll be trouble, of course. What can you expect these days? Everything is trouble since independence. Not that I'm against independence, far from it. But everything new brings new trouble here in addition to all the old troubles, so that the troubles get more and more. On Bow Island no troubles ever go away. Why is that?"

But Miss Izzy did not stop for an answer. "No, I'm all for independence and I shall tell you all about that, my dear"—she turned to Jemima and put one damp hand on her sleeve—"on your program. I'm being a Bo'lander born and bred, you know." It was true that Miss Izzy, unlike Tina for example, spoke with the peculiar, slightly sing-song intonation of the islanders—not unattractive to Jemima's ears.

"I was born in this very house eighty-two years ago in April," went on Miss Izzy. "You shall come to my birthday party. I was born during a hurricane. A good start! But my mother died in childbirth, they should never have got in that new-fangled doctor, just because he came from England. A total fool he was, I remember him well. They should have had a good Bo'lander midwife, then my mother wouldn't have died and my father would have had sons—"

Miss Izzy was drifting away into a host of reminiscences—and while these were supposed to be what Jemima had come to hear, her thoughts were actually racing off in quite a different direction. Trouble? What trouble? Where did Greg Harrison, for example, stand in all this—Greg Harrison who wanted Miss Izzy to be left to "die in peace"? Greg Harrison who had been married to Tina and was no longer? Tina Archer, now heiress to a fortune.

Above all, why was this forthright old lady intending to leave everything to her companion? For one thing, Jemima did not know how seriously to treat the matter of Tina's surname. Joseph Archer had laughed off the whole subject of Sir Valentine's innumerable descendants. But perhaps the beautiful Tina was in some special way connected to Miss Izzy. She might be the product of some rather more recent union between a rakish

Archer and a Bo'lander maiden. More recent than the seventeenth century, that is.

Her attention was wrenched back to Miss Izzy's reminiscing monologue by the mention of the Archer Tomb.

"You've seen the grave? Tina has discovered it's all a fraud. A great big lie, lying under the sun—yes, Tina dear, you once said that. Sir Valentine Archer, my great great great—" An infinite number of greats followed before Miss Izzy finally pronounced the word "grandfather," but Jemima had to admit that she did seem to be counting. "He had a great big lie perpetuated on his tombstone."

"What Miss Izzy means—" This was the first time Tina had spoken since they entered the darkened drawing room. She was still standing, while Jemima and Miss Izzy sat.

"Don't tell me what I mean, child," rapped out the old lady; her tone was imperious rather than indulgent. Tina might for a moment have been a plantation worker two hundred years earlier rather than an independent-minded girl in the late twentieth century. "It's the inscription which is a lie. She wasn't his only wife. The very inscription should have warned us. Tina wants to see justice done to poor little Lucie Anne and so do I. Independence indeed! I've been independent all my life and I'm certainly not stopping now. Tell me, Miss Shore, you're a clever young woman from television. Why do you bother to contradict something unless it's true all along? That's the way you work all the time in television, don't you?"

Jemima was wondering just how to answer this question diplomatically and without traducing her profession when Tina firmly, and this time successfully, took over from her employer.

"I read history at university in the UK, Jemima. Genealogical research is my speciality. I was helping Miss Izzy put her papers in order for the museum—or what was to be the museum. Then the request came for your program and I began to dig a little deeper. That's how I found the marriage certificate. Old Sir Valentine *did* marry his young Carib mistress, known as Lucie

Anne. Late in life—long after his first wife died. That's Lucie Anne who was the mother of his youngest two children. He was getting old, and for some reason he decided to marry her. The church, maybe. In its way, this has always been a God-fearing island. Perhaps Lucie Anne, who was very young and very beautiful, put pressure on the old man, using the church. At any rate, these last two children of all the hundreds he sired would have been legitimate!"

"And so?" questioned Jemima in her most encouraging manner.

"I'm descended from Lucie Anne—and Sir Valentine, of course." Tina returned sweet smile for sweet smile. "I've traced that, too, from the church records—not too difficult, given the strength of the church here. Not too difficult for an expert, at all events. Oh, I've got all sorts of blood, like most of us round here, including a Spanish grandmother and maybe some French blood, too. But the Archer descent is perfectly straightforward and clear."

Tina seemed aware that Jemima was gazing at her with respect. Did she, however, understand the actual tenor of Jemima's thoughts? This is a formidable person, Jemima was reflecting. Charming, yes, but formidable. And ruthless, maybe, on occasion. Jemima was also, to be frank, wondering just how she was going to present this sudden change of angle in her program on Megalith Television. On the one hand, it might now be seen as a romantic rags-to-riches story, the discovery of the lost heiress. On the other hand, just supposing Tina Archer was not so much an heiress as an adventuress? In that case, what would Megalith— what did Jemima Shore—make of a bright young woman putting across a load of false history on an innocent old lady? In those circumstances, Jemima could understand how the man by the sunny grave might display his contempt for Tina Archer.

"I met Greg Harrison by the Archer Tomb this morning," Jemima commented deliberately. "Your ex-husband, I take it."

"Of course he's her ex-husband." It was Miss Izzy who chose to answer. "That no-good. Gregory Harrison has been a no-good since the day he was born. And that sister of his. Drifters. Not a job between them. Sailing. Fishing. As if the world owes them a living."

"Half sister. Coralie is his half sister. And she works in a hotel boutique." Tina spoke perfectly equably, but once again Jemima guessed that she was in some way put out. "Greg is the no-good in that family." For all her calm, there was a hint of suppressed anger in her reference to her former husband. With what bitterness that marriage must have ended!

"No-good, the pair of them. You're well out of that marriage, Tina dear," exclaimed Miss Izzy. "And do sit down, child—you're standing there like some kind of housekeeper. And where is Hazel, anyway? It's nearly half past five. It'll begin to get dark soon. We might go down to the terrace to watch the sun sink. Where is Henry? He ought to be bringing us some punch. The Archer Plantation punch, Miss Shore—wait till you taste it. One secret ingredient, my father always said—"

Miss Izzy was happily returning to the past.

"I'll get the punch," said Tina, still on her feet. "Didn't you say Hazel could have the day off? Her sister is getting married over at Tamarind Creek. Henry has taken her."

"Then where's the boy? Where's what's-his-name? Little Joseph." The old lady was beginning to sound petulant.

"There isn't a boy any longer," explained Tina patiently. "Just Hazel and Henry. As for Joseph—well, little Joseph Archer is quite grown up now, isn't he?"

"Of course he is! I didn't mean that Joseph—he came to see me the other day. Wasn't there another boy called Joseph? Perhaps that was before the war. My father had a stable boy—"

"I'll get the rum punch." Tina vanished swiftly and gracefully.

"Pretty creature," murmured Miss Izzy after her. "Archer blood. It always shows. They do say the best-looking Bo'landers are still called Archer."

But when Tina returned, the old lady's mood had changed again.

"I'm cold and damp," she declared. "I might get a chill sitting

here. And soon I'm going to be all alone in the house. I hate
being left alone. Ever since I was a little girl I've hated being
alone. Everyone knows that. Tina, you have to stay to dinner.
Miss Shore, you must stay, too. It's so lonely here by the sea. What
happens if someone breaks in?—Don't frown, there are plenty
of bad people about. That's one thing that hasn't gotten better
since independence."

"Of course I'm staying," replied Tina easily. "I've arranged it
with Hazel." Jemima was wondering guiltily if she, too, ought to
stay. But it was the night of her hotel's weekly party on the
beach—barbecue followed by dancing to a steel band. Jemima,
who loved to dance in the Northern Hemisphere, was longing to
try it here. Dancing under the stars by the sea sounded idyllic.
Did Miss Izzy really need extra company? Her eyes met those of
Tina Archer across the old lady's straw-hatted head. Tina shook
her head slightly.

After a sip of the famous rum punch—whatever the secret
ingredient, it was the strongest she had yet tasted on the island—
Jemima was able to make her escape. In any case, the punch was
having a manifestly relaxing effect on Miss Izzy herself. She
became rapidly quite tipsy and Jemima wondered how long she
would actually stay awake. The next time they met must be in
the freshness of a morning.

Jemima drove away just as the enormous red sun was rushing
down below the horizon. The beat of the waves from the shore
pursued her. Archer Plantation House was set in a lonely position on its own spit of land at the end of its own long avenue.
She could hardly blame Miss Izzy for not wanting to be abandoned there. Jemima listened to the sound of the waves until the
very different noise of the steel band in the next village along the
shore took over. That transferred her thoughts temporarily from
recent events at Archer Plantation House to the prospect of her
evening ahead. One way or another, for a brief space of time, she
would stop thinking altogether about Miss Isabella Archer.

*

That was because the beach party was at first exactly what Jemima had expected—relaxed, good-natured, and noisy. She found her cares gradually floating away as she danced and danced again with a series of partners, English, American, and Bo'lander, to the beat of the steel band. That rum punch of Miss Izzy's, with its secret ingredient, must have been lethal because its effects seemed to stay with her for hours. She decided she didn't even need the generous profferings of the hotel mixture—a good deal weaker than Miss Izzy's beneath its lavish surface scattering of nutmeg. Others, however, decided that the hotel punch was exactly what they did need. All in all, it was already a very good party long before the sliver of the new moon became visible over the now-black waters of the Caribbean. Jemima, temporarily alone, tilted back her head as she stood by the lapping waves at the edge of the beach and fixed the moon in her sights.

"You going to wish on that new little moon?" She turned. A tall man—at least a head taller than she was—was standing beside her on the sand. She had not heard him, the gentle noise of the waves masking his approach. For a moment she didn't recognize Joseph Archer in his loose flowered shirt and long white trousers, so different did he look from the fisherman encountered that noon at the graveside.

In this way it came about that the second part of the beach party was quite unexpected, at least from Jemima's point of view.

"I ought to wish. I ought to wish to make a good program, I suppose. That would be a good, professional thing to do."

"Miss Izzy Archer and all that?"

"Miss Izzy, Archer Plantation House, Bow Island—to say nothing of the Archer Tomb, old Sir Valentine, and all that." She decided not to mention Tina Archer and all that for the time being.

"All that!" He sighed. "Listen, Jemima—it's good, this band. We're saying it's about the best on the island these days. Let's be dancing, shall we? Then you and me can talk about all that in the morning. In my office, you know."

It was the distinct authority with which Joseph Archer spoke quite as much as the mention of his office which intrigued Jemima. Before she lost herself still further in the rhythm of the dance—which she had a feeling that with Joseph Archer to help her she was about to do—she must find out just what he meant. And, for that matter, just who he was.

The second question was easily answered. It also provided the answer to the first. Joseph Archer might or might not go fishing from time to time when he was off-duty, but he was also a member of the newly formed Bo'lander government. Quite an important one, in fact. Important in the eyes of the world in general, and particularly important in the eyes of Jemima Shore, Investigator. For Joseph Archer was the minister dealing with tourism, his brief extending to such matters as conservation, the Bo'lander historic heritage, and—as he described it to her—"the future National Archer Plantation House Museum."

Once again it didn't seem the appropriate moment to mention Tina Archer and her possible future ownership of the plantation house. As Joseph himself had said, the morning would do for all that. In his office in Bowtown.

They danced on for a while, and it was as Jemima had suspected it would be: something to lose herself in, perhaps dangerously so. The tune to "This is my island in the sun" was played and Jemima never once heard the graveyard words in her imagination. Then Joseph Archer, most politely and apparently regretfully, said he had to leave. He had an extremely early appointment—and not with a fish, either, he added with a smile. Jemima felt a pang which she hoped didn't show. But there was plenty of time, wasn't there? There would be other nights and other parties, other nights on the beach as the moon waxed to full in the two weeks she had before she must return to England.

Jemima's personal party stopped, but the rest of the celebration went on late into the night, spilling onto the sands, even into the sea, long after the sliver of the moon had vanished. Jemima, sleeping fitfully and visited by dreams in which Joseph Archer, Tina, and Miss Izzy executed some kind of elaborate dance, not at all like the kind of island jump-up she had recently been enjoying, heard the noise in the distance.

Far away on Archer Plantation's lonely peninsula, the peace was broken not by a steel band but by the rough sound of the waves bashing against the rocks at its farthest point. A stranger might have been surprised to see that the lights were still on in the great drawing room, the shutters having been drawn back once the sun was gone, but nobody born on Bow Island—a fisherman out to sea, for example—would have found it at all odd. Everyone knew that Miss Izzy Archer was frightened of the dark and liked to go to bed with all her lights blazing. Especially when Hazel had gone to her sister's wedding and Henry had taken her there—another fact of island life which most Bo'landers would have known.

In her room overlooking the sea, tossing in the big four-poster bed in which she had been born over eighty years ago, Miss Izzy, like Jemima Shore, slept fitfully. After a while, she got out of bed and went to one of the long windows. Jemima would have found her nightclothes, like her swimming costume, bizarre, for Miss Izzy wasn't wearing the kind of formal Victorian nightdress which might have gone with the house. Rather, she was "using up," as she quaintly put it, her father's ancient burgundy-silk pajamas, purchased many aeons ago in Jermyn Street. And as the last Sir John Archer, Baronet, had been several feet taller than his plump little daughter, the long trouser legs trailed on the floor behind her.

Miss Izzy continued to stare out of the window. Her gaze followed the direction of the terrace, which led in a series of parterres, once grandly planted, now overgrown, down to the rocks and the sea. Although the waters themselves were mostly blackness, the Caribbean night was not entirely dark. Besides, the light from the drawing-room windows streamed out onto the nearest terrace. Miss Izzy rubbed her eyes, then she turned back into the bedroom, where the celebrated oil painting of Sir Valentine hung over the mantelpiece dominated the room. Rather confusedly—she must have drunk far too much of that punch—she decided that her ancestor was trying to encourage her to be valiant in the face of danger for the first time in her life. She, little Isabella Archer, spoilt and petted Izzy, his last legitimate descendant—no, not his last legitimate descendant, but the habits of a lifetime were difficult to break—was being spurred on to something courageous by the hawklike gaze of the fierce old autocrat.

But I'm so old, thought Miss Izzy. Then: But not *too* old. Once you let people know you're not, after all, a coward—

She looked out of the window once more. The effects of the punch were wearing off. Now she was quite certain of what she was seeing. Something dark, darkly clad, dark-skinned— What did it matter, someone dark had come out of the sea and was now proceeding silently in the direction of the house.

I must be brave, thought Miss Izzy. She said aloud: "Then he'll be proud of me. His brave girl." Whose brave girl? No, not Sir Valentine's—Daddy's brave girl. Her thoughts began to float away again into the past. I wonder if Daddy will take me on a swim with him to celebrate?

Miss Izzy started to go downstairs. She had just reached the door of the drawing room and was standing looking into the decaying red-velvet interior, still brightly illuminated, at the moment when the black-clad intruder stepped into the room through the open window.

Even before the intruder began to move softly toward her, dark-gloved hands outstretched, Miss Izzy Archer knew without doubt in her rapidly beating old heart that Archer Plantation, the house in which she had been born, was also the house in which she was about to die.

"Miss Izzy Archer is dead. Some person went and killed her last night. A robber, maybe." It was Joseph Archer who broke the news to Jemima the next morning.

He spoke across the broad desk of his formal office in Bowtown. His voice was hollow and distant, only the Bo'lander sing-song to connect him with Jemima's handsome dancing partner of the night before. In his short-sleeved but official-looking white shirt and dark trousers, he looked once again completely different from the cheerful ragged fisherman Jemima had first encountered. This was indeed the rising young Bo'lander politician she was seeing: a member of the newly formed government of Bow Island. Even the tragic fact of the death—the murder, as it seemed—of an old lady seemed to strike no chord of emotion in him.

Then Jemima looked again and saw what looked suspiciously like tears in Joseph Archer's eyes.

"I just heard myself, you know. The Chief of Police, Sandy Marlow, is my cousin." He didn't attempt to brush away the tears. If that was what they were. But the words were presumably meant as an explanation. Of what? Of shock? Grief? Shock he must surely have experienced, but grief? Jemima decided at this point that she could at least inquire delicately about his precise relationship to Miss Izzy.

It came back to her that he had visited the old lady the week previously, if Miss Izzy's rather vague words concerning "Little Joseph" were to be trusted. She was thinking not so much of a possible blood relationship as some other kind of connection. After all, Joseph Archer himself had dismissed the former idea in the graveyard. His words about Sir Valentine and his numerous progeny came back to her: "Don't pay too much attention to the stories. Otherwise, how come we're not all living in that fine old Archer Plantation House?" At which Greg Harrison had commented with such fury: "Instead of merely my ex-wife." The exchange made more sense to her now, of course, that she knew of the position of Tina Harrison, now Tina Archer, in Miss Izzy's will.

The will! Tina would now inherit! And she would inherit in the light of a will signed the very morning of the day of Miss

Izzy's death. Clearly, Joseph had been correct when he dismissed the claim of the many Bo'landers called Archer to be descended in any meaningful fashion from Sir Valentine. There was already a considerable difference between Tina, the allegedly sole legitimate descendant other than Miss Izzy, and the rest of the Bo'lander Archers. In the future, with Tina come into her inheritance, the gap would widen even more.

It was extremely hot in Joseph's office. It was not so much that Bow Island was an unsophisticated place as that the persistent breeze made air-conditioning generally unnecessary. The North American tourists who were beginning to request air-conditioning in the hotels, reflected Jemima, would only succeed in ruining the most perfect kind of natural ventilation. But a government office in Bowtown was rather different. A huge fan in the ceiling made the papers on Joseph's desk stir uneasily. Jemima felt a ribbon of sweat trickle down beneath her long loose white T-shirt, which she had belted as a dress to provide some kind of formal attire to call on a Bo'lander minister in working hours.

By this time, Jemima's disbelieving numbness on the subject of Miss Izzy's murder was wearing off. She was struck by the frightful poignancy of that last encounter in the decaying grandeur of Archer Plantation House. Worse still, the old lady's pathetic fear of loneliness was beginning to haunt her. Miss Izzy had been so passionate in her determination not to be abandoned. "Ever since I was a little girl I've hated being alone. Everyone knows that. It's so lonely here by the sea. What happens if someone breaks in?"

Well, someone had broken in. Or so it was presumed. Joseph Archer's words: "A robber, maybe." And this robber—maybe—had killed the old lady in the process.

Jemima began hesitantly: "I'm so sorry, Joseph. What a ghastly tragedy! You knew her? Well, I suppose everyone round here must have known her—"

"All the days of my life, since I was a little boy. My mama was one of her maids. Just a little thing herself, and then she died. She's in that churchyard, you know, in a corner. Miss Izzy was very good to me when my mama died, oh, yes. She was kind. Now you'd think that independence, *our* independence, would be hard for an old lady like her, but Miss Izzy she just liked it very much. 'England's no good to me any more, Joseph,' she said, 'I'm a Bo'lander just like the rest of you.'"

"You saw her last week, I believe. Miss Izzy told me that herself."

Joseph gazed at Jemima steadily—the emotion had vanished. "I went to talk with her, yes. She had some foolish idea of changing her mind about things. Just a fancy, you know. But that's over. May she rest in peace, little old Miss Izzy. We'll have our National Museum now, that's for sure, and we'll remember her with it. It'll make a good museum for our history. Didn't they tell you in London, Jemima?" There was pride in his voice as he concluded: "Miss Izzy left everything in her will to the people of Bow Island."

Jemima swallowed hard. Was it true? Or rather, was it still true? Had Miss Izzy really signed a new will yesterday? She had been quite circumspect on the subject, mentioning someone called Thompson—her lawyer, no doubt—who thought there would be "trouble" as a result. "Joseph," she said, "Tina Archer was up at Archer Plantation House yesterday afternoon, too."

"Oh, that girl, the trouble she made, tried to make. Tina and her stories and her fine education and her history. And she's so pretty!" Joseph's tone was momentarily violent but he finished more calmly. "The police are waiting at the hospital. She's not speaking yet, she's not even conscious." Then even more calmly: "She's not so pretty now, I hear. That robber beat her, you see."

It was hotter than ever in the Bowtown office and even the papers on the desk were hardly stirring in the waft of the fan. Jemima saw Joseph's face swimming before her. She absolutely must not faint—she never fainted. She concentrated desperately on what Joseph Archer was telling her, the picture he was re-creating of the night of the murder. The shock of learning that

Tina Archer had also been present in the house when Miss Izzy was killed was irrational, she realized that. Hadn't Tina promised the old lady she would stay with her?

Joseph was telling her that Miss Izzy's body had been found in the drawing room by the cook, Hazel, returning from her sister's wedding at first light. It was a grisly touch that because Miss Izzy was wearing red-silk pajamas—her daddy's—and all the furnishings of the drawing room were dark-red as well, poor Hazel had not at first realized the extent of her mistress's injuries. Not only was there blood everywhere, there was water, too— pools of it. Whatever—whoever—had killed Miss Izzy had come out of the sea. Wearing rubber shoes—or flippers—and probably gloves as well.

A moment later, Hazel was in no doubt about what had hit Miss Izzy. The club, still stained with blood, had been left lying on the floor of the front hall. (She herself, deposited by Henry, had originally entered by the kitchen door.) The club, although not of Bo'lander manufacture, belonged to the house. It was a relic, African probably, of Sir John Archer's travels in other parts of the former British Empire, and hung heavy and short-handled on the drawing-room wall. Possibly Sir John had in mind to wield it against unlawful intruders but to Miss Izzy it had been simply one more family memento. She never touched it. Now it had killed her.

"No prints anywhere," Joseph said. "So far."

"And Tina?" asked Jemima with dry lips. The idea of the pools of water stagnant on the floor of the drawing room mingled with Miss Izzy's blood reminded her only too vividly of the old lady when last seen—soaking wet in her bizarre swimming costume, defiantly sitting down on her own sofa.

"The robber ransacked the house. Even the cellar. The champagne cases Miss Izzy boasted about must have been too heavy, though. He drank some rum. The police don't know yet what he took—silver snuff-boxes maybe, there were plenty of those about." Joseph sighed. "Then he went upstairs."

"And found Tina?"

"In one of the bedrooms. He didn't hit her with the same weapon—lucky for her, as he'd have killed her just like he killed Miss Izzy. He left that downstairs and picked up something a good deal lighter. Probably didn't reckon on seeing her or anyone there at all. 'Cept for Miss Izzy, that is. Tina must have surprised him. Maybe she woke up. Robbers—well, all I can say is that robbers here don't generally go and kill people unless they're frightened."

Without warning, Joseph slumped down in front of her and put his head in his hands. He murmured something like: "When we find who did it to Miss Izzy—"

It wasn't until the next day that Tina Archer was able to speak even haltingly to the police. Like most of the rest of the Bow Island population, Jemima Shore was informed of the fact almost immediately. Claudette, manageress of her hotel, a sympathetic if loquacious character, just happened to have a niece who was a nurse. But that was the way information always spread about the island—no need for newspapers or radio, this private telegraph was far more efficient.

Jemima had spent the intervening twenty-four hours swimming rather aimlessly, sunbathing, and making little tours of the island in her Mini. She was wondering at what point she should inform Megalith Television of the brutal way in which her projected program had been terminated and make arrangements to return to London. After a bit, the investigative instinct, that inveterate curiosity which would not be stilled, came to the fore. She found she was speculating all the time about Miss Izzy's death. A robber? A robber who had also tried to kill Tina Archer? Or a robber who had merely been surprised by her presence in the house? What connection, if any, had all this with Miss Izzy's will?

The will again. But that was one thing Jemima didn't have to speculate about for very long. For Claudette, the manageress, also just happened to be married to the brother of Hazel, Miss Izzy's cook. In this way, Jemima was apprised—along with the rest of Bow Island, no doubt—that Miss Izzy had indeed signed a new will down in Bowtown on the morning of her death, that Eddie Thompson, the solicitor, had begged her not to do it, that Miss Izzy *had* done it, that Miss Izzy had still looked after Hazel all right, as she had promised (and Henry who had worked for her even longer), and that some jewelry would go to a cousin in England, "seeing as Miss Izzy's mother's jewels were in an English bank anyway since long back." But for the rest, well, there would be no National Bo'lander Museum now, that was for sure. Everything else—that fine old Archer Plantation House, Miss Izzy's fortune, reputedly enormous but who knew for sure?— would go to Tina Archer.

If she recovered, of course. But the latest cautious bulletin from Claudette via the niece-who-was-a-nurse, confirmed by a few other loquacious people on the island, was that Tina Archer *was* recovering. The police had already been able to interview her. In a few days she would be able to leave the hospital. And she was determined to attend Miss Izzy's funeral, which would be held, naturally enough, in that little English-looking church with its incongruous tropical vegetation overlooking the sunny grave. For Miss Izzy had long ago made clear her own determination to be buried in the Archer Tomb along with Governor Sir Valentine and "his only wife, Isabella."

"As the last of the Archers. But she still had to get permission since it's a national monument. And of course the government couldn't do enough for her. So they gave it. Then. Ironic, isn't it?" The speaker making absolutely no attempt to conceal her disgust was Coralie Harrison. "And now we learn that she wasn't the last of the Archers, not officially, and we shall have the so-called Miss Tina Archer as chief mourner. And while the Bo'lander government desperately looks for ways to get round the will and grab the house for their precious museum, nobody quite had the bad taste to go ahead and say no—no burial in the

Archer Tomb for naughty old Miss Izzy. Since she hasn't, after all, left the people of Bow Island a penny."

"It should be an interesting occasion," Jemima murmured. She was sitting with Coralie Harrison under the conical thatched roof of the hotel's beach bar. This was where she first danced, then sat out with Joseph Archer on the night of the new moon—the night Miss Izzy had been killed. Now the sea sparkled under the sun as though there were crystals scattered on its surface. Today there were no waves at all and the happy water-skiers crossed and recrossed the wide bay with its palm-fringed shore. Enormous brown pelicans perched on some stakes which indicated where rocks lay. Every now and then, one would take off like an unwieldy airplane and fly slowly and inquisitively over the heads of the swimmers. It was a tranquil, even an idyllic scene, but somewhere in the distant peninsula lay Archer Plantation House, not only shuttered but now, she imagined, also sealed by the police.

Coralie had sauntered up to the bar from the beach. She traversed the few yards with seeming casualness—all Bo'landers frequently exercised their right to promenade along the sands unchecked (as in most Caribbean islands, no one owned any portion of the beach in Bow Island, even outside the most stately mansion like Archer Plantation House, except the people). Jemima, however, was in no doubt that this was a planned visit. She had not forgotten that first meeting, and Coralie's tentative approach to her, interrupted by Greg's peremptory cry.

It was the day after the inquest on Miss Izzy's death. Her body had been released by the police and the funeral would soon follow. Jemima admitted to herself that she was interested enough in the whole Archer family, and its various branches, to want to attend it, quite apart from the tenderness she felt for the old lady herself, based on that brief meeting. To Megalith Television, in a telex from Bowtown, she had spoken merely of tying up a few loose ends resulting from the cancellation of her program.

There had been an open verdict at the inquest. Tina Archer's evidence in a sworn statement had not really contributed much that wasn't known or suspected already. She had been asleep upstairs in one of the many fairly derelict bedrooms kept ostensibly ready for guests. The bedroom chosen for her by Miss Izzy had not faced onto the sea. The chintz curtains in this back room, bearing some dated rosy pattern from a remote era, weren't quite so bleached and tattered since they had been protected from the sun and salt.

Miss Izzy had gone to bed in good spirits, reassured by the fact that Tina Archer was going to spend the night. She had drunk several more rum punches and had offered to have Henry fetch some of her father's celebrated champagne from the cellar. As a matter of fact, Miss Izzy often made this offer after a few draughts of punch, but Tina reminded her that Henry was away and the subject was dropped.

In her statement, Tina said she had no clue as to what might have awakened the old lady and induced her to descend the stairs—it was right out of character in her own opinion. Isabella Archer was a lady of independent mind but notoriously frightened of the dark, hence Tina's presence at the house in the first place. As to her own recollection of the attack, Tina had so far managed to dredge very few of the details from her memory—the blow to the back of the head had temporarily or permanently expunged all the immediate circumstances from her consciousness. She had a vague idea that there had been a bright light, but even that was rather confused and might be part of the blow she had suffered. Basically, she could remember nothing between going to bed in the tattered, rose-patterned four-poster and waking up in hospital.

Coralie's lip trembled. She bowed her head and sipped at her long drink through a straw—she and Jemima were drinking some exotic mixture of fruit juice, alcohol-free, invented by Matthew, the barman. There was a wonderful soft breeze coming in from the sea and Coralie was dressed in a loose flowered cotton dress, but she looked hot and angry. "Tina schemed for everything all her life and now she's got it. That's what I wanted to warn you about that morning in the churchyard—don't trust Tina Archer, I wanted to say. Now it's too late, she's got it all. When she was married to Greg, I tried to like her, Jemima, honestly I did. Little Tina, so cute and so clever, but always trouble—"

"Joseph Archer feels rather the same way about her, I gather," Jemima said. Was it her imagination or did Coralie's face soften slightly at the sound of Joseph's name?

"Does he? I'm glad. He fancied her, too, once upon a time. She is quite pretty." Their eyes met. "Well, not all that pretty, but if you like the type—" Jemima and Coralie both laughed. The fact was that Coralie Harrison was quite appealing, if you liked *her* type, but Tina Archer was ravishing by any standards.

"Greg absolutely loathes her now, of course," Coralie continued firmly, "especially since he heard the news about the will. When we met you that morning up at the church he'd just been told. Hence, well, I'm sorry, but he was very rude, wasn't he?"

"More hostile than rude." But Jemima had begun to work out the timing. "You mean your brother knew about the will *before* Miss Izzy was killed?" she exclaimed.

"Oh, yes. Someone from Eddie Thompson's office told Greg—Daisy Marlow, maybe, he takes her out. Of course, we all knew it was on the cards, except we hoped Joseph had argued Miss Izzy out of it. And he *would* have argued her out of it given time. That museum is everything to Joseph."

"Your brother and Miss Izzy—that wasn't an easy relationship, I gather."

Jemima thought she was using her gentlest and most persuasive interviewer's voice, but Coralie countered with something like defiance: "You sound like the police!"

"Why, have they—?"

"Well, of course they have!" Coralie answered the question before Jemima had completed it. "Everyone knows that Greg absolutely hated Miss Izzy—blamed her for breaking up his marriage, for taking little Tina and giving her ideas!"

"Wasn't it rather the other way around—Tina delving into the family records for the museum and then my program? You *said* she was a schemer."

"Oh, I *know* she was a schemer! But did Greg? He did not. Not then. He was besotted with her at the time, so he had to blame the old lady. They had a frightful row—very publicly. He went round to the house one night, went in by the sea, shouted at her. Hazel and Henry heard, so then everyone knew. That was when Tina told him she was going to get a divorce and throw in her lot with Miss Izzy for the future. I'm afraid my brother is rather an extreme person—his temper is certainly extreme. He made threats—"

"But the police don't think—" Jemima stopped. It was clear what she meant.

Coralie swung her legs off the bar stool. Jemima handed her the huge straw bag with the archer logo on it and she slung it over her shoulder in proper Bo'lander fashion.

"How pretty," Jemima commented politely.

"I sell them at the hotel on the North Point. For a living." The remark sounded pointed. "No," Coralie went on rapidly before Jemima could say anything more on that subject, "of course the police don't *think*, as you put it. Greg might have assaulted Tina— but Greg kill Miss Izzy when he knew perfectly well that by so doing he was handing his ex-wife a fortune? No way. Not even the Bo'lander police would believe that."

That night Jemima Shore found Joseph Archer again on the beach under the stars. But the moon had waxed since their first encounter. Now it was beginning to cast a silver pathway on the waters of the night. Nor was this meeting unplanned as that first one had been. Joseph had sent her a message that he would be free and they had agreed to meet down by the bar.

"What do you say I'll take you on a night drive round our island, Jemima?"

"No. Let's be proper Bo'landers and walk along the sands." Jemima wanted to be alone with him, not driving past the rows of lighted tourist hotels, listening to the eternal beat of the steel bands. She felt reckless enough not to care how Joseph himself would interpret this change of plan.

They walked for some time along the edge of the sea, in silence except for the gentle lap of the waves. After a while, Jemima took off her sandals and splashed through the warm receding waters, and a little while after that Joseph took her hand and led her back onto the sand. The waves grew conspicuously rougher as they rounded the point of the first wide bay. They stood for a moment together, Joseph and Jemima, he with his arm companionably round her waist.

"Jemima, even without that new moon, I'm going to wish—" Then Joseph stiffened. He dropped the encircling arm, grabbed her shoulder, and swung her around. "Jesus, oh sweet Jesus, do you see that?"

The force of his gesture made Jemima wince. For a moment she was distracted by the flickering moonlit swathe on the dark surface of the water. There were multitudinous white—silver—horses out beyond the land where high waves were breaking over an outcrop of rocks. She thought Joseph was pointing out to sea. Then she saw the lights.

"The Archer house!" she cried. "I thought it was shut up!" It seemed that all the lights of the house were streaming out across the promontory on which it lay. Such was the illumination that you might have supposed some great ball was in progress, a thousand candles lit as in the days of Governor Archer. More somberly, Jemima realized that was how the plantation house must have looked on the night of Miss Izzy's death. Tina Archer and others had borne witness to the old lady's insistence on never leaving her house in darkness. The night her murderer had come in from the sea, this is how the house must have looked to him.

"Come on!" said Joseph. The moment of lightness—or loving,

perhaps?—had utterly vanished. He sounded both grim and determined.

"To the police?"

"No, to the house. I need to know what's happening there."

As they half ran along the sands, Joseph said, "This house should have been *ours*."

Ours: the people of Bow Island.

His restlessness on the subject of the museum struck Jemima anew since her conversation with Coralie Harrison. What would a man—or a woman, for that matter—do for an inheritance? And there was more than one kind of inheritance. Wasn't a national heritage as important to some people as a personal inheritance to others? Joseph Archer was above all a patriotic Bo'lander. And he had not known of the change of will on the morning after Miss Izzy's death. She herself had evidence of that. Might a man like Joseph Archer, a man who had already risen in his own world by sheer determination, decide to take the law into his own hands in order to secure the museum for his people while there was still time?

But to kill the old lady who had befriended him as a boy? Batter her to death? As he strode along, so tall in the moonlight, Joseph was suddenly a complete and thus menacing enigma to Jemima.

They had reached the promontory, had scrambled up the rocks, and had got as far as the first terrace when all the lights in the house went out. It was as though a switch had been thrown. Only the cold eerie glow of the moon over the sea behind them remained to illuminate the bushes, now wildly overgrown, and the sagging balustrades.

But Joseph strode on, helping Jemima up the flights of stone steps, some of them deeply cracked and uneven. In the darkness, Jemima could just see that the windows of the drawing room were still open. There had to be someone in there behind the ragged red-brocade curtains which had been stained by Miss Izzy's blood.

Joseph, holding Jemima's hand, pulled her through the center window.

There was a short cry like a suppressed scream and then a low sound, as if someone was laughing at them there in the dark. An instant later, all the lights were snapped on at once.

Tina was standing at the door, her hand at the switch. She wore a white bandage on her head like a turban—and she wasn't laughing, she was sobbing.

"Oh, it's you, Jo-seph and Je-mi-ma Shore." For the first time, Jemima was aware of the sing-song Bo'lander note in Tina's voice. "I was so fright-ened."

"Are you all right, Tina?" asked Jemima hastily, to cover the fact that she had been quite severely frightened herself. The atmosphere of angry tension between the two other people in the room, so different in looks yet both of them, as it happened, called Archer, was almost palpable. She felt she was in honor bound to try to relieve it. "Are you all alone?"

"The police said I could come." Tina ignored the question. "They have finished with everything here. And besides—" her terrified sobs had vanished, there was something deliberately provocative about her as she moved toward them "why ever not?" To neither of them did she need to elaborate. The words "since it's all mine" hung in the air.

Joseph spoke for the first time since they had entered the room. "I want to look at the house," he said harshly.

"Jo-seph Archer, you get out of here. Back where you came from, back to your off-ice and that's not a great fine house." Then she addressed Jemima placatingly, in something more like her usual sweet manner. "I'm sorry, but, you see, we've not been friends since way back. And, besides, you gave me such a shock."

Joseph swung on his heel. "I'll see you at the funeral, Miss Archer." He managed to make the words sound extraordinarily threatening.

*

That night it seemed to Jemima Shore that she hardly slept, although the threads of broken, half remembered dreams disturbed her and indicated that she must actually have fallen into some kind of doze in the hour before dawn. The light was still gray when she looked out of her shutters. The tops of the tall palms were bending—there was quite a wind.

Back on her bed, Jemima tried to recall just what she had been dreaming. There had been some pattern to it: she knew there had. She wished rather angrily that light would suddenly break through into her sleepy mind as the sun was shortly due to break through the eastern fringe of palms on the hotel estate. No gentle, slow-developing, rosy-fingered dawn for the Caribbean: one brilliant low ray was a herald of what was to come, and then, almost immediately, hot relentless sunshine for the rest of the day. She needed that kind of instant clarity herself.

Hostility. That was part of it all—the nature of hostility. The hostility, for example, between Joseph and Tina Archer the night before, so virulent and public—with herself as the public—that it might almost have been managed for effect.

Then the management of things: Tina Archer, always managing, always a schemer (as Coralie Harrison had said—and Joseph Archer, too). That brought her to the other couple in this odd, four-pointed drama: the Harrisons, brother and sister, or rather *half* brother and sister (a point made by Tina to correct Miss Izzy).

More hostility: Greg, who had once loved Tina and now loathed her. Joseph, who had once also perhaps loved Tina. Coralie, who had once perhaps—very much perhaps, this one—loved Joseph and certainly loathed Tina. Cute and clever little Tina, the Archer Tomb, the carved figures of Sir Valentine and his wife, the inscription. Jemima was beginning to float back into sleep, as the four figures, all Bo'landers, all sharing some kind of common past, began to dance to a calypso whose wording, too, was confused:

*

"This is your graveyard in the sun
Where my people have toiled since time begun—"

An extraordinarily loud noise on the corrugated metal roof above her head recalled her, trembling, to her senses. The racket had been quite immense, almost as if there had been an explosion or at least a missile fired at the chalet. The thought of a missile made her realize that it had in fact been a missile: it must have been a coconut which had fallen in such a startling fashion on the corrugated roof. Guests were officially warned by the hotel against sitting too close under the palm trees, whose innocuous-looking fronds could suddenly dispense their heavily lethal nuts. COCONUTS CAN CAUSE INJURY ran the printed notice.

That kind of blow on my head would certainly have caused injury, thought Jemima, if not death.

Injury, if not death. And the Archer Tomb: my only wife.

At that moment, straight on cue, the sun struck low through the bending fronds to the east and onto her shutters. And Jemima realized not only why it had been done but how it had been done. Who of them all had been responsible for consigning Miss Izzy Archer to the graveyard in the sun.

The scene by the Archer Tomb a few hours later had that same strange mixture of English tradition and Bo'lander exoticism which had intrigued Jemima on her first visit. Only this time she had a deeper, sadder purpose than sheer tourism. Traditional English hymns were sung at the service, but outside a steel band was playing at Miss Izzy's request. As one who had been born on the island, she had asked for a proper Bo'lander funeral.

The Bo'landers, attending in large numbers, were by and large dressed with that extreme formality—dark suits, white shirts, ties, dark dresses, dark straw hats, even white gloves—which Jemima had observed in churchgoers of a Sunday and in the Bo'lander children, all of them neatly uniformed on their way to school. No Bow Island T-shirts were to be seen, although many of the highly colored intricate and lavish wreaths were in the bow shape of the island's logo. The size of the crowd was undoubtedly a genuine mark of respect. Whatever the disappointments of the will to their government, to the Bo'landers Miss Izzy Archer had been part of their heritage.

Tina Archer wore a black scarf wound round her head which almost totally concealed her bandage. Joseph Archer, standing far apart from her and not looking in her direction, looked both elegant and formal in his office clothes, a respectable member of the government. The Harrisons stood together, Coralie with her head bowed. Greg's defiant aspect, head lifted proudly, was clearly intended to give the lie to any suggestions that he had not been on the best of terms with the woman whose body was now being lowered into the family tomb.

As the coffin—so small and thus so touching—vanished from view, there was a sigh from the mourners. They began to sing again: a hymn, but with the steel band gently echoing the tune in the background.

Jemima moved discreetly in the crowd and stood by the side of the tall man.

"You'll never be able to trust her," she said in a low voice. "She's managed you before, she'll manage you again. It'll be someone else who will be doing the dirty work next time. On you. You'll never be able to trust her, will you? Once a murderess, always a murderess. You may wish one day you'd finished her off."

The tall man looked down at her. Then he looked across at Tina Archer with one quick savagely doubting look. Tina Archer Harrison, his only wife.

"Why, you—" For a moment, Jemima thought Greg Harrison would actually strike her down there at the graveside, as he had struck down old Miss Izzy and—if only on pretense—struck down Tina herself.

"Greg darling." It was Coralie Harrison's pathetic, protesting murmur. "What are you saying to him?" she demanded of Jemima in a voice as low as Jemima's own. But the explanations—for Coralie and the rest of Bow Island—of the conspiracy of Tina Archer and Greg Harrison were only just beginning.

The rest was up to the police, who with their patient work of investigation would first amplify, then press, finally concluding the case. And in the course of the investigations; the conspirators would fall apart, this time for real. To the police fell the unpleasant duty of disentangling the new lies of Tina Archer, who now swore that her memory had just returned, that it had been Greg who had half killed her that night, that she had had absolutely nothing to do with it. And Greg Harrison denounced Tina in return, this time with genuine ferocity. "It was her plan, her plan all along. She managed everything. I should never have listened to her!"

Before she left Bow Island, Jemima went to say goodbye to Joseph Archer in his Bowtown office. There were many casualties of the Archer tragedy beyond Miss Izzy herself. Poor Coralie was one: she had been convinced that her brother, for all his notorious temper, would never batter down Miss Izzy to benefit his ex-wife. Like the rest of Bow Island, she was unaware of the deep plot by which Greg and Tina would publicly display their hostility, advertise their divorce, and all along plan to kill Miss Izzy once the new will was signed. Greg, ostentatiously hating his ex-wife, would not be suspected, and Tina, suffering such obvious injuries, could only arouse sympathy.

Another small casualty, much less important, was the romance which just might have developed between Joseph Archer and Jemima Shore. Now, in his steamingly hot office with its perpetually moving fan, they talked of quite other things than the new moon and new wishes.

"You must be happy you'll get your museum," said Jemima.

"But that's not at all the way I wanted it to happen," he replied. Then Joseph added: "But you know, Jemima, there has been justice done. And in her heart of hearts Miss Izzy did really want us to have this National Museum. I'd have talked her round to good sense again if she had lived."

"That's why they acted when they did. They didn't dare wait given Miss Izzy's respect for you," suggested Jemima. She stopped but her curiosity got the better of her. There was one thing she had to know before she left. "The Archer Tomb and all that. Tina being descended from Sir Valentine's lawful second marriage. Is that true?"

"Yes, it's true. Maybe. But it's not important to most of us here. You know something, Jemima? I, too, am descended from that well-known second marriage. Maybe. And a few others maybe. Lucie Anne had two children, don't forget, and Bo'landers have large families. It was important to Tina Archer, not to me. That's not what I want. That's all past. Miss Izzy was the last of the Archers, so far as I'm concerned. Let her lie in her tomb."

"What *do* you want for yourself? Or for Bow Island, if you prefer."

Joseph smiled and there was a glimmer there of the handsome fisherman who had welcomed her to Bow Island, the cheerful dancing partner. "Come back to Bow Island one day, Jemima. Make another program about us, our history and all that, and I'll tell you then."

"I might just do that," said Jemima Shore.

The Case of the Pietro Andromache

SARA PARETSKY

Sara Paretsky (b. 1947) was born in Ames, Iowa, and educated at the University of Kansas, Lawrence, and the University of Chicago, where she attained a Ph.D. in history. After working as a business writer and direct-mail marketing manager for an insurance company, she turned to fiction writing with *Indemnity Only,* which introduced Chicago private detective V. I. Warshawski, one of two renowned female p.i.'s to debut in the watershed year of 1982. As fictional sleuths go, Warshawski is a specialist. Paretsky writes in *St. James Guide to Crime & Mystery Writers* (4th edition, 1996), "Like Lew Archer before her she looks beyond the surface to 'the far side of the dollar,' the side where power and money corrupt people into making criminal decisions to preserve their positions. All of her cases explore some aspect of white-collar crime where senior executives preserve position or bolster their companies without regard for the ordinary people who work for them." These guidelines provide scope for plenty of variety of background from medicine to politics to religion to law enforcement.

Along with producing her own fiction, Paretsky has done much to advance the cause of women crime writers generally, editing anthologies of their work and founding the highly successful Sisters in Crime.

Paretsky's name is invariably bracketed with that of Sue Grafton, who also introduced her female private eye Kinsey Millhone in 1982. The two writers are about equally capable, though V. I. Warshawski is a bit harder-edged and certainly more overtly political in her point of view than Millhone. One result of the continual comparison, Paretsky admits in a recent interview in *Crime Time* magazine, is that she is no longer able to read Grafton, whom she previously enjoyed, for fear of being unconsciously influenced.

Like many of the female private eyes, V. I. Warshawski has an extended family of friends that recur from book to book. Two of them, Lotty Herschel and Max Loewenthal, appear in "The Case of the Pietro Andromache," a story that has achieved the status of a modern classic judging by the number of times it has been anthologized.

Y ou only agreed to hire him because of his art collection. Of that I'm sure." Lotty Herschel bent down to adjust her stockings. "And don't waggle your eyebrows like that—it makes you look like an adolescent Groucho Marx."

Max Loewenthal obediently smoothed his eyebrows, but said, "It's your legs, Lotty; they remind me of my youth. You know, going into the Underground to wait out the air raids, looking at the ladies as they came down the escalators. The updraft always made their skirts billow."

"You're making this up, Max. I was in those Underground stations, too, and as I remember the ladies were always bundled in coats and children."

Max moved from the doorway to put an arm around Lotty. "That's what keeps us together, *Lottchen:* I am a romantic and you are severely logical. And you know we didn't hire Caudwell because of his collection. Although I admit I am eager to see it. The board wants Beth Israel to develop a transplant program. It's the only way we're going to become competitive—"

"Don't deliver your publicity lecture to me," Lotty snapped. Her thick brows contracted to a solid black line across her forehead. "As far as I am concerned he is a cretin with the hands of a Caliban and the personality of Attila."

Lotty's intense commitment to medicine left no room for the mundane consideration of money. But as the hospital's executive director, Max was on the spot with the trustees to see that Beth Israel ran at a profit. Or at least at a smaller loss than they'd achieved in recent years. They'd brought Caudwell in part to attract more paying patients—and to help screen out some of the indigent who made up 12 percent of Beth Israel's patient load. Max wondered how long the hospital could afford to support personalities as divergent as Lotty and Caudwell with their radically differing approaches to medicine.

He dropped his arm and smiled quizzically at her. "Why do you hate him so much, Lotty?"

"*I* am the person who has to justify the patients I admit to this—this troglodyte. Do you realize he tried to keep Mrs. Mendes from the operating room when he learned she had AIDS? He wasn't even being asked to sully his hands with her blood and he didn't want me performing surgery on her."

Lotty drew back from Max and pointed an accusing finger at him. "You may tell the board that if he keeps questioning my judgment they will find themselves looking for a new perinatologist. I am serious about this. You listen this afternoon, Max, you hear whether or not he calls me 'our little baby doctor.' I am fifty-eight years old, I am a Fellow of the Royal College of Surgeons besides having enough credentials in this country to support a whole hospital, and to him I am a 'little baby doctor.'"

Max sat on the daybed and pulled Lotty down next to him. "No, no, *Lottchen*: don't fight. Listen to me. Why haven't you told me any of this before?"

"Don't be an idiot, Max: you are the director of the hospital. I cannot use our special relationship to deal with problems I have with the staff. I said my piece when Caudwell came for his final interview. A number of the other physicians were not happy with his attitude. If you remember, we asked the board to bring him in as a cardiac surgeon first and promote him to chief of staff after a year if everyone was satisfied with his performance."

"We talked about doing it that way," Max admitted. "But he wouldn't take the appointment except as chief of staff. That was the only way we could offer him the kind of money he could get at one of the university hospitals or Humana. And, Lotty, even if you don't like his personality you must agree that he is a first-class surgeon."

"I agree to nothing." Red lights danced in her black eyes. "If he patronizes me, a fellow physician, how do you imagine he treats his patients? You cannot practice medicine if—"

"Now it's my turn to ask to be spared a lecture," Max interrupted gently. "But if you feel so strongly about him, maybe you shouldn't go to his party this afternoon."

"And admit that he can beat me? Never."

"Very well then." Max got up and placed a heavily brocaded wool shawl over Lotty's shoulders. "But you must promise me to behave. This is a social function we are going to, remember, not a gladiator contest. Caudwell is trying to repay some hospitality this afternoon, not to belittle you."

"I don't need lessons in conduct from you: Herschels were attending the emperors of Austria while the Loewenthals were operating vegetable stalls on the Ring," Lotty said haughtily.

Max laughed and kissed her hand. "Then remember these regal Herschels and act like them, *Eure Hoheit.*"

II

Caudwell had bought an apartment sight unseen when he moved to Chicago. A divorced man whose children are in college only has to consult with his own taste in these matters. He asked the Beth Israel board to recommend a realtor, sent his requirements to them—twenties construction, near Lake Michigan, good security, modern plumbing—and dropped seven hundred and fifty thousand for an eight-room condo facing the lake at Scott Street.

Since Beth Israel paid handsomely for the privilege of retaining Dr. Charlotte Herschel as their perinatologist, nothing required her to live in a five-room walkup on the fringes of Uptown, so it was a bit unfair of her to mutter "Parvenu" to Max when they walked into the lobby.

Max relinquished Lotty gratefully when they got off the elevator. Being her lover was like trying to be companion to a Bengal tiger: you never knew when she'd take a lethal swipe at you. Still, if Caudwell were insulting her—and her judgment—maybe he needed to talk to the surgeon, explain how important Lotty was for the reputation of Beth Israel.

Caudwell's two children were making the obligatory Christmas visit. They were a boy and a girl, Deborah and Steve, within a year of the same age, both tall, both blond and poised, with a hearty sophistication born of a childhood spent on expensive ski slopes. Max wasn't very big, and as one took his coat and the other performed brisk introductions, he felt himself shrinking, losing in self-assurance. He accepted a glass of special *cuvée* from one of them—was it the boy or the girl, he wondered in confusion—and fled into the melee.

He landed next to one of Beth Israel's trustees, a woman in her sixties wearing a gray textured mini-dress whose black stripes were constructed of feathers. She commented brightly on Caudwell's art collection, but Max sensed an undercurrent of hostility: wealthy trustees don't like the idea that they can't out-buy the staff.

While he was frowning and nodding at appropriate intervals, it dawned on Max that Caudwell did know how much the hospital needed Lotty. Heart surgeons do not have the world's smallest egos: when you ask them to name the world's three leading practitioners, they never can remember the names of the other two. Lotty was at the top of her field, and she, too, was used to having things her way. Since her confrontational style was reminiscent more of the Battle of the Bulge than the Imperial Court of Vienna, he didn't blame Caudwell for trying to force her out of the hospital.

Max moved away from Martha Gildersleeve to admire some of the paintings and figurines she'd been discussing. A collector himself of Chinese porcelains, Max raised his eyebrows and mouthed a soundless whistle at the pieces on display. A small Watteau and a Charles Demuth watercolor were worth as much as Beth Israel paid Caudwell in a year. No wonder Mrs. Gildersleeve had been so annoyed.

"Impressive, isn't it."

Max turned to see Arthur Gioia looming over him. Max was shorter than most of the Beth Israel staff, shorter than everyone but Lotty. But Gioia, a tall muscular immunologist, loomed over everyone. He had gone to the University of Arkansas on a football scholarship and had even spent a season playing tackle for Houston before starting medical school. It had been twenty years since he last lifted weights, but his neck still looked like a redwood stump.

Gioia had led the opposition to Caudwell's appointment. Max had suspected at the time that it was due more to a medicine man's not wanting a surgeon as his nominal boss than from any other cause, but after Lotty's outburst he wasn't so sure. He was debating whether to ask the doctor how he felt about Caudwell now that he'd worked with him for six months when their host surged over to him and shook his hand.

"Sorry I didn't see you when you came in, Loewenthal. You like the Watteau? It's one of my favorite pieces. Although a collector shouldn't play favorites any more than a father should, eh, sweetheart?" The last remark was addressed to the daughter, Deborah, who had come up behind Caudwell and slipped an arm around him.

Caudwell looked more like a Victorian seadog than a surgeon. He had a round red face under a shock of yellow-white hair, a hearty Santa Claus laugh, and a bluff, direct manner. Despite Lotty's vituperations, he was immensely popular with his patients. In the short time he'd been at the hospital, referrals to cardiac surgery had increased 15 percent.

His daughter squeezed his shoulder playfully. "I know you don't play favorites with us, Dad, but you're lying to Mr. Loewenthal about your collection; come on, you know you are."

She turned to Max. "He has a piece he's so proud of he doesn't like to show it to people—he doesn't want them to see he's got vulnerable spots. But it's Christmas, Dad, relax, let people see how you feel for a change."

Max looked curiously at the surgeon, but Caudwell seemed pleased with his daughter's familiarity. The son came up and added his own jocular cajoling.

"This really is Dad's pride and joy. He stole it from Uncle Griffen when Grandfather died and kept Mother from getting her mitts on it when they split up."

Caudwell did bark out a mild reproof at that. "You'll be giving my colleagues the wrong impression of me, Steve. I didn't steal it from Grif. Told him he could have the rest of the estate if he'd leave me the Watteau and the Pietro."

"Of course he could've bought ten estates with what those two would fetch," Steve muttered to his sister over Max's head.

Deborah relinquished her father's arm to lean over Max and whisper back, "Mom, too."

Max moved away from the alarming pair to say to Caudwell, "A Pietro? You mean Pietro d'Alessandro? You have a model, or an actual sculpture?"

Caudwell gave his staccato admiral's laugh. "The real McCoy, Loewenthal. The real McCoy. An alabaster."

"An alabaster?" Max raised his eyebrows. "Surely not. I thought Pietro worked only in bronze and marble."

"Yes, yes," chuckled Caudwell, rubbing his hands together. "Everyone thinks so, but there were a few alabasters in private collections. I've had this one authenticated by experts. Come take a look at it—it'll knock your breath away. You come, too, Gioia," he barked at the immunologist. "You're Italian, you'll like to see what your ancestors were up to."

"A Pietro alabaster?" Lotty's clipped tones made Max start—he hadn't noticed her joining the little group. "I would very much like to see this piece."

"Then come along, Dr. Herschel, come along." Caudwell led them to a small hallway, exchanging genial greetings with his guests as he passed, pointing out a John William Hill miniature they might not have seen, picking up a few other people who for various reasons wanted to see his prize.

"By the way, Gioia, I was in New York last week, you know. Met an old friend of yours from Arkansas. Paul Nierman."

"Nierman?" Gioia seemed to be at a loss. "I'm afraid I don't remember him."

"Well, he remembered you pretty well. Sent you all kinds of messages—you'll have to stop by my office on Monday and get the full strength."

Caudwell opened a door on the right side of the hall and let them into his study. It was an octagonal room carved out of the corner of the building. Windows on two sides looked out on Lake Michigan. Caudwell drew salmon drapes as he talked about the room, why he'd chosen it for his study even though the view kept his mind from his work.

Lotty ignored him and walked over to a small pedestal which stood alone against the paneling on one of the far walls. Max followed her and gazed respectfully at the statue. He had seldom seen so fine a piece outside a museum. About a foot high, it depicted a woman in classical draperies hovering in anguish over the dead body of a soldier lying at her feet. The grief in her beautiful face was so poignant that it reminded you of every sorrow you had ever faced.

"Who is it meant to be?" Max asked curiously.

"Andromache," Lotty said in a strangled voice. "Andromache mourning Hector."

Max stared at Lotty, astonished equally by her emotion and her knowledge of the figure—Lotty was totally uninterested in sculpture.

Caudwell couldn't restrain the smug smile of a collector with a true coup. "Beautiful, isn't it? How do you know the subject?"

"I should know it." Lotty's voice was husky with emotion. "My grandmother had such a Pietro. An alabaster given her great-grandfather by the Emperor Joseph the Second himself for his help in consolidating imperial ties with Poland."

She swept the statue from its stand, ignoring a gasp from Max, and turned it over. "You can see the traces of the imperial stamp here still. And the chip on Hector's foot which made the Hapsburg wish to give the statue away to begin with. How came you to have this piece? Where did you find it?"

The small group that had joined Caudwell stood silent by the entrance, shocked at Lotty's outburst. Gioia looked more horrified than any of them, but he found Lotty overwhelming at the best of times—an elephant confronted by a hostile mouse.

"I think you're allowing your emotions to carry you away, doctor." Caudwell kept his tone light, making Lotty seem more gauche by contrast. "I inherited this piece from my father, who bought it—legitimately—in Europe. Perhaps from your—grandmother, was it? But I suspect you are confused about something you may have seen in a museum as a child."

Deborah gave a high-pitched laugh and called loudly to her brother, "Dad may have stolen it from Uncle Grif, but it looks like Grandfather snatched it to begin with anyway."

"Be quiet, Deborah," Caudwell barked sternly.

His daughter paid no attention to him. She laughed again and joined her brother to look at the imperial seal on the bottom of the statue.

Lotty brushed them aside. "*I* am confused about the seal of Joseph the Second?" she hissed at Caudwell. "Or about this chip on Hector's foot? You can see the line where some Philistine filled in the missing piece. Some person who thought his touch would add value to Pietro's work. Was that you, *doctor*? Or your father?"

"Lotty." Max was at her side, gently prizing the statue from her shaking hands to restore it to its pedestal. "Lotty, this is not the place or the manner to discuss such things."

Angry tears sparkled in her black eyes. "Are you doubting my word?"

Max shook his head. "I'm not doubting you. But I'm also not supporting you. I'm asking you not to talk about this matter in this way at this gathering."

"But, Max: either this man or his father is a thief!"

Caudwell strolled up to Lotty and pinched her chin. "You're

working too hard, Dr. Herschel. You have too many things on your mind these days. I think the board would like to see you take a leave of absence for a few weeks, go someplace warm, get yourself relaxed. When you're this tense, you're no good to your patients. What do you say, Loewenthal?"

Max didn't say any of the things he wanted to—that Lotty was insufferable and Caudwell intolerable. He believed Lotty, believed that the piece had been her grandmother's. She knew too much about it, for one thing. And for another, a lot of artworks belonging to European Jews were now in museums or private collections around the world. It was only the most god-awful coincidence that the Pietro had ended up with Caudwell's father.

But how dare she raise the matter in the way most likely to alienate everyone present? He couldn't possibly support her in such a situation. And at the same time, Caudwell's pinching her chin in that condescending way made him wish he were not chained to a courtesy that would have kept him from knocking the surgeon out even if he'd been ten years younger and ten inches taller.

"I don't think this is the place or the time to discuss such matters," he reiterated as calmly as he could. "Why don't we all cool down and get back together on Monday, eh?"

Lotty gasped involuntarily, then swept from the room without a backward glance.

Max refused to follow her. He was too angry with her to want to see her again that afternoon. When he got ready to leave the party an hour or so later, after a long conversation with Caudwell that taxed his sophisticated urbanity to the utmost, he heard with relief that Lotty was long gone. The tale of her outburst had of course spread through the gathering at something faster than the speed of sound; he wasn't up to defending her to Martha Gildersleeve who demanded an explanation of him in the elevator going down.

He went home for a solitary evening in his house in Evanston.

Normally such time brought him pleasure, listening to music in his study, lying on the couch with his shoes off, reading history, letting the sounds of the lake wash over him.

Tonight, though, he could get no relief. Fury with Lotty merged into images of horror, the memories of his own disintegrated family, his search through Europe for his mother. He had never found anyone who was quite certain what became of her, although several people told him definitely of his father's suicide. And stamped over these wisps in his brain was the disturbing picture of Caudwell's children, their blond heads leaning backward at identical angles as they gleefully chanted, "Grandpa was a thief, Grandpa was a thief," while Caudwell edged his visitors out of the study.

By morning he would somehow have to reconstruct himself enough to face Lotty, to respond to the inevitable flood of calls from outraged trustees. He'd have to figure out a way of soothing Caudwell's vanity, bruised more by his children's behavior than anything Lotty had said. And find a way to keep both important doctors at Beth Israel.

Max rubbed his gray hair. Every week this job brought him less joy and more pain. Maybe it was time to step down, to let the board bring in a young MBA who would turn Beth Israel's finances around. Lotty would resign then, and it would be an end to the tension between her and Caudwell.

Max fell asleep on the couch. He awoke around five muttering, "By morning, by morning." His joints were stiff from cold, his eyes sticky with tears he'd shed unknowingly in his sleep.

But in the morning things changed. When Max got to his office he found the place buzzing, not with news of Lotty's outburst but word that Caudwell had missed his early morning surgery. Work came almost completely to a halt at noon when his children phoned to say they'd found the surgeon strangled in his own study and the Pietro Andromache missing. And on Tuesday, the police arrested Dr. Charlotte Herschel for Lewis Caudwell's murder.

III

Lotty would not speak to anyone. She was out on two hundred fifty thousand dollars' bail, the money raised by Max, but she had gone directly to her apartment on Sheffield after two nights in County Jail without stopping to thank him. She would not talk to reporters, she remained silent during all conversations with the police, and she emphatically refused to speak to the private investigator who had been her close friend for many years.

Max, too, stayed behind an impregnable shield of silence. While Lotty went on indefinite leave, turning her practice over to a series of colleagues, Max continued to go to the hospital every day. But he, too, would not speak to reporters: he wouldn't even say, "No comment." He talked to the police only after they threatened to lock him up as a material witness, and then every word had to be pried from him as if his mouth were stone and speech Excalibur. For three days V. I. Warshawski left messages which he refused to return.

On Friday, when no word came from the detective, when no reporter popped up from a nearby urinal in the men's room to try to trick him into speaking, when no more calls came from the state's attorney, Max felt a measure of relaxation as he drove home. As soon as the trial was over he would resign, retire to London. If he could only keep going until then, everything would be—not all right, but bearable.

He used the remote release for the garage door and eased his car into the small space. As he got out he realized bitterly he'd been too optimistic in thinking he'd be left in peace. He hadn't seen the woman sitting on the stoop leading from the garage to the kitchen when he drove in, only as she uncoiled herself at his approach.

"I'm glad you're home—I was beginning to freeze out here."

"How did you get into the garage, Victoria?"

The detective grinned in a way he usually found engaging.

Now it seemed merely predatory. "Trade secret, Max. I know you don't want to see me, but I need to talk to you."

He unlocked the door into the kitchen. "Why not just let yourself into the house if you were cold? If your scruples permit you into the garage, why not into the house?"

She bit her lip in momentary discomfort but said lightly, "I couldn't manage my picklocks with my fingers this cold."

The detective followed him into the house. Another tall monster; five foot eight, athletic, light on her feet behind him. Maybe American mothers put growth hormones or steroids in their children's cornflakes. He'd have to ask Lotty. His mind winced at the thought.

"I've talked to the police, of course," the light alto continued behind him steadily, oblivious to his studied rudeness as he poured himself a cognac, took his shoes off, found his waiting slippers, and padded down the hall to the front door for his mail.

"I understand why they arrested Lotty—Caudwell had been doped with a whole bunch of Xanax and then strangled while he was sleeping it off. And, of course, she was back at the building Sunday night. She won't say why, but one of the tenants ID'd her as the woman who showed up around ten at the service entrance when he was walking his dog. She won't say if she talked to Caudwell, if he let her in, if he was still alive."

Max tried to ignore her clear voice. When that proved impossible he tried to read a journal which had come in the mail.

"And those kids, they're marvelous, aren't they? Like something out of the *Fabulous Furry Freak Brothers*. They won't talk to me but they gave a long interview to Murray Ryerson over at the *Star*.

"After Caudwell's guests left, they went to a flick at the Chestnut Street Station, had a pizza afterwards, then took themselves dancing on Division Street. So they strolled in around two in the morning—confirmed by the doorman—saw the light on in the old man's study. But they were feeling no pain and he kind of overreacted—their term—if they were buzzed, so they didn't stop in to say goodnight. It was only when they got up around noon and went in that they found him."

V. I. had followed Max from the front hallway to the door of his study as she spoke. He stood there irresolutely, not wanting his private place desecrated with her insistent, air-hammer speech, and finally went on down the hall to a little-used living room. He sat stiffly on one of the brocade armchairs and looked at her remotely when she perched on the edge of its companion.

"The weak piece in the police story is the statue," V.I. continued.

She eyed the Persian rug doubtfully and unzipped her boots, sticking them on the bricks in front of the fireplace.

"Everyone who was at the party agrees that Lotty was beside herself. By now the story has spread so far that people who weren't even in the apartment when she looked at the statue swear they heard her threaten to kill him. But if that's the case, what happened to the statue?"

Max gave a slight shrug to indicate total lack of interest in the topic.

V.I. plowed on doggedly. "Now some people think she might have given it to a friend or a relation to keep for her until her name is cleared at the trial. And these people think it would be either her Uncle Stefan here in Chicago, her brother Hugo in Montreal, or you. So the Mounties searched Hugo's place and are keeping an eye on his mail. And the Chicago cops are doing the same for Stefan. And I presume someone got a warrant and went through here, right?"

Max said nothing, but he felt his heart beating faster. Police in his house, searching his things? But wouldn't they have to get his permission to enter? Or would they? Victoria would know, but he couldn't bring himself to ask. She waited for a few minutes, but when he still wouldn't speak, she plunged on. He could see it was becoming an effort for her to talk, but he wouldn't help her.

"But I don't agree with those people. Because I know that Lotty is innocent. And that's why I'm here. Not like a bird of prey, as you think, using your misery for carrion. But to get you to help me. Lotty won't speak to me, and if she's that miserable I won't force her to. But surely, Max, you won't sit idly by and let her be railroaded for something she never did."

Max looked away from her. He was surprised to find himself holding the brandy snifter and set it carefully on a table beside him.

"Max!" Her voice was shot with astonishment. "I don't believe this. You actually think she killed Caudwell."

Max flushed a little, but she'd finally stung him into a response. "And you are God who sees all and knows she didn't?"

"I see more than you do," V.I. snapped. "I haven't known Lotty as long as you have, but I know when she's telling the truth."

"So you are God." Max bowed in heavy irony. "You see beyond the facts to the innermost souls of men and women."

He expected another outburst from the young woman, but she gazed at him steadily without speaking. It was a look sympathetic enough that Max felt embarrassed by his sarcasm and burst out with what was on his mind.

"What else am I to think? She hasn't said anything, but there's no doubt that she returned to his apartment Sunday night."

It was V.I.'s turn for sarcasm. "With a little vial of Xanax that she somehow induced him to swallow? And then strangled him for good measure? Come on, Max, you know Lotty: honesty follows her around like a cloud. If she'd killed Caudwell, she'd say something like, 'Yes, I bashed the little vermin's brains in." Instead she's not speaking at all."

Suddenly the detective's eyes widened with incredulity. "Of course. She thinks you killed Caudwell. You're doing the only thing you can to protect her—standing mute. And she's doing the same thing. What an admirable pair of archaic knights."

"No!" Max said sharply. "It's not possible. How could she think such a thing? She carried on so wildly that it was embarrassing to be near her. I didn't want to see her or talk to her. That's why I've felt so terrible. If only I hadn't been so obstinate, if only I'd called her Sunday night. How could she think

I would kill someone on her behalf when I was so angry with her?"

"Why else isn't she saying anything to anyone?" Warshawski demanded.

"Shame, maybe," Max offered. "You didn't see her on Sunday. I did. That is why I think she killed him, not because some man let her into the building."

His brown eyes screwed shut at the memory. "I have seen Lotty in the grip of anger many times, more than is pleasant to remember, really. But never, never have I seen her in this kind of—uncontrolled rage. You could not talk to her. It was impossible."

The detective didn't respond to that. Instead she said, "Tell me about the statue. I heard a couple of garbled versions from people who were at the party, but I haven't found anyone yet who was in the study when Caudwell showed it to you. Was it really her grandmother's, do you think? And how did Caudwell come to have it if it was?"

Max nodded mournfully. "Oh, yes. It was really her family's, I'm convinced of that. She could not have known in advance about the details, the flaw in the foot, the imperial seal on the bottom. As to how Caudwell got it, I did a little looking into that myself yesterday. His father was with the Army of Occupation in Germany after the war. A surgeon attached to Patton's staff. Men in such positions had endless opportunities to acquire artworks after the war."

V.I. shook her head questioningly.

"You must know something of this, Victoria. Well, maybe not. You know the Nazis helped themselves liberally to artwork belonging to Jews everywhere they occupied Europe. And not just to Jews—they plundered Eastern Europe on a grand scale. The best guess is that they stole sixteen million pieces—statues, paintings, altarpieces, tapestries, rare books. The list is beyond reckoning, really."

The detective gave a little gasp. "Sixteen million! You're joking."

"Not a joke, Victoria. I wish it were so, but it is not. The U.S. Army of Occupation took charge of as many works of art as they found in the occupied territories. In theory, they were to find the rightful owners and try to restore them. But in practice few pieces were ever traced, and many of them ended up on the black market.

"You only had to say that such-and-such a piece was worth less than five thousand dollars and you were allowed to buy it. For an officer on Patton's staff, the opportunities for fabulous acquisitions would have been endless. Caudwell said he had the statue authenticated, but of course he never bothered to establish its provenance. Anyway, how could he?" Max finished bitterly. "Lotty's family had a deed of gift from the Emperor, but that would have disappeared long since with the dispersal of their possessions."

"And you really think Lotty would have killed a man just to get this statue back? She couldn't have expected to keep it. Not if she'd killed someone to get it, I mean."

"You are so practical, Victoria. You are too analytical, sometimes, to understand why people do what they do. That was not just a statue. True, it is a priceless artwork, but you know Lotty, you know she places no value on such possessions. No, it meant her family to her, her past, her history, everything that the war destroyed forever for her. You must not imagine that because she never discusses such matters that they do not weigh on her."

V.I. flushed at Max's accusation. "You should be glad I'm analytical. It convinces me that Lotty is innocent. And whether you believe it or not I'm going to prove it."

Max lifted his shoulders slightly in a manner wholly European. "We each support Lotty according to our lights. I saw that she met her bail, and I will see that she gets expert counsel. I am not convinced that she needs you making her innermost secrets public."

V.I.'s gray eyes turned dark with a sudden flash of temper. "You're dead wrong about Lotty. I'm sure the memory of the war is a pain that can never be cured, but Lotty lives in the present, she works in hope for the future. The past does not obsess and consume her as, perhaps, it does you."

Max said nothing. His wide mouth turned in on itself in a narrow line. The detective laid a contrite hand on his arm.

"I'm sorry, Max. That was below the belt."

He forced the ghost of a smile to his mouth.

"Perhaps it's true. Perhaps it's why I love these ancient things so much. I wish I could believe you about Lotty. Ask me what you want to know. If you promise to leave as soon as I've answered and not to bother me again, I'll answer your questions."

IV

Max put in a dutiful appearance at the Michigan Avenue Presbyterian Church Monday afternoon for Lewis Caudwell's funeral. The surgeon's former wife came, flanked by her children and her husband's brother Griffen. Even after three decades in America Max found himself puzzled sometimes by the natives' behavior: since she and Caudwell were divorced, why had his ex-wife draped herself in black? She was even wearing a veiled hat reminiscent of Queen Victoria.

The children behaved in a moderately subdued fashion, but the girl was wearing a white dress shot with black lightning forks which looked as though it belonged at a disco or a resort. Maybe it was her only dress or her only dress with black in it, Max thought, trying hard to look charitably at the blond Amazon— after all, she had been suddenly and horribly orphaned.

Even though she was a stranger both in the city and the church, Deborah had hired one of the church parlors and managed to find someone to cater coffee and light snacks. Max joined the rest of the congregation there after the service.

He felt absurd as he offered condolences to the divorced widow: did she really miss the dead man so much? She accepted his conventional words with graceful melancholy and leaned slightly against her son and daughter. They hovered near her with what struck Max as a stagey solicitude. Seen next to her daughter, Mrs. Caudwell looked so frail and undernourished that she seemed like a ghost. Or maybe it was just that her children had a hearty vitality that even a funeral couldn't quench.

Caudwell's brother Griffen stayed as close to the widow as the children would permit. The man was totally unlike the hearty seadog surgeon. Max thought if he'd met the brothers standing side by side he would never have guessed their relationship. He was tall, like his niece and nephew, but without their robustness. Caudwell had had a thick mop of yellow-white hair; Griffen's domed head was covered by thin wisps of gray. He seemed weak and nervous, and lacked Caudwell's outgoing *bonhomie;* no wonder the surgeon had found it easy to decide the disposition of their father's estate in his favor. Max wondered what Griffen had gotten in return.

Mrs. Caudwell's vague, disoriented conversation indicated that she was heavily sedated. That, too, seemed strange. A man she hadn't lived with for four years and she was so upset at his death that she could only manage the funeral on drugs? Or maybe it was the shame of coming as the divorced woman, not a true widow? But then why come at all?

To his annoyance, Max found himself wishing he could ask Victoria about it. She would have some cynical explanation— Caudwell's death meant the end of the widow's alimony and she knew she wasn't remembered in the will. Or she was having an affair with Griffen and was afraid she would betray herself without tranquilizers. Although it was hard to imagine the uncertain Griffen as the object of a strong passion.

Since he had told Victoria he didn't want to see her again when she left on Friday, it was ridiculous of him to wonder what she was doing, whether she was really uncovering evidence that would clear Lotty. Ever since she had gone he had felt a little flicker of hope in the bottom of his stomach. He kept trying to drown it, but it wouldn't quite go away.

Lotty, of course, had not come to the funeral, but most of the rest of the Beth Israel staff was there, along with the trustees. Arthur Gioia, his giant body filling the small parlor to the bursting point, tried finding a tactful balance between honesty and courtesy with the bereaved family; he made heavy going of it.

A sable-clad Martha Gildersleeve appeared under Gioia's elbow, rather like a furry football he might have tucked away. She made bright, unseemly remarks to the bereaved family about the disposal of Caudwell's artworks.

"Of course, the famous statue is gone now. What a pity. You could have endowed a chair in his honor with the proceeds from that piece alone." She gave a high, meaningless laugh.

Max sneaked a glance at his watch, wondering how long he had to stay before leaving would be rude. His sixth sense, the perfect courtesy that governed his movements, had deserted him, leaving him subject to the gaucheries of ordinary mortals. He never peeked at his watch at functions, and at any prior funeral he would have deftly pried Martha Gildersleeve from her victim. Instead he stood helplessly by while she tortured Mrs. Caudwell and other bystanders alike.

He glanced at his watch again. Only two minutes had passed since his last look. No wonder people kept their eyes on their watches at dull meetings: they couldn't believe the clock could move so slowly.

He inched stealthily toward the door, exchanging empty remarks with the staff members and trustees he passed. Nothing negative was said about Lotty to his face, but the comments cut off at his approach added to his misery.

He was almost at the exit when two newcomers appeared. Most of the group looked at them with indifferent curiosity, but Max suddenly felt an absurd stir of elation. Victoria, looking sane and modern in a navy suit, stood in the doorway, eyebrows raised, scanning the room. At her elbow was a police sergeant Max had met with her a few times. The man was in charge of Caudwell's death, too: it was that unpleasant association that kept the name momentarily from his mind.

V.I. finally spotted Max near the door and gave him a discreet sign. He went to her at once.

"I think we may have the goods," she murmured. "Can you get everyone to go? We just want the family, Mrs. Gildersleeve, and Gioia."

"*You* may have the goods," the police sergeant growled. "I'm here unofficially and reluctantly."

"But you're here." Warshawski grinned, and Max wondered how he ever could have found the look predatory. His own spirits rose enormously at her smile. "You know in your heart of hearts that arresting Lotty was just plain dumb. And now I'm going to make you look real smart. In public, too."

Max felt his suave sophistication return with the rush of elation that an ailing diva must have when she finds her voice again. A touch here, a word there, and the guests disappeared like the hosts of Sennacherib. Meanwhile he solicitously escorted first Martha Gildersleeve, then Mrs. Caudwell to adjacent armchairs, got the brother to fetch coffee for Mrs. Gildersleeve, the daughter and son to look after the widow.

With Gioia he could be a bit more ruthless, telling him to wait because the police had something important to ask him. When the last guest had melted away, the immunologist stood nervously at the window rattling his change over and over in his pockets. The jingling suddenly was the only sound in the room. Gioia reddened and clasped his hands behind his back.

Victoria came into the room beaming like a governess with a delightful treat in store for her charges. She introduced herself to the Caudwells.

"You know Sergeant McGonnigal, I'm sure, after this last week. I'm a private investigator. Since I don't have any legal standing, you're not required to answer any questions I have. So I'm not going to ask you any questions. I'm just going to treat you to a travelogue. I wish I had slides, but you'll have to imagine the visuals while the audio track moves along."

"A private investigator!" Steve's mouth formed an exaggerated "O"; his eyes widened in amazement. "Just like Bogie."

He was speaking, as usual, to his sister. She gave her high-pitched laugh and said, "We'll win first prize in the 'How I Spent My Winter Vacation' contests. Our daddy was murdered. Zowie. Then his most valuable possession was snatched. Powie. But he'd already stolen it from the Jewish doctor who killed him. Yowie! And then a PI to wrap it all up. Yowie! Zowie! Powie!"

"Deborah, please," Mrs. Caudwell sighed. "I know you're excited, sweetie, but not right now, okay?"

"Your children keep you young, don't they, ma'am?" Victoria said. "How can you ever feel old when your kids stay seven all their lives?"

"Oo, ow, she bites, Debbie, watch out, she bites!" Steve cried.

McGonnigal made an involuntary movement, as though restraining himself from smacking the younger man. "Ms. Warshawski is right: you are under no obligation to answer any of her questions. But you're bright people, all of you: you know I wouldn't be here if the police didn't take her ideas very seriously. So let's have a little quiet and listen to what she's got on her mind."

Victoria seated herself in an armchair near Mrs. Caudwell's. McGonnigal moved to the door and leaned against the jamb. Deborah and Steve whispered and poked each other until one or both of them shrieked. They then made their faces prim and sat with their hands folded on their laps, looking like bright-eyed choirboys.

Griffen hovered near Mrs. Caudwell. "You know you don't have to say anything, Vivian. In fact, I think you should return to your hotel and lie down. The stress of the funeral—then these strangers—"

Mrs. Caudwell's lips curled bravely below the bottom of her veil. "It's all right, Grif; if I managed to survive everything else, one more thing isn't going to do me in."

"Great." Victoria accepted a cup of coffee from Max. "Let me just sketch events for you as I saw them last week. Like everyone else in Chicago, I read about Dr. Caudwell's murder and saw it on television. Since I know a number of people attached to Beth Israel, I may have paid more attention to it than the average viewer, but I didn't get personally involved until Dr. Herschel's arrest on Tuesday."

She swallowed some coffee and set the cup on the table next to her with a small snap. "I have known Dr. Herschel for close to twenty years. It is inconceivable that she would commit such a murder, as those who know her well should have realized at once. I don't fault the police, but others should have known better: she is hot-tempered. I'm not saying killing is beyond her—I don't think it's beyond any of us. She might have taken the statue and smashed Dr. Caudwell's head in in the heat of rage. But it beggars belief to think she went home, brooded over her injustices, packed a dose of prescription tranquilizer, and headed back to the Gold Coast with murder in mind."

Max felt his cheeks turn hot at her words. He started to interject a protest but bit it back.

"Dr. Herschel refused to make a statement all week, but this afternoon, when I got back from my travels, she finally agreed to talk to me. Sergeant McGonnigal was with me. She doesn't deny that she returned to Dr. Caudwell's apartment at ten that night—she went back to apologize for her outburst and to try to plead with him to return the statue. He didn't answer when the doorman called up, and on impulse she went around to the back of the building, got in through the service entrance, and waited for some time outside the apartment door. When he neither answered the doorbell nor returned home himself, she finally went away around eleven o'clock. The children, of course, were having a night on the town."

"*She* says," Gioia interjected.

"Agreed." V.I. smiled. "I make no bones about being a partisan: I accept her version. The more so because the only reason she didn't give it a week ago was that she herself was protecting an old friend. She thought perhaps this friend had bestirred himself on her behalf and killed Caudwell to avenge deadly insults against her. It was only when I persuaded her that these suspicions were as unmerited as—well, as accusations against herself—that she agreed to talk."

Max bit his lip and busied himself with getting more coffee for the three women. Victoria waited for him to finish before continuing.

"When I finally got a detailed account of what took place at Caudwell's party, I heard about three people with an axe to grind. One always has to ask, what axe and how big a grindstone? That's what I've spent the weekend finding out. You might as well know that I've been to Little Rock and to Havelock, North Carolina."

Gioia began jingling the coins in his pockets again. Mrs. Caudwell said softly, "Grif, I am feeling a little faint. Perhaps—"

"Home you go, Mom," Steve cried out with alacrity.

"In a few minutes, Mrs. Caudwell," the sergeant said from the doorway. "Get her feet up, Warshawski."

For a moment Max was afraid that Steve or Deborah was going to attack Victoria, but McGonnigal moved over to the widow's chair and the children sat down again. Little drops of sweat dotted Griffen's balding head; Gioia's face had a greenish sheen, foliage on top of his redwood neck.

"The thing that leapt out at me," Victoria continued calmly, as though there had been no interruption, "was Caudwell's remark to Dr. Gioia. The doctor was clearly upset, but people were so focused on Lotty and the statue that they didn't pay any attention to that.

"So I went to Little Rock, Arkansas, on Saturday and found the Paul Nierman whose name Caudwell had mentioned to Gioia. Nierman lived in the same fraternity with Gioia when they were undergraduates together twenty-five years ago. And he took Dr. Gioia's anatomy and physiology exams his junior year when Gioia was in danger of academic probation, so he could stay on the football team.

"Well, that seemed unpleasant, perhaps disgraceful. But there's no question that Gioia did all his own work in medical school, passed his boards, and so on. So I didn't think the board would demand a resignation for this youthful indiscretion. The question was whether Gioia thought they would, and if he would have killed to prevent Caudwell making it public."

She paused, and the immunologist blurted out, "No. No. But Caudwell—Caudwell knew I'd opposed his appointment. He and I—our approaches to medicine were very opposite. And as soon as he said Nierman's name to me, I knew he'd found out and that he'd torment me with it forever. I—I went back to his place Sunday night to have it out with him. I was more determined than Dr. Herschel and got into his unit through the kitchen entrance; he hadn't locked that.

"I went to his study, but he was already dead. I couldn't believe it. It absolutely terrified me. I could see he'd been strangled and—well, it's no secret that I'm strong enough to have done it. I wasn't thinking straight. I just got clean away from there—I think I've been running ever since."

"You!" McGonnigal shouted. "How come we haven't heard about this before?"

"Because you insisted on focusing on Dr. Herschel," V.I. said nastily. "I knew he'd been there because the doorman told me. He would have told you if you'd asked."

"This is terrible," Mrs. Gildersleeve interjected. "I am going to talk to the board tomorrow and demand the resignations of Dr. Gioia and Dr. Herschel."

"Do," Victoria agreed cordially. "Tell them the reason you got to stay for this was because Murray Ryerson at the *Herald-Star* was doing a little checking for me here in Chicago. He found out that part of the reason you were so jealous of Caudwell's collection is that you're living terribly in debt. I won't humiliate you in public by telling people what your money has gone to, but you've had to sell your husband's art collection and you have a third mortgage on your house. A valuable statue with no documented history would have taken care of everything."

Martha Gildersleeve shrank inside her sable. "You don't know anything about this."

"Well, Murray talked to Pablo and Eduardo . . . Yes, I won't say anything else. So anyway, Murray checked whether either Gioia or Mrs. Gildersleeve had the statue. They didn't, so—"

"You've been in my house?" Mrs. Gildersleeve shrieked.

V.I. shook her head. "Not me. Murray Ryerson." She looked apologetically at the sergeant. "I knew you'd never get a warrant for me, since you'd made an arrest. And you'd never have got it in time, anyway."

She looked at her coffee cup, saw it was empty and put it down again. Max took it from the table and filled it for her a third time. His fingertips were itching with nervous irritation; some of the coffee landed on his trouser leg.

"I talked to Murray Saturday night from Little Rock. When he came up empty here, I headed for North Carolina. To Havelock, where Griffen and Lewis Caudwell grew up and where Mrs. Caudwell still lives. And I saw the house where Griffen lives, and talked to the doctor who treats Mrs. Caudwell, and—"

"You really are a pooper snooper, aren't you," Steve said.

"Pooper snooper, pooper snooper," Deborah chanted. "Don't get enough thrills of your own so you have to live on other people's shit."

"Yeah, the neighbors talked to me about you two." Victoria looked at them with contemptuous indulgence. "You've been a two-person wolfpack terrifying most of the people around you since you were three. But the folks in Havelock admired how you always stuck up for your mother. You thought your father got her addicted to tranquilizers and then left her high and dry. So you brought her newest version with you and were all set—you just needed to decide when to give it to him. Dr. Herschel's outburst over the statue played right into your hands. You figured your father had stolen it from your uncle to begin with—why not send it back to him and let Dr. Herschel take the rap?"

"It wasn't like that," Steve said, red spots burning in his cheeks.

"What was it like, son?" McGonnigal had moved next to him.

"Don't talk to them—they're tricking you," Deborah shrieked. "The pooper snooper and her gopher gooper."

"She—Mommy used to love us before Daddy made her take all this shit. Then she went away. We just wanted him to see what it was like. We started putting Xanax in his coffee and stuff; we wanted to see if he'd fuck up during surgery, let his life get ruined. But then he was sleeping there in the study after his stupid-ass party, and we thought we'd just let him sleep through his morning surgery. Sleep forever, you know, it was so easy, we used his own Harvard necktie. I was so fucking sick of hearing 'Early to bed, early to rise' from him. And we sent the statue to Uncle Grif. I suppose the pooper snooper found it there. He can sell it and Mother can be all right again."

"Grandpa stole it from Jews and Daddy stole it from Grif, so we thought it worked out perfectly if we stole it from Daddy," Deborah cried. She leaned her blond head next to her brother's and shrieked with laughter.

V

Max watched the line of Lotty's legs change as she stood on tiptoe to reach a brandy snifter. Short, muscular from years of racing at top speed from one point to the next, maybe they weren't as svelte as the long legs of modern American girls, but he preferred them. He waited until her feet were securely planted before making his announcement.

"The board is bringing in Justin Hardwick for a final interview for chief of staff."

"Max!" She whirled, the Bengal fire sparkling in her eyes. "I know this Hardwick and he is another like Caudwell, looking for cost-cutting and no poverty patients. I won't have it."

"We've got you and Gioia and a dozen others bringing in so many non-paying patients that we're not going to survive another five years at the present rate. I figure it's a balancing act. We need someone who can see that the hospital survives so that you and Art can practice medicine the way you want to. And when he knows what happened to his predecessor, he'll be very careful not to stir up our resident tigress."

"Max!" She was hurt and astonished at the same time. "Oh. You're joking, I see. It's not very funny to me, you know."

"My dear, we've got to learn to laugh about it: it's the only way we'll ever be able to forgive ourselves for our terrible misjudgments." He stepped over to put an arm around her. "Now where is this remarkable surprise you promised to show me."

She shot him a look of pure mischief, Lotty on a dare as he first remembered meeting her at eighteen. His hold on her tightened and he followed her to her bedroom. In a glass case in the corner, complete with a humidity-control system, stood the Pietro Andromache.

Max looked at the beautiful, anguished face. I understand your sorrows, she seemed to say to him. I understand your grief for your mother, your family, your history, but it's all right to let go of them, to live in the present and hope for the future. It's not a betrayal.

Tears pricked his eyelids, but he demanded, "How did you get this? I was told the police had it under lock and key until lawyers decided on the disposition of Caudwell's estate."

"Victoria," Lotty said shortly. "I told her the problem and she got it for me. On the condition that I not ask how she did it. And Max, you know—*damned* well that it was not Caudwell's to dispose of."

It was Lotty's. Of course it was. Max wondered briefly how Joseph the Second had come by it to begin with. For that matter, what had Lotty's great-great-grandfather done to earn it from the emperor? Max looked into Lotty's tiger eyes and kept such reflections to himself. Instead he inspected Hector's foot where the filler had been carefully scraped away to reveal the old chip.

Afraid All the Time

NANCY PICKARD

Nancy Pickard (b. 1945) was born in Kansas City, Missouri, and graduated from the Missouri School of Journalism, working for a time as a reporter and editor before turning to freelance writing. Her series about Jenny Cain, foundation director in a small Massachusetts town, began with the paperback original *Generous Death* (1984), graduating to hardcovers with the third book, *No Body* (1986). Noted from the beginning for their humor, the Cain books gradually became darker in tone and theme. In an interview with Robert J. Randisi (*Speaking of Murder*, volume II [1999]) Pickard explained why, using Susan Wittig Albert's term, the " 'mega-book' mystery series . . . a new phenomenon . . . which denotes a series of novels which are essentially one long book. Each novel in the series is rather like a 'chapter' in the mega-book." Unlike the series of writers like Agatha Christie and John D. MacDonald, in which sleuths like Miss Marple and Travis McGee remained essentially the same from book to book, "in a 'mega-book' series, you can't count on each succeeding book being much like the last . . . It's more like real life (if . . . any amateur sleuth is *ever* like real life), because the protagonist goes through some real changes . . . As we (and they) mature, things do come to assume a more substantial feeling, a weightiness, which can sometimes carry a feeling of greater 'darkness.'"

In several books, beginning with *The 27 Ingredient Chile Con Carne Murders* (1993), Pickard has adopted the character of Eugenia Potter, introduced in three novels by the late Virginia Rich. Pickard's continuation of the series, the first based on Rich's notes and the later ones on original stories, brought a sense of pace, craft, and complexity missing from some cooking mysteries and others in the domestic cozy category. Asked by Randisi if she is a cozy writer, Pickard has fun with the concept: "I don't know what I am. What's between cozy and uncomfortable? If mystery writers were chairs, I wouldn't quite be a chintz rocking chair, but I wouldn't be a hard metal folding chair, either. A nice, swivel office chair, perhaps?"

Some novelists who also write short stories produce the same sort of narrative, only shorter. Others use the short form to experiment with theme, mood, and subject matter. Pickard is in the latter category, as shown in her collection *Storm Warnings* (1999) and in the Edgar-nominated story, "Afraid All the Time."

R ibbon a darkness over me . . ."
Mel Brown, known variously as Pell Mell and Animel, sang the line from the song over and over behind his windshield as he flew from Missouri into Kansas on his old black Harley-Davidson motorcycle.

Already he loved Kansas, because the highway that stretched ahead of him was like a long, flat, dark ribbon unfurled just for him.

"Ribbon a darkness over me . . ."

He flew full throttle into the late-afternoon glare, feeling as if he were soaring gloriously drunk and blind on a skyway to the sun. The clouds in the far distance looked as if they'd rain on him that night, but he didn't worry about it. He'd heard there were plenty of empty farm and ranch houses in Kansas where a man could break in to spend the night. He'd heard it was like having your choice of free motels, Kansas was.

"Ribbon a darkness over me . . ."

Three hundred miles to the southwest, Jane Baum suddenly stopped what she was doing. The fear had hit her again. It was always like that, striking out of nowhere, like a fist against her heart. She dropped her clothes basket from rigid fingers and stood as if paralyzed between the two clotheslines in her yard. There was a wet sheet to her right, another to her left. For once the wind had died down, so the sheets hung as still and silent as walls. She felt enclosed in a narrow, white, sterile room of cloth, and she never wanted to leave it.

Outside of it was danger.

On either side of the sheets lay the endless prairie where she felt like a tiny mouse exposed to every hawk in the sky.

It took all of her willpower not to scream.

She hugged her own shoulders to comfort herself. It didn't help. Within a few moments she was crying, and then shaking with a palsy of terror.

She hadn't known she'd be so afraid.

Eight months ago, before she had moved to this small farm she'd inherited, she'd had romantic notions about it, even about such simple things as hanging clothes on a line. It would feel so good, she had imagined, they would smell so sweet. Instead, everything had seemed strange and threatening to her from the start, and it was getting worse. Now she didn't even feel protected by the house. She was beginning to feel as if it were fear instead of electricity that lighted her lamps, filled her tub, lined her cupboards and covered her bed—fear that she breathed instead of air.

She hated the prairie and everything on it.

The city had never frightened her, not like this. She knew the city, she understood it, she knew how to avoid its dangers and its troubles. In the city there were buildings everywhere, and now she knew why—it was to blot out the true and terrible openness of the earth on which all of the inhabitants were so horribly exposed to danger.

The wind picked up again. It snapped the wet sheets against her body. Janie bolted from her shelter. Like a mouse with a hawk circling overhead, she ran as if she were being chased. She ran out of her yard and then down the highway, racing frantically, breathlessly, for the only other shelter she knew.

When she reached Cissy Johnson's house, she pulled open the side door and flung herself inside without knocking.

"Cissy?"

"I'm afraid all the time."

"I know, Janie."

Cissy Johnson stood at her kitchen sink peeling potatoes for supper while she listened to Jane Baum's familiar litany of fear. By now Cissy knew it by heart. Janie was afraid of: being alone in the house she had inherited from her aunt; the dark; the crack of every twig in the night; the storm cellar; the horses that might step on her, the cows that might trample her, the chickens that might peck her, the cats that might bite her and have rabies, the coyotes that might attack her; the truckers who drove by her house, especially the flirtatious ones who blasted their horns when they saw her in the yard; tornadoes, blizzards, electrical storms; having to drive so far just to get simple groceries and supplies.

At first Cissy had been sympathetic, offering daily doses of coffee and friendship. But it was getting harder all the time to remain patient with somebody who just burst in without knocking and who complained all the time about imaginary problems and who—

"You've lived here all your life," Jane said, as if the woman at the sink had not previously been alert to that fact. She sat in a kitchen chair, huddled into herself like a child being punished. Her voice was low, as if she were talking more to herself than to Cissy. "You're used to it, that's why it doesn't scare you."

"Um," Cissy murmured, as if agreeing. But out of her neighbor's sight, she dug viciously at the eye of a potato. She rooted it out—leaving behind a white, moist, open wound in the vegetable—and flicked the dead black skin into the sink where the water running from the faucet washed it down the garbage disposal. She thought how she'd like to pour Janie's fears down the sink and similarly grind them up and flush them away. She held the potato to her nose and sniffed, inhaling the crisp, raw smell.

Then, as if having gained strength from that private moment, she glanced back over her shoulder at her visitor. Cissy was ashamed of the fact that the mere sight of Jane Baum now repelled her. It was a crime, really, how she'd let herself go. She wished

Jane would comb her hair, pull her shoulders back, paint a little coloring onto her pale face, and wear something else besides that ugly denim jumper that came nearly to her heels. Cissy's husband, Bob, called Janie "Cissy's pup," and he called that jumper the "pup tent." He was right, Cissy thought, the woman did look like an insecure, spotty adolescent, and not at all like a grown woman of thirty-five-plus years. And darn it, Janie did follow Cissy around like a neurotic nuisance of a puppy.

"Is Bob coming back tonight?" Jane asked.

Now she's even invading my mind, Cissy thought. She whacked resentfully at the potato, peeling off more meat than skin. "Tomorrow." Her shoulders tensed.

"Then can I sleep over here tonight?"

"No." Cissy surprised herself with the shortness of her reply. She could practically feel Janie radiating hurt, and so she tried to make up for it by softening her tone. "I'm sorry, Janie, but I've got too much book work to do, and it's hard to concentrate with people in the house. I've even told the girls they can take their sleeping bags to the barn tonight to give me some peace." The girls were her daughters, Tessie, thirteen, and Mandy, eleven. "They want to spend the night out there 'cause we've got that new little blind calf we're nursing. His mother won't have anything to do with him, poor little thing. Tessie has named him Flopper, because he tries to stand up but he just flops back down. So the girls are bottle-feeding him, and they want to sleep near . . ."

"Oh." It was heavy with reproach.

Cissy stepped away from the sink to turn her oven on to 350°. Her own internal temperature was rising too. God forbid she should talk about her life! God forbid they should ever talk about anything but Janie and all the damned things she was scared of! She could write a book about it: *How Jane Baum Made a Big Mistake by Leaving Kansas City and How Everything About the Country Just Scared Her to Death.*

"Aren't you afraid of anything, Cissy?"

The implied admiration came with a bit of a whine to it—
*any*thing—like a curve on a fastball.

"Yes." Cissy drew out the word reluctantly.

"You *are?* What?"

Cissy turned around at the sink and laughed self-consciously.
"It's so silly . . . I'm even afraid to mention it."

"Tell me! I'll feel better if I know you're afraid of things, too."

There! Cissy thought. *Even my fears come down to how they
affect you!*

"All right." She sighed. "Well, I'm afraid of something
happening to Bobby, a wreck on the highway or something, or
to one of the girls, or my folks, things like that. I mean, like
leukemia or a heart attack or something I can't control. I'm always
afraid there won't be enough money and we might have to sell
this place. We're so happy here. I guess I'm afraid that might
change." She paused, dismayed by the sudden realization that she
had not been as happy since Jane Baum moved in down the road.
For a moment, she stared accusingly at her neighbor. "I guess
that's what I'm afraid of." Then Cissy added deliberately, "But I
don't think about it all the time."

"I think about mine all the time," Jane whispered.

"I know."

"I hate it here!"

"You could move back."

Janie stared reproachfully. "You know I can't afford that!"

Cissy closed her eyes momentarily. The idea of having to listen
to *this* for who knew how many years . . .

"I love coming over here," Janie said wistfully, as if reading
Cissy's mind again. "It always makes me feel so much better. This
is the only place I feel safe anymore. I just hate going home to
the big old house all by myself."

I will not *invite you to supper*, Cissy thought.

Janie sighed.

Cissy gazed out the big square window behind Janie. It was
October, her favorite month, when the grass turned as red as the

curly hair on a Hereford's back and the sky turned a steel gray like the highway that ran between their houses. It was as if the whole world blended into itself—the grass into the cattle, the roads into the sky, and she into all of it. There was an electricity in the air, as if something more important than winter were about to happen, as if all the world were one and about to burst apart into something brand-new. Cissy loved the prairie, and it hurt her feelings a little that Janie didn't. How could anyone live in the middle of so much beauty, she puzzled, and be frightened of it?

"We'll never get a better chance." Tess ticked off the rationale for the adventure by holding up the fingers of her right hand, one at a time, an inch from her sister's scared face. "Dad's gone. We're in the barn. Mom'll be asleep. It's a new moon." She ran out of fingers on that hand and lifted her left thumb. "And the dogs know us."

"They'll find out!" Mandy wailed.

"*Who'll* find out?"

"Mom and Daddy will!"

"They won't! Who's gonna tell 'em? The gas-station owner? You think we left a trail of toilet paper he's going to follow from his station to here? And he's gonna call the sheriff and say lock up those Johnson girls, boys, they stole my toilet paper!"

"Yes!"

Together they turned to gaze—one of them with pride and cunning, the other with pride and trepidation—at the small hill of hay that was piled, for no apparent reason, in the shadows of a far corner of the barn. Underneath that pile lay their collection of six rolls of toilet paper—a new one filched from their own linen closet, and five partly used ones (stolen one trip at a time and hidden in their school jackets) from the ladies' bathroom at the gas station in town. Tess's plan was for the two of them to "t.p." their neighbor's house that night, after dark. Tess had lovely visions of how it would look—all ghostly and spooky, with streamers of white hanging down from the tree limbs and waving eerily in the breeze.

"They do it all the time in Kansas City, jerk," Tess proclaimed. "And I'll bet they don't make any big deal crybaby deal out of it." She wanted to be the first one in her class to do it, and she wasn't about to let her little sister chicken out on her. This plan would, Tess was sure, make her famous in at least a four-county area. No grown-up would ever figure out who had done it, but all the kids would know, even if she had to tell them.

"Mom'll kill us!"

"Nobody'll know!"

"It's gonna rain!"

"It's not gonna rain."

"We shouldn't leave Flopper!"

Now they looked, together, at the baby bull calf in one of the stalls. It stared blindly in the direction of their voices, tried to rise, but was too frail to do it.

"Don't be a dope. We leave him all the time."

Mandy sighed.

Tess, who recognized the sound of surrender when she heard it, smiled magnanimously at her sister.

"You can throw the first roll," she offered.

In a truck stop in Emporia, Mel Brown slopped up his supper gravy with the last third of a cloverleaf roll. He had a table by a window. As he ate, he stared with pleasure at his bike outside. If he moved his head just so, the rays from the setting sun flashed off the handle bars. He thought about how the leather seat and grips would feel soft and warm and supple, the way a woman in leather felt, when he got back on. At the thought he got a warm feeling in his crotch, too, and he smiled.

God, he loved living like this.

When he was hungry, he ate. When he was tired, he slept. When he was horny, he found a woman. When he was thirsty, he stopped at a bar.

Right now Mel felt like not paying the entire $5.46 for this lousy chicken-fried steak dinner and coffee. He pulled four dollar bills out of his wallet and a couple of quarters out of his right front pocket and set it all out on the table, with the money sticking out from under the check.

Mel got up and walked past the waitress.

"It's on the table," he told her.

"No cherry pie?" she asked him.

It sounded like a proposition, so he grinned as he said, "Nah." *If you weren't so ugly*, he thought, *I just might stay for dessert.*

"Come again," she said.

You wish, he thought.

If they called him back, he'd say he couldn't read her handwriting. Her fault. No wonder she didn't get a tip. Smiling, he lifted a toothpick off the cashier's counter and used it to salute the man behind the cash register.

"Thanks," the man said.

"You bet."

Outside, Mel stood in the parking lot and stretched, shoving his arms high in the air, letting anybody who was watching get a good look at him. Nothin' to hide. Eat your heart out, baby. Then he strolled over to his bike and kicked the stand up with his heel. He poked around his mouth with the toothpick, spat out a sliver of meat, then flipped the toothpick onto the ground. He climbed back on his bike, letting out a breath of satisfaction when his butt hit the warm leather seat.

Mel accelerated slowly, savoring the surge of power building between his legs.

Jane Baum was in bed by 10:30 that night, exhausted once again by her own fear. Lying there in her late aunt's double bed, she obsessed on the mistake she had made in moving to this dreadful, empty place in the middle of nowhere. She had expected to feel nervous for a while, as any other city dweller might who moved to the country. But she hadn't counted on being actually phobic about it—of being possessed by a fear so strong that it seemed to inhabit every cell of her body until at night, every night, she felt she could die from it. She hadn't known—how could she have known?—she would be one of those people who is terrified by the vastness of the prairie. She had visited the farm only a few times as a child, and from those visits she had remembered only warm and fuzzy things like caterpillars and chicks. She had only dimly remembered how antlike a human being feels on the prairie.

Her aunt's house had been broken into twice during the period between her aunt's death and her own occupancy. That fact cemented her fantasies in a foundation of terrifying reality. When Cissy said, "It's your imagination," Janie retorted, "But it happened twice before! Twice!" She wasn't making it up! There *were* strange, brutal men—that's how she imagined them, they were never caught by the police—who broke in and took whatever they wanted—cans in the cupboard, the radio in the kitchen. It could happen again, Janie thought obsessively as she lay in the bed; it could happen over and over. *To me, to me, to me.*

On the prairie, the darkness seemed absolute to her. There were millions of stars but no streetlights. Coyotes howled, or cattle bawled. Occasionally the big night-riding semis whirred by out front. Their tire and engine sounds seemed to come out of nowhere, build to an intolerable whine and then disappear in an uncanny way. She pictured the drivers as big, rough, intense men hopped up on amphetamines; she worried that one night she would hear truck tires turning into her gravel drive, that an engine would switch off, that a truck door would quietly open and then close, that careful footsteps would slur across her gravel.

Her fear had grown so huge, so bad, that she was even frightened of it. It was like a monstrous balloon that inflated every time she breathed. Every night the fear got worse. The balloon got bigger. It nearly filled the bedroom now.

The upstairs bedroom where she lay was hot because she had the windows pulled down and latched, and the curtains drawn.

She could have cooled it with a fan on the dressing table, but she was afraid the fan's noise might cover the sound of whatever might break into the first floor and climb the stairs to attack her. She lay with a sheet and a blanket pulled up over her arms and shoulders, to just under her chin. She was sweating, as if her fear-frozen body were melting, but it felt warm and almost comfortable to her. She always wore pajamas and thin wool socks to bed because she felt safer when she was completely dressed. She especially felt more secure in pajama pants, which no dirty hand could shove up onto her belly as it could a nightgown.

Lying in bed like a quadriplegic, unmoving, eyes open, Janie reviewed her precautions. Every door was locked, every window was permanently shut and locked, so that she didn't have to check them every night; all the curtains were drawn; the porch lights were off; and her car was locked in the barn so no trucker would think she was home.

Lately she had taken to sleeping with her aunt's loaded pistol on the pillow beside her head.

Cissy crawled into bed just before midnight, tired from hours of accounting. She had been out to the barn to check on her giggling girls and the blind calf. She had talked to her husband when he called from Oklahoma City. Now she was thinking about how she would try to start easing Janie Baum out of their lives.

"I'm sorry, Janie, but I'm awfully busy today. I don't think you ought to come over . . ."

Oh, but there would be that meek, martyred little voice, just like a baby mouse needing somebody to mother it. How would she deny that need? She was already feeling guilty about refusing Janie's request to sleep over.

"Well, I will. I just will do it, that's all. If I could say no to the FHA girls when they were selling fruitcakes, I can start saying no more often to Janie Baum. Anyway, she's never going to get over her fears if I indulge them."

Bob had said as much when she'd complained to him

long-distance. "Cissy, you're not helping her," he'd said. "You're just letting her get worse." And then he'd said something new that had disturbed her. "Anyway, I don't like the girls being around her so much. She's getting too weird, Cissy."

She thought of her daughters—of fearless Tess and dear little Mandy—and of how *safe* and *nice* it was for children in the country . . .

"Besides," Bob had said, "she's *got* to do more of her own chores. We need Tess and Mandy to help out around our place more; we can't be having them always running off to mow her grass and plant her flowers and feed her cows and water her horse and get her eggs, just because she's scared to stick her silly hand under a damned hen . . ."

Counting the chores put Cissy to sleep.

"Tess!" Mandy hissed desperately. "Wait!"

The older girl slowed, to give Mandy time to catch up to her, and then to touch Tess for reassurance. They paused for a moment to catch their breath and to crouch in the shadow of Jane Baum's porch. Tess carried three rolls of toilet paper in a makeshift pouch she'd formed in the belly of her black sweatshirt. ("We gotta wear black, remember!") and Mandy was similarly equipped. Tess decided that now was the right moment to drop her bomb.

"I've been thinking," she whispered.

Mandy was struck cold to her heart by that familiar and dreaded phrase. She moaned quietly. "What?"

"It might rain."

"I told you!"

"So I think we better do it inside."

"*Inside?*"

"Shh! It'll scare her to death, it'll be great! Nobody else'll ever have the guts to do anything as neat as this! We'll do the kitchen, and if we have time, maybe the dining room."

"Ohhh, noooo."

"*She* thinks she's got all the doors and windows locked, but she doesn't!" Tess giggled. She had it all figured out that when Jane Baum came downstairs in the morning, she'd take one look, scream, faint, and then, when she woke up, call everybody in town. The fact that Jane might also call the sheriff had occurred to her, but since Tess didn't have any faith in the ability of adults to figure out anything important, she wasn't worried about getting caught. "When I took in her eggs, I unlocked the down-stairs bathroom window Come on! This'll be great!"

The ribbon of darkness ahead of Mel Brown was no longer straight. It was now bunched into long, steep hills. He hadn't expected hills. Nobody had told him there was any part of Kansas that wasn't flat. So he wasn't making as good time, and the couldn't run full-bore. But then, he wasn't in a hurry, except for the hell of it. And this was more interesting, more dangerous, and he liked the thrill of that. He started edging closer to the centerline every time he roared up a hill, playing a game of highway roulette in which he was the winner as long as what-ever coming from the other direction had its headlights on.

When that got boring, he turned his own headlights off.

Now he roared past cars and trucks like a dark demon.

Mel laughed every time, thinking how surprised they must be, and how frightened. They'd think, *Crazy fool, I could have hit him . . .*

He supposed he wasn't afraid of anything, except maybe going back to prison, and he didn't think they'd send him down on a speeding ticket. Besides, if Kansas was like most states, it was long on roads and short on highway patrolmen . . .

Roaring downhill was even more fun, because of the way his stomach dropped out. He felt like a kid, yelling "Fuuuuck," all the way down the other side. What a goddamned roller coaster of a state this was turning out to be.

The rain still looked miles away.

Mel felt as if he could ride all night. Except that his eyes were gritty, the first sign that he'd better start looking for a likely place to spend the night. He wasn't one to sleep under the stars, not if he could find a ceiling.

Tess directed her sister to stack the rolls of toilet paper underneath the bathroom window on the first floor of Jane Baum's house. The six rolls, all white, stacked three in a row, two high, gave Tess the little bit of height and leverage she needed to push up the glass with her palms. She stuck her fingers under the bottom edge and laboriously attempted to raise the window. It was stiff in its coats of paint.

"Damn!" she exclaimed, and let her arms slump. Beneath her feet, the toilet paper was getting squashed.

She tried again, and this time she showed her strength from lifting calves and tossing hay. With a crack of paint and a thump of wood on wood, the window slid all the way up.

"Shhh!" Mandy held her fists in front of her face and knocked her knuckles against each other in excitement and agitation. Her ears picked up the sound of a roaring engine on the highway, and she was immediately sure it was the sheriff, coming to arrest her and Tess. She tugged frantically at the calf of her sister's right leg.

Tess jerked her leg out of Mandy's grasp and disappeared through the open window.

The crack of the window and the thunder of the approaching motorcycle confused themselves in Jane's sleeping consciousness, so that when she awoke from dreams full of anxiety—her eyes flying open, the rest of her body frozen—she imagined in a confused, hallucinatory kind of way that somebody was both coming to get her and already there in the house.

Jane then did as she had trained herself to do. She had practiced over and over every night, so that her actions would be instinctive. She turned her face to the pistol on the other pillow and placed her thumb on the trigger.

Her fear—of rape, of torture, of kidnapping, of agony, of

death—was a balloon, and she floated horribly in the center of it. There were thumps and other sounds downstairs, and they joined her in the balloon. There was an engine roaring, and then suddenly it was silent, and a slurring of wheels in her gravel drive, and these sounds joined her in her balloon. When she couldn't bear it any longer, she popped the balloon by shooting herself in the forehead.

In the driveway, Mel Brown heard the gun go off.

He slung his leg back onto his motorcycle and roared back out onto the highway. So the place had looked empty. So he'd been wrong. So he'd find someplace else. But holy shit. Get the fuck outta here.

Inside the house, in the bathroom, Tess also heard the shot and, being a ranch child, recognized it instantly for what it was, although she wasn't exactly sure where it had come from. Cussing and sobbing, she clambered over the sink and back out the window, falling onto her head and shoulders on the rolls of toilet paper.

"It's the sheriff!" Mandy was hysterical. "He's shooting at us!"

Tess grabbed her little sister by a wrist and pulled her away from the house. They were both crying and stumbling. They ran in the drainage ditch all the way home and flung themselves into the barn.

Mandy ran to lie beside the little blind bull calf. She lay her head on Flopper's side. When he didn't respond, she jerked to her feet. She glared at her sister.

"He's dead!"

"Shut up!"

Cissy Johnson had awakened, too, although she hadn't known why. Something, some noise, had stirred her. And now she sat up in bed, breathing hard, frightened for no good reason she could fathom. If Bob had been home, she'd have sent him out to the barn to check on the girls. But why? The girls were all right, they must be, this was just the result of a bad dream. But she didn't remember having any such dream.

Cissy got out of bed and ran to the window.

No, it wasn't a storm, the rain hadn't come.

A motorcycle!

That's what she'd heard, that's what had awakened her!

Quickly, with nervous fingers, Cissy put on a robe and tennis shoes. Darn you, Janie Baum, she thought, your fears are contagious, that's what they are. The thought popped into her head: If you don't have fears, they can't come true.

Cissy raced out to the barn.

The Young Shall See Visions, and the Old Dream Dreams

KRISTINE KATHRYN RUSCH

There has long been a substantial crossover between writers of science fiction and writers of crime and suspense fiction, but most of the early names that come readily to mind (Poul Anderson, Anthony Boucher, Fredric Brown, Isaac Asimov) are male, simply because in its earlier years, few women wrote sci-fi. Now, of course, there are many women in that field, and a number of them—Kate Wilhelm, for example—have also contributed to mystery fiction.

Kristine Kathryn Rusch (b. 1960) was born in Oneonta, New York, attended the University of Wisconsin and Clarion Writers Workshop, and now lives in Oregon. A freelance journalist and editor and a radio news director earlier in her career, she edited *The Magazine of Fantasy and Science Fiction,* the venerable journal founded by Boucher at mid-century, from 1991 to 1997. With her husband, Dean Wesley Smith, she founded Pulphouse Publishing (1987–92).

While Rusch is better known as a science fiction than a mystery writer, having won the prestigious John W. Campbell Award for new writers in 1991, she has a solid record of achievement in both genres. Among her sci-fi works are Star Trek (in collaboration with her husband) and Star Wars novels. The cross-genre *Afterimage* (1992), written with Kevin J. Anderson, is a fantasy serial-killer novel. Her mystery novel *Hitler's Angel* (1998) was a critical success, and in 1999, she scored a rare hat trick, winning Reader's Choice Awards from three different periodicals: *Science Fiction Age, Isaac Asimov's Science Fiction Magazine,* and (with the World War II–era mystery "Details") *Ellery Queen's Mystery Magazine.*

"The Young Shall See Visions and the Old Dream Dreams" first appeared in *EQMM*'s stablemate, *Alfred Hitchcock's Mystery Magazine.*

N ell rubs a hand on her knickers and grips the bat tightly. Her topknot is coming loose. She can see strands of hair hanging in front of the wire frames of her glasses.

"What's the matter, four-eyes? You nervous?"

She concentrates on the ball Pete holds in his right hand instead of the boys scattered across the dusty back lot. Any minute now, he'll pitch, and if she thinks about the ball instead of the names, she'll hit it.

"You hold that bat like a girl," T.J. says from first base.

Nell keeps staring at the ball. She can see the stitches running along its face, the dirty surface disappearing into Pete's fist. "That's because I am a girl," she says. It doesn't matter if T.J. hears her. All that matters is that she spoke.

"Pitch already!" Chucky yells from the grassy sideline.

Pete spits and Nell grimaces. She hates it when he spits. With a sharp snap of the wrist, he releases the ball. It curves toward her. She jumps out of its way and swings at the same time. The ball hits the skinny part of the bat, close to her fingers, and bounces forward.

"Ruuun!" Chucky screams.

She drops the bat and takes off, the air caught in her throat. She's not good at running; someone always tags her before she gets to base. But the sweater-wrapped rock that is first base is getting closer and still she can't hear anyone running behind her. She leaps the last few inches and lands in the middle of the rock, leaving a large footprint in the wool. A few seconds later, the ball slams into T.J.'s palm.

"You didn't have to move," T.J. says. "The ball was gonna hit you anyway."

"Pete always does that so that I can't swing." Nell tugs on her ripped, high-buttoned blouse. "He knows I hit better than any of you guys, so he cheats. And besides, the last time he did that I was bruised for a week. Papa wasn't gonna let me play anymore."

T.J. shrugs, his attention already on the next batter.

"Nell?"

She looks up. Edmund is standing behind third base. His three-piece suit is dusty and he looks tired. "Jeez," she says under her breath.

"What?" T.J. asks.

"Nothing," she says. "I gotta go."

"Why? The game's not over."

"I know." She pushes a strand of hair out of her face. "But I gotta go anyway."

She walks across the field in front of the pitcher's mound. Pete spits and barely misses her shoe. She stops and slowly looks up at him in a conscious imitation of her father's most frightening look.

"Whatcha think you're doing?" he asks.

"Leaving." Her glasses have slid to the edge of her nose, but she doesn't push them back. Touching them would remind him that she can't see very well.

"Can't. You're on first."

"Chucky can take my place."

"Can't neither. He's gotta bat soon."

She glances at Chucky. He's too far away to hear anything. "I can't do anything about it, Pete. I gotta go."

Pete tugs his cap over his eyes and squints at her. "Then you can't play with us no more. It was dumb to let a girl play in the first place."

"It is not dumb! And you've gone home in the middle of a game before." She hates Pete. Someday she'll show him that a girl can be just as good as a boy, even at baseball.

"Nell." Edmund sounds weary. "Let's go."

"He's not your pa," Pete says. "How come you gotta go with him?"

"He's my sister's boyfriend." She pushes her glasses up with her knuckle and trudges the rest of the way across the yard. When she reaches Edmund, he takes her arm and they start walking.

"Why do you play with them?" he asks softly. "Baseball isn't a game for young ladies."

He always asks her that, and once he yelled at her for wearing the knickers that Karl had given her. "I don't like playing dollies with Louisa."

"I don't suppose I'd like that much either," he says. When they get far enough away from the field, he stops and turns her to him. There are deep shadows under his eyes and his face looks pinched. "I'm not going to take you all the way home. I just came because I promised I would."

"You're not gonna see Bess?"

He shakes his head, then reaches into his pocket and pulls out the slender ring that cost him three months' wages. The diamond glitters in the sunlight. "Karl's back," he says.

Nell traced the nameplate. Karl Krupp. She hadn't imagined it; the name didn't disappear under her touch like so many other things did. Her fingers, with their swollen knuckles and fragile bones, looked defenseless beside that name. Slowly she let her hand fall back onto the cold metal rim of her walker. He would be how old now? When she had been ten, he had been twenty-five—a fifteen-year difference that would now make him . . . ninety-five. She glanced at the door to his room. It hadn't been open since he arrived, and that frustrated her. She wanted to see how badly age had changed him.

She supposed it hadn't changed him much, since he was in Household 5. The other residents were reasonably intelligent and ambulatory—except for Sophronia. But the nurses had removed her as soon as her senility became evident. Nell's own memory lapses and growing tendency to daydream worried her. She wasn't sure how much provocation the nurses needed before they moved her to a more restrictive household.

Nell lifted her walker and moved away from the door. She didn't want Karl to catch her snooping. Her name was different and she certainly didn't look like the scrawny tomboy he had known, but she didn't want him to know that she was watching him until she knew exactly what she was going to do.

Karl slouches indolently in the settee. His long legs stretch out before him and cross at the ankles, his left arm is draped across the armrest, and his finely chiseled head rests against the upholstered back. He should not be comfortable, but he clearly is.

Bess sits in the armchair across from him, leaning forward. Wisps of hair frame her flushed face, her eyes sparkle, and her hands—looking naked without Edmund's ring—nervously toy with her best skirt.

Nell lets the door swing shut. Karl doesn't turn at the click, but instead says in his deep, rich baritone, "Is that my Nell?"

She freezes, not expecting the well of emotion that voice raises in her. She imagines herself running to him and burying her face in his neck, then pulling back and slapping him with all her strength.

"Nelly, it's Karl." Bess can't quite keep the happiness from her voice.

"I know," she says, flicking dried mud off her thumb. She is covered with sweat, her glasses are dirty, and her topknot is coming loose. She probably doesn't even look like a little girl.

"Nelly . . ."

She hates the nickname almost as much as she hates Bess's tone. "I'm gonna go wash up."

"Go around front so you don't get mud on the floor."

Nell suppresses a sigh and turns around to let herself out. Just then her father opens the door, bringing with him the scents of tobacco and hair tonic. He ignores his youngest daughter's appearance and starts to go into the parlor.

"Who owns the fancy Model-T? Is it yours, Edm—?"

He stops just inside the parlor and Nell takes a step forward so that she can see everything. Karl rises quickly and extends his hand. Bess is biting her lower lip, and Papa has flushed a deep scarlet.

"I told you," he says in his lowest, angriest voice, "never to cross my threshold again."

"Mr. Richter, things have changed."

"I don't care if you've become the richest man in the world. You are not welcome here." Papa's voice grows even softer. "Now get out."

"Sir, please—"

"Get. Out. Or must I escort you?"

With one swift, graceful movement, Karl sweeps his hat off the table and places it jauntily on his head. He nods at Bess, steps around Papa, and musses Nell's hair as he goes out the door.

Papa doesn't move until he hears the automobile crank up. Then he says tightly to Bess, "You know he's not allowed to be here."

"But he's different. He's got a new job in Milwaukee, and he's got *prospects*, Papa."

"Fine. Let him find another girl."

Nell leans back against the door. They have forgotten that she's there.

"Papa." Bess rises out of the armchair. In her high-buttoned shoes, she is almost as tall as her father. "Things are better. He promised."

"Oh? Did he promise he would never hit you again, or did he just talk about money?"

Bess whirls away and looks out the window. "Papa, that's not fair."

"No, it's not fair." Papa pulls his watch from his pocket, opens it, and then closes it without looking at the face. "But I don't want him back. After he hit you, I heard Nelly crying herself to sleep every single night."

Nell's face grows warm. She thought no one knew.

Papa stuffs his watch back into his pocket and adjusts his waistcoat. "Now, I would like some dinner."

Nell slips out the front door and heads around the house to the pump. Her body is shaking. She remembers Bess's swollen and bruised face, but she also remembers the fun they had laughing on the front porch with Karl. Her tears those nights hadn't been just for Bess. They had also been for those summer afternoons filled with laughter, lemonade, and Karl mussing her hair!

Even though it was difficult, Nell liked to walk. She felt that each slow step added a minute to her life. Without her walker, she would have to use a wheelchair—and the wheelchair was a sign of weakness. Lifting the walker and then taking a step gave her the same sure feel that she used to have after hitting a home run the way Karl had taught her to.

Sometimes she spent the entire day walking up and down the hallways. She got to go outside on those rare occasions when her family visited. They took her out so that they could avoid talking.

Each household was painted a different color. The walls in Household 5 were robin's egg blue and covered with artwork done by the residents. Shortly after Karl arrived, a painting of a multi-colored spiral had gone up beside his door.

Nell found her gaze drawn to the painting. She pushed her glasses up so that she could study it. The spiral had rungs, like a ladder. At the bottom, instead of a signature, was a notation that tugged at a memory she couldn't reach: deoxyribose nucleic acid. She read the phrase twice, then saw with a start that Karl's door was open. Strains of a Chopin étude slipped into the hallway. Intrigued, she leaned closer.

The residents were encouraged to fill their rooms with their personal effects. Most rooms had a television set, a stuffed armchair covered with a quilt, and a cross on prominent display. But Karl's room was lined with bookcases, and the bookcases were full. Karl stood near the door, holding a book in his hand.

"It's the pretty woman from across the hall." His voice hadn't changed. It was still rich and full, and it still sent shivers down her back. His black hair had become silver and his skin was covered with delicately etched lines. Age hadn't bent him. He extended his hand. His movements were as graceful as ever. "Would you care to come and visit for a moment?"

Nell found herself staring at his hand. The last time she had seen it, it had been covered with blood. "No, thank you," she said. "I'm taking my walk."

"Surely you have just a moment—?" He inclined his head toward her, waiting for her to give him her name.

"Eleanor," she said.

"Eleanor?" He took a step back so that she could pass him. She hesitated, then smiled a little bit at herself, realizing that this was the man who had given her a taste for charm.

"A moment." She turned her walker and started toward him, feeling awkward for the first time in years.

He watched her shuffling movements. "Arthritis?"

She shook her head. "I broke both hips pinch-hitting for some Little Leaguers in 1975. The doctors said I'd never walk again."

"Did you win?"

She looked up at him, startled to find herself only a foot away. "I'm walking, aren't I?"

He chuckled. "No, no. The game."

"Oh." She pushed the walker through the doorway. Bookcases made the entrance narrow. His room smelled like ink and old books. "We lost by three runs."

"It's a shame," he said quietly. "You should always win your last game."

She stopped near the window. He had a view of the back parking lot. "Who says it was my last game?"

She turned and looked at his room, then. It was filled with books. A desk covered with papers stood in the center of the floor and a stereo, like the one her granddaughter was so proud of, took up a shelf of one of the bookcases. The bed in the far corner was neatly made and covered with a manufactured spread.

"Would you like to sit?" He pulled a chair back for her. Nell shook her head.

"Tea then?" He reached behind him and plugged in a coffee machine. Cups, canisters, and vials filled with liquid rested beside the machine.

"What are you doing here?" Nell's question slipped out. He turned sharply to look at her. Nell felt herself blush. "I mean, you don't look as if you need to be here."

He smiled and the lines cascaded into wrinkles. "My grand-nephew runs this place. He figures I'm getting too old to live alone."

"But there are other places to stay if you're in good health. You don't seem to need medical care."

"I don't yet." He hooked his thumb in his front pockets and leaned against the door frame. Nell wondered if he'd stop her if she tried to leave. "I'm helping him with some research."

Nell glanced again at the desk. Some of the papers lying there were covered with the same spiral that was near the door.

"We're trying to find a way to slow down the aging process," he said. "You've heard of Leonard Hayflick?"

"No."

"Hayflick is a biologist who found that cells have a clearly defined life span. He figured that the life span was determined by the number of cell divisions instead of chronological age. But some cells deteriorate before they reach their maximum divisions. And that, some believe, causes aging. Follow me?"

Nell realized she had been staring at him blankly. "Sorry."

"Let me put it simply," he said. "Everyone can live to a certain maximum age, but not everyone reaches that age because of physical deterioration. What we're trying to do is prevent that physical deterioration so that people can live out their entire lives."

"What is this maximum age?" Nell asked.

Karl shrugged. "We don't know. But some people have claimed

that they were well over a hundred. And I just read about a woman recently whose baptismal records prove she is a hundred and twenty."

"Why are you telling me?"

"You asked, Nelly."

Nell's entire body went cold. She gripped her walker tightly and tried to think of a way she could get out of the room.

He took a step toward her, and she cringed.

"I'm sorry," he said softly. "I should have let you know right away that I knew who you were. My family stayed in Wisconsin, Nell. They let me know what was going on in your life. I knew you were here well before I came."

"What are you going to do?" Her voice trembled.

He took another cautious step toward her. "Well, first, Nelly, I'd like to explain about Bess."

"No," she said and her fear was as real as it had been that sunlit July morning when he had clamped his bloody hand against her mouth. "If you don't let me out of here, I'm going to scream."

"Nelly—"

"I mean it, Karl, I'm going to scream."

He opened his hands wide. "You're free to go, Nell. If I wanted to hurt you, I could have done it a long time ago."

She pushed the walker before her like a shield. Her hands were slipping on the metal. As she passed Karl, she didn't look at him.

The walls seemed narrower and the distance to her room much too short. When she got inside, she closed the door, wishing that it would lock. But she knew that part of her fear was irrational. There wasn't much a ninety-five-year-old man could do to her here, not in this home filled with bright lights and young nurses. All she had to do was scream and someone would come to her. They didn't ignore screams in Household 5.

Nell tugs at her knickers. No matter how tightly she ties them, they always stay uncomfortably loose about the waist. She has been reluctant to slide into a base like Chucky tells her to because she's afraid that if she does her knickers will come off.

She takes the path that goes through Kirschman's apple orchard. Mr. Kirschman hates it when the kids take the shortcut through his orchard, but they do anyway.

As she turns the corner to the center of the orchard, someone clamps a hand over her mouth and drags her back against the tree. The hand is tight and slippery. It smells like iron.

"Nelly, promise not to scream if I let you go?"

The voice is Karl's. She nods. Slowly he releases her.

"What were you trying to do?"

He raises a grimy finger to his lips. His dark hair stands out in sharp relief to his pale skin. "I don't want you to go any farther, okay? I want you to go back and get your father right away. Promise?"

Nell nods again. She's staring at his stained white shirt and she realizes that it is covered with blood. She wipes at her mouth and her hand comes away bloody.

"Nell—"

She turns and starts to run, not realizing until she's rounded the corner that she's disobeyed Karl. There, lying across the orchard path, is her sister. Bess's hair is strewn about her, and her blouse is covered with blood.

"Nell, it'll be okay, just—"

Nell screams. Karl is standing behind her. She pushes him out of her way and runs down the orchard path toward home. This time running seems easy although the air still catches in her throat. She can't hear Karl behind her, and as she nears the house, she knows she's safe. Karl won't hurt her, Karl would never hurt her. The only one Karl hurts is Bess, and that is Bess's fault because she doesn't listen to Papa and now it's too late, it's all too late because Nell has left her there, bleeding and helpless, with Karl, the man who hurts her, the man whose hands are covered with blood.

*

"Did I ever tell you that my sister was murdered?"

Anna smoothed her already neat skirt and sighed. "Yes, Mother." Her tone said, *A thousand times, Mother. Do I have to hear it again?*

Nell clutched her hands in her lap, trying to decide if she should continue. Anna would never believe her. Even though she was fifty-five, Anna rarely thought about anything more serious than clothing and makeup. And, of course, she had never known her Aunt Bess.

"I saw the man who killed her."

Anna suddenly became stiff, and her eyes focused on something beyond Nell's shoulder.

Nell's heart was pounding. Her oldest, Elizabeth, would have listened. But Bess had been dead for six years. "I think I told you this once," Nell said. "But the man who killed her—his name was Karl—also killed her fiancé, Edmund. And they never caught him. And it used to frighten me, thinking that someday he'd come back for me."

"That was a long time ago, Mother." Anna's voice had an edge to it.

"I know." Nell's fingers had grown cold. "But I wouldn't be telling you now if it weren't important."

Anna looked at her mother full in the face, a deep, piercing look. "Why is it important now?"

"Because he's here," Nell whispered. The words sounded too melodramatic, but she couldn't take them back. "He's across the hall."

Anna took a deep breath. "Mother, even if he were here, there's nothing he could do. He probably doesn't even remember you."

"He remembers," Nell said. "I talked to him."

"Even so." Anna reached out and took Nell's hand. Her palm was warm and moist. "He's an elderly man. He probably won't live long. If we called the police and they verified what you said, he probably wouldn't even make it to trial. I mean, who else knows about the murder, besides you?"

"My father knew and—"

"Anyone living?"

"No." Tears were building in Nell's eyes. She blinked rapidly.

"Then it would be your word against his, and frankly, Mother, I don't think it's worth it. I mean, what can you gain now? He'll die soon and then you won't have to worry."

"No." A tear traced its way down Nell's cheek and stopped on her lips. She licked it away quickly, hoping Anna didn't see. "He won't die soon."

Anna frowned. "Why not?"

"He's working on an experiment to prolong his life."

"Oh, for God's sake, Mother." Anna pulled her hand away. "How many other people have you told this piece of nonsense to?"

"I haven't—"

A nurse knocked on the door and walked in. She set a tray next to Nell's armchair. "I have your medication, Nell."

Nell reached over and took the Dixie cup. The liquid inside was brown. "This doesn't look like my medication."

She looked up in time to see Anna shaking her head at the nurse.

"Just drink it, Nell," the nurse said in her fakely sweet voice, "and it'll be all right."

Nell took a sniff of the cup. The contents smelled bitter. "I really don't want it."

"Mother," Anna snapped. Then in a confidential tone to the nurse, she said, "Mother is having a bad day."

"The past few days have been difficult," the nurse said. "She hasn't gone to meals and she won't leave her room at all."

"Is that true, Mother?"

Nell swirled the liquid in her cup. Sediment floated around the bottom. Suddenly she realized that it didn't matter. No one would care if Karl poisoned her. She put the cup to her lips and drank before she could change her mind.

The liquid bit at her tongue like homemade whiskey. She coughed once and then set the cup down. "I don't see why you want to know," she said.

Anna pursed her lips. "Mother, really."

Nell rubbed her tongue against the roof of her mouth, but she couldn't make the taste go away. She grabbed the side of her chair and got to her feet. Her hips cracked slightly when she stood. The nurse handed her the walker.

"Where are you going, Nell?"

Nell didn't reply. She moved the walker toward the sink, and got herself a drink of water.

"I'm afraid my mother may not be well," Anna said softly. "She was just telling me that the man across the hall murdered her sister, and she's afraid that he's after her."

"Mr. Krupp? I wouldn't think so. He's been bedridden since he came here."

"Maybe you should say something." Anna stopped speaking as Nell turned around. Nell made her way back to the armchair. The nurse took her arm as she sat down.

"Nell, I understand the man across the hall frightens you."

Nell looked up at the nurse's round face, trying to remember her name without glancing at the name tag. "No. Whatever gave you that idea?"

"Your daughter was saying that he made you nervous."

The name tag said DANA, L.P.N. "I haven't even seen him and he's very quiet. Why would that make me nervous?"

The nurse smiled and picked up the tray. "I was just checking, Nell."

Anna waited until the nurse left before speaking. "Why did you lie to her, Mother?"

"I don't know why you come visit me," Nell said.

Anna slid her chair back and stood up. "I don't know either sometimes. But I'm sure I'll be back." She picked up her coat and slung it around her shoulder. "And, Mother, it's better for you to socialize, you know, than to stay locked up in your room. Talking to other people will give you something to think about, so that your mind won't wander."

She walked out. Nell waited until she could no longer hear the click of Anna's high heels on the tile floor. "My mind doesn't wander," she murmured. But the nurse had said that Karl was bedridden, and he had looked so healthy to her. Nell sighed and then frowned. What would he be doing in Household 5 if he couldn't get out of bed?

Nell picks up the bat and takes a practice swing. Her dress sways with her, but she won't wear the knickers Karl gave her. Bess has been dead for a week, and Nell is lonely.

"What are you doing here?" Chucky asks. They are alone. The other boys haven't arrived yet.

"Wanna play," she says.

He frowns. "In a dress? Where are your knickers?"

"Threw them out." She hits the bat against the dirt like she's seen Pete do.

"You can't run in a dress."

"I can try." Her anger is sharp and quick. She hasn't been able to control her moods since Bess died. "I'm sorry."

Chucky ducks his head and looks away. "It's okay."

"I'm sorry," she says again, and looks at the playing field. The grass has been ruined near the bases. Sometimes she thinks baseball is the only dream she has left. Now, with Bess dead and Karl gone, even that seems impossible. "I'll just go home."

"No," Chucky says. "I mean, you can play."

She smiles a little and shakes her head. "Not in a dress. You were right."

"Wait." He touches her arm and then runs to his house, letting the porch door slam behind him. She goes to home base and swings the bat again, pretending that she has hit a home run. It is a good feeling, to send the ball whistling across the creek. She loves nothing more. If only she were a little boy, she could play baseball forever. Karl once told her that she could turn into a boy when she kissed her elbow. She tried for weeks before she realized that kissing her own elbow was impossible. She will never be a boy, but she will be good at baseball.

Chucky comes back. He thrusts some cloth into her hand. "Here," he says.

She unfolds it. He's given her a pair of frayed and poorly mended knickers. "Chucky?"

"They don't fit me no more. Maybe they'll fit you."

"But isn't your brother supposed to get them?"

"Nah," he says, but doesn't meet her eyes.

"I don't want to take them if it'll get you in trouble."

"It won't." He studies her, sees that she's unconvinced. "Look, you're the best hitter on the team. I don't want to lose you."

She smiles, a real smile this time, one that she feels. "Thanks, Chucky."

Nell resumed her walks again, making sure that she took them around medication time.

Karl's door remained closed for days, but she finally caught him in the hallway, switching Dixie cups on the trays.

"You're switching my medication," she said. She stood straight, leaning on her walker, knowing that he couldn't touch her in the halls.

"Yes, I am," he replied.

She swallowed heavily. She hadn't expected him to admit it. "Why?"

"I guess I kinda feel like I owe you, Nell."

"For killing Bess?"

He set the cup down on the tray marked with her room number. His hand was trembling. "I didn't kill Bess," he said quietly. "I killed Edmund."

"You're lying."

He shook his head. "I was going to meet Bess that morning in the orchard. We were going to run away together. Edmund got there first, and he killed her. So I went and I killed him."

Nell could feel the power of that morning, the sunlight against her skin, his bloody fingers across her lips. "Why—didn't you tell somebody?"

"I still committed a murder, Nelly."

That's why he had told her to get her father. That's why he had never come back to kill her, too. "Why—" She shook her head in an attempt to clear it. "Why did you come back here?"

"Wisconsin is my home, Nell." He was leaning on the cart for support. "I wanted to die at home."

"But your experiment?"

He smiled. "I've outlived most of my siblings for a good twenty years. And the formula wasn't quite right for me at first. We've changed it, so yours is better from the start."

"Mine?"

"Nelly." He bowed his head slightly and ran his fingers through his thick, silver hair. The gesture made her think of the old Karl, the one who had taught her how to laugh and how to hit home runs. "What did you think? That I was poisoning you?"

She nodded.

"I'm not. I'm trying the drug on you. I know I should have asked, but you didn't trust me, and it was just easier to do it this way."

"Why me?" she asked.

"Lots of reasons." The cart slid forward slightly and he had to catch himself to keep from falling. "I don't know many people who still play baseball when they're seventy years old. Or learn to walk again when the doctors say they can't. You're strong, Nelly. The power of your mind is amazing."

"But what if I don't want to live any longer?"

"You do or you wouldn't be out here, trying to catch me."

"I have caught you." The hallway was empty. Usually it was full of people walking back and forth.

"I know," Karl said. "What are you going to do? Call a nurse, tell them to arrest me? There's no statute of limitations on murder, you know."

Nell studied him for a moment. He was thin and his skin was pale. He was ninety-five. How much longer could he live?

"I don't want any more of your medication," she said.

He stood motionlessly, waiting for her to say something else.

She moved her walker forward, on the other side of the cart. "And I don't want to talk anymore."

She didn't let herself look back as she slowly made her way down the hall. Imagine if she could walk without a walker, without pain. Imagine if she could live longer than her father, who had died when he was ninety-eight. She wasn't ready to give up living yet. Some days she felt as if she had only just started.

When she reached her own door, she stopped and looked back at Karl's. Once she had believed in Karl and his miracles. She did no longer.

The world has reduced itself to the ball clutched in Pete's hand. "Throw it straight," Chucky yells.

Pete spits. Nell barely notices. She watches that ball, knowing that when he throws it she will hit it with all her strength. Time seems to slow down as the ball whizzes toward her. She knows how the ball will fly, where it will end up, and she swings the bat down to meet it. There is a satisfying crack as they hit and time speeds up again.

"Holy cow!" Chucky cries, but Nell ignores him as she drops the bat. Out of the corner of her eye, she sees the ball sail over the creek. She runs as fast as she can. Her right foot hits first base, and she keeps going, flying, like the ball. It disappears into the weeds behind the creek as her left foot hits second. Her glasses bounce off her nose between second and third, and she is navigating according to color. Her lungs are burning as her left foot hits the rock that is third base.

"Go, Nelly! Go!"

She runs toward the blurred shapes behind home. There is a stitch in her side and her entire body aches, but she keeps moving. She leaps on home base and her team cheers, but she can't stop. She has run too hard to stop right away, and she crashes into Chucky, who hugs her.

"Great!" he says. "That was great!"

She stands there, savoring the moment. Karl would have been proud of her. But Karl would never know. She wipes the sweat off her forehead and says, "I lost my glasses."

As Chucky trudges out to retrieve them, she realizes she can get no higher than this; her tiny girl's body, for all its batting accuracy, will prevent her from going on. But she doesn't care. If she can't play on a real team, she will hit home runs until she is a hundred, long after these boys are dead.

"That was great, Nelly," Chucky says as he hands her her glasses. "Really great."

She checks the lenses, which haven't cracked, and then bends the frame back into shape. "Not bad for a girl," she says with a glance at T.J. Then she goes over to the grass and sits at the end of the line, hoping that she'll get another chance at bat.

The sound of running feet woke Nell up. She had heard that sound before. Someone had died or was dying and they wanted to get him out before the other residents knew.

She grabbed her glasses and got out of bed, carefully making her way to the door. They were gathered in front of Karl's room. Two men wheeled a stretcher out. The body was strapped in and the face was covered. Quickly they pushed him out of sight.

She crossed the empty hallway. The tile beneath her feet felt cold and gritty. They had left Karl's door open, and she stopped just outside it, catching the smell of death under the scent of ink and books.

"Nell?" One of the nurses started down the hall toward her.

"Is he dead?" she asked.

"Mr. Krupp? I'm afraid so. I'm sorry if it disturbed you."

"No, not really," Nell said. She drew her nightgown closely about her chest. She was getting cold.

"He probably shouldn't have been in this household," the nurse said. "He was much too sick, but his family wanted him to have a private room."

Nell wondered how the nurse expected her to believe that.

One glance inside Karl's room made it obvious that he hadn't been bedridden. Nell surveyed the room once more. The desk top was bare and the vials were gone, but otherwise it looked the same.

The nurse finally reached her side. Nell recognized her as the round-faced one who usually gave her her medicine, Dana, LPN.

"How did you get out here?" Dana LPN asked.

"Walked," Nell said.

Dana LPN shot her a perplexed look. "Well, let's get you back to bed, shall we?"

She put her arm around Nell's waist and helped her back to the room. The support wasn't necessary until they reached the door. When Nell saw her walker in its usual place beside the bed, her knees buckled.

"Nell?"

Nell straightened herself and pushed out of the nurse's grasp. She made her way to the side of the bed and lightly touched her walker. "I'm fine," she said.

She climbed into the bed and lay there until she heard the nurse's footsteps echo down the hall. Then she got up and walked slowly around her room.

You're strong, Nelly, he had said. *The power of your mind is amazing.*

She walked to the door and stared at Karl's empty room across the hall. The drawing was still there, its spirals twisting like a malformed ladder. Beneath the stunned joy that she was feeling, frustration beat at her stomach. She would never know if it was her own determination or Karl's bitter medicine that made her legs work again, just as she would never know if he had actually killed her sister or if he had been lying. She wanted to believe that it was the power of her own mind, but her mind's healing took time. She had started to walk within days of receiving the medication.

Nell went back to the bed and sat down, wondering what Anna would say when she learned that her mother could walk again.

Then Nell decided that it didn't matter. What mattered was that her feet which had run bases, chased two children, and carried her through decades of living worked again. Once she had vowed to hit home runs until she was a hundred. And maybe, just maybe, she would.

A Predatory Woman

SHARYN McCRUMB

Sharyn McCrumb (b. 1948), who holds degrees from the University of North Carolina and Virginia Tech, lives in Virginia's Blue Ridge Mountains but travels the United States and the world lecturing on her work, most recently leading a writer's workshop in Paris in summer 2001.

McCrumb's Ballad series, beginning with *If Ever I Return, Pretty Peggy-O* (1990), has won her numerous honors, including the Appalachian Writers Association's Award for Outstanding Contribution to Appalachian Literature and several listings as *New York Times* and *Los Angeles Times* notable books. In the introduction to her short-story collection *Foggy Mountain Breakdown and Other Stories* (1997), she details the family history in North Carolina and Tennessee that contributed to her Appalachian fiction. One of the continuing characters, Sheriff Spencer Arrowood, takes his surname from ancestors on her father's side, while Frankie Silver ("the first woman hanged for murder in the state of North Carolina"), whose story McCrumb would incorporate in *The Ballad of Frankie Silver* (1998), was a distant cousin. "My books are like Appalachian quilts," she writes. "I take brightly colored scraps of legends, ballads, fragments of rural life, and local tragedy, and I place them together into a complex whole that tells not only a story, but also a deeper truth about the nature of the mountain south." The sixth and most recent title in the series, *The Songcatcher*, appeared in summer 2001.

McCrumb describes "A Predatory Woman" as "my own meditation on what might happen if 1966's Moors Murderer Myra Hindley were released from prison in Britain. Although Myra never killed anyone (she was the girlfriend and accomplice of child-killer Ian Brady) she has now served more time in prison for her crime than any actual murderer in British history."

S he looks a proper murderess, doesn't she?" said Ernie Sleaford tapping the photo of a bleached blonde. His face bore that derisive grin he reserved for the "puir doggies," his term for unattractive women.

With a self-conscious part of her own more professionally lightened hair, Jackie Duncan nodded. Because she was twenty-seven and petite she had never been the object of Ernie's derision. When he shouted at her, it was for more professional reasons—a missed photo opportunity or a bit of careless reporting. She picked up the unappealing photograph. "She looks quite tough. One wonders that children would have trusted her in the first place."

"What did they know, poor lambs? We never had a woman like our Erma before, had we?"

Jackie studied the picture, wondering if the face were truly evil, or if their knowledge of its possessor had colored the likeness. Whether or not it was a cruel face, it was certainly a plain one. Erma Bradley had dumpling features with gooseberry eyes, and that look of sullen defensiveness that plain women often have in anticipation of slights to come.

Ernie had marked the photo "Page One." It was not the sort of female face that usually appeared in the pages of *Stellar,* a tabloid known for its daily photo of Princess Diana, and for its bosomy beauties on page three. A beefy woman with a thatch of badly bleached hair had to earn her way into the tabloids, which Erma Bradley certainly had. Convicted of four child murders in 1966, she was serving a life sentence in Holloway Prison in north London.

Gone, but not forgotten. Because she was Britain's only female serial killer, the tabloids kept her memory green with frequent stories about her, all accompanied by that menacing 1965 photo of the scowling, just-arrested Erma. Most of the recent articles about her didn't even attempt to be plausible: "Erma Bradley: Hitler's Illegitimate Daughter"; "Children's Ghosts Seen Outside Erma's Cell"; and, the October favorite, "Is Erma Bradley a Vampire?" That last one was perhaps the most apt, because it acknowledged the fact that the public hardly thought of her as a real person anymore; she was just another addition to the pantheon of monsters, taking her place alongside Frankenstein, Dracula, and another overrated criminal, Guy Fawkes. Thinking up new excuses to use the old Erma picture was Ernie Sleaford's speciality. Erma's face was always good for a sales boost.

Jackie Duncan had never done an Erma story. Jackie had been four years old at the time of the infamous trial, and later, with the crimes solved and the killers locked away, the case had never particularly interested her. "I thought it was her boyfriend, Sean Hardie, who actually did the killing," she said, frowning to remember details of the case.

Stellar's editor sneered at her question. "Hardie? I never thought he had a patch on Erma for toughness. Look at him now. He's completely mental, in a prison hospital, making no more sense than a vegetable marrow. That's how you *ought* to be with the lives of four kids on your conscience. But not our Erma! Got her university degree by telly, didn't she? Learned to talk posh in the cage? And now a bunch of bloody do-gooders have got her out!"

Jackie, who had almost tuned out this tirade as she contemplated her new shade of nail varnish, stared at him with renewed interest. "I hadn't heard that, Sleaford! Are you sure it isn't another of your fairy tales?" She grinned. " 'Erma Bradley, Bride of Prince Edward?' That was my favorite."

Ernie had the grace to blush at the reminder of his last Erma headline, but he remained solemn. "S'truth, Jackie. I had it on the quiet from a screw in Holloway. She's getting out next week."

"Go on! It would have been on every news show in Britain by now! Banner headlines in the *Guardian.* Questions asked in the House."

"The prison officials are keeping it dark. They don't want Erma to be pestered by the likes of us upon her release. She wants to be let alone." He smirked. "I had to pay dear for this bit of information, I can tell you."

Jackie smiled. "Poor mean Ernie! Where do I come into it, then?"

"Can't you guess?"

"I think so. You want Erma's own story, no matter what."

"Well, we can write that ourselves in any case. I have Paul working on that already. What I really need is a new picture, Jackie. The old cow hasn't let herself be photographed in twenty years. Wants her privacy, does our Erma. I think *Stellar*'s readers would like to take a butcher's at what Erma Bradley looks like today, don't you?"

"So they don't hire her as the nanny." Jackie let him finish laughing before she turned the conversation round to money.

The cell was beginning to look the way it had when she first arrived. Newly swept and curtainless, it was a ten-by-six-foot rectangle containing a bed, a cupboard, a table and a chair, a wooden wash basin, a plastic bowl and jug, and a bucket. Gone were the posters and the photos of home. Her books were stowed away in a Marks & Spencers shopping bag.

Ruthie, whose small, sharp features earned her the nickname Minx, was sitting on the edge of the bed, watching her pack. "Taking the lot, are you?" she asked cheerfully.

The thin dark woman stared at the array of items on the table. "I suppose not," she said, scowling. She held up a tin of green tooth powder. "Here. D'you want this, then?"

The Minx shrugged and reached for it. "Why not? After all, you're getting out, and I've a few years to go. Will you write to me when you're on the outside?"

"You know that isn't permitted."

The younger woman giggled. "As if that ever stopped you." She reached for another of the items on the bed. "How about your Christmas soap? You can get more on the outside, you know."

She handed it over. "I shan't want freesia soap ever again."

"Taking your posters, love? Anyone would think you'd be sick of them by now."

"I am. I've promised them to Senga." She set the rolled-up posters on the bed beside Ruthie, and picked up a small framed photograph. "Do you want this, then, Minx?"

The little blonde's eyes widened at the sight of the grainy snapshot of a scowling man. "Christ! It's Sean, isn't it? Put it away. I'll be glad when you've taken that out of here."

Erma Bradley smiled and tucked the photograph in among her clothes. "I shall keep this."

Jackie Duncan seldom wore her best silk suit when she conducted interviews, but this time she felt that it would help to look both glamorous and prosperous. Her blond hair, shingled into a stylish bob, revealed shell-shaped earrings of real gold, and her calf leather handbag and shoes were an expensive matched set. It wasn't at all the way a working *Stellar* reporter usually dressed, but it lent Jackie an air of authority and professionalism that she needed in order to profit from this interview.

She looked around the shabby conference room, wondering if Erma Bradley had ever been there, and, if so, where she had sat. In preparation for the new assignment, Jackie had read everything she could find on the Bradley case: the melodramatic book by the BBC journalist; the measured prose of the prosecuting attorney; and a host of articles from more reliable newspapers than *Stellar*. She had begun to be interested in Erma Bradley and her deadly lover, Sean Hardie: *the couple who slays together stays together?* The analyses of the case had made much of the evidence and horror at the thought of child murder, but they had been at a loss to provide motive, and they had been reticent about details of the killings themselves. There was a book in that, and it would earn a fortune for whoever could get the material to write it. Jackie intended to find out more than she had uncovered, but first she had to find Erma Bradley.

Her Sloane Ranger outfit had charmed the old cats in the prison office into letting her in to pursue the story in the first place. The story they thought she was after. Jackie glanced at herself in the mirror. Very useful for impressing old sahibs, this posh outfit. Besides, she thought, why not give the prison birds a bit of a fashion show?

The six inmates, dressed in shapeless outfits of polyester, sprawled in their chairs and stared at her with no apparent interest. One of them was reading a Barbara Cartland novel.

"Hello, girls!" said Jackie in her best nursing-home voice. She was used to jollying up old ladies for feature stories, and she decided that this couldn't be much different. "Did they tell you what I'm here for?"

More blank stares, until a heavyset redhead asked, "You ever do it with a woman?"

Jackie ignored her. "I'm here to do a story about what it's like in prison. Here's your chance to complain, if there are things you want changed."

Grudgingly then, they began to talk about the food, and the illogical, unbending rules that governed every part of their lives. The tension eased as they talked, and she could tell that they were becoming more willing to confide in her. Jackie scribbled a few cursory notes to keep them talking. Finally one of them said that she missed her children: Jackie's cue.

As if on impulse, she put down her notepad. "Children!" she said breathlessly. "That reminds me! Wasn't Erma Bradley a prisoner here?"

They glanced at each other. "So?" said the dull-eyed woman with unwashed hair.

A ferrety blonde, who seemed more taken by Jackie's glamour than the older ones, answered eagerly, "I knew her! We were best friends!"

"To say the least, Minx," said the frowsy embezzler from Croydon.

Jackie didn't have to feign interest anymore. "Really?" she said to the one called Minx. "I'd be terrified! What was she like!"

They all began to talk about Erma now.

"A bit reserved," said one. "She never knew who she could trust, because of her rep, you know. A lot of us here have kids of our own, so there was feeling against her. In the kitchen, they used to spit in her food before they took it to her. And sometimes, new girls would go at her to prove they were tough."

"That must have taken nerve!" cried Jackie. "I've seen her pictures!"

"Oh, she didn't look like that anymore!" said Minx. "She'd let her hair go back to its natural dark color, and she was much smaller. Not bad, really. She must have lost fifty pounds since the trial days!"

"Do you have a snapshot of her?" asked Jackie, still doing her best impression of breathless and impressed.

The redhead laid a meaty hand on Minx's shoulder. "Just a minute. What are you really here for?"

Jackie took a deep breath. "I need to find Erma Bradley. Can you help me? I'll pay you."

A few minutes later, Jackie was saying a simpering goodbye to the warden, telling her that she'd have to come back in a few days for a follow-up. She had until then to come up with a way to smuggle in two bottles of Glenlivet: the price on Erma Bradley's head. Ernie would probably make her pay for the liquor out of her own pocket. It would serve him right if she got a good book deal out of it on the side.

*

The flat could have used a coat of paint, and some better quality furniture, but that could wait. She was used to shabbiness. What she liked best about it was its high ceiling and the big casement window overlooking the moors. From that window you could see nothing but hills and heather and sky; no roads, no houses, no people. After twenty-four years in the beehive of a women's prison, the solitude was blissful. She spent hours each day just staring out that window, knowing that she could walk on the moors whenever she liked, without guards or passes or physical restraints.

Erma Bradley tried to remember if she had ever been alone before. She had lived in a tiny flat with her mother until she finished O levels, and then, when she'd taken the secretarial job at Hadlands, there had been Sean. She had gone into prison at the age of twenty-three, an end to even the right to privacy. She could remember no time when she could have had solitude, to get to know her own likes and dislikes. She had gone from Mum's shadow to Sean's. She kept his picture, and her mother's, not out of love, but as a reminder of the prisons she had endured before Holloway.

Now she was learning that she liked plants, and the music of Sibelius. She liked things to be clean, too. She wondered if she could paint the flat by herself. It would never look clean until she covered those dingy green walls.

She reminded herself that she could have had a house, *if*. If she had given up some of that solitude. Sell your story to a book publisher; sell the film rights to this movie company. Keith, her long-suffering solicitor, dutifully passed along all the offers for her consideration. The world seemed willing to throw money at her, but all she wanted was for it to go away. The dowdy but slender Miss Emily Kay, newborn at forty-seven, would manage on her own, with tinned food and secondhand furniture, while the pack of journalists went baying after Erma Bradley, who didn't exist anymore. She wanted solitude. She never thought about those terrible months with Sean, the things they did together. For twenty-four years she had not let herself remember any of it.

Jackie Duncan looked up at the gracefully ornamented stone building, carved into apartments for working-class people. The builders in that gentler age had worked leaf designs into the stonework framing the windows, and they had set gargoyles at a corner of each roof. Jackie made a mental note of this useful detail; yet another monster has been added to the building.

In the worn but genteel hallway, Jackie checked the names on mailboxes to make sure that her information was correct. There it was: E. Kay. She hurried up the stairs with only a moment's thought to the change in herself these past few weeks. When Ernie first gave her the assignment, she might have been fearful of confronting a murderess, or she might have gone upstairs with the camera poised to take the shot just as Erma Bradley opened her door, and then she would have fled. But now she was as anxious to meet the woman as she could be to interview a famous film star. More so, because this celebrity was hers alone. She had not even told Ernie that she had found Erma. This was her show, not *Stellar*'s. Without another thought about what she would say, Jackie knocked at the lair of the beast.

After a few moments, the door opened partway, and a small dark-haired woman peered nervously out at her. The woman was thin, and dressed in a simple green jumper and skirt. She was no longer the brassy blonde of the sixties. But the eyes were the same. The face was still Erma Bradley's.

Jackie was brisk. "May I come in, Miss *Kay?* You wouldn't want me to pound on your door calling out your real name, would you?"

The woman fell back and let her enter. "I suppose it wouldn't help to tell you that you're mistaken?" No trace remained of her Midlands accent. She spoke in quiet, cultured tones.

"Not a hope. I swotted for weeks to find you, dear."

"Couldn't you just leave me alone?"

Jackie sat down on the threadbare brown sofa and smiled up at her hostess. "I suppose I could arrange it. I could, for instance, *not* tell the BBC, the tabloids, and the rest of the world what you look like, and where you are."

The woman looked down at her ringless hands. "I haven't any money," she said.

"Oh, but you're worth a packet all the same, aren't you? In all the years you've been locked up, you never said anything except, *I didn't do it,* which is rubbish, because the world knows you did. You taped the Doyle boy's killing on a bloody tape recorder!"

The woman hung her head for a moment, turning away. "What do you want?" she said at last, sitting in the chair by the sofa.

Jackie Duncan touched the other woman's arm. "*I want you to tell me about it.*"

"No. I can't. I've forgotten."

"No, you haven't. Nobody could. And that's the book the world wants to read. Not this mealymouthed rubbish the others have written about you. I want you to tell me every single detail, all the way through. That's the book I want to write." She took a deep breath, and forced a smile. "And in exchange, I'll keep your identity and whereabouts a secret, the way Ursula Bloom did when she interviewed Crippen's mistress in the fifties."

Erma Bradley shrugged. "I don't read crime stories," she said.

The light had faded from the big window facing the moors. On the scarred pine table a tape recorder was running, and in the deepening shadows, Erma Bradley's voice rose and fell with weary resignation, punctuated by Jackie's eager questions.

"I don't know," she said again.

"Come on. Think about it. Have a biscuit while you think. Sean didn't have sex with the Allen girl, but did he make love to *you* afterwards? Do you think he got an erection while he was doing the strangling?"

A pause. "I didn't look."

"But you made love after he killed her?"

"Yes."

"On the same bed?"

"But later. A few hours later. After we had taken away the body. It was Sean's bedroom, you see. It's where we always slept."

"Did you picture the child's ghost watching you do it?"

"I was twenty-two. He said— He used to get me drunk—and I—"

"Oh, come on, Erma. There's no bloody jury here. Just tell me if it turned you on to watch Sean throttling kids. When he did it, were both of you naked or just him?"

"Please, I— Please!"

"All right, Erma. I can have the BBC here in time for the wake-up news."

"Just him."

An hour later. "Do stop snivelling, Erma. You lived through it once, didn't you? What's the harm in talking about it? They can't try you again. Now come on, dear, answer the question."

"Yes. The little boy—Brian Doyle—he was quite brave, really. Kept saying he had to take care of his mum, because she was divorced now, and asking us to let him go. He was only eight, and quite small. He even offered to fight us if we'd untie him. When Sean was getting the masking tape out of the cupboard, I went up to him, and I whispered to him to let the boy go, but he . . ."

"There you go again, Erma. Now, I've got to shut the machine off again while you get hold of yourself."

She was alone now. At last, the reporter woman was gone. Just before eleven, she had scooped up her notes and her tape recorder, and the photos of the dead children she had brought from the photo archives, and she'd gone away, promising to return in a few days to "put the finishing touches on the interview." The dates and places and forensic details she could get from the other sources, she'd said.

The reporter had gone, and the room was empty, but Miss

Emily Kay wasn't alone anymore. Now Erma Bradley had got in as well.

She knew, though, that no other journalists would come. This one, Jackie, would keep her secret well enough, but only to ensure the exclusivity of her own book. Other than that, Miss Emily Kay would be allowed to enjoy her freedom in the shabby little room overlooking the moors. But it wasn't a pleasant retreat any longer, now that she wasn't alone. Erma had brought the ghosts back with her.

Somehow the events of twenty-five years ago had become more real when she told them than when she lived them. It had been so confused back then. Sean drank a lot, and he liked her to keep him company in that. And it happened so quickly the first time, and then there was no turning back. But she never let herself think about it. It was Sean's doing, she would tell herself, and then part of her mind would close right down, and she would turn her attention to something else. At the trial, she had thought about the hatred that she could almost touch, flaring at her from nearly everyone in the courtroom. She couldn't think then, for if she broke down, they would win. They never put her on the stand. She answered no questions, except to say when a microphone was thrust in her face, *I didn't do it*. And then later in prison there were adjustments to make, and bad times with the other inmates to be faced. She didn't need a lot of sentiment dragging her down as well. *I didn't do it* came to have a truth for her: it meant, I am no longer the somebody who did that. I am small, and thin, and well-spoken. The ugly, ungainly monster is gone.

But now she had testified. Her own voice had conjured up the images of Sarah Allen calling out for her mother, and of Brian Doyle, offering to sell his bike to ransom himself, for his mum's sake. The hatchet-faced blonde, who had told them to shut up, who had held them down . . . she was here. And she was going to live here, too, with the sounds of weeping, and the screams. And every tread on the stair would be Sean, bringing home another little lad for a wee visit.

I didn't do it, she whispered. And it had come to have another meaning. *I didn't do it*. Stop Sean Hardie from hurting them. Go to the police. Apologize to the parents during the years in prison. Kill myself from the shame of it. *I didn't do it*, she whispered again. *But I should have.*

Ernie Sleaford was more deferential to her now. When he heard about the new book, and the size of her advance, he realized that she was a player, and he had begun to treat her with a new deference. He had even offered her a rise in case she was thinking of quitting. But she wasn't going to quit. She quite enjoyed her work. Besides, it was so amusing now to see him stand up for her when she came into his grubby little office.

"We'll need a picture for the front page, love," he said in his most civil tones. "Would you mind if Denny took your picture, or is there one you'd rather use?"

Jackie shrugged. "Let him take one. I just had my hair done. So I make the front page as well?"

"Oh yes. We're devoting the whole page to Erma Bradley's suicide, and we want a sidebar of your piece. "I Was the Last to See the Monster Alive." It will make a nice contrast. Your picture beside pudding-faced Erma."

"I thought she looked all right for forty-seven. Didn't the picture I got turn out all right?"

Ernie looked shocked. "We're not using that one, Jackie. We want to remember her the way she *was*. A vicious ugly beastie in contrast to a pure young thing like yourself. Sort of a moral statement, like."

Jack Be Quick

BARBARA PAUL

Barbara Paul (b. 1931) was born in Maysville, Kentucky, and educated at Bowling Green State University, University of Redlands, and the University of Pittsburgh, where she received her Ph.D. in Theater in 1969. Before becoming a full-time novelist, she worked as a college professor and drama director. Her first novel, *An Exercise for Madmen* (1978) was science fiction, but beginning with *The Fourth Wall* (1979), she would devote most of her energies to mysteries, often with a theatrical background. Among her works are a series of opera-related historical mysteries in which Enrico Caruso and Geraldine Farrar figure as amateur sleuths (Farrar is the smart one, Caruso the Watson), beginning with *A Cadenza for Caruso* (1984), and a contemporary police procedural series about homicide detective Marian Larch, beginning with *The Renewable Virgin* (1984).

Paul's work in the field shows an unusual variety and versatility, reflected in her gift for striking titles like *Liars and Tyrants and People Who Turn Blue* (1980), *Your Eyelids Are Growing Heavy* (1981), *He Huffed and He Puffed* (1989), *Good King Sauerkraut* (1990), and *Inlaws and Outlaws* (1990). The whimsically titled *But He Was Already Dead When I Got There* (1986) suggests her pleasure in playing with genre conventions.

In "Jack Be Quick," Paul suggests a solution to one of the most notorious unsolved cases in criminal history. Jack the Ripper, killer of prostitutes in 1880s London, operated in a time and place, sadly unlike here and now, where serial killers were rare. Non-fictional accounts of the case could fill a library, and fictional treatments, direct and indirect, go back at least as far as Marie Belloc Lowndes's *The Lodger* (1913). Paul's approach to the mystery, in the 1991 anthology *Solved,* is among the most original, as well as being notable for a highly appropriate feminist slant.

30 September 1888, St. Jude's Vicarage, Whitechapel.

He took two, this time, and within the same hour, Inspector Abberline told us. The first victim was found this morning less than an hour after midnight, in a small court off Berner Street. The second woman was killed in Mitre Square forty-five minutes later. He did his hideous deed and escaped undetected, as he always does. Inspector Abberline believes he was interrupted in Berner Street, because he did not . . . do to that woman what he'd done to his other victims. My husband threw the Inspector a warning look, not wanting me exposed to such distressing matters more than necessary. "But the second woman was severely mutilated," Inspector Abberline concluded, offering no details. "He finished in Mitre Square what he'd begun in Berner Street."

My husband and I knew nothing of the double murder, not having left the vicarage all day. When no one appeared for morning services, Edward was angry. Customarily we can count on a Sunday congregation of a dozen or so; we should have suspected something was amiss. "Do you know who the women were, Inspector?" I asked.

"One of them," he said. "His Mitre Square victim was named Catherine Eddowes. We have yet to establish the identity of the Berner Street victim."

Inspector Abberline looked exhausted; I poured him another cup of tea. He undoubtedly would have preferred something stronger, but Edward permitted no spirits in the house, not even sherry. I waited until the Inspector had taken a sip before I put my next question to him. "Did he cut out Catherine Eddowes's womb the way he did Annie Chapman's?"

Edward looked shocked that I should know about that, but the police investigator was beyond shock. "Yes, Mrs. Wickham, he did. But this time he did not take it away with him."

It was one of the many concerns that baffled and horrified me about the series of grisly murders haunting London. Annie Chapman's disemboweled body had been found in Hanbury Street three weeks earlier; all the entrails had been piled above her shoulder except the womb. Why had he stolen her womb? "And the intestines?"

"Heaped over the left shoulder, as before."

Edward cleared his throat. "This Eddowes woman . . . she was a prostitute!"

Inspector Abberline said she was. "And I have no doubt that the Berner Street victim will prove to have been on the game as well. That's the only common ground among his victims—they were all prostitutes."

"Evil combating evil," Edward said with a shake of his head. "When will it end?"

Inspector Abberline put down his cup. "The end, alas, is not yet in sight. We are still conducting door-to-door searches, and the populace is beginning to panic. We have our hands full dispersing the mobs."

"Mobs?" Edward asked. "Has there been trouble?"

"I regret to say there has. Everyone is so desperate to find someone to blame . . ." The Inspector allowed the unfinished sentence to linger a moment. "Earlier today a constable was chasing a petty thief through the streets, and someone who saw them called out, 'It's the Ripper!' Several men joined in the chase, and then others, as the word spread that it was the Ripper the constable was pursuing. That mob was thirsting for blood—nothing less than a lynching would have satisfied them. The thief and the constable ended up barricading themselves in a building together until help could arrive."

Edward shook his head sadly. "The world has gone mad."

"It's why I have come to you, Vicar," Inspector Abberline said. "You can help calm them down. You could speak to them, persuade them to compose themselves. Your presence in the streets will offer a measure of reassurance."

"Of course," Edward said quickly. "Shall we leave now? I'll get my coat."

The Inspector turned to me. "Mrs. Wickham, thank you for the tea. Now we must be going." I saw both men to the door.

The Inspector did not know he had interrupted a disagreement between my husband and me, one that was recurring with increasing frequency of late. But I had no wish to revive the dispute when Edward returned; the shadow of these two new murders lay like a shroud over all other concerns. I retired to my sewing closet, where I tried to calm my spirit through prayer. One could not think dispassionately of this unknown man wandering the streets of London's East End, a man who hated women so profoundly that he cut away those parts of the bodies that proclaimed his victims to be female. I tried to pray for *him*, lost soul that he is; God forgive me, I could not.

1 October 1888, St. Jude's Vicarage.

Early the next morning the fog lay so thick about the vicarage that the street gaslights were still on. They performed their usual efficient function of lighting the *tops* of the poles; looking down from our bedroom window, I could not see the street below.

Following our morning reading from the Scriptures, Edward called my attention to an additional passage. "Since you are aware of what the Ripper does to his victims, Beatrice, it will be to your benefit to hear this. Attend. 'Let the breast be torn open and the heart and vitals be taken from hence and thrown over the shoulder.'"

A moment of nausea overtook me. "The same way Annie Chapman and the others were killed."

"Exactly," Edward said with a hint of triumph in his voice. "Those are Solomon's words, ordering the execution of three murderers. I wonder if anyone has pointed this passage out to Inspector Abberline? It could be of assistance in ascertaining the rationale behind these murders, perhaps revealing something of the killer's mental disposition . . ." He continued in this speculative vein for a while longer.

I was folding linen as I listened. When he paused for breath, I asked Edward about his chambray shirt. "I've not seen it these two weeks."

"Eh? It will turn up. I'm certain you have put it away somewhere."

I was equally certain I had not. Then, with some trepidation, I reintroduced the subject of our disagreement the night before. "Edward, would you be willing to reconsider your position concerning charitable donations? If parishioners can't turn to their church for help—"

"Allow me to interrupt you, my dear," he said. "I am convinced that suffering *cannot* be reduced by indiscriminately passing out money but only through the realistic appraisal of each man's problems. So long as the lower classes depend upon charity to see them through hard times, they will never learn thrift and the most propitious manner of spending what money they have."

Edward's "realistic appraisal" of individual problems always ended the same way, with little lectures on how to economize. "But surely in cases of extreme hardship," I said, "a small donation would not be detrimental to their future well-being."

"Ah, but how are we to determine who are those in true need? They will tell any lie to get their hands on a few coins which they promptly spend on hard drink. And then they threaten us when those coins are not forthcoming! This is the legacy my predecessor at St. Jude's has left us, this expectancy that the church *owes* them charity!"

That was true; the vicarage had been stoned more than once when Edward had turned petitioners away. "But the children,

Edward—surely we can help the children! They are not to blame for their parents' wastrel ways."

Edward sat down next to me and took my hand. "You have a soft heart and a generous nature, Beatrice, and I venerate those qualities in you. Your natural instinct for charity is one of your most admirable traits." He smiled sadly. "Nevertheless, how will these poor, desperate creatures ever learn to care for their own children if we do it for them? And there is this. Has it not occurred to you that God may be testing *us*? How simple it would be, to hand out a few coins and convince ourselves we have done our Christian duty! No, Beatrice, God is asking more of us than that. We must hold firm in our resolve."

I acquiesced, seeing no chance of prevailing against such unshakable certitude that God's will was dictating our course of action. Furthermore, Edward Wickham was my husband and I owed him obedience, even when my heart was troubled and filled with uncertainty. It was his decision to make, not mine.

"Do not expect me until tea time," Edward said as he rose and went to fetch his greatcoat. "Mr. Lusk has asked me to attend a meeting of the Whitechapel Vigilance Committee, and I then have my regular calls to make. Best you not go out today, my dear, at least until Inspector Abberline has these riots under control." Edward's duties were keeping him away from the vicarage more and more. He sometimes would return in the early hours of the morning, melancholy and exhausted from trying to help a man find night work or from locating shelter for a homeless widow and her children. At times he seemed not to remember where he'd been; I was concerned for his health and his spirit.

The fog was beginning to lift by the time he departed, but I still could not see very far—except in my mind's eye. If one were to proceed down Commercial Street and then follow Aldgate to Leadenhall and Cornhill on to the point where six roads meet at a statue of the Duke of Wellington, one would find onself in front of the imposing Royal Exchange, its rich interior murals and Turkish floor paving a proper setting for the transactions undertaken there. Across Threadneedle Street, the Bank of England, with its windowless lower stories, and the rocklike Stock Exchange both raise their impressive façades. Then one could turn to the opposite direction and behold several other banking establishments clustered around Mansion House, the Lord Mayor's residence. It still dumbfounds me to realize that the wealth of the nation is concentrated there, in so small an area . . . all within walking distance of the worst slums in the nation.

Do wealthy bankers ever spare a thought for the *appalling* poverty of Whitechapel and Spitalfields? The people living within the boundaries of St. Jude's parish are crowded like animals into a labyrinth of courts and alleys, none of which intersect major streets. The crumbling, hazardous buildings fronting the courts house complete families in each room, some-times numbering as many as a dozen people; in such circum-stances, incest is common . . . and, some say, inevitable. The buildings reek from the liquid sewage accumulated in the base-ments, while the courts themselves stink of garbage that attracts vermin, dogs, and other scavengers. Often one standing pipe in the courtyard serves as the sole source of water for all the inhab-itants of three or four buildings, an outdoor pipe that freezes with unremitting regularity during the winter. Once Edward and I were called out in the middle of the night to succor a woman suffering from scarlet fever; we found her in a foul-smelling single room with three children and four pigs. Her husband, a cabman, had committed suicide the month before; and it wasn't until we were leaving that we discovered one of the children had been lying there dead for thirteen days.

The common lodging houses are even worse—filthy and infested and reservoirs of disease. In such doss houses a bed can be rented for fourpence for the night, strangers often sharing a bed because neither has the full price alone. There is no such thing as privacy, since the beds are lined up in crowded rows in the manner of dormitories. Beds are rented indiscriminately to men and women alike; consequently many of the doss houses are in truth brothels, and even those that are not have no compunction about renting a bed to a prostitute when she brings a paying customer with her. Inspector Abberline once told us the police estimate there are twelve hundred prostitutes in Whitechapel alone, fertile hunting grounds for the man who pleasures himself with the butchering of ladies of the night.

Ever since the Ripper began stalking the East End, Edward has been campaigning for more police to patrol the back alleys and for better street lighting. The problem is that Whitechapel is so poor it cannot afford the rates to pay for these needed improvements. If there is to be help, it must come from outside. Therefore I have undertaken a campaign of my own. Every day I write to philanthropists, charitable establishments, government officials. I petition every personage of authority and good will with whose name I am conversant, pleading the cause of the *children* of Whitechapel, especially those ragged, dirty street arabs who sleep wherever they can, eat whatever they can scavenge or steal, and perform every unspeakable act demanded of them in exchange for a coin they can call their own.

12 October 1888, Golden Lane Mortuary, City of London.

Today I did something I have never done before: I wilfully disobeyed my husband. Edward had forbidden me to attend the inquest of Catherine Eddowes, saying I should not expose myself to such unsavory disclosures as were bound to be made. Also, he said it was unseemly for the vicar's wife to venture abroad unaccompanied, a dictum that impresses me as more appropriately belonging to another time and place. I waited until Edward left the vicarage and then hurried on my way. My path took me past one of the larger slaughterhouses in the area; with my handkerchief covering my mouth and nose to keep out the stench, I had to cross the road to avoid the blood and urine flooding the pavement. Once I had left Whitechapel, however, the way was unencumbered.

Outside the Golden Lane Mortuary I was pleased to encounter Inspector Abberline; he was surprised to see me there and immediately offered himself as my protector. "Is the Reverend Mr. Wickham not with you?"

"He has business in Shoreditch," I answered truthfully, not adding that Edward found inquests distasteful and would not have attended in any event.

"This crowd could turn ugly, Mrs. Wickham," Inspector Abberline said. "Let me see if I can obtain us two chairs near the door."

That he did, with the result that I had to stretch in a most unladylike manner to see over other people's heads. "Inspector," I said, "have you learned the identity of the other woman who was killed the same night as Catherine Eddowes?"

"Yes, it was Elizabeth Stride—Long Liz, they called her. About forty-five years of age and homely as sin, if you'll pardon my speaking ill of the dead. They were all unattractive, all the Ripper's victims. One thing is certain, he didn't choose them for their beauty."

"Elizabeth Stride was a prostitute?"

"That she was, Mrs. Wickham, I'm sorry to say. She had nine children somewhere, and a husband, until he could tolerate her drunkenness no longer and turned her out. A woman with a nice big family like that and a husband who supported them—what reasons could she have had to turn to drink?"

I could think of nine or ten. "What about Catherine Eddowes? Did she have children too?"

Inspector Abberline rubbed the side of his nose. "Well, she had a daughter, that much we know. We haven't located her yet, though."

The inquest was ready to begin. The small room was crowded, with observers standing along the walls and even outside in the passageway. The presiding coroner called the first witness, the police constable who found Catherine Eddowes's body.

The remarkable point to emerge from the constable's testimony was that his patrol took him through Mitre Square, where he'd found the body, every fourteen or fifteen minutes. The Ripper had only fifteen minutes to inflict so much damage? How swift he was, how sure of what he was doing!

It came out during the inquest that the Eddowes woman had been strangled before her killer had cut her throat, thus explaining why she had not cried out. In response to my whispered question, Inspector Abberline said yes, the other victims had also been strangled first. When the physicians present at the postmortem testified, they were agreed that the killer had sound anatomical knowledge but they were not in accord as to the extent of his actual skill in removing the organs. Their reports of what had been done to the body were disturbing; I grew slightly faint during the description of how the flaps of the abdomen had been peeled back to expose the intestines.

Inspector Abberline's sworn statement was succinct and free of speculation; he testified as to the course of action pursued by the police following the discovery of the body. There were other witnesses, people who had encountered Catherine Eddowes on the night she was killed. At one time she had been seen speaking to a middle-aged man wearing a black coat of good quality which was now slightly shabby; it was the same description that had emerged during the investigation of one of the Ripper's earlier murders. But at the end of it all we were no nearer to knowing the Ripper's identity than ever; the verdict was "Willful murder by some person unknown."

I refused Inspector Abberline's offer to have one of his assistants escort me home. "That makes six women he's killed now, this Ripper," I said. "You need all of your men for your investigation."

The Inspector rubbed the side of his nose, a mannerism I was coming to recognize indicated uncertainty. "As a matter of fact, Mrs. Wickham, I am of the opinion that only four were killed by the same man. You are thinking of the woman murdered near St. Jude's Church? And the one on Osborn Street?" He shook his head. "Not the Ripper's work, I'm convinced of it."

"What makes you think so, Inspector?"

"Because while those two women did have their throats cut, they weren't cut in the same manner as the later victims." There is viciousness in the way the Ripper slashes his victims' throats ... he is left-handed, we know, and he slashes twice, once each way. The cuts are deep, brutal . . . he almost took Annie Chapman's head off. No, Polly Nichols was his first victim, then Chapman. And now this double murder, Elizabeth Stride and Catherine Eddowes. Those four are all the work of the same man."

I shuddered. "Did the four women know one another?"

"Not that we can determine," Inspector Abberline replied. "Evidently they had nothing in common except the fact that they were all four prostitutes."

More questions occurred to me, but I had detained the Inspector long enough. I bade him farewell and started back to St. Jude's, a long walk from Golden Lane. The daylight was beginning to fail, but I had no money for a hansom cab. I pulled my shawl tight about my shoulders and hurried my step, not wishing to be caught out of doors after dark. It was my husband's opinion that since the Ripper killed only prostitutes, respectable married women had nothing to fear. It was my opinion that my husband put altogether too much faith in the Ripper's ability to tell the difference.

I was almost home when a most unhappy incident ensued. A distraught woman approached me on Middlesex Street, carrying what looked like a bundle of rags which she thrust into my arms. Inside the rags was a dead baby. I cried out and almost dropped the cold little body.

"All he needed were a bit o' milk," the mother said, tears running down her cheeks.

"Oh, I am so sorry!" I gasped helplessly. The poor woman looked half-starved herself.

"They said it was no use a-sending to the church," she sobbed, "for you didn't never give nothing though you spoke kind."

I was so ashamed I had to lower my head. Even then I didn't

have tuppence in my pocket to give her. I slipped off my shawl and wrapped it around the tiny corpse. "Bury him in this."

She mumbled something as she took the bundle from me and staggered away. She would prepare to bury her child in the shawl, but at the last moment she would snatch back the shawl's warmth for herself. She would cry over her dead baby as she did it, but she would do it. I prayed that she would do it.

16 October 1888, St. Jude's Vicarage.

This morning I paid an out-of-work bricklayer fourpence to clean out our fireplaces. In the big fireplace in the kitchen, he made a surprising discovery: soot-blackened buttons from my husband's missing chambray shirt turned up. When later I asked Edward why he had burned his best shirt, he looked at me in utter astonishment and demanded to know why I had burned it. Yet we two are the only ones living at the vicarage.

22 October 1888, Spitalfields Market.

The chemist regretfully informed me that the price of arsenic had risen, so of necessity I purchased less than the usual quantity, hoping Edward would find the diminished volume sufficient. Keeping the vicarage free of rats was costly. When first we took up residence at St. Jude's, we believed the rats were coming from the warehouses farther along Commercial Street; but then we came to understand that every structure in Whitechapel was plagued with vermin. As fast as one killed them, others appeared to take their place.

A newspaper posted outside an alehouse caught my eye; I had made it a point to read every word published about the Ripper. The only new thing was that all efforts to locate the family of Catherine Eddowes, the Ripper's last victim, had failed. A front-page editorial demanded the resignation of the Commissioner of Police and various other men in authority. Three weeks had passed since the Ripper had taken two victims on the same night, and the police still had no helpful clues and no idea of who the Ripper was or when he would strike next. That he would strike again, no one doubted; that the police could protect the women of Whitechapel, no one believed.

In the next street I came upon a posted bill requesting anyone with information concerning the identity of the murderer to step forward and convey that information to the police. The request saddened me; the police could not have formulated a clearer admission of failure.

25 October 1888, St. Jude's Vicarage.

Edward is ill. When he had not appeared at the vicarage by tea time yesterday, I began to worry. I spent an anxious evening awaiting his return; it was well after midnight before I heard his key in the lock.

He looked like a stranger. His eyes were glistening and his clothes in disarray; his usual proud bearing had degenerated into a stoop, his shoulders hunched as if he were cold. The moment he caught sight of me he began berating me for failing to purchase the arsenic he needed to kill the rats; it was only when I led him to the pantry where he himself had spread the noxious powder around the rat holes did his reprimands cease. His skin was hot and dry, and with difficulty I persuaded him into bed.

But sleep would not come. I sat by the bed and watched him thrashing among the covers, throwing off the cool cloth I had placed on his forehead. Edward kept waving his hands as if trying to fend someone off; what nightmares was he seeing behind those closed lids? In his delirium he began to cry out. At first the words were not clear, but then I understood my husband to be saying, "Whores! Whores! All whores!"

When by two in the morning his fever had not broken, I knew I had to seek help. I wrapped my cloak about me and set forth, not permitting myself to dwell on what could be hiding in the shadows. I do not like admitting it, but I was terrified; nothing less than Edward's illness could have driven me into the streets of Whitechapel at night. But I reached my destination with nothing untoward happening; I roused Dr. Phelps from a sound sleep and rode back to the vicarage with him in his carriage.

When Dr. Phelps bent over the bed, Edward's eyes flew open; he seized the doctor's upper arm in a grip that made the man wince. "They must be stopped!" my husband whispered hoarsely. "They . . . must be stopped!"

"We will stop them," Dr. Phelps replied gently and eased Edward's hand away. Edward's eyes closed and his body resumed its thrashing.

The doctor's examination was brief. "The fever is making him hallucinate," he told me. "Sleep is the best cure, followed by a period of bed rest." He took a small vial from his bag and asked me to bring a glass of water. He tapped a few drops of liquid into the water, which he then poured into Edward's mouth as I held his head.

"What did you give him?" I asked.

"Laudanum, to make him sleep. I will leave the vial with you." Dr. Phelps rubbed his right arm where Edward had gripped him. "Strange, I do not recall Mr. Wickham as being left-handed."

"He is ambidextrous. This fever . . . will he recover?"

"The next few hours will tell. Give him more laudanum only if he awakes in this same disturbed condition, and then only one drop in a glass of water. I will be back later to see how he is."

When Dr. Phelps had gone, I replaced the cool cloth on Edward's forehead and resumed my seat by the bed. Edward did seem calmer now, the wild thrashing at an end and only the occasional twitching of the hands betraying his inner turmoil. By dawn he was in a deep sleep and seemed less feverish.

My spirit was too disturbed to permit me to sleep. I decided to busy myself with household chores. Edward's black greatcoat was in need of a good brushing, so that came first. It was then that I discovered the rust-colored stains on the cuffs; they did not look fresh, but I could not be certain. Removing them was a delicate matter. The coat had seen better days and the cloth would not withstand vigorous handling. But eventually I got the worst of the stains out and hung the coat in the armoire.

Then I knelt by the bedroom window and prayed. I asked God to vanquish the dark suspicions that had begun to cloud my mind.

Whitechapel had changed Edward. Since he had accepted the appointment to St. Jude's, he had become more distant, more aloof. He had always been a reserved man, speaking rarely of himself and never of his past. I knew nothing of his childhood, only that he had been born in London; he had always discouraged my inquiring about the years before we met. If my parents had still been living when Edward first began to pay court, they would never have permitted me to entertain a man with no background, no family, and no connections. But by then I had passed what was generally agreed to be a marriageable age, and I was enchanted by the appearance out of nowhere of a gentleman of compatible spirit who desired me to spend my life with him. All I knew of Edward was that he was a little older than most new curates were, suggesting that he had started in some other profession, or had at least studied for one, before joining the clergy. Our twelve years together had been peaceful ones, and I had never regretted my choice.

But try as he might to disguise the fact, Edward's perspective had grown harsher during our tenure in Whitechapel. Sadly, he held no respect for the people whose needs he was here to minister to. I once heard him say to a fellow vicar, "The lower classes render no useful service. They create no wealth—more often they destroy it. They degrade whatever they touch, and as individuals are most probably incapable of improvement. Thrift and good management mean nothing to them. I resist terming them hopeless, but perhaps that is what they are." The Edward Wickham I married would never have spoken so.

"Beatrice."

I glanced toward the bed; Edward was awake and watching me. I rose from my knees and went to his side. "How do you feel, Edward?"

"Weak, as if I've lost a lot of blood." He looked confused. "Am I ill?"

I explained about the fever. "Dr. Phelps says you need a great deal of rest."

"Dr. Phelps? He was here?" Edward remembered nothing of the doctor's visit. Nor did he remember where he'd been the night before or even coming home. "This is frightening," he said shakily. His speech was slurred, an effect of the laudanum. "Hours of my life missing and no memory of them?"

"We will worry about that later. Right now you must try to sleep some more."

"Sleep . . . yes." I sat and held his hand until he drifted off again.

When he awoke a second time a few hours later, I brought him a bowl of broth, which he consumed with reawakening appetite. My husband was clearly on the mend; he was considering getting out of bed when Dr. Phelps stopped by.

The doctor was pleased with Edward's progress. "Spend the rest of the day resting," he said, "and then tomorrow you may be allowed up. You must be careful not to overtax yourself or the fever may recur."

Edward put up a show of protesting, but I think he was secretly relieved that nothing was required of him except that he lie in bed all day. I escorted the doctor to the door.

"Make sure he eats," he said to me. "He needs to rebuild his strength."

I said I'd see to it. Then I hesitated; I could not go on without knowing. "Dr. Phelps, did anything happen last night?"

"I beg your pardon?"

He didn't know what I meant. "Did the Ripper strike again?"

Dr. Phelps smiled. "I am happy to say he did not. Perhaps we've seen an end of these dreadful killings, hmm?"

My relief was so great it was all I could do not to burst into tears. When the doctor had gone, I again fell to my knees and prayed, this time asking God to forgive me for entertaining such treacherous thoughts about my own husband.

1 November 1888, Leman Street Police Station, Whitechapel.

It was with a light heart that I left the vicarage this bright, crisp Tuesday morning. My husband was recovered from his recent indisposition and busy with his daily duties. I had received two encouraging replies to my petitions for charitable assistance for Whitechapel's children. And London had survived the entire month of October without another Ripper killing.

I was on my way to post two letters, my responses to the philan-thropists who seemed inclined to listen to my plea. In my letters I had pointed out that over half the children born in Whitechapel die before they reach the age of five. The ones that do not die are mentally and physically underdeveloped; many of them that are taken into pauper schools are adjudged abnormally dull if not actual mental defectives. Children frequently arrive at school crying from hunger and then collapse at their benches. In winter they are too cold to think about learning their letters or doing their sums. The schools themselves are shamefully mismanaged and the children sometimes mistreated; there are school direc-tors who pocket most of the budget and hire out the children to sweatshop owners as cheap labor.

What I proposed was the establishment of a boarding school for the children of Whitechapel, a place where the young would be provided with hygienic living conditions, wholesome food to eat, and warm clothing to wear—all before they ever set foot in a classroom. Then when their physical needs had been attended to, they would be given proper educational and moral instruc-tion. The school was to be administered by an honest and consci-entious director who could be depended upon never to exploit the downtrodden. All this would cost a great deal of money.

My letters went into the post accompanied by a silent prayer. I was then in Leman Street, not far from the police station. I stopped in and asked if Inspector Abberline was there.

He was; he greeted me warmly and offered me a chair. After inquiring after my husband's health, he sat back and looked at me expectantly.

Now that I was there, I felt a tinge of embarrassment. "It is presumptuous of me, I know," I said, "but may I make a suggestion? Concerning the Ripper, I mean. You've undoubtedly thought of every possible approach, but . . ." I didn't finish my sentence because he was laughing.

"Forgive me, Mrs. Wickham," he said, still smiling. "I would like to show you something." He went into another room and returned shortly carrying a large box filled with papers. "These are letters," he explained, "from concerned citizens like yourself. Each one offers a plan for capturing the Ripper. And we have two more boxes just like this one."

I flushed and rose to leave. "Then I'll not impose—"

"Please, Mrs. Wickham, take your seat. We read every letter that comes to us and give serious consideration to every suggestion made. I show you the box only to convince you we welcome suggestions."

I resumed my seat, not fully convinced but nevertheless encouraged by the Inspector's courtesy. "Very well." I tried to gather my thoughts. "The Ripper's first victim, you are convinced, was Polly Nichols?"

"Correct. Buck's Row, the last day of August."

"The *Illustrated Times* said that she was forty-two years old and separated from her husband, to whom she had borne five children. The cause of their separation was her propensity for strong drink. Mr. Nichols made his wife an allowance, according to the *Times,* until he learned of her prostitution—at which time he discontinued all pecuniary assistance. Is this account essentially correct?"

"Yes, it is."

"The Ripper's next victim was Annie Chapman, about forty, who was murdered early in September?"

"The night of the eighth," Inspector Abberline said, "although her body wasn't found until six the next morning. She was killed on Hanbury Street, less than half a mile from the Buck's Row site of Polly Nichols's murder."

I nodded. "Annie Chapman also ended on the streets because of drunkenness. She learned her husband had died only when her allowance stopped. When she tried to find her two children, she discovered they had been separated and sent to different schools, one of them abroad."

Inspector Abberline raised an eyebrow. "How did you ascertain that, Mrs. Wickham?"

"One of our parishioners knew her," I said. "Next came the double murder of Elizabeth Stride and Catherine Eddowes, during the small hours of the thirtieth of September. Berner Street and Mitre Square, a fifteen-minute walk from each other. The Stride woman was Swedish by birth and claimed to be a widow, but I have heard that may not be true. She was a notorious inebriate, according to one of the constables patrolling Fairclough Street, and she may simply have been ashamed to admit her husband would not allow her near the children—the *nine* children. Is this also correct?"

The Inspector was looking bemused. "It is."

"Of Catherine Eddowes I know very little. But the *Times* said she had spent the night before her death locked up in the Cloak Lane Police Station, because she'd been found lying drunk in the street somewhere in Aldgate. And you yourself told me she had a daughter. Did she also have a husband, Inspector?"

He nodded slowly. "A man named Conway. We've been unable to trace him."

The same pattern in each case. "You've said on more than one occasion that the four victims had only their prostitution in common. But in truth, Inspector, they had a great deal in common. They were all in their forties. They were all lacking in beauty. They had all been married. They all lost their homes through a weakness for the bottle." I took a breath. "And they were all mothers."

Inspector Abberline looked at me quizzically.

"They were all mothers *who abandoned their children.*"

He considered it. "You think the Ripper had been abandoned?"

"Is it not possible? Or perhaps he too had a wife he turned out because of drunkenness. I don't know where he fits into the pattern. But consider. The nature of the murders makes it quite clear that these women are not just killed the way the unfortunate victim of a highwayman is killed—the women are being *punished.*" I was uncomfortable speaking of such matters, but speak I must. "The manner of their deaths, one might say, is a grotesque version of the way they earned their livings."

The Inspector was also uncomfortable. "They were not raped, Mrs. Wickham."

"But of course they were, Inspector," I said softly. "They were raped with a knife."

I had embarrassed him. "We should not be speaking of this," he said, further chagrined at seeming to rebuke the vicar's wife. "These are not matters that concern you."

"All I ask is that you consider what I have said."

"Oh, I can promise you that," he answered wryly, and I believed him. "I do have some encouraging news," he continued, desirous of changing the subject. "We have been given more men to patrol the streets—more than have even before been concentrated in one section of London! The next time the Ripper strikes, we'll be ready for him."

"Then you think he will strike again."

"I fear so. He's not done yet."

It was the same opinion that was held by everyone else, but it was more ominous coming from the mouth of a police investigator. I thanked Inspector Abberline for his time and left.

The one thing that had long troubled me about the investigation of the Ripper murders was the refusal of the investigators to acknowledge that there was anything carnal about these violent acts. The killings were the work of a madman, the police and the newspapers agreed . . . as if that explained everything. But unless Inspector Abberline and the rest of those in authority could see the fierce hatred of women that drove the Ripper, I despaired of his ever being caught.

10 November 1888, Miller's Court, Spitalfields.

At three in the morning, I was still fully dressed, awaiting Edward's return to the vicarage. It had been hours since I'd made my last excuse to myself for his absence; his duties frequently kept him out late, but never this late. I was trying to decide whether I should go to Dr. Phelps for help when a frantic knocking started at the door.

It was a young market porter named Macklin who occasionally attended services at St. Jude's, and he was in a frantic state. "It's the missus," he gasped. "'Er time is come and the midwife's too drunk to stand up. Will you come?"

I said I would. "Let me get a few things." I was distracted, wanting to send him away; but this was the Macklins' first child and I couldn't turn down his plea for help.

We hurried off in the direction of Spitalfields; the couple had recently rented a room in a slum building facing on Miller's Court. I knew the area slightly. Edward and I had once been called to a doss house there to minister to a dying man. That was the first time I'd ever been inside one of the common lodging houses; it was a big place, over three hundred beds and every one of them rented for the night.

Miller's Court was right across the street from the doss house. As we went into the courtyard, a girl of about twelve unfolded herself from the doorway where she had been huddled and tugged at my skirt. "Fourpence for a doss, lady?"

"Get out of 'ere!" Macklin yelled. "Go on!"

"Just a moment," I stopped him. I asked the girl if she had no home to go to.

"Mam turned me out," the girl answered sullenly. "Says don't come back 'til light."

I understood; frequently the women here put their children out on the street while they rented their room for immoral purposes. "I have no money," I told the girl, "but you may come inside."

"Not in my room, she don't!" Macklin shouted.

"She can be of help, Mr. Macklin," I said firmly.

He gave in ungraciously. The girl, who said her name was Rose Howe, followed us inside. Straightaway I started to sneeze; the air was filled with particles of fur. Someone in the building worked at plucking hair from dogs, rabbits, and perhaps even rats for sale to a furrier. There were other odors as well; the building held at least one fish that had not been caught yesterday. I could smell paste, from drying match boxes, most likely. It was all rather overpowering.

Macklin led us up a flight of stairs from which the banisters had been removed—for firewood, no doubt. Vermin-infested wallpaper was hanging in strips above our heads. Macklin opened a door upon a small room where his wife lay in labor. Mrs. Macklin was still a girl herself, only a few years older than Rose Howe. She was lying on a straw mattress, undoubtedly infested with fleas, on a broken-down bedstead. A few boxes were stacked against one wall; the only other piece of furniture was a plank laid across two stacks of bricks. I sent Macklin down to fill a bucket from the water pipe in the courtyard, and then I put Rose Howe to washing some rags I found in a corner.

It was a long labor. Rose curled up on the floor and went to sleep. Macklin wandered out for a few pints.

Day had broken before the baby came. Macklin was back, sobriety returning with each cry of pain from his young wife. Since it was daylight, Rose Howe could have returned to her own room but instead stayed and helped; she stood like a rock, letting Mrs. Macklin grip her thin wrists during the final bearing-down.

The baby was undersized; but as I cleared out her mouth and nose, she voiced a howl that announced her arrival to the world in no uncertain terms. I watched a smile light the faces of both girls as Rose cleaned the baby and placed her in her mother's arms. Then Rose held the cord as I tied it off with thread in two places and cut it through with my sewing scissors.

Macklin was a true loving husband. "Don't you worry none, love," he said to his wife. "Next 'un'll be a boy."

I told Rose Howe I'd finish cleaning up and for her to go home. Then I told Macklin to bring his daughter to St. Jude's for christening. When at last I was ready to leave, the morning sun was high in the sky.

To my surprise the small courtyard was crowded with people, one of whom was a police constable. I tried to work my way through to the street, but no one would yield a passage for me; I'm not certain they even knew I was there. They were all trying to peer through the broken window of a ground-floor room. "Constable?" I called out. "What has happened here?"

He knew me; he blocked the window with his body and said, "You don't want to look in there, Mrs. Wickham."

A fist of ice closed around my heart; the constable's facial expression already told me, but I had to ask nonetheless. I swallowed and said, "Is it the Ripper?"

He nodded slowly. "It appears so, ma'am. I've sent for Inspector Abberline—you there, stand back!" Then, to me again: "He's not never killed indoors afore. This is new for him."

I was having trouble catching my breath. "That means . . . he didn't have to be quick this time. That means he could take as much time as he liked."

The constable was clenching and unclenching his jaw. "Yes'm. He took his time."

Oh dear God. "Who is she, do you know?"

"The rent-collector found her. Here, Thomas, what's her name again?"

A small, frightened-looking man spoke up. "Mary . . . Mary

Kelly. Three months behind in 'er rent, she was. I thought she was hidin' from me."

The constable scowled. "So you broke the window to try to get in?"

"'Ere, now, that winder's been broke these past six weeks! I pulled out the bit o' rag she'd stuffed in the hole so I could reach through and push back the curtain—just like you done, guv'nor, when you wanted to see in!" The rent-collector had more to say, but his words were drowned out by the growing noise of the crowd, which by now had so multiplied in its numbers that it overflowed from Miller's Court into a passageway leading to the street. A few women were sobbing, one of them close to screaming.

Inspector Abberline arrived with two other men, all three of them looking grim. The Inspector immediately tried the door and found it locked. "Break out the rest of the window," he ordered. "The rest of you, stand back. Mrs. Wickham, what are you doing here? Break in the window, I say!"

One of his men broke out the rest of the glass and crawled over the sill. We heard a brief, muffled cry, and then the door was opened from the inside. Inspector Abberline and his other man pushed into the room . . . and the latter abruptly rushed back out again, retching. The constable hastened to his aid, and without stopping to think about it, I stepped into the room.

What was left of Mary Kelly was lying on a cot next to a small table. Her throat had been cut so savagely that her head was nearly severed. Her left shoulder had been chopped through so that her arm remained attached to the body only by a flap of skin. Her face had been slashed and disfigured, and her nose had been hacked away . . . and carefully laid on the small table beside the cot. Her breasts had been sliced off and placed on the same table. The skin had been peeled from her forehead; her thighs had also been stripped of their skin. The legs themselves had been spread in an indecent posture and then slashed to the bone. And Mary Kelly's abdomen had been ripped open, and between her feet lay one of her internal organs . . . possibly the liver. On the table lay a piece of the victim's brown plaid woolen petticoat half-wrapped around still another organ. The missing skin had been carefully mounded on the table next to the other body parts, as if the Ripper were rebuilding his victim. But this time the killer had not piled the intestines above his victim's shoulder as he'd done before; this time, he had taken them away with him. Then as a final embellishment, he had pushed Mary Kelly's right hand into her ripped-open stomach.

Have you punished her enough, Jack? Don't you want to hurt her some more?

I felt a hand grip my arm and steer me firmly outside. "You shouldn't be in here, Mrs. Wickham," Inspector Abberline said. He left me leaning against the wall of the building as he went back inside; a hand touched my shoulder and Thomas the rent-collector said, "There's a place to sit, over 'ere." He led me to an upended wooden crate, where I sank down gratefully. I sat with my head bent over my knees for some time before I could collect myself enough to utter a prayer for Mary Kelly's soul.

Inspector Abberline's men were asking questions of everyone in the crowd. When one of them approached me, I explained I'd never known Mary Kelly and was here only because of the birth of the Macklin baby in the same building. The Inspector himself came over and commanded me to go home; I was not inclined to dispute the order.

"It appears this latest victim does not fit your pattern," the Inspector said as I was leaving. "Mary Kelly was a prostitute, but she was still in her early twenties. And from what we've learned so far, she had no husband and no children."

So the last victim had been neither middle-aged, nor married, nor a mother. It was impossible to tell whether poor Mary Kelly had been homely or not. But the Ripper had clearly chosen a woman this time who was markedly different from his earlier victims, deviating from his customary pattern. I wondered what it meant; had some change taken place in his warped, evil mind? Had he progressed one step deeper into madness?

I thought about that on the way home from Miller's Court. I thought about that, and about Edward.

10 November 1888, St. Jude's Vicarage.

It was almost noon by the time I reached the vicarage. Edward was there, fast asleep. Normally he never slept during the day, but the small vial of laudanum Dr. Phelps had left was on the bedside table; Edward had drugged himself into a state of oblivion.

I picked up his clothes from the floor where he'd dropped them and went over every piece carefully; not a drop of blood anywhere. But the butchering of Mary Kelly had taken place indoors; the butcher could simply have removed his clothing before beginning his "work." Next I checked all the fireplaces, but none of them had been used to burn anything. It *could* be happenstance, I told myself. I didn't know how long Edward had been blacking out; it was probably not as singular as it seemed that one of his spells should coincide with a Ripper slaying. That's what I told myself.

The night had exhausted me. I had no appetite but a cup of fresh tea would be welcome. I was on my way to the kitchen when a knock at the door stopped me. It was the constable I'd spoken to at Miller's Court.

He handed me an envelope. "Inspector Abberline said to give you this." He touched his cap and was gone.

I went to stand by the window where the light was better. Inside the envelope was a hastily scrawled note.

My dear Mrs. Wickham,
Further information has come to light that makes it appear that your theory of a pattern in the Ripper murders may not be erroneous after all. Although Mary Kelly currently had no

*husband, she had at one time been married. At the age of
sixteen she wed a collier who died less than a year later. During
her widowhood she found a series of men to support her for
brief periods until she ended on the streets. And she was given
to strong drink, as the other four victims were. But the most
cogent revelation is the fact that Mary Kelly was pregnant.
That would explain why she was so much younger than the
Ripper's earlier victims: he was stopping her before she could
abandon her children.*

Yrs,

Frederick Abberline

So. Last night the Ripper had taken two lives instead of one,
assuring that a fertile young woman would never bear children
to suffer the risk of being forsaken. It was not in the Ripper's
nature to consider that his victims had themselves been abandoned in their time of need. Polly Nichols, Annie Chapman,
Elizabeth Stride, and Catherine Eddowes had all taken to drink
for reasons no one would ever know and had subsequently been
turned out of their homes. And now there was Mary Kelly, widowed
while little more than a child and with no livelihood—undoubtedly she lacked the education and resources to support herself
honorably. Polly, Annie, Elizabeth, Catherine, and Mary . . . they
had all led immoral and degraded lives, every one of them. But
in not even one instance had it been a matter of choice.

I put Inspector Abberline's note in a drawer in the writing
table and returned to the kitchen; I'd need to start a fire to make
the tea. The wood box had recently been filled, necessitating my
moving the larger pieces to get at the twigs underneath.
Something else was underneath as well. I pulled out a long strip
of brown plaid wool cloth with brown stains on it. Brown plaid
wool. Mary Kelly's petticoat. Mary Kelly's blood.

The room began to whirl. There it was. No more making of
excuses. No more denying the truth. I was married to the Ripper.
For twelve years Edward had kept the odious secret of his

abnormal inner being, hiding behind a mask of gentility and even godliness. He had kept his secret well. But no more. The masquerade was ended. I sank to my knees and prayed for guidance. More than anything in the world I wanted to send for Inspector Abberline and have him take away the monster who was sleeping upstairs. But if the laudanum-induced sleep had the same effect this time as when he was ill, Edward would awake as his familiar rational self. If I could speak to him, make him understand what he'd done, give him the opportunity to surrender voluntarily to the police, surely that would be the most charitable act I could perform under these hideous circumstances. If Edward were to have any chance at all for redemption, he must beg both God and man for forgiveness.

With shaking hands I tucked the strip of cloth away in my pocket and forced myself to concentrate on the routine of making tea. The big kettle was already out; but when I went to fill it with water, it felt heavy. I lifted the lid and found myself looking at a pile of human intestines.

I did not faint . . . most probably because I was past all feeling by then. I tried to think. The piece of cloth Edward could have used to wipe off the knife; then he would have put the cloth in the wood box with the intention of burning it later. But why wait? And the viscera in the tea kettle . . . was I meant to find that? Was this Edward's way of asking for help? And where was the knife? Systematically I began to look for it; but after nearly two hours' intensive search, I found nothing. He could have disposed of the knife on his way home. He could have hidden it in the church. He could have it under his pillow.

I went into the front parlor and forced myself to sit down. I was frightened; I didn't want to stay under the same roof with him, I didn't want to fight for his soul. Did he even have a soul any more? The Edward Wickham I had lain beside every night for twelve years was a counterfeit person, one whose carefully fabricated personality and demeanor had been devised to control and constrain the demon imprisoned inside. The deception had worked well until we came to Whitechapel, when the constraints began to weaken and the demon escaped. What had caused the change—was it the place itself? The constant presence of prostitutes in the streets? It was beyond my comprehension.

The stresses of the past twenty-four hours eventually proved too much for me; my head fell forward, and I slept.

Edward's hand on my shoulder awoke me. I started, and gazed at him with apprehension; but his face showed only gentle concern. "Is something wrong, Beatrice? Why are you sleeping in the afternoon?"

I pressed my fingertips against my eyes. "I did not sleep last night. The Macklin baby was born early this morning."

"Ah! Both mother and child doing well, I trust? I hope you impressed upon young Macklin the importance of an early christening. But Beatrice, the next time you are called out, I would be most grateful if you could find a way to send me word. When you had not returned by midnight, I began to grow worried."

That was the first falsehood Edward had ever told me that I could recognize as such; it was I who had been waiting for him at midnight. His face was so open, so seemingly free of guile . . . did he honestly have no memory of the night before, or was he simply exceptionally skilled in the art of deception? I stood up and began to pace. "Edward, we must talk about last night . . . about what you did last night."

His eyebrow shot up. "I?"

I couldn't look at him. "I found her intestines in the tea kettle. Mary Kelly's intestines."

"Intestines?" I could hear the distaste in his voice. "What is this, Beatrice? And who is Mary Kelly?"

"She's the woman you killed last night!" I cried. "Surely you knew her name!" I turned to confront him . . . and saw a look of such loathing on his face that I took a step back. "Oh!" I gasped involuntarily. "Please don't . . ." Edward? Jack?

The look disappeared immediately—he knew, he knew what he was doing! "I killed someone last night, you say?" he asked, his rational manner quickly restored. "And then I put her intestines . . . in the tea kettle? Why don't you show me, Beatrice?"

Distrustful of his suggestion, I nevertheless led the way to the kitchen. As I'd half expected, the tea kettle was empty and spotlessly clean. With a heavy heart I pulled the piece of brown plaid cloth out of my pocket. "But here is something you neglected to destroy."

He scowled. "A dirty rag?"

"Oh, Edward, stop professing you know nothing of this! It is a strip from Mary Kelly's petticoat, as you well realize! Edward, you must go to the police. Confess all, make your peace with God. No one else can stop your nocturnal expeditions—you must stop yourself! Go to Inspector Abberline."

He held out one hand. "Give me the rag," he said expressionlessly.

"Think of your soul, Edward! This is your one chance for salvation! You *must* confess!"

"The rag, Beatrice."

"I cannot! Edward, do you not understand? You are accursed—your own actions have damned you! You must go down on your knees and beg for forgiveness!"

Edward lowered his hand. "You are ill, my dear. This delusion of yours that I am the Ripper—that is the crux of your accusation, is it not? This distraction is most unbefitting the wife of the vicar of St. Jude's. I cannot tolerate the thought that before long you may be found raving in the street. We will pray together, we will ask God to send you self-control."

I thought I understood what that meant. "Very well . . . if you will not turn yourself over to the police, there is only one alternate course of action open to you. You must kill yourself."

"Beatrice!" He was shocked. "Suicide is a *sin!*"

His reaction was so absurd that I had to choke down a hysterical laugh. But it made me understand that further pleading would be fruitless. He was hopelessly insane; I would never be able to reach him.

Edward was shaking his head. "I am most disturbed, Beatrice. This dementia of yours is more profound than I realized. I must tell you I am unsure of my capacity to care for you while you are subject to delusions. Perhaps an institution is the rightful solution."

I was stunned. "You would put me in an asylum?"

He sighed. "Where else will we find physicians qualified to treat dementia? But if you cannot control these delusions of yours, I see no other recourse. You must pray, Beatrice, you must pray for the ability to discipline your thoughts."

He *could* have me locked away; he could have me locked away and then continue unimpeded with his ghastly killings, never having to worry about a wife who noticed too much. It was a moment before I could speak. "I will do as you say, Edward. I will pray."

"Excellent! I will pray with you. But first—the rag, please."

Slowly, reluctantly, I handed him the strip of Mary Kelly's petticoat. Edward took a fireplace match and struck it, and the evidence linking him to murder dissolved into thin black smoke that spiralled up the chimney. Then we prayed; we asked God to give me the mental and spiritual willpower I lacked.

Following that act of hypocrisy, Edward suggested that I prepare our tea; I put the big tea kettle aside and used my smaller one. Talk during tea was about several church duties Edward still needed to perform. I spoke only when spoken to and was careful to give no offense. I did everything I could to assure my husband that I deferred to his authority.

Shortly before six Edward announced he was expected at a meeting of the Whitechapel Vigilance Committee. I waited until he was out of sight and went first to the cupboard for a table knife and then to the writing table for a sheet of foolscap. Then I stepped into the pantry and began to scrape up as much of the arsenic from the rat holes as I could.

*23 February 1892, Whitechapel Charitable
Institute for Indigent Children.*

Inspector Abberline sat in my office, nodding approval at everything he'd seen. "It's difficult to believe," he said, "that these are
the same thin and dirty children who only months ago used to
sleep in doorways and under wooden crates. You have worked
wonders, Mrs. Wickham. The board of trustees could not have
found a better director. Are the children learning to read and
write? *Can* they learn?"

"Some can," I answered. "Others are slower. The youngest are the
quickest, it seems. I have great hopes for them."

"I wonder if they understand how fortunate they are. What a
pity the Reverend Mr. Wickham didn't live to see this. He would
have been so pleased with what you've accomplished."

"Yes." Would he have? Edward always believed the poor should
care for their own.

The Inspector was still thinking of my late husband. "I had an
aunt who succumbed to gastric fever," he said. "Dreadful way to
die, dreadful." He suddenly realized I might not care to be
reminded of the painful method of Edward's passing. "I do beg
your pardon—that was thoughtless of me."

I told him not to be concerned. "I am reconciled to his death
now, as much as I can ever be. My life is here now, in the school,
and it is a most rewarding way to spend my days."

He smiled. "I can see you are in your element." Then he
sobered. "I came not only to see your school but also to tell you
something." He leaned forward in his chair. "The file on the
Ripper is officially closed. It's been more than two years since his
last murder. For whatever reason he stopped, he *did* stop. That
particular reign of terror is over. The case is closed."

My heart lifted. Keeping up my end of the conversation, I
asked, "Why do you think he stopped, Inspector?"

He rubbed the side of his nose. "He stopped either because
he's dead or because he's locked up somewhere, in an asylum or

perhaps in prison for some other crime. Forgive my bluntness, Mrs. Wickham, but I earnestly hope it is the former. Inmates have been known to escape from asylums and prisons."

"I understand. Do you think the file will ever be reopened?"

"Not for one hundred years. Once a murder case is marked closed, the files are sealed and the date is written on the outside when they can be made public. It will be a full century before anyone looks at those papers again."

It couldn't be more official than that; the case was indeed closed. "A century . . . why so long a time?"

"Well, the hundred-year rule was put into effect to guarantee the anonymity of all those making confidential statements to the police during the course of the investigation. It's best that way. Now no one will be prying into our reports on the Ripper until the year 1992. It is over."

"Thank Heaven for that."

"Amen."

Inspector Abberline chatted a little longer and then took his leave. I strolled through the halls of my school, a former church building adapted to its present needs. I stopped in one of the classrooms. Some of the children were paying attention to the teacher, others were daydreaming, a few were drawing pictures. Just like children everywhere.

Not all the children who pass through here will be helped; some will go on to better themselves, but others will slide back into the life of the streets. I can save none of them. I must not add arrogance to my other offenses by assuming the role of deliverer; God does not entrust the work of salvation to one such as I. But I am permitted to offer the children a chance, to give them the opportunity to lift themselves above the life of squalor and crime that is all they have ever known. I do most earnestly thank God for granting me this privilege.

Periodically I return to Miller's Court. I go there not because it is the site of Edward's final murder, but because it is where I last saw Rose Howe, the young girl who helped me deliver the

Macklin baby. There is a place for Rose in my school. I have not found her yet, but I will keep searching.

My life belongs to the children of Whitechapel now. My prayers are for them; those prayers are the only ones of mine ever likely to be answered. When I do pray for myself, it is always and only to ask for an easier place in Hell.

Ghost Station

CAROLYN WHEAT

Carolyn Wheat (b. 1946), was a New York legal aid attorney for twenty-three years and later an administrative law judge. When she introduced Brooklyn lawyer Cass Jameson in *Dead Men's Thoughts* (1983), the torrent of lawyer novelists (male and female) that would be unleashed by the success of Scott Turow and John Grisham had not yet begun. That first novel was well received, receiving an Edgar nomination, but Wheat proved the opposite of prolific, the second Jameson novel appearing three years later, the third not for another eleven. When she stepped up production with books like *Mean Streak* (1996) and *Troubled Waters* (1997), a novel that looked back on radical 1960s activism much more briefly but just as effectively as Turow's *Laws of Our Fathers* (1996), it became obvious that Wheat ranks near the top not just among lawyer novelists but contemporary crime writers generally. After leaving the practice of law, she became a valued teacher of writing, including a stint as Writer in Residence at the University of Central Oklahoma.

Wheat's short stories, collected in *Tales Out of School* (2000), display a variety nearly as remarkable as their uniform excellence. Some of them have the expected legal background, including the chilling jury-room tale "Cruel and Unusual" and a rare Sherlock Holmes court-room story, "The Adventure of the Angel's Trumpet," but many of them do not. "Ghost Station," about a New York transit cop, she credits to her experience working for the NYPD.

I f there's one thing I can't stand, it's a woman drunk. The words burned my memory the way Irish whiskey used to burn my throat, only there was no pleasant haze of alcohol to follow. Just bitter heartburn pain.

It was my first night back on the job, back to being Sergeant Maureen Gallagher instead of "the patient." Wasn't it hard enough being a transit cop, hurtling beneath the streets of Manhattan on a subway train that should have been in the Transit Museum? Wasn't it enough that after four weeks of detox I felt empty instead of clean and sober? Did I *have* to have some rookie's casually cruel words ricocheting in my brain like a wild-card bullet?

Why couldn't I remember the good stuff? Why couldn't I think about O'Hara's beefy handshake, Greenspan's "Glad to see ya, Mo," Ianuzzo's smiling welcome? Why did I have to run the tape in my head of Manny Delgado asking Captain Lomax for a different partner?

"Hey, I got nothing against a lady sarge, Cap," he'd said. "Don't get me wrong. It's just that if there's one thing I can't stand . . ." Et cetera.

Lomax had done what any standup captain would—kicked Delgado's ass and told him the assignment stood. What he hadn't known was that I'd heard the words and couldn't erase them from my mind.

Even without Delgado, the night hadn't gotten off to a great start. Swinging in at midnight for a twelve-to-eight, I'd been greeted with the news that I was on Graffiti Patrol, the dirtiest, most mind-numbing assignment in the whole transit police duty roster. I was a sergeant, damn it, on my way to a gold shield, and I wasn't going to earn it dodging rats in tunnels or going after twelve-year-olds armed with spray paint.

Especially when the rest of the cop world, both under- and aboveground, was working overtime on the torch murders of homeless people. There'd been four human bonfires in the past six weeks, and the cops were determined there wouldn't be a fifth.

Was Lomax punishing me, or was this assignment his subtle way of easing my entry back into the world? Either way, I resented it. I wanted to be a real cop again, back with Sal Minucci, my old partner. He was assigned to the big one, in the thick of the action, where both of us belonged. I should have been with him. I was Anti-Crime, for God's sake, I should have been assigned—

Or should I? Did I really want to spend my work nights prowling New York's underground skid row, trying to get information from men and women too zonked out to take care of legs gone gangrenous, whose lives stretched from one bottle of Cool Breeze to another?

Hell, yes. If it would bring me one step closer to that gold shield, I'd interview all the devils in hell. On my day off.

If there's one thing I can't stand, it's a woman drunk.

What did Lomax think—that mingling with winos would topple me off the wagon? That I'd ask for a hit from some guy's short dog and pass out in the Bleecker Street station? Was that why he'd kept me off the big one and had me walking a rookie through routine Graffiti Patrol?

Was I getting paranoid, or was lack of alcohol rotting my brain?

Manny and I had gone to our respective locker rooms to suit up. Plain clothes—and I do mean plain. Long johns first; damp winter had a way of seeping down into the tunnels and into your very blood. Then a pair of denims the Goodwill would have turned down. Thick wool socks, fisherman's duck boots, a black turtleneck, and a photographer's vest with lots of pockets. A black knit hat pulled tight over my red hair.

Then the gear: flashlight, more important than a gun on this assignment, handcuffs, ticket book, radio, gun, knife. A slapper, an oversize blackjack, hidden in the rear pouch of the vest. They were against regulations; I'd get at least a command discipline if caught with it, but experience told me I'd rather have it than a gun going against a pack of kids.

I'd forgotten how heavy the stuff was; I felt like a telephone lineman.

I looked like a cat burglar.

Delgado and I met at the door. It was obvious he'd never done vandal duty before. His tan chinos were immaculate, and his hiking boots didn't look waterproof. His red plaid flannel shirt was neither warm enough nor the right dark color. With his Latin good looks, he would have been stunning in an L. L. Bean catalog, but after ten minutes in a subway tunnel, he'd pass for a chimney sweep.

"Where are we going?" he asked, his tone a shade short of sullen. And there was no respectful "Sergeant" at the end of the question, either. This boy needed a lesson in manners.

I took a malicious delight in describing our destination. "The Black Hole of Calcutta," I replied cheerfully, explaining that I meant the unused lower platform of the City Hall station downtown. The oldest, darkest, dankest spot in all Manhattan. If there were any subway alligators, they definitely lurked in the Black Hole.

The expression on Probationary Transit Police Officer Manuel Delgado's face was all I could have hoped for. I almost—but not quite—took pity on the kid when I added, "And after that, we'll try one or two of the ghost stations."

"Ghost stations?" Now he looked really worried. "What are those?"

This kid wasn't just a rookie; he was a suburbanite. Every New Yorker knew about ghost stations, abandoned platforms where trains no longer stopped. They were still lit, though, and showed up in the windows of passing trains like ghost towns on the prairie. They were ideal canvases for the aspiring artists of the underground city.

I explained on the subway, heading downtown. The car, which

rattled under the city streets like a tin lizzie, was nearly riderless at 1:00 a.m. A typical Monday late hour.

The passengers were one Orthodox Jewish man falling asleep over his Hebrew Bible, two black women, both reading thick paperback romances, the obligatory pair of teenagers making out in the last seat, and an old Chinese woman.

I didn't want to look at Delgado. More than once I'd seen a fleeting smirk on his face when I glanced his way. It wasn't enough for insubordination; the best policy was to ignore it.

I let the rhythm of the subway car lull me into a litany of the A.A. slogans I was trying to work into my life: EASY DOES IT. KEEP IT SIMPLE, SWEETHEART. ONE DAY AT A TIME. I saw them in my mind the way they appeared on the walls at meetings, illuminated, like old Celtic manuscripts.

This night I had to take one hour at a time. Maybe even one minute at a time. My legs felt wobbly. I was a sailor too long from the sea. I'd lost my subway legs. I felt white and thin, as though I'd had several major organs removed.

Then the drunk got on. One of the black women got off, the other one looked up at the station sign and went back to her book, and the drunk got on.

If there's one thing I can't stand, it's a woman drunk.

ONE DAY AT A TIME. EASY DOES IT.

I stiffened. The last thing I wanted was to react in front of Delgado, but I couldn't help it. The sight of an obviously intoxicated man stumbling into our subway car brought the knowing smirk back to his face.

There was one at every A.A. meeting. No matter how nice the neighborhood, how well-dressed most people attending the meeting were, there was always a drunk. A real drunk, still reeling, still reeking of cheap booze. My sponsor, Margie, said they were there for a reason, to let us middle-class, recovery-oriented types remember that "there but for the grace of God . . ."

I cringed whenever I saw them, especially if the object lesson for the day was a woman.

"Hey, kid," the drunk called out to Delgado, in a voice as inappropriately loud as a deaf man's, "how old are you?" The doors closed and the car lurched forward; the drunk all but fell into his seat.

"Old enough," Manny replied, flashing the polite smile a well-brought-up kid saves for his maiden aunt.

The undertone wasn't so pretty. Little sidelong glances at me that said, *See how nice I am to this old fart. See what a good boy I am. I like drunks, Sergeant Gallagher.*

To avoid my partner's face, I concentrated on the subway ads as though they contained all the wisdom of the Big Book. "Here's to birth defects," proclaimed a pregnant woman about to down a glass of beer. Two monks looked to heaven, thanking God in Spanish for the fine quality of their brandy.

Weren't there any signs on this damn train that didn't involve booze? Finally an ad I could smile at: the moon in black space; on it, someone had scrawled, "Alice Kramden was here, 1959."

My smile faded as I remembered Sal Minucci's raised fist, his Jackie Gleason growl. "One of these days, Gallagher, you're goin' to the moon. To the moon!"

It wasn't just the murder case I missed. It was Sal. The easy partnership of the man who'd put up with my hangovers, my depressions, my wild nights out with the boys.

"Y'know how old I am?" the drunk shouted, almost falling over in his seat. He righted himself. "Fifty-four in September," he announced, an expectant look on his face.

After a quick smirk in my direction, Manny gave the guy what he wanted. "You don't look it," he said. No trace of irony appeared on his Spanish altar boy's face. It was as though he'd never said the words that were eating into me like battery-acid A.A. coffee.

The sudden jab of anger that stabbed through me took me by surprise, especially since it wasn't directed at Delgado. *No, you don't look it,* I thought. *You look more like seventy.* White wisps of hair over a bright pink scalp. The face more than pink; a slab of raw calves' liver. Road maps of broken blood vessels on his nose and cheeks. Thin white arms and matchstick legs under too-big trousers. When he lifted his hand, ropy with bulging blue veins, it fluttered like a pennant in the breeze.

Like Uncle Paul's hands.

I turned away sharply. I couldn't look at the old guy anymore. The constant visual digs Delgado kept throwing in my direction were nothing compared to the pain of looking at a man dying before my eyes. I didn't want to see blue eyes in that near-dead face. *As blue as the lakes of Killarney,* Uncle Paul used to say in his mock-Irish brogue.

I focused on the teenagers making out in the rear of the car. A couple of Spanish kids, wearing identical pink T-shirts and black leather jackets. If I stared at them long enough, would they stop groping and kissing, or would an audience spur their passion?

Uncle Paul. After Daddy left us, he was my special friend, and I was his best girl.

I squeezed my eyes shut, but the memories came anyway. The red bike Uncle Paul gave me for my tenth birthday. The first really big new thing, bought just for me, that I'd ever had. The best part was showing it off to cousin Tommy. For once I didn't need his hand-me-downs, or Aunt Bridget's clucking over me for being poor. *God bless the child who's got her own.*

I opened my eyes just as the Lex passed through the ghost station at Worth Street. Closed off to the public for maybe fifteen years, it seemed a mirage, dimly seen through the dirty windows of the subway car. Bright color on the white tile walls told me graffiti bombers had been there. A good place to check, but not until after City Hall. I owed Manny Delgado a trip to the Black Hole.

"Uh, Sergeant?"

I turned; a patronizing smile played on Delgado's lips. He'd apparently been trying to get my attention. "Sorry," I said, feigning a yawn. "Just a little tired."

Yeah, sure, his look remarked. "We're coming to Brooklyn Bridge. Shouldn't we get off the train?"

"Right." *Leave Uncle Paul where he belongs.*

At the Brooklyn Bridge stop, we climbed up the steps to the upper platform, showed our ID to the woman token clerk, and told her we were going into the tunnel toward City Hall. Then we went back downstairs, heading for the south end of the downtown platform.

As we were about to go past the gate marked NO UNAUTHO-RIZED PERSONNEL BEYOND THIS POINT, I looked back at the lighted platform, which made a crescent-shaped curve behind us. Almost in a mirror image, the old drunk was about to pass the forbidden gate and descend into the tunnel heading uptown.

He stepped carefully, holding on to the white, bathroom-tile walls, edging himself around the waist-high gate. He lowered himself down the stone steps, the exact replica of the ones Manny and I were about to descend, then disappeared into the blackness.

I couldn't let him go. There were too many dangers in the subway, dangers beyond the torch killer everyone was on the hunt for. How many frozen bodies had I stumbled over on the catwalks between tunnels? How many huddled victims had been hit by trains as they lay in sodden sleep? And yet, I had to be careful. My friend Kathy Denzer had gone after a bum sleeping on the catwalk, only to have the man stab her in the arm for trying to save his life.

I couldn't let him go. Turning to Delgado, I said, "Let's save City Hall for later. I saw some graffiti at Worth Street on the way here. Let's check that out first."

He shrugged. At least he was being spared the Black Hole, his expression said.

Entering the tunnel's blackness, leaving behind the brightly lit world of sleepy riders, a tiny rush of adrenaline, like MSG after a Chinese dinner, coursed through my bloodstream. Part of it was pure reversion to childhood's fears. Hansel and Gretel. Snow White. Lost in dark woods with enemies all around. In this case, rats. Their scuffling sent shivers up my spine as we balanced our way along the catwalk above the tracks.

The other part was elation. This was my job. I was good at it. I could put aside my fears and step boldly down into murky depths where few New Yorkers ever went.

Our flashlights shone dim as fireflies. I surveyed the gloomy underground world I'd spent my professional life in.

My imagination often took over in the tunnels. They became caves of doom. Or an evil wood, out of *Lord of the Rings*. The square columns holding up the tunnel roof were leafless trees, the constant trickle of foul water between the tracks a poisonous stream from which no one drank and lived.

Jones Beach. Uncle Paul's huge hand cradling my foot, then lifting me high in the air and flinging me backward, laughing with delight, into the cool water. Droplets clinging to his red beard, and Uncle Paul shaking them off into the sunlight like a wet Irish setter.

Me and Mo, we're the only true Gallaghers. The only redheads. I got straight A's in English; nobody's grammar was safe from me—except Uncle Paul's.

I thought all men smelled like him: whiskey and tobacco.

As Manny and I plodded along the four-block tunnel between the live station and the dead one, we exchanged no words. The acrid stench of an old track fire filled my nostrils the way memories flooded my mind. Trying to push Uncle Paul away, I bent all my concentration on stepping carefully around the foul-smelling water, the burned debris I didn't want to identify.

I suspected Delgado's silence was due to fear; he wouldn't want a shaking voice to betray his tension. I knew how he felt. The first nighttime tunnel trek was a landmark in a young transit cop's life.

When the downtown express thundered past, we ducked into the coffin-sized alcoves set aside for transit workers. My heart pounded as the wind wake of the train pulled at my clothes; the fear of falling forward, landing under those relentless steel wheels, never left me, no matter how many times I stood in the well. I always thought of Anna Karenina; once in a while, in my drinking days, I'd wondered how it would feel to edge forward, to let the train's undertow pull me toward death.

I could never do it. I'd seen too much blood on the tracks.

Light at the end of the tunnel. The Worth Street station sent rays of hope into the spidery blackness. My step quickened; Delgado's pace matched mine. Soon we were almost running toward the light, like cavemen coming from the hunt to sit by the fire of safety.

We were almost at the edge of the platform when I motioned Delgado to stop. My hunger to bathe in the light was as great as his, but our post was in the shadows, watching.

A moment of panic. I'd lost the drunk. Had he fallen on the tracks, the electrified third rail roasting him like a pig at a barbecue? Not possible; we'd have heard, and smelled.

I had to admit, the graffiti painting wasn't a mindless scrawl. It was a picture, full of color and life. Humanlike figures in bright primary shades, grass green, royal blue, orange, sun yellow, and carnation pink—colors unknown in the black-and-gray tunnels—stood in a line, waiting to go through a subway turnstile. Sexless, they were cookie-cutter replicas of one another, the only difference among them the color inside the black edges.

A rhythmic clicking sound made Delgado jump. "What the hell—?"

"Relax, Manny," I whispered. "It's the ball bearing in the spray-paint can. The vandals are here. As soon as the paint hits the tiles, we jump out and bust them."

Four rowdy teenagers, ranging in color from light brown to ebony, laughed raucously and punched one another with a theatrical style that said *We bad. We* real *bad.* They bounded up the steps from the other side of the platform and surveyed their artwork, playful as puppies, pointing out choice bits they had added to their mural.

It should have been simple. Two armed cops, with the advantage of surprise, against four kids armed with Day-Glo spray paint. Two things kept it from being simple: the drunk, wherever the hell he was, and the fact that one of the kids said, "Hey, bro, when Cool and Jo-Jo gettin' here?"

A very black kid with a nylon stocking on his head answered, "Jo-Jo be comin' with Pinto. Cool say he might be bringin' Slasher and T.P."

Great. Instead of two against four, it sounded like all the graffiti artists in New York City were planning a convention in the Worth Street ghost station.

"Sarge?" Delgado's voice was urgent. "We've gotta—"

"I know," I whispered back. "Get on the radio and call for backup."

Then I remembered. Worth Street was a dead spot. Lead in the ceiling above our heads turned our radios into worthless toys.

"Stop," I said wearily as Manny pulled the antenna up on his handheld radio. "It won't work. You'll have to go back to Brooklyn Bridge. Alert Booth Robert two-twenty-one. Have them call Operations. Just ask for backup, don't make it a ten-thirteen." A 10-13 meant "officer in trouble," and I didn't want to be the sergeant who cried wolf.

"Try the radio along the way," I went on. "You never know when it will come to life. I'm not sure where the lead ends."

Watching Delgado trudge back along the catwalk, I felt lonely, helpless, and stupid. No one knew we'd gone to Worth Street instead of the Black Hole, and that was my fault.

"Hey," one of the kids called, pointing to a pile of old clothes in the corner of the platform, "what this dude be doin' in our crib?"

Dude? What dude? Then the old clothes began to rise; it was the drunk from the train. He was huddled into a fetal ball, hoping not to be noticed by the graffiti gang.

Nylon Stocking boogied over to the old drunk, sticking a finger in his ribs. "What you be doin' here, ol' man? Huh? Answer me."

A fat kid with a flat top walked over, sat down next to the drunk, reached into the old man's jacket pocket, and pulled out a half-empty pint bottle.

A lighter-skinned, thinner boy slapped the drunk around, first lifting him by the scruff of the neck, then laughing as he flopped back to the floor. The old guy tried to rise, only to be kicked in the ribs by Nylon Stocking.

The old guy was bleeding at the mouth. Fat Boy held the pint of booze aloft, teasing the drunk the way you tease a dog with a bone. The worst part was that the drunk was reaching for it, hands flapping wildly, begging. He'd have barked if they'd asked him to.

I was shaking, my stomach starting to heave. God, where was Manny? Where was my backup? I had to stop the kids before their friends got there, but I felt too sick to move. *If there's one thing I can't stand, it's a woman drunk.* It was as though every taunt, every kick, was aimed at me, not just at the old man.

I reached into my belt for my gun, then opened my vest's back pouch and pulled out the slapper. Ready to charge, I stopped cold when Nylon Stocking said, "Yo, y'all want to do him like we done the others?"

Fat Boy's face lit up. "Yeah," he agreed. "Feel like a cold night. We needs a little fire."

"You right, bro," the light-skinned kid chimed in. "I got the kerosene. Done took it from my momma heater."

"What he deserve, man," the fourth member of the gang said, his voice a low growl. "Comin' into our crib, pissin' on the art, smellin' up the place. This here *our* turf, dig?" He prodded the old man in the chest.

"I—I didn't mean nothing," the old man whimpered. "I just wanted a place to sleep."

Uncle Paul, sleeping on our couch when he was too drunk for Aunt Rose to put up with him. He was never too drunk for Mom to take him in. Never too drunk to give me one of his sweet Irish smiles and call me his best girl.

The light-skinned kid opened the bottle—ironically, it looked as if it once contained whiskey—and sprinkled the old man the way my mother sprinkled clothes before ironing them. Nylon Stocking pulled out a book of matches.

By the time Delgado came back, with or without backup, there'd be one more bonfire if I didn't do something. Fast.

Surprise was my only hope. Four of them, young and strong. One of me, out of shape and shaky.

I shot out a light. I cracked the bulb on the first shot. Target shooting was my best asset as a cop, and I used it to give the kids the impression they were surrounded.

The kids jumped away from the drunk, moving in all directions. "Shit," one said, "who shootin'?"

I shot out the second and last bulb. In the dark, I had the advantage. They wouldn't know, at least at first, that only one cop was coming after them.

"Let's book," another cried. "Ain't worth stayin' here to get shot."

I ran up the steps, onto the platform lit only by the moonlike rays from the other side of the tracks. Yelling "Stop, police," I waded into the kids, swinging my illegal slapper.

Thump into the ribs of the kid holding the kerosene bottle. He dropped it, clutching his chest and howling. I felt the breath whoosh out of him, heard the snap of rib cracking. I wheeled and slapped Nylon Stocking across the knee, earning another satisfying howl.

My breath came in gasps, curses pouring out of me. Blood pounded in my temples, a thumping noise that sounded louder than the express train.

The advantage of surprise was over. The other two kids jumped me, one riding my back, the other going for my stomach with hard little fists. All I could see was a maddened teenage tornado circling me with blows. My arm felt light as I thrust my gun deep into the kid's stomach. He doubled, groaning.

It was like chugging beer at a cop racket. Every hit, every satisfying *whack* of blackjack against flesh made me hungry for the next. I whirled and socked. The kids kept coming, and I kept knocking them down like bowling pins.

The adrenaline rush was stupendous, filling me with elation. I was a real cop again. There was life after detox.

At last they stopped. Panting, I stood among the fallen, exhausted. My hair had escaped from my knit hat and hung in matted tangles over a face red-hot as a griddle.

I pulled out my cuffs and chained the kids together, wrist to wrist, wishing I had enough sets to do each individually. Together, even cuffed, they could overpower me. Especially since they were beginning to realize I was alone.

I felt weak, spent. As though I'd just made love.

I sat down on the platform, panting, my gun pointed at Nylon Stocking. "You have the right to remain silent," I began.

As I finished the last Miranda warning on the last kid, I heard the cavalry coming over the hill. Manny Delgado, with four reinforcements.

As the new officers took the collars, I motioned Manny aside, taking him to where the drunk lay sprawled in the corner, still shaking and whimpering.

"Do you smell anything?" I asked.

Manny wrinkled his nose. I looked down at the drunk.

A trickle of water seeped from underneath him; his crotch was soaked.

Uncle Paul, weaving his way home, singing off-key, stopping to take a piss under the lamppost. Nothing unusual in that, except that this time Julie Ann Mackinnon, my eighth-grade rival, watched from across the street. My cheeks burned as I recalled how she'd told the other kids what she'd seen, her hand cupped over her giggling mouth.

"Not that," I said, my tone sharp, my face reddening. "The kerosene. These kids are the torch killers. They were going to roast this guy. That's why I had to take them on alone."

Delgado's face registered the scepticism I'd seen lurking in his eyes all night. Could he trust me? He'd been suitably impressed at my chain gang of prisoners, but now I was talking about solving the crime that had every cop in the city on overtime.

"Look, just go back to Brooklyn Bridge and radio"—I was going to say Captain Lomax, when I thought better—"Sal Minucci in

Anti-Crime. He'll want to have the guy's coat analyzed. And make sure somebody takes good care of that bottle." I pointed to the now-empty whiskey bottle the light-skinned boy had poured kerosene from.

"Isn't that his?" Manny indicated the drunk.

"No, his is a short dog," I said, then turned away as I realized the term was not widely known in nondrunk circles.

Just go, kid, I prayed. *Get the hell out of here before—*

He turned, following the backup officers with their chain gang. "And send for Emergency Medical for this guy," I added. "I'll stay here till they come."

I looked down at the drunk. His eyes were blue, a watery, no-color blue with all the life washed out of them. Uncle Paul's eyes.

Uncle Paul, blurry-faced and maudlin, too blitzed to care that I'd come home from school with a medal for the best English composition. I'd put my masterpiece by his chair, so he could read it after dinner. He spilled whiskey on it; the blue-black ink ran like tears and blotted out my carefully chosen words.

Uncle Paul, old, sick, and dying, just like this one. Living by that time more on the street than at home, though there were people who would take him in. His eyes more red than blue, his big frame wasted. I felt a sob rising, like death squeezing my lungs. I heaved, grabbing for air. My face was wet with tears I didn't recall shedding.

I hate you, Uncle Paul. I'll never be like you. Never.

I walked over to the drunk, still sprawled on the platform. I was a sleepwalker; my arm lifted itself. I jabbed the butt of my gun into old, thin ribs, feeling it bump against bone. It would be a baseball-size bruise. First a raw red-purple, then blue-violet, finally a sickly yellow-gray.

I lifted my foot, just high enough to land with a thud near the kidneys. The old drunk grunted, his mouth falling open. A drizzle of saliva fell to the ground. He put shaking hands to his face and squeezed his eyes shut. I lifted my foot again. I wanted to kick and kick and kick.

Uncle Paul, a frozen lump of meat found by some transit cop on the aboveground platform at 161st Street. The Yankee Stadium stop, where he took me when the Yanks played home games. We'd eat at the Yankee Tavern, me wolfing down a corned beef on rye and cream soda, Uncle Paul putting away draft beer after draft beer.

Before he died, Uncle Paul had taken all the coins out of his pocket, stacking them in neat little piles beside him. Quarters, dimes, nickels, pennies. An inventory of his worldly goods.

I took a deep, shuddering breath, looked down at the sad old man I'd brutalized. A hot rush of shame washed over me.

I knelt down, gently moving the frail, blue-white hands away from the near-transparent face. The fear I saw in the liquid blue eyes sent a piercing ray of self-hatred through me.

If there's anything I can't stand, it's a woman drunk. Me too, Manny, I can't stand women drunks either.

The old man's lips trembled; tears filled his eyes and rolled down his thin cheeks. He shook his head from side to side, as though trying to wake himself from a bad dream.

"Why?" he asked, his voice a raven's croak.

"Because I loved you so much." The words weren't in my head anymore, they were slipping out into the silent, empty world of the ghost station. As though Uncle Paul weren't buried in Calvary Cemetery but could hear me with the ears of this old man who looked too damn much like him. "Because I wanted to be just like you. And I am." My voice broke. "I'm just like you, Uncle Paul. I'm a drunk." I put my head on my knee and sobbed like a child. All the shame of my drinking days welled up in my chest. The stupid things I'd said and done, the times I'd had to be taken home and put to bed, the times I'd thrown up in the street outside the bar. *If there's one thing I can't stand . . .*

"Oh, God, I wish I were dead."

The bony hand on mine felt like a talon. I started, then looked into the old man's watery eyes. I sat in the ghost station and saw in this stranger the ghost that had been my dying uncle.

"Why should you wish a thing like that?" the old man asked. His voice was clear, no booze-blurred slurring, no groping for words burned out of the brain by alcohol. "You're a young girl. You've got your whole life ahead of you."

My whole life. To be continued . . .

One day at a time. One night at a time.

When I got back to the District, changed out of my work clothes, showered, would there be a meeting waiting for me? Damn right; in the city that never sleeps, A.A. never sleeps either.

I reached out to the old man. My fingers brushed his silver stubble.

"I'm sorry, Uncle Paul," I said. "I'm sorry."

New Moon and Rattlesnakes

WENDY HORNSBY

Wendy Hornsby (b. 1947) was born in Los Angeles and educated at UCLA and California State University, Long Beach. Since 1975, she has been a Professor of History at Long Beach City College. Her first novel, *No Harm* (1987), featured history teacher Kate Teague, who figured in one more case before she was succeeded by the better-known documentary filmmaker Maggie MacGowen in *Telling Lies* (1992) and several subsequent books. Though both series characters are technically amateur detectives, their law enforcement connections put Hornsby's books into the police procedural category. Asked to identify influences, Hornsby pays obeisance to the California hardboiled triumvirate of Dashiell Hammett, Raymond Chandler, and Ross Macdonald but identifies as her real role model the wife of Macdonald, Margaret Millar. Outside the mystery genre, she noted in *Deadly Women* (1998), "As a kid I read my way through Dickens, a huge influence on a budding hard-boiled writer, and Mark Twain who is the master of characterization, and Ambrose Bierce because he was so wicked."

In recent times, the distinctions between tough and cozy, masculine and feminine approaches to crime fiction have become less pronounced and in most cases less important than they used to be. Hornsby's "New Moon and Rattlesnakes" is a noir-ish story that would have been right at home in the great 1950s digest *Manhunt*, a periodical to which few women writers contributed.

Lise caught a ride at a truck stop near Riverside, in a big rig headed for Phoenix. The driver was a paunchy, lonely old geek whose come-on line was a fatherly routine. She helped him play his line because it got her inside the air-conditioned cab of his truck and headed east way ahead of her schedule.

"Sweet young thing like you shouldn't be thumbing rides," he said, helping Lise with her seat belt. "Desert can be awful damn dangerous in the summertime."

"I know the desert. Besides . . ." She put her hand over his hairy paw. "I'm not so young and there's nothing sweet about me."

He laughed, but he looked at her more closely. Looked at the heavy purse she carried with her, too. After that long look, he dropped the fatherly routine. She was glad, because she didn't have a lot of time to waste on preliminaries.

The tired old jokes he told her got steadily gamier as he drove east out Interstate 10. Cheap new housing tracts and pink stucco malls gave way to a landscape of razor-sharp yucca and shimmering heat, and all the way Lise laughed at his stupid jokes only to let him know she was hanging in with him.

Up the steep grade through Beaumont and Banning and Cabazon she laughed on cue, watching him go through his gears, deciding whether she could drive the truck without him. Or not. Twice, to speed things along, she told him jokes that made his bald head blush flame red.

Before the Palm Springs turnoff, he suggested they stop at an Indian bingo palace for cold drinks and a couple of games. Somehow, while she was distracted watching how the place operated, his hand kept finding its way into the back of her spandex tank top.

The feel of him so close, his suggestive leers, the smell of him, the smoky smell of the place, made her clammy all over. But she kept up a good front, didn't retch when her stomach churned. She had practice; for five years she had kept up a good front, and survived because of it. Come ten o'clock, she encouraged herself, there would be a whole new order of things.

After bingo, it was an hour of front-seat wrestling, straight down the highway to a Motel 6—all rooms $29.95, cable TV and a phone in every room. He told her what he wanted; she asked him to take a shower first.

In Riverside, he'd said his name was Jack. But the name on the Louisiana driver's license she found in his wallet said Henry LeBeau. He was in the shower, singing, when she made this discovery. Lise practiced writing the name a couple of times on motel stationery while she placed a call on the room phone. Mrs. Henry LeBeau, Lise LeBeau . . . she wrote it until the call was answered.

"I'm out," Lise said.

"You're lying."

"Not me," she said. "Penalty for lying's too high."

"I left my best man at the house with you. He would have called me."

"If he could. Maybe your best man isn't as good as you thought he was. Maybe I'm better."

Waiting for more response from the other end, she wrote LeBeau's name a few more times, wrote it until it felt natural to her hand.

Finally, she got more than heavy breathing from the phone. "Where are you, Lise?"

"I'm a long way into somewhere else. Don't bother to go looking, because this time you won't find me."

"Of course I will."

She hung up.

Jack/Henry turned off the shower. Before he was out of the bathroom, fresh and clean and looking for love, Lise was out of the motel and down the road. With his wallet in her bag.

The heat outside was like a frontal assault after the cool dim room; hundred and ten degrees, zero percent humidity according to a sign. Afternoon sun slanted directly into Lise's eyes and the air smelled like truck fuel and hot pavement, but it was better than the two-day sweat that had filled the big-rig cab and had followed them into the motel. She needed a dozen hot breaths to get his stench out of her.

The motel wasn't in a place, nothing but a graded spot at the end of a freeway off-ramp halfway between L.A. and Phoenix: a couple of service stations and a minimart, a hundred miles of scrubby cactus and sharp rocks for neighbors. Shielding her eyes, Lise quick-walked toward the freeway, looking for possibilities even before she crossed the road to the Texaco station.

The meeting she needed to attend would be held in Palm Springs, and she had to find a way to get there. She knew for a dead certainly she didn't want to get into another truck, and she couldn't stay in the open.

Heat blazed down from the sky, bounced up off the pavement, and caught her both ways. Lise began to panic. Fifteen minutes, maybe twenty, under the sun and she knew she would be fried. But it wasn't the heat that made her run for the shelter of the covered service station. After being confined for so long, she was sometimes frightened by open space.

The Texaco and its minimart were busy with a transient olio show: cranky families in vans, chubby truckers, city smoothies in desert vacation togs and too much shiny jewelry, everyone in a hurry to fill up, scrape the bugs off the windshield, and get back on the road with the air-conditioning buffering them from the relentless heat.

As she walked past the pumps, waiting for opportunity to present itself, an old white-haired guy in a big new Cadillac slid past her, pulled up next to the minimart. He was a very clean-looking man, the sort, she thought, who doesn't like to get hot and mussed. Like her father. When he got out of his car to go into the minimart, the cream puff left his engine running and his air conditioner blowing to keep the car's interior cool.

Lise saw the man inside the store, spinning a rack of road maps, as she got into his car and drove away.

When she hit the on-ramp, backtracking west, she saw Mr. Henry LeBeau, half dressed and sweating like a comeback wrestler, standing out in front of the motel, looking upset, peering around like he'd lost something.

"Goodbye, Mr. LeBeau." Lise smiled at his tiny figure as it receded in her rearview mirror. "Thanks for the ride." Then she looked all around, half expecting to spot a tail, to find a fleet of long, shiny black cars deployed to find her, surround her, take her back home; escape couldn't be this easy. But the only shine she saw came from mirages, like silver puddles splashed across the freeway. She relaxed some, settled against the leather uphol-stery, aimed the air vents on her face and changed the Caddy's radio station from a hundred violins to Chopin.

Her transformation from truck-stop dolly to mall matron took less than five minutes. She wiped off the heavy makeup she had acquired in Riverside, covered the skimpy tank top with a blouse from her bag, rolled down the cuffs of her denim shorts to cover three more inches of her muscular thighs, traded the hand-tooled boots for graceful leather sandals, and tied her windblown hair into a neat ponytail at the back of her neck. When she checked her face in the mirror, she saw any lady in a checkout line looking back at her.

Lise took the Bob Hope Drive off-ramp, sighed happily as the scorched and barren virgin desert gave way to deep-green golf courses, piles of chichi condos, palm trees, fountains, and posh restaurants whose parking lots were garnished with Jags, Caddies, and Benzes.

She pulled into one of those lots and, with the motor running, took some time to really look over what she had to work with. American Express card signed H. G. LeBeau. MasterCard signed Henry LeBeau. Four hundred in cash. The wallet also had some gas company cards, two old condoms, a picture of an ugly wife, and a slip of paper with a four-digit number. Bless his heart, she thought, smiling; Henry had given her a PIN number, contributed to her range of possibilities.

Lise committed the four digits to memory, put the credit cards and cash into her pocket, then got out into the blasting heat to stuff the wallet into a trash can before she drove on to the Palm Desert Mall.

Like a good scout, Lise left the Caddy in the mall parking lot just as she had found it, motor running, doors unlocked, keys inside. Without a backward glance, she headed straight for I. Magnin. Wardrobe essentials and a beautiful leather-and-brocade suitcase to carry it consumed little more than an hour. She signed for purchases alternately as Mrs. Henry LeBeau or H. G. LeBeau as she alternated the credit cards. She felt safe doing it; in Magnin's, no one ever dared ask for ID.

Time was a problem, and so was cash enough to carry through the next few days, until she could safely use other resources.

As soon as Henry got himself pulled together, she knew he would report his cards lost. She also knew he wouldn't have the balls to confess the circumstances under which the cards got away from him, so she wasn't worried about the police. But once the cards were reported, they would be useless. How much longer would it take him? she wondered.

From a teller machine, she pulled the two-hundred-dollar cash advance limit off the MasterCard, then used the card a last time to place another call.

"You're worried," she said into the receiver. "You have that meeting tonight, and I have distracted you. You have a problem, because if I'm not around to sign the final papers, everything falls apart. Now you're caught in a bind: you can't stand up the congressman and you can't let me get away, and you sure as hell can't be in two places at once. What are you going to do?"

"This is insane." The old fury was in his voice this time. "Where are you?"

"Don't leave the house. Don't even think about it. I'll know if you do. I'll see the lie in your eyes. I'll smell it on every lying word that comes out of your mouth." It was easy; the words just came, like playing back an old, familiar tape. The words did sound funny to her, though, coming out of her own mouth. She wondered how he came up with such garbage and, more to the point, how he had persuaded her over the years that death could be any worse than living under his dirty thumb.

The true joy of talking to him over the telephone was having the power to turn him off. She hung up, took a deep breath, blew out the sound of him.

In the soft soil of a planter next to the phone bank, she dug a little grave for the credit card and covered it over.

After a late lunch, accompanied by half a bottle of very cold champagne, Lise had her hair done, darkened back to its original color and cut very short. The beauty parlor receptionist was accommodating, added a hundred dollars to the American Express bill and gave Lise the difference in cash.

Lise had been moderately surprised when the card flew through clearance, but risked using it one last time. From a gourmet boutique, she picked up some essentials of another kind: a few bottles of good wine, a basket of fruit, a variety of expensive little snacks. On her way out of the store, she jettisoned the American Express into a bin of green jelly beans.

Every transaction fed her confidence, assured her she had the courage to go through with the plan that would set her free forever. By the time she had finished her chores, her accumulation of bags was almost more than she could carry, and she was exhausted. But she felt better than she had for a very long time.

When she headed for the mall exit on the far side from where she had left Mr. Clean's Cadillac, Lise was not at all sure what would happen next. She still had presentiments of doom; she still looked over her shoulder and at reflections of the crowd in every window she passed. Logic said she was safe; conditioning kept her wary, kept her moving.

Hijacking a car with its motor running had worked so well once, she decided to try it again. She had any number of prospects to choose from. The mall's indoor ice-skating rink—bizarrely, the rink overlooked a giant cactus garden—and the movie theater complex next to it, meant parents waiting at the curb for kids. Among that row of cars, Lise counted three with motors running, air-conditioning purring, and no drivers in sight.

Lise considered her choices: a Volvo station wagon, a small Beemer, and a teal-blue Jag. She ran through "eeny, meeny," though she had targeted the Jag right off; the Jag was the first car in the row.

Bags in the backseat, Lise in the driver's seat and pulling away from the curb before she had the door all the way shut. After a stop on a side street to pack her new things into the suitcase, she drove straight to the Palm Springs airport. She left the Jag in a passenger loading zone and, bags in hand, rushed into the terminal like a tourist late for a flight.

She stopped at the first phone.

"You've checked, haven't you?" she said when he picked up "You sent your goons to look in on me. You know I'm out. We're so close, I know everything you've done. I can hear your thoughts running through my head. You're thinking the deal is dead without me. And I'm in another time zone."

"You won't get away from me."

"I think you're angry. If I don't correct you when you have bad thoughts, you'll ruin everything."

"Stop it."

She looked at her nails, kept her voice flat. "You're everything to me. I'd kill you before I let you go."

"Please, Lise." His voice had a catch, almost like a sob, when she hung up.

She left the terminal by a different door, came out at the cab stand, where a single cab waited. The driver looked like a cousin of the Indians at the bingo palace, and because of the nature of the meeting scheduled that night, she hesitated. In the end, she handed the cabbie her suitcase and gave him the address of a hotel in downtown Palm Springs, an address she had memorized a long time ago.

"Pretty dead over there," the driver said, fingering the leather grips of her bag. "Hard to get around without a car when you're so far out. I can steer you to nicer places closer in. Good rates off season, too."

"No, thank you," she said.

He talked the entire way. He asked more questions than she answered, and made her feel uneasy. Why should a stranger need to know so much? Could the driver possibly be a plant sent to bring her back? Was the conversation normal chitchat? That last question bothered her: she had been cut off for so long, would she know normal if she met it head-on?

When the driver dropped her at a funky old place on the block behind the main street through Palm Springs, she was still wary. She waited until he was gone before she picked up her bag and walked inside.

Off season, the hotel felt empty. The manager was old enough to be her mother; a desert woman with skin like a lizard and tiny black eyes.

"I need a room for two nights," Lise told her.

The manager handed her a registration card. "Put it on a credit card or cash in advance?"

Lise paid cash for the two nights and gave the woman a fifty-dollar deposit for the use of the telephone.

"It's quiet here," the manager said, handing over a key. "Too hot this time of year for most people."

"Quiet is what I'm counting on," Lise said. "I'm not expecting any calls, but if someone asks for me, I'd appreciate it if you never heard of me."

When the manager smiled, her black eyes nearly disappeared among the folds of dry skin. "Man trouble, honey?"

"Is there another kind?"

"From my experience, it's always either a man or money. And from the look of you," the manager said, glancing at the suitcase and the gourmet shop's handled bag, "I'd put my nickel on the former. Don't worry, honey, I didn't get a good look at you, and I already forgot your name."

The name Lise wrote on the registration card was the name on a bottle of chardonnay in her bag: Rutherford Hill.

The hotel was built like an old adobe ranch house, with thick walls and rounded corners, Mexican tile on the floors, dark, open-beamed ceilings. Lise's room was a bit threadbare, but it was larger, cleaner, nicer than she had expected for the price. The air conditioner worked, and there was a kitchenette with a little, groaning refrigerator for her wine. For the first time in five years, she had her own key, and used it to lock the door from the inside.

From her tiny balcony Lise could see both the pool in the patio below and the rocky base of Mount San Jacinto a quarter mile away. Already the sun had slipped behind the crest of the mountain, leaving the hotel in blue shade. Finally, Lise was able to smell the real desert, dry sage and blooming oleander, air without exhaust fumes.

A gentle breeze blew in off the mountain. Lise left the window open and lay down on the bed to rest for just a moment. When she opened her eyes again, floating on the cusp between sleep and wakefulness, the room was washed in soft lavender light—hot, but fragrant with the flowers on the patio below. She could hear a fountain somewhere, now and then voices at a distance. For the first time in a long time, she didn't go straight to the door and listen for breathing on the other side.

Lise slipped into the new swimsuit. A little snug in the rear—she hadn't taken time to try it on before she bought it. She needed the ice pick she found on the sink to free the ice in the trays so she could fill the paper ice bucket. She liked the heavy feel of the tool. While she opened a bottle of wine and cut some fruit and cheese, she made a call.

"Sunset will be exactly eight thirty-two. No moon tonight. Rattlesnakes love a moonless night. You better stay indoors, or you might get bitten."

"What is your game?"

"Your game. I'm a quick learner. Remember when you said that? I think I have all your moves down. Let's see how they play."

"You're a rookie, Lise. You won't make it in the big leagues. And every game I play, baby, is the big one." He'd had some time to get over the initial surprise and anger, so he was back on the offensive. He scared her, but because he couldn't touch her, her resolve held firm as she listened to him. "You'll be back, Lise. You'll take a few hard ones to the head and realize how cold and cruel that world out there is. You'll beg me to take you in and watch over you again. You can be mad at me all you want, but it isn't my fault you're such a princess you can't find your way across the street alone. Blame your asshole father for spoiling you. If it wasn't for me—"

"If it wasn't for you, my father would be alive," she said, cutting off his windup. "I have the proof with me."

The moment of silence told her she had hit home. She hung up.

Lise swam in the small pool until she felt clean again, until the heat and the sweat and the layer of fine sand had all been washed away, until the warm, chlorinated water had bleached away the fevered touch of Henry LeBeau. Some of her new hair color was bleached away too; it left a shadow on the towel when she got out and dried off.

Lise poured a bathroom tumbler full of straw-colored wine and stretched out on a chaise beside the pool. There was still some blue in the sky when the manager came out to switch on the pool lights.

"Sure was a hot one." The manager nursed a drink of her own. "Course, till October they're pretty much all hot ones. Let me know when you're finished with the pool. Sun heats it up so much that every night I let out some of the water and replace it with cold. Otherwise I'll have parboiled guests on my hands."

"How many guests are in the hotel?" Lise asked.

"Just you, honey." The manager drained her glass. "One guest is one more than I had all last week."

Lise offered her the tray of cheese. "Can you sit down for a minute? Have a little happy hour with the registered guests."

"I don't mind." The manager pulled up a chaise next to Lise and let Lise fill her empty glass with chardonnay. "I have to say, off season it does get lonely now and then. We used to close up from Memorial Day to Labor Day—the whole town did. We're more year-round now. Hell, there's talk we'll have gambling soon and become the new Vegas."

"Vegas is noisy."

"Vegas is full of crooks." The manager nibbled some cheese. "I wouldn't mind having my rooms booked up again. But the high rollers would stay in the big new hotels and I'd get their hookers and pushers. Who needs that?"

Lise sipped from her glass and stayed quiet. The manager sighed as she looked up into the darkening sky. "Was a time when this place hopped with Hollywood people and their carryings-on. Liberace and a bunch of them had places just up the road here, you know. We used to get the overflow, and were they ever a wild crowd. I miss them. That set has moved on east, fancier places like Palm Desert. I still get an old-timer now and then, but most of my guests are Canadian snowbirds. They start showing up around Thanksgiving, spend the winter. Nice bunch, but awful tame." She winked at Lise. "Tame, but easier to deal with than Vegas hookers."

"I'm sure," Lise said.

With a thoughtful tilt to her head, the manager looked again, and more closely, at Lise. "I'm pretty far off the beaten track. How'd you ever find my place?"

"I passed the hotel when I was up here visiting. It seemed so . . ." Lise refilled their glasses. "It seemed peaceful."

Lise could feel the manager's shiny black eyes on her. "You okay, honey?"

Lise held up the empty bottle. "I'm getting there."

"That kind of medicine is only going to last so long. It's none of my business, but you want to talk about it?"

"I'm sure you've heard it all before. Long-suffering wife skips out on asshole husband."

"I've not only heard it, I've lived it. Twice." The manager put her weathered hand on Lise's bare knee and smiled sweetly. "You're going to be fine. Just give it some time."

The wine, fatigue, the sweet concern on the old woman's face all combining, Lise felt the cracks inside open up and let in some light. The last time anyone had shown her genuine concern had been five years ago, when her father was still alive. There was a five-year accumulation of moss on her father's marble headstone. Lise began to cry softly.

The manager pulled a packet of tissues out of her pocket. "Atta girl. Let the river flow."

Lise laughed then.

"Does he know where you are?"

Lise shook her head. "Not yet."

"Not yet?"

"Given time, he'll find me. He always does. No matter how far I run, he can find me. He's a powerful man with powerful friends."

"What are you going to do?"

Lise shrugged, though she knew very well. The answer was in the bag upstairs in the closet.

"Well, don't you worry, honey. No one knows about this old place. And I already told you, I don't remember what you look like and I don't recall your name." The manager picked up the empty bottle and looked at the Rutherford Hill label, sly humour folding the corners of her creased face. "Though come to think of it, the name does have a familiar ring."

The sun set at exactly 8:32. Lise showered and changed into long khakis and a pale-peach shirt, both in tones of the desert floor. She took her bag out of the closet and held it on her lap while she waited for the last reflected light of the day to fade.

The big story on the local TV news was what the manager had been talking about, the growing controversy over the proposal to build a Vegas-style casino on Tahquitz Indian tribal land at the southern city limits of Palm Springs. A congressional delegation had come to town to investigate. As the videotaped congressmen, wearing sober gray and big smiles, paraded across the barren hillside site, Lise felt chilled; her husband, wearing his own big smile, was among the entourage. She knew why he was in town and who he would be meeting with. But she hadn't expected to see him before . . .

She pulled the bag closer against her and checked the clock beside the bed. If the clock was correct, he had nearly run out of time.

When Lise walked downstairs, she could see the flickering light of a television behind the front desk, could hear the manager moving around and further coverage of the big story spieling across the empty lobby. Quietly, Lise went out through the patio, the bag hanging heavily from her shoulder.

Maybe rattlesnakes do like a moonless night, she thought. But they hate people and slither away pretty fast. Lise walked along a sandy path that paralleled the road, feeling the stored heat in the earth soak through her sneakers. Palms rustled overhead like the rattle of a snake and set her on edge.

Lise slipped on a pair of surgical gloves and, being excruciatingly careful not to disturb the beautiful, five-year-old set of prints on the barrel, took the .380 out of her bag, pumped a round into the chamber in case of emergency, and walked on.

The house where the meeting would take place had belonged to her father. Before her marriage, she used to drive out on weekends and school vacations to visit him. After her marriage, after her father's funeral, her husband had taken the place over to use when he had deals to make in the desert. Now and then, when he couldn't make other arrangements for her, Lise had come along. It had been during a recent weekend, when she was banished to the bedroom during a business meeting, that Lise had figured out a way to get free of him. Forever.

The house sat in a shallow box canyon at the end of the same street the hotel was on. Her father had built the house in the Spanish style, a long string of rooms that all opened onto a central patio. Like the hotel, it had thick walls to keep out the worst of the heat. And like the hotel, like a fort, it was very quiet.

All the lights were on. Lise knew that for a meeting this delicate, there would be no entourage. Inside the house, there would be only three people: the non-English-speaking housekeeper, Lise's husband, and the congressman. She knew the routine well; the congressman was as much a part of her husband's inheritance from her father as Lise and the house were.

Outside, there was a guard on the front door and one on the back patio, standing away from the windows so that his presence wouldn't offend the congressman. Both of the guards were big and ugly, snakes of another kind, and more intimidating than they were smart. By circling wide, Lise got past the man in front, made it to the edge of the patio before she was seen. It wasn't the hired muscle who spotted her first.

Luther; her father's old rottweiler guard dog, ambled across the patio to greet Lise. She pushed his head aside to keep him from muzzling her crotch, made him settle for a head scratch.

The guard, Rollmeyer; hand on his holstered gun butt, hit her with the beam of his flashlight, smiled when he recognized who she was. Part of his job was forestalling interruptions, so he walked over to her without calling out.

Lise hadn't been sure about what would happen when she got to this point, couldn't know who the guard would be or how he would react to her. How much he might know. She had gone over several possibilities and decided to let the guard lead the way into this wilderness.

"Didn't know you was here, ma'am." Rollmeyer kept his voice low, standing close beside her on the soft sand. "They're going to be a while yet. You want me to take you around front, let you in that way?"

"The house is so hot. I'll wait out here until they're finished." She had her hand inside her bag, trading the automatic for something more appropriate to the situation. "Been a long time, Rollmeyer. Talk to me. How've you been?"

"Can't complain."

Hand in the bag, she wrapped her fingers around the wooden handle of the hotel ice pick. "Don't you have a hug for an old friend?"

Rollmeyer, whose job was to follow orders, and whose inclination was to cop any feel he could, seemed confused for just a moment. Then he opened his big arms and took a step toward her. She used the forward thrust of his body to help drive the ice pick up into his chest. Holding on to the handle, she could feel his heart beating around the slender blade, pump, pump, pump, before he realized something had happened to him. By then it was too late. She stepped back, withdrawing the blade, met his dumb gaze for another three-count, watched the dark trickle spill from the tiny hole in his shirt, before he fell, face down. His eyes were still open, sugared with grains of white sand, when she left him.

Luther stayed close to her, his bulk providing a shield while she lay on her belly beside the pool and rinsed away Rollmeyer's blood from her glove and from the ice pick. With the dog, she ducked back into the shelter of the oleander hedge to watch the meeting proceed inside.

Creatures of habit, her husband and the congressman were holding to schedule. By the time Lise arrived, they had eaten dinner in the elegant dining room and the housekeeper had cleared the table, leaving the two men alone with coffee and brandy. Genteel preliminaries over, Lise's husband went to the silver closet and brought out a large briefcase, which he set on the table. He opened the case and, smiling like Santa, turned it to show the contents to the congressman, showed them to Lise also in the reflection in the mirror over the antique sideboard: money in bank wrappers, three-quarters of a million dollars of it, the going price for a crucial vote on the federal level—the vote in question of course having to do with permits for Vegas-style casinos on tribal land.

There was a toast with brandy snifters, handshakes, then goodbyes. Once business had been taken care of, she knew her husband would leave immediately and the congressman would stay over for his special treat.

Lise dropped low behind the hedge when her husband, smiling still, crossed the patio and headed for the garage. She had the .380 in firing position in case he came looking for Rollmeyer. But he didn't. He went straight to the garage, started his Rolls.

As soon as he was out of sight, Lise moved quickly. Her husband would back down the drive to the road and signal the call girl who was waiting there in her own car, the call girl who always came as part of the congressman's package. Lise knew she had to be finished within the time it would take for the whore to drive into the vacant slot in the garage, freshen her makeup, spray on new perfume, plump her cleavage, and walk up to the house.

With Luther lumbering at her side, Lise crept into the dining room through the patio door just as her husband's lights cleared the corner of the house. The congressman had already closed his case of booty and set it on the floor, was just finishing his brandy when she stepped onto the deep carpet.

"Lise, dear," he said, surprised but not displeased to see her. He rose and held out his arms toward her. "I had not expected the pleasure of your company."

Lise said nothing as she walked up within a few feet of him. Her toe was touching the case full of money when she raised the .380, took aim the way her father had taught her, and fired a round into the congressman's chest, followed it, as her father had taught her, with a shot into the center of his forehead.

Luther, startled by the noise, began to bark. The housekeeper, in the kitchen, made "ah ah" noises and dropped something on the floor. Lise tucked the gun under the congressman's chest, picked up the case of money, and left.

Behind the hedge again, Lise waited for the call girl to walk in and help the housekeeper make her discovery. The timing was good. Both women faced each other from their respective doorways, shocked pale, within seconds of the shooting.

Through the quiet, moonless night, Lise walked back to the hotel along the same sandy path. She stowed the case behind a planter near the pool and continued onward a block to place a call.

Rollmeyer would be a complication, but the police could explain him any way they wanted to. Lise dialled 911.

"There's been a shooting," she said. She gave the address, identified the congressman as the victim and her husband as the shooter. Then she went to another phone, further down the street, and made a similar call to the press and to the local TV station.

When she heard the first siren heading up the road to the house, she was mailing an unsigned note to the detective who had investigated her father's death five years ago, a note that explained exactly why her husband and the congressman were meeting in the desert in the middle of the summer and what her husband's motives might be for murder—for two murders. And why the bullets taken from the congressman should be compared with the two taken from her father. And where the assets were hidden. Chapter and verse, a fitting eulogy for a man who would never again see much open sky, whose every movement would be monitored in a place where punishment came swiftly, where he would never, ever have a key to his own door or the right to make the game plans. Trapped, for the rest of his life.

When the note was out of her hand, she finally took off the surgical gloves. Lise raised her face to catch a breeze that was full of sweet, clean desert air, looked up at the extravagance of stars in the moonless sky, and yawned. It was over: agenda efficiently covered, meeting adjourned.

On her way back to the hotel, Lise stopped at an all-night drugstore and bought an ice cream bar with some of Henry LeBeau's money. She ate it as she walked.

The manager was standing in front of the hotel, watching the police and the paramedics speed past, when Lise strolled up.

"Big fuss." Lise stood on the sidewalk with the manager and finished her ice cream. "You told me it was dead around here this time of year."

"It's dead, all right." The manager laughed her dry, lizard laugh. "Lot of old folks out here. Bet you one just keeled over."

Lise watched with her until the coroner's van passed them. Then she took the manager by the arm and walked inside with her.

Lise saw the light of excitement still dancing in the manager's dark eyes. Lise herself was too keyed up to think about sleep. So she said. "I have another bottle of wine in my room. Let's say we have a little nightcap. Talk about crooks and the good old days."

Death of a Snowbird

J. A. JANCE

Judith Ann Jance (b. 1944) was born in Watertown, South Dakota, and educated at the University of Arizona and Bryn Mawr. She now lives in Bellevue, Washington. Before taking up writing, she worked as a high school teacher, Indian school librarian, and insurance salesperson, her father's profession. In an interview with Rylla Goldberg (*Speaking of Murder,* volume II [1999]), she credits her family background with her ability to promote her mystery novels effectively. "I started in sales early—homemade jewelry, Girl Scout cookies, newspaper subscriptions, and all-occasion greeting cards. In our family, selling was everybody's business with my mother dishing out the "leads" about new people in town over the breakfast table. Once my first book was published, I took up where my mother left off."

Jance's two series feature Seattle police detective J. P. Beaumont, beginning with *Until Proven Guilty* (1985), and Arizona sheriff Joanna Brady, beginning with *Desert Heat* (1993). She has also written non-fiction for children on such topics as parental kidnapping, sexual molestation, and family alcoholism. She remarked to *Contemporary Authors* (volume 61, new revision series, 1998), "Writing has provided a means of rewriting my own history, both in terms of the children's books and the murder thrillers. The children's books confront difficult issues . . . The murder thrillers are escapist fare with no redeeming social value." That last statement (though presumably facetious) invites a response: how could a story as entertaining and as unpredictable and as sensitive in its depiction of senior citizens as "Death of a Snowbird" lack redeeming social value?

Agnes Barkley did the dishes. She always did the dishes. After breakfast. After lunch. After dinner. For forty-six years she had done them. Maybe "always" was a slight exaggeration. Certainly there must have been a time or two when she had goofed off, when she had just rinsed them and stacked them in the sink to await the next meal; but mostly she kept the sink clear and the dishes dried and put away where they belonged. It was her job. Part of her job.

Back home in Westmont, Illinois, the single kitchen window was so high overhead that Agnes couldn't see out at all. Here, in Oscar's RV, the sink was situated directly in front of an eye-level window. Agnes could stand there with her hands plunged deep in warm, sudsy dishwater and enjoy the view. While doing her chores she occasionally caught sight of hawks circling in a limitless blue sky. In the evening she reveled in the flaming sunsets, with their spectacular orange glows that seemed to set the whole world on fire.

Even after years of coming back time and again, she wasn't quite used to it. Every time Agnes looked out a January window, she couldn't help being amazed. There before her, instead of Chicago's gray, leaden cloud cover and bone-chilling cold, she found another world—the wide-open, brown desert landscape, topped by a vast expanse of sunny blue sky.

Agnes couldn't get over the clean, clear air. She delighted in the crisp, hard-edged shadows left on the ground by the desert sun, and she loved the colors. When some of her neighbors back home had wondered how she could stand to live in such a barren, ugly place three months out of the year, Agnes had tried in vain to explain the lovely contrast of newly leafed mesquite against a red, rockbound earth. Her friends had looked at her sympathetically, smiled, shaken their heads, and said she was crazy.

And in truth she was—crazy about the desert. Agnes loved the stark wild plants that persisted in growing despite a perpetual lack of moisture—the spiny, leggy ocotillos and the sturdy, low-growing mesquite; the majestic saguaro; the cholla with its glowing halo of dangerous thorns. She loved catching glimpses of desert wildlife—coyotes and jackrabbits and kangaroo rats. She even loved the desert floor itself—the smooth sands and rocky shales, the expanses of rugged reds and soothing, round-rocked grays, all of which, over the great visible distances, would fade to uniform blue.

At first she had been dreadfully homesick for Westmont, but now all that had changed. Agnes Barkley's love affair with the desert was such that, had she been in charge, their snowbird routine would have been completely reversed. They would have spent nine to ten months out of the year in Arizona and only two or so back home in Illinois.

No one could have been more surprised by this turn of events than Agnes Barkley herself. When Oscar had first talked about retiring from the post office and becoming a snowbird—about buying an RV and wintering in Arizona—Agnes had been dead set against it. She had thought she would hate the godforsaken place, and she had done her best to change Oscar's mind. As if anyone could do that.

In the end, she had given in gracefully. As she had in every other aspect of her married existence, Agnes put the best face on it she could muster and went along for the ride, just as Oscar must have known she would. After forty-six years of marriage, there weren't that many surprises left.

In the past she would have grudgingly tolerated whatever it was Oscar wanted and more or less pretended to like it. But when it came to Arizona, no pretense was necessary. Agnes adored the place—once they got out of Mesa, that is.

Oscar couldn't stand Mesa, either. He said there were too many old people there.

"What do you think you are?" Agnes had been tempted to ask him, although she never did, because the truth of the matter was, Agnes agreed with him—and for much the same reason. It bothered her to see all those senior citizens more or less locked up in the same place, year after year.

The park itself was nice enough, with a pool and all the appropriate amenities. Still, it made Agnes feel claustrophobic somehow, especially when, for two years running, their motor home was parked next to that of a divorced codger who snored so loudly that the racket came right through the walls into the Barkleys' own bedroom—even with the RV's air conditioner cranked up and running full blast.

So they set out to find someplace else to park their RV someplace a little off the beaten track, as Oscar said. That's how they had ended up in Tombstone—The Town Too Tough to Die. Outside the Town Too Tough to Die was more like it.

The trailer park—that's what they called it: the OK Trailer Park, Overnighters Welcome—was several miles out of town. The individual lots had been carved out of the desert by terracing up the northern flank of a steep hillside. Whoever had designed the place had done a good job of it. Each site was far enough below its neighbor that every RV or trailer had its own unobstructed view of the hillside on the opposite side of a rocky draw. The western horizon boasted the Huachuca Mountains. To the east were the Wheststones and beyond those the Chiricahuas.

The views of those distant purple mountain majesties were what Agnes Barkley liked most about the OK Trailer Park. The views and the distances and the clear, clean air. And the idea that she didn't have to go to sleep listening to anyone snoring—anyone other than Oscar, that is. She was used to him.

"Yoo-hoo, Aggie. Anybody home?" Gretchen Dixon tapped on the doorframe. She didn't bother to wait for Agnes to answer before shoving open the door and popping her head inside. "Ready for a little company?"

Agnes took one last careful swipe at the countertop before wringing out the dishrag and putting it away under the sink. "What are you up to, Gretchen?"

At seventy-nine, Gretchen Dixon was given to chartreuse tank tops and Day-Glo Bermuda shorts—a color combination that showed off her tanned hide to best advantage. She wore her hair in a lank pageboy that hadn't changed—other than color—for forty years. It was one of fate's great injustices that someone like Gretchen, who had spent years soaking ultraviolet rays into her leathery skin, should be walking around bareheaded and apparently healthy, while Dr. Forsythe, Aggie's physician back home in Westmont, after burning off a spot of skin cancer, had forbidden Aggie to venture outside at all without wearing sunblock and a hat.

Agnes Barkley and Gretchen Dixon were friends, but there were several things about Gretchen that annoyed hell out of Agnes. The main one at this moment was the fact that despite the midday sun, Gretchen was bareheaded. Agnes loathed hats.

Gretchen lounged against the cupboard door and shook a cigarette out of a pack she always kept handy in some pocket or other. "So where's that worthless husband of yours?" she asked.

Not that Gretchen was really all that interested in knowing Oscar's whereabouts. She didn't like Oscar much, and the feeling was mutual. Rather than being worried about their mutual antipathy, Agnes found it oddly comforting. In fact, it was probably a very good idea to have friends your husband didn't exactly approve of. Years earlier, there had been one or two of Aggie's friends that Oscar had been crazy about. Too much so, in fact— with almost disastrous results for all concerned.

"Tramping around looking for arrowheads as per usual," Aggie said. "Out along the San Pedro, I think. He and Jim Rathbone went off together right after lunch. They'll be back in time for supper."

"That figures," Gretchen said disdainfully, rolling her eyes and blowing a plume of smoke high in the air as she slipped into the bench by the table.

"Aggie," she said, "do you realize you're the only woman around here who still cooks three square meals a day—breakfast, lunch, and dinner?"

"Why not?" Agnes objected. "I like to cook."

Gretchen shook her head. "You don't understand, Aggie. It gives all the rest of us a bad name. You maybe ought to let Oscar know that he's not the only one who's retired. It wouldn't kill the man to take you into town once in a while. He could buy you a nice dinner at the Wagon Wheel or at one of those newer places over on Allen Street."

"Oscar doesn't like to eat anybody else's cooking but mine," Aggie said.

Gretchen was not impressed. "He likes your cooking because he's cheap. Oscar's so tight his farts squeak."

Agnes Barkley laughed out loud. Gretchen Dixon was the most outrageous friend she had ever had. Agnes liked to listen to Gretchen just to hear what words would pop out of her mouth next. Even so, Agnes couldn't let Gretchen's attack on Oscar go unchallenged. After all, he was her husband.

"You shouldn't be so hard on him," she chided. "You'd like him if you ever spent any time with him."

"How can I spend time with the man?" Gretchen returned sarcastically. "Whenever I'm around him, all he does is grouse about how it isn't ladylike for women to smoke."

"Oscar was raised a Southern Baptist," Agnes countered.

"Oscar Barkley was raised under a rock."

Agnes changed the subject. "Would you like some lemonade? A cup of coffee?"

"Aggie Barkley, I'm not your husband. I didn't come over here to have you wait on me hand and foot the way you do him. I came to ask you a question. The senior citizens in town have chartered a bus to go up to Phoenix to the Heard Museum day after tomorrow. Me and Dolly Ann Parker and Lola Carlson are going to go. We were wondering if you'd like to come along."

"You mean Oscar and me?"

"No, I mean you, silly. Aggie Barkley by her own little lonesome. It's an overnight. We'll be staying someplace inexpensive, especially if we all four bunk in a single room. So you see, there wouldn't be any place for Oscar to sleep. Besides, it'll be fun. Just us girls. Think about it. It'll be like an old-fashioned slumber party. Remember those?"

Agnes was already shaking her head. "Oscar would never let me go. Never in a million years."

"Let?" Gretchen yelped, as though the very word wounded her. "Do you mean to tell me that at your age you have to ask that man for permission to be away from home overnight?"

"Not really. It's just that . . ."

"Say you'll go, then. The bus is filling up fast, and Dolly Ann needs to call in our reservation by five this afternoon."

"Where did you say it's going?"

Gretchen grinned triumphantly and ground out her cigarette in the ashtray Agnes had unobtrusively slipped in front of her. "The Heard Museum. In Phoenix. It's supposed to be full of all kinds of Indian stuff. Artifacts and baskets and all like that. I'm not that wild about Indians myself—I can take them or leave them—but the trip should be fun."

Agnes thought about it for a minute. She didn't want Gretchen to think she was a complete stick-in-the-mud. "If it's only overnight, I suppose I could go."

"That's my girl," Gretchen said. "I'll go right home and call Dolly Ann." She stood up and started briskly toward the door, then paused and turned back to Agnes. "By the way, have you ever played strip poker?"

"Me?" Agnes Barkley croaked. "Strip poker? Never!"

"Hold your breath, honey, because you're going to learn. The trick is to start out wearing plenty of clothes to begin with, so if you lose some it doesn't matter."

With that Gretchen Dixon was out the door, her flip-flops slapping noisily on the loose gravel as she headed down the hill toward her own mobile, parked two doors away. Agnes sat at the table, stunned. They would be playing strip poker? What on earth had she let herself in for?

Agnes wasn't so sure she had said yes outright, but she certainly had implied that she would go. She could have jumped up right then, swung the door open, and called out to Gretchen that she'd changed her mind, but she didn't. Instead she just sat there like a lump until she heard Gretchen's screen door slam shut behind her.

In the silence that followed, Agnes wondered what Oscar would say. It wasn't as though she had never left him alone. For years, she had spent one weekend in May—three whole days—at a Women's Bible Study retreat held each year at the YMCA camp at Lake Zurich, north of Buffalo Grove. And always, before she left, she had cooked and frozen and labeled enough food to last two weeks rather than three days. All Oscar and the girls ever had to do was thaw it out and heat it up.

Well, a Bible study retreat at a YMCA camp and four old ladies sitting around playing strip poker in a cheap hotel room weren't exactly the same thing, but Oscar didn't need to know about the poker part of it. Actually, the idea of Agnes going off someplace with Gretchen Dixon and her pals might be enough to set Oscar off all by itself.

And what if it did? Agnes Barkley asked herself, with a sudden jolt of self-determination. Sauce for the goose and sauce for the gander, right? After all, she never balked at the idea of him going off and spending hours on end wandering all over the desert with Jimmy Rathbone, that windy old crony of his, did she? So if Oscar Barkley didn't like the idea of her going to Phoenix with Gretchen, he could just as well lump it.

That was what Agnes thought at two o'clock in the afternoon, but by evening she had softened up some. Not that she'd changed her mind. She was still determined to go, but she'd figured out a way to ease it past Oscar.

As always her first line of attack was food. She made his favorite dinner—Italian meat loaf with baked potatoes and frozen French-cut green beans; a tossed salad with her own homemade Thousand Island dressing; and a lemon meringue pie for dessert. Agnes never failed to be amazed by the amount of food she could coax out of that little galley-sized kitchen with its tiny oven and stove. All it took was a little talent for both cooking and timing.

Dinner was ready at six, but Oscar wasn't home. He still wasn't there at six thirty or seven o'clock, either. Finally, at seven fifteen, with the meat loaf tough and dry in the cooling oven and with the baked potatoes shrivelled to death in their wrinkled, crusty skins, Agnes heard Oscar's Honda crunch to a stop outside the RV. By then, Agnes had pushed the plates and silverware aside and was playing a game of solitaire on the kitchen-nook table.

When Oscar stepped in through the door, Agnes didn't even glance up at him. "Sorry I'm so late, Aggie," he said, pausing long enough to hang his jacket and John Deere cap in the closet. "I guess we just got a little carried away with what we were doing."

"I just guess you did," she returned coolly.

With an apprehensive glance in her direction, Oscar hurried to the kitchen sink, rolled up his sleeves, and began washing his hands. "It smells good," he said.

"It probably was once," she replied. "I expect it'll be a little past its prime by the time I get it on the table."

"Sorry," he muttered again.

Deliberately, one line of cards at a time, she folded the solitaire hand away and then moved the dishes and silverware back to their respective places.

"Sit down and get out of the way," she ordered. "There isn't enough room for both of us to be milling around between the stove and the table while I'm trying to put food on the table."

Obediently, Oscar sank into the bench. While Agnes shifted the lukewarm food from the stove to the table, he struggled his way out of the nylon fanny pack he customarily wore on his walking jaunts. Agnes wasn't paying that much attention to what he was doing, but when she finished putting the last serving bowl on the table and went to sit down, she found a small earthen pot sitting next to her plate.

Agnes had seen Mexican *ollas* for sale at various curio shops on their travels through the Southwest. This one was shaped the same way most *ollas* were, with a rounded base and a small, narrow-necked lip. But most of those commercial pots were generally unmarked and made of a smooth reddish-brown clay. This was much smaller than any of the ones she had ever seen for sale. It was gray—almost black—with a few faintly etched white markings dimly visible.

"What's that?" she asked, sitting down at her place and leaning over so she could get a better view of the pot.

"Aggie, honey," Oscar said, "I believe you are looking at a winning lottery ticket."

Agnes Barkley sat up and stared across the tiny tabletop at her husband. It wasn't like Oscar to make jokes. Working in the post office all those years had pretty well wrung all the humor out of the man. But when she saw his face, Agnes was startled. Oscar was actually beaming. He reminded her of the grinning young man who had been waiting beside the altar for her forty-six years earlier.

"It doesn't look like any lottery ticket I've ever seen," Agnes answered, with a disdainful sniff. "Have some meat loaf and pass it before it gets any colder."

"Agnes," he said, not moving a finger toward the platter, "you don't understand. I think this is very important. Very valuable. I found it today. Down along the San Pedro just south of Saint David. There's a place where one of last winter's floods must have caused a cave-in. This pot was just lying there in the sand, sticking up in the air and waiting for someone like me to come along and pick it up."

Agnes regarded the pot with a little more respect. "You think it's old, then?"

"Very."

"And it could be worth a lot of money?"

"Tons of money. Well, maybe not tons." Oscar Barkley never allowed himself to indulge in unnecessary exaggeration. "But enough to make our lives a whole lot easier."

"It's just a little chunk of clay. Why would it be worth money?"

"Because it's all in one piece, dummy," he replied with certainty. Agnes was so inured to Oscar's customary arrogance that she didn't even notice it, much less let it bother her.

"If you read *Archaeology,* or *Discovery,* or *National Geographic,* once in a while," he continued, "or if you even bothered to look at the pictures, you'd see that stuff like this is usually found smashed into a million pieces. People have to spend months and years fitting them all back together."

Agnes reached out to pick up the pot. She had planned on examining it more closely, but as soon as she touched it, she inexplicably changed her mind and pushed it aside.

"It still doesn't look like all that much to me," she said. "Now, if you're not going to bother with the meat loaf, would you please go ahead and pass it?"

The grin disappeared from Oscar's face. He passed the platter without another word. Agnes saw at once that she had hurt his feelings. Usually, just a glimpse of that wounded look on his face would have been enough to melt her heart and cause her to make up with him, but tonight, for some reason, she still felt too hurt herself. Agnes was in no mood for making apologies.

"By the way," she said, a few minutes later, as she slathered margarine on a stone-cold potato, "Gretchen and Dolly Ann invited me to come up to Phoenix with them on a senior citizen bus tour the day after tomorrow. I told them I'd go."

"Oh? For how long?" Oscar asked.

"Just overnight. Why, do you have a problem with that?"

"No. No problem at all."

He said it so easily—it slipped out so smoothly—that for a moment Agnes almost missed it. "You mean you don't mind if I go, then?"

Oscar focused on her vaguely, as though his mind was preoccupied with something far away. "Oh, no," he said. "Not at all. You go right ahead and have a good time. Just one thing, though."

Agnes gave him a sharp look. "What's that?"

"Don't mention a word about this pot to anyone. Not Gretchen, not Dolly Ann."

"This is yours and Jimmy's little secret, I suppose?" Agnes asked.

Oscar shook his head. "Jimmy was a good half mile down the river when I found it," he said. "I brushed it off and put it straight in my pack. He doesn't even know I found it, and I'm not going to tell him, either. After all, I'm the one who found it. If it turns out to be worth something, there's no sense in splitting it with someone who wasn't any help at all in finding it, do you think?"

Agnes thought about that for a moment. "No," she said finally. "I don't suppose there is."

The meat loaf tasted like old shoe leather. The potatoes were worse. When chewed, the green beans snapped tastelessly against their teeth like so many boiled rubber bands. Oscar and Agnes picked at their food with little interest, no appetite, and even less conversation. Finally, Agnes stood up and began clearing away the dishes.

"How about some lemon pie," she offered, conciliatory at last. "At least that's *supposed* to be served cold."

They went to bed right after the ten o'clock news ended on TV. Oscar fell asleep instantly, planted firmly in the middle of the bed and snoring up a storm, while Agnes clung to her side of the mattress and held a pillow over her ear to help shut out some of the noise. Eventually she fell asleep as well. It was close to morning when the dream awakened her.

Agnes was standing on a small knoll, watching a young child play in the dirt. The child—apparently a little girl—wasn't one of Agnes Barkley's own children. Both of her girls were fair-skinned blondes. This child was brown-skinned, with a mane of thick black hair and white, shiny teeth. The child was bathed in warm sunlight, laughing and smiling. She spun around and around, kicking up dirt from around her, looking for all the world like a child-sized dust devil dancing across the desert floor.

Suddenly, for no clear reason, the scene darkened as though a huge cloud had passed in front of the sun. Somehow sensing danger, Agnes called out to the child: "Come here. Quick."

The little girl looked up at her and frowned, but she didn't seem to understand the warning Agnes was trying to give, and she didn't move. Agnes heard the sound then, heard the incredible roar and rush of water and knew that a flash flood was bearing down on them from somewhere upstream.

"Come here!" she cried again, more urgently this time. "Now!"

The child looked up at Agnes once more, and then she glanced off to her side. Her eyes widened in terror at the sight of a solid wall of murky brown water, twelve to fourteen feet high, churning toward her. The little girl scrambled to her feet and started away, darting toward Agnes and safety. But then, when she was almost out of harm's way, she stopped, turned, and went back. She was bending over to retrieve something from the dirt—something small and round and black—when the water hit. Agnes watched in helpless horror while the water crashed over her. Within seconds, the child was swept from view.

Agnes awakened drenched in sweat, just as she had years before when she was going through the change of life. Long after her heart quit pounding, the vivid, all-too-real dream stayed with her. Was that where the pot had come from? she wondered. Had the pot's owner, some small Indian child—no one in Westmont ever used the term Native American—been swept to her death before her mother's horrified eyes? And if it was true, if what Agnes had seen in the dream had really happened, it must have been a long time ago. How was it possible that it could be passed on to her—to a rock-solid Lutheran lady from Illinois, one not given to visions or wild flights of imagination?

Agnes crawled out of bed without disturbing the sleeping Oscar. She fumbled on her glasses, then slipped into her robe and went to the bathroom. When she emerged she stopped by the kitchen table, where the pot, sitting by itself, was bathed in a shaft of silver moonlight. It seemed to glow and shimmer in that strange, pearlescent light, but rather than being frightened of it, Agnes found herself drawn to it.

Without thinking, she sat down at the table, pulled the pot toward her, and let her fingers explore its smooth, cool surface. How did you go about forming such a pot? Agnes wondered. Where did you find the clay? How was it fired? What was it used for? There were no answers to those questions, but Agnes felt oddly comforted simply by asking them. A few minutes later she slipped back into bed and slept soundly until well after her usual time to get up and make coffee.

Two nights later, at the hotel in Phoenix, Agnes Barkley was down to nothing but her bra and panties when Gretchen Dixon's irritated voice brought her back to herself. "Well?" Gretchen demanded. "Do you want a card or not, Aggie? Either get in the game or get out."

Agnes put down her cards. "I'm out," she said. "I'm not very good at this. I can't concentrate."

"We should have played hearts instead," Lola offered.

"Strip hearts isn't all the same thing as strip poker," Gretchen snapped. "How many cards?"

"Two," Lola answered.

Agnes got up and pulled on her nightgown and robe. She had followed Gretchen's advice and started the game wearing as many clothes as she could manage. It hadn't helped. Although she was usually a quick study at games, she was hopeless when it came to the intricacies of poker. And now, with the room aswirl in a thick cloud of cigarette smoke, she was happy to be out of the game.

Agnes opened the sliding door and slipped out onto the tiny balcony. Although the temperature hovered in the low forties, it wasn't that cold—not compared to Chicago in January. In fact, it seemed downright balmy. She looked out at the sparse traffic waiting for the light on Grand Avenue and heard the low, constant rumble of trucks on the Black Canyon Freeway behind her. The roar reminded her once more of the noise the water had made as it crashed down around the little girl and overwhelmed her.

Although she wasn't cold, Agnes shivered and went back inside. She propped three pillows behind her, then sat on the bed with a book positioned in front of her face. The other women may have thought she was reading, but she wasn't.

Agnes Barkley was thinking about flash floods—remembering the real one she and Oscar had seen last winter. January had been one of the wettest ones on record. The fill-in manager at the trailer park commuted from Benson. He had told them one afternoon that a flood crest was expected over by Saint David shortly and that if they hurried, it would probably be worth seeing. They had been standing just off the bridge at Saint David when the wall of water came rumbling toward them, pushing ahead of it a jumbled collection of tires and rusty car fenders and even an old refrigerator, which bobbed along in the torrent as effortlessly as if it were nothing more than a bottle cork floating in a bathtub.

Agnes Barkley's dream from the other night—that still too vivid dream—might very well have been nothing more than a holdover from that. But she was now convinced it was more than that, especially after what she'd learned that day at the Heard Museum. Just as Gretchen Dixon had told her, the museum had been loaded with what Agnes now knew enough to call Native American artifacts—baskets, pottery, beadwork.

Their group had been led through the tour by a fast-talking docent who had little time or patience for dawdlers or questions. Afterward, while the others milled in the gift shop or lined up for refreshments, Agnes made her way back to one display in particular, where she had seen a single pot that very closely resembled the one she had last seen sitting on the kitchen table of the RV.

The display was a mixture of *Tohono O'othham* artifacts. Some of the basketry was little more than fragments. And just as Oscar had mentioned, the pots all showed signs of having been broken and subsequently glued back together. What drew Agnes to this display was not only the pot but also the typed legend on a nearby wall, which explained how, upon the death of the potmaker, her pots were always destroyed lest her spirit remain trapped forever in that which she had made.

Oscar's pot was whole, but surely the person who had crafted it was long since dead. Could the potmaker's spirit somehow still be captured, inside that little lump of blackened clay? Had the mother made that tiny pot as some kind of plaything for her child? Was that what had made it so precious to the little girl? Did that explain why she had bolted back into the path of certain death in a vain attempt to save it? And had the mother's restless spirit somehow managed to create a vision in order to convey the horror of that terrible event to Agnes?

As she stood staring at the lit display in the museum, that's how Agnes came to see what had happened to her. She hadn't dreamed a dream so much as she had seen a vision. And now, two days later, with the book positioned in front of her face and with the three-handed poker game continuing across the room, Agnes tried to sort out what it all meant and what she was supposed to do about it.

The poker game ended acrimoniously when Lola and Dolly Ann, both with next to nothing on, accused the fully dressed Gretchen of cheating. The other three women were still arguing about that when they came to bed. Not wanting to be drawn into the quarrel, Agnes closed her eyes and feigned sleep.

Long after the others were finally quiet, Agnes lay awake, puzzling about her responsibility to a woman she had never seen but through whose eyes she had witnessed that ancient and yet all too recent drowning. The child swept away in the rolling brown water was not Agnes Barkley's own child, yet the Indian child's death grieved Agnes as much as if she had been one of her own. It was growing light by the time Agnes reached a decision and was finally able to fall asleep.

The tour bus seemed to take forever to get them back to Tombstone. Oscar came to town to meet the bus and pick Agnes up. He greeted her with an exultant grin on his face and with an armload of library books sliding this way and that in the back seat of the Honda.

"I took a quick trip up to Tucson while you were gone," he explained. "They made an exception and let me borrow these books from the university library. Wait until I show you."

"I don't want to see," Agnes replied.

"You don't? Why not? I pored over them half the night and again this morning, until my eyes were about to fall out of my head. That pot of ours really is worth a fortune."

"You're going to have to take it back," Agnes said quietly.

"Take it back?" Oscar echoed in dismay. "What's the matter with you? Have you gone nuts or something? All we have to do is sell the pot, and we'll be on easy street from here on out."

"That pot is not for sale," Agnes asserted. "You're going to have to take it right back where you found it and break it."

Shaking his head, Oscar clamped his jaw shut, slammed the car in gear, and didn't say another word until they were home at the trailer park and had dragged both the books and Agnes Barkley's luggage inside.

"What in the hell has gotten into you?" Oscar demanded at last, his voice tight with barely suppressed anger.

Agnes realized she owed the man some kind of explanation. "There's a woman's spirit caught inside that pot," she began. "We have to let her out. The only way to do that is to break the pot. Otherwise she stays trapped in there forever."

"That's the craziest bunch of hocus-pocus nonsense I ever heard. Where'd you come up with something like that? It sounds like something that fruitcake Gretchen Dixon would come up with. You didn't tell her about this, did you?"

"No. I read about it. In a display at the museum, but I think I already knew it, even before I saw it there."

"You already *knew* it?" Oscar sneered. "What's that supposed to mean? Are you trying to tell me that the spirit who's suppos-edly trapped in my pot is telling you I have to break it?"

"That's right. And put it back where you found it."

"Like hell I will!" Oscar growled.

He stomped outside and stayed there, making some pretense of checking fluids under the hood of the Honda. Oscar may have temporarily abandoned the field of battle, but Agnes knew the fight was far from over. She sat down and waited. It was two o'clock in the afternoon—time to start some arrangements about dinner—but she didn't make a move toward either the stove or the refrigerator.

For forty-six years, things had been fine between them. Every time a compromise had been required, Agnes had made it cheer-fully and without complaint. That was the way it had always been, and it was the way Oscar expected it to be now. But this time—this one time—Agnes Barkley was prepared to stand firm. This one time, she wasn't going to bend.

Oscar came back inside half an hour later. "Look," he said, his manner amiable and apologetic. "I'm sorry I flew off the handle. You didn't know the whole story, because I didn't have a chance to tell you. While I was up in Tucson, I made some preliminary inquiries about the pot. Anonymously, of course. Hypothetically. I ended up talking to a guy who runs a trading post up near Oracle. He's a dealer, and he says he could get us a ton of money. You'll never guess how much."

"How much?"

"One hundred thou. Free and clear. That's what comes to us after the dealer's cut. And that's at a bare minimum. He says that if the collectors all end up in a bidding war, the price could go a whole lot higher than that. Do you have any idea what we could do with that kind of money?"

"I don't care how much money it is," Agnes replied stubbornly. "It isn't worth it. We've got to let her out, Oscar. She's been trapped in there for hundreds of years."

"Trapped?" Oscar demanded. "I'll tell you about trapped. Trapped is having to go to work every day for thirty years, rain or shine, hoping some goddamned dog doesn't take a chunk out of your leg. Trapped is hoping like hell you won't slip and fall on someone's icy porch and break your damned neck. Trapped is always working and scrimping and hoping to put enough money together so that someday we won't have to worry about outliving our money. And now, just when it's almost within my grasp, you—"

He broke off in midsentence. They were sitting across from each other in the tiny kitchen nook. Agnes met and held Oscar's eyes, her gaze serene and unwavering. He could see that nothing he said was having the slightest effect.

Suddenly it was all too much. How could Agnes betray him like that? Oscar lunged to his feet, his face contorted with outraged fury. "So help me, Aggie . . ."

He raised his hand as if to strike her. For one fearful moment, Agnes waited for the blow to fall. It didn't. Instead Oscar's eyes bulged. The unfinished threat died in his throat. The only sound that escaped his distorted lips was a strangled sob.

Slowly, like a giant old-growth tree falling victim to a logger's saw, Oscar Barkley began to tip over. Stiff and still, like a cigar store Indian, he tottered toward the wall and then bounced against the cupboard. Only then did the sudden terrible rigidity desert his body. His bones seemed to turn to jelly. Disjointed and limp, he slid down the face of the cupboard like a lifeless Raggedy Andy doll.

Only when he landed on the floor was there any sound at all, and that was nothing but a muted thump—like someone dropping a waist-high bag of flour.

Agnes watched him fall and did nothing. Later, when the investigators asked her about the ten-minute interval between the time Oscar's broken watch stopped and the time the 911 call came in to the emergency communications center, she was unable to explain them. Not that ten minutes one way or another would have made that much difference. Oscar Barkley's one and only coronary episode was instantly fatal.

Oh, he had been warned to cut down on fat, to lower his cholesterol, but Oscar had never been one to take a doctor's advice very seriously.

The day after the memorial service, Gretchen Dixon popped her head in the door of the RV just as Agnes, clad in jeans, a flannel shirt, and a straw hat, was tying the strings on her tennis shoes.

"How are you doing?" Gretchen asked.

"I'm fine," Agnes answered mechanically. "Really I am."

"You look like you're going someplace."

Agnes nodded toward the metal box of ashes the mortician had given her. "I'm going out to scatter the ashes," she said. "Oscar always said he wanted to be left along the banks of the San Pedro."

"Would you like me to go along?" Gretchen asked.

"No, thank you. I'll be fine."

"Is someone else going with you, then? The girls, maybe?"

"They caught a plane back home early this morning."

"Don't tell me that rascal Jimmy Rathbone is already making a move on you."

"I'm going by myself," Agnes answered firmly. "I don't want any company."

"Oh," Gretchen said. "Sorry."

When Agnes Barkley drove the Honda away from the RV a few minutes later, it looked as though she was all alone in the car, but strangely enough, she didn't feel alone. And although Oscar hadn't told Agnes exactly where along the riverbank he had found the pot, it was easy for Agnes to find her way there— almost as though someone were guiding each and every foot-step.

As soon as she reached the crumbled wall of riverbank, Agnes Barkley fell to her knees. It was quiet there, with what was left of the river barely trickling along in its sandy bed some thirty paces behind her. The only sound was the faint drone of a Davis-Monthan Air Force Base jet flying far overhead. Part of Agnes heard the sound and recognized it for what it was—an airplane. Another part of her jumped like a startled hare when what she thought was a bee turned out to be something totally beyond her understanding and comprehension.

When Agnes had arrived home with Oscar's ashes, she had immediately placed the pot inside the metal container. Now, with fumbling fingers, she drew it out. For one long moment, she held it lovingly to her breast. Then, with tears coursing down her face, she smashed the pot to pieces. Smashed it to smithereens on the metal container that held Oscar Barkley's barely cooled ashes.

Now Agnes snatched up the container. Holding it in front of her, she let the contents cascade out as she spun around and around, imitating someone else who once had danced exactly the same way in this very place sometime long, long ago.

At last, losing her balance, Agnes Barkley fell to the ground, gasping and out of breath. Minutes later she realized, as if for the first time, that Oscar was gone. Really gone. And there, amid his scattered ashes and the broken potsherds, she wept real tears. Not only because Oscar was dead but also because she had done nothing to help him. Because she had sat there helplessly and watched him die, as surely as that mysterious other woman had watched the surging water overwhelm her child.

At last Agnes seemed to come to herself. When she stopped crying, she was surprised to find that she felt much better. Relieved somehow. Maybe it was just as well Oscar was dead, she thought. He would not have liked being married to both of them—to Agnes and to the ghost of that other woman, to the mother of that poor drowned child.

This is the only way it could possibly work, Agnes said to herself. She picked up a tiny piece of black pottery, held it between her fingers, and let it catch the full blazing light of the warm afternoon sun.

This was the only way all three of them could be free.

The River Mouth

LIA MATERA

From the time of Wilkie Collins, a large number of crime fiction writers have been drawn from the ranks of lawyers, but the past twenty years have seen a veritable flood of attorneys hoping to escape the billable-hour rat race and emulate the success of John Grisham and Scott Turow. For a time, legal fiction, and indeed the practice of law itself, was largely a male province, but recent years have changed that. Lia Matera (b. 1952), who was born in Canada to an Italian-American family, received her law degree from the University of California's Hastings College of Law, where she was the editor in chief of the *Hastings Constitutional Law Quarterly*. She was later a teaching fellow at Stanford Law School. The author of two separate series about lawyer sleuths, Matera is one of the best of the lawyers-turned-mystery-writers. Her first series, beginning with *Where Lawyers Fear to Tread* (1987), which draws on her background as a law review editor, introduces Willa Jansson, the daughter of fiercely left-wing parents. The family political background gives a political charge to the series that often results in widely divergent critical reaction. As *Contemporary Authors* (volume 110, 1999) points out in a discussion of *Hidden Agenda* (1987), "Though a reviewer for *Publishers Weekly* felt that the novel 'is angry, and devoid of humor or emotions other than hate,' a *Booklist* critic praised the novel as 'offbeat and very funny.'" *The Smart Money* (1988) began a shorter series about a sharper-edged, higher-profile advocate, Laura DiPalma.

Matera has written relatively few short stories, and several of those few were originally envisioned as novels. All her stories to date are collected in *Counsel for the Defense and Other Stories* (2000). In introducing that collection, she identifies "The River Mouth," an outdoor account of gathering menace, as among those stories that have "given [her] a welcome break from writing about lawyers."

To reach the mouth of the Klamath River, you head west off 101 just south of the Oregon border. You hike through an old Yurok meeting ground, an overgrown glade with signs asking you to respect native spirits and stay out of the cooking pits and the split-long amphitheater. The trail ends at a sand cliff. From there you can watch the Klamath rage into the sea, battering the tide. Waves break in every direction, foam blowing off like rising ghosts. Sea lions by the dozens bob in the swells, feeding on eels flushed out of the river.

My boyfriend and I made our way down to the wet-clay beach. The sky was every shade of gray, and the Pacific looked like mercury. We were alone except for five Yurok in rubber boots and checkered flannel, fishing in the surf. We watched them flick stiff whips of sharpened wire mounted on pick handles. When the tips lashed out of the waves, they had eels impaled on them. With a rodeo windup, they flipped the speared fish over their shoulders into pockets they'd dug in the sand. We passed shallow pits seething with creatures that looked like short, mean-faced snakes.

We continued for maybe a quarter mile beyond the river mouth. We climbed some small, sharp rocks to get to a tall, flat one midway between the shore and the cliff. From there we could see the fishermen but not have our conversation carry down to them.

Our topic of the day (we go to the beach to hash things out) was if we wanted to get married. Because it was a big, intimidating topic, we'd driven almost four hundred miles to find the right beach. We'd had to spend the night in a tacky motel, but this was the perfect spot, no question.

Patrick uncorked the champagne—we had two bottles; it was likely to be a long talk. I set out the canned salmon and crackers on paper plates on the old blue blanket. I kicked off my shoes so I could cross my legs. I watched Pat pour, wondering where we'd end up on the marriage thing.

When he handed me the paper cup of bubbles, I tapped it against his. "To marriage or not."

"To I do or I don't," he agreed.

The air smelled like cold beach, like wet sky and slick rocks and storms coming. At home, the beach stinks like fish and shored seaweed buzzing with little flies. If there are sunbathers on blankets, you can smell their beer and coconut oil.

"So, Pat?" I looked him over, trying to imagine being married to him. He was a freckly, baby-faced Scot with strange hair and hardly any meat on him. Whereas I was a black-haired mutt who tended to blimp out in the winter and get it back under control in the summer. But the diets were getting harder; and I knew fat women couldn't be choosers. I was thinking it was time to lock in. And worrying that was an unworthy motive. "Maybe we're fine the way we are now."

Right away he frowned.

"I just mean it's okay with me the way it is."

"Because you were married to Mr. Perfect and how could I ever take his place?"

"Hearty-har." Mr. Perfect meaning my ex-husband had plenty of money and good clothes. Pat had neither right now. He'd just got laid off, and there were a thousand other software engineers answering every ad he did.

"I guess *he* wasn't an 'in-your-face child,'" Pat added.

Aha. Here we had last night's fight.

"With Mr. Perfect you didn't even have arguments. *He* knew when to stop."

Me and Pat fight on long drives. I say things. I don't necessarily mean them. It was too soon to call the caterer, I guess.

I held out my paper cup for more. "All I meant was he had more experience dealing with—"

"Oh, it goes without saying!" He poured refills so fast they bubbled over. "I'm a mere infant! About as cleanly as a teenager and as advanced in my political analysis as a college freshman."

"What is this, a retrospective of old fights? Okay, so it takes some adjustment living with a person. I've said things in crabby moments. On the drive up—"

"Crabby moments? You? No, you're an *artist*." You could have wrung the scorn out of the word and still had it drip sarcasm. "Reality's just more *complicated* for you."

I felt my eyes narrow. "I hate that, Patrick."

"Oh, she's calling me Patrick."

Usually I got formal when I got mad. "I'm not in the best mood when I write. If you could just learn to leave me alone then." Like I said in the car.

His pale brows pinched as he flaked salmon onto crackers. I made a show of shading my eyes and watching a Yurok woman walk toward us. When she got to the bottom of our rock, she called up, "Got a glass for me?"

Usually we were antisocial, which is why we did our drinking at the beach instead of in bars. But the conversation wasn't going the greatest. A diversion, a few minutes to chill—why not?

"Sure," I said.

Pat hit me with the angry-bull look, face lowered, brows down, nostrils flared. As she clattered up the rocks, he muttered, "I thought we came here to be alone."

"Hi there," she said, reaching the top. She was slim, maybe forty, with long brown hair and a semi-flat nose and darkish skin just light enough to show some freckles. She had a great smile but bad teeth. She wore a black hat almost like a cowboy's but not as western. She sat on a wet part of the rock to spare our blanket whatever funk was on her jeans (as if we cared):

"Picnic, huh? Great spot."

I answered, "Yeah," because Pat was sitting in pissy silence.

She drank some champagne. "Not many people know about this beach. You expecting other folks?"

"No. We're pretty far from home."

"This is off the beaten path, all right." She glanced over her shoulder, waving at her friends.

"We had to hike through Yurok land to get here," I admitted. "Almost elven, and that wonderful little amphitheater." I felt embarrassed, didn't know how to assure her we hadn't been disrespectful. I'd had to relieve myself behind a bush, but we didn't do war cries or anything insensitive. "I hope it isn't private property. I hope this beach isn't private."

"Nah. That'd be a crime against nature, wouldn't it?" She grinned. "There's a trailer park up the other way. That *is* private property. But as long as you go out the way you came in, no problem."

"Thanks, that's good to know. We heard about this beach on our last trip north, but we didn't have a chance to check it out. We didn't expect all the seals or anything."

"Best time of year; eels come upriver to spawn in the ocean. Swim twenty-five hundred miles, some of them," she explained. "It's a holy spot for the Yurok, the river mouth." A break in the clouds angled light under her hat brim, showing leathery lines around her eyes. "This place is about mouths, really. In the river, the eel is the king mouth. He hides, he waits, he strikes fast. But time comes when he's got to heed that urge. And he swims right into the jaws of the sea lion. Yup." She motioned behind her. "Here and now, this is the eel's judgment day."

Pat was giving me crabby little get-rid-of-her looks. I ignored him. Okay, we had a lot to talk about. But what are the odds of a real-McCoy Yurok explaining the significance of a beach?

She lay on her side on the blanket, holding out her paper cup for a refill and popping some salmon into her mouth. "Salmon means renewal," she said. "Carrying on the life cycle, all that. You should try the salmon jerky from the rancheria."

Pat hesitated before refilling her cup. I let him fill mine too.

"King mouth of the river, that's the eel," she repeated. "Of course, the Eel River's named after him. But it's the Klamath that's his castle. They'll stay alive out of water longer than any other fish I know. You see them flash that ugly gray-green in the surf, and thwack, you get them on your whipstick and flip them onto the pile. You do that awhile, you know, and get maybe fifteen, and when you go back to put them in your bucket, maybe eight of the little monsters have managed to jump out of the pit and crawl along the sand. You see how far some of them got and you have to think they stayed alive a good half hour out of the water. Now how's that possible?"

I lay on my side too, sipping champagne, listening, watching the gorgeous spectacle behind her in the distance: seals bobbing and diving, the river crashing into the sea, waves colliding like hands clapping. Her Yurok buddies weren't fishing anymore; they were talking. One gestured toward our rock. I kind of hoped they'd join us. Except Pat would really get cranky then.

Maybe I did go too far on the drive up. But I wished he'd let it go.

"So it's not much of a surprise, huh?" the woman continued. "That they're king of the river. They're mean and tough, they got teeth like nails. If they were bigger, man, sharks wouldn't stand a chance, never mind seals." She squinted at me, sipping. "Because the cussed things can hide right in the open. Their silt-bark color, they can sit right in front of a rock, forget behind it. They can look like part of the scenery. And you swim by feeling safe and cautious, whoever you are—maybe some fancy fish swum upriver—and munch! You're eel food. But the river ends some-where, you know what I mean? Every river has its mouth. There's always that bigger mouth out there waiting for you to wash in, no matter how sly and bad you are at home. You heed those urges and leave your territory, and you're dinner."

Pat was tapping the bottom of my foot with his. Tapping, tapping urgently like I should do something.

That's when I made up my mind: Forget marriage. He was too young. Didn't want to hear this Yurok woman talk and was tapping on me like, Make her go away, Mom. I had kids, two of them, and they were grown now and out of the house. And not much later, their dad went too (though I didn't miss him and I did miss the kids, at least sometimes). And I didn't need someone fifteen years younger than me always putting the responsibility on me. I paid most of the bills, got the food together (didn't cook, but knew my delis), picked up around the house, told Pat what he should read, because engineers don't know squat about literature or history; and every time someone needed getting rid of or something social had to be handled or even just a business letter had to be written, it was tap-tap-tap, oh, Maggie, could you please . . . ?

I reached behind me and shoved Pat's foot away. If he wanted to be antisocial, he could think of a way to make the woman leave himself. We had plenty of time to talk, just the two of us. I didn't want her to go yet.

"Got any more?" the Yurok asked.

I pulled the second bottle out of our beat-up backpack and opened it, trying not to look at Pat, knowing he'd have that hermity scowl now big-time.

"You picnic like this pretty often?" she asked.

"Yeah, we always keep stuff in the trunk—wine, canned salmon, crackers. Gives us the option." That was the other side of it: Pat was fun, and he let me have control. If I said let's go, he said okay. That means everything if you spent twenty years with a stick-in-the-mud.

"You come here a lot?" she asked.

"No. This was a special trip."

"It was supposed to be," Pat fussed.

I hastily added, "Our beaches down around Santa Cruz and Monterey are nice, but we've been to them a thousand times."

"Mmm." She let me refill her cup. I had more too. Pat didn't seem to be drinking.

"Now, the sea lion is a strange one," she said. "There's little it won't eat, and not much it won't do to survive, but it has no guile. It swims along, do-de-do, and has a bite whenever it can. It doesn't hide or trick. It's lazy. If it can find a place to gorge, it'll do that and forget about hunting. It doesn't seem to have the hunting instinct. It just wants to eat and swim and jolly around. Mate. Be playful." She broke another piece of salmon off, holding it in fingers with silt and sand under the nails. "Whereas an eel is always lurking, even when it's just eaten. It never just cavorts. It's always thinking ahead, like a miser worrying how to get more."

"Until it leaves home and washes into the sea lion's mouth." I concluded the thought for her.

"What the eel needs"—she sat up—"is a way to say, Hell no. Here it is, the smarter, stealthier creature. And what does nature do but use its own instinct against it. Favor some fat, lazy thing that's not even a fish, it's a mammal that lives in the water, that doesn't really belong and yet has food poured down its gullet just for being in the right place." She pointed at the sea lion heads bobbing in the waves. "Look at them. This is their welfare cafeteria. They do nothing but open their mouths."

Pat put in, "You could say you're like the seals. You're out there with those steel-pronged things, spearing eels."

I wanted to hit him. It seemed a rude thing to say.

"The Yurok are like the eels." She removed her hat. Her dark hair, flattened on top, began to blow in the wind coming off the water. "The Yurok were king because the Yurok knew how to blend in. The Yurok thought always of food for tomorrow because Yurok nightmares were full of yesterday's starvation. The Yurok were part of the dark bottom of history's river, silent and ready. And they got swept out into the bigger mouths that waited without deserving."

She leaped to her feet. She looked majestic, her hair blowing against a background of gray-white clouds, her arms and chin raised to the heavens. "This is where the ancient river meets the thing that is so much bigger, the thing the eel can't bear to understand because the knowledge is too bitter."

Behind me, Pat whispered, "This is weird. Look at her friends."

On the beach, the Yurok men raised their arms too. They stood just like the woman, maybe imitating her to tease her, maybe just coincidence.

"Where the ancient river meets the thing that is much bigger, and the eel can't understand because the knowledge is too bitter," she repeated to the sky.

Pat was poking me now, hardly bothering to whisper. "I don't like this! She's acting crazy!"

I smacked him with an absent-minded hand behind my back, like a horse swatting off a fly. Maybe this was too much for a software engineer—why had I ever thought I could marry someone as unlyrical as that?—but it was a writer's dream. It was real-deal Yurok lore. If she quit because of him, I'd push Pat's unimaginative damn butt right off the rock.

She shook her head from side to side, hair whipping her cheeks. "At the mouth of the river, you learn the truth: follow your obsession, and the current carries you into a hundred waiting mouths. But if you lie quiet"—she bent forward so I could see her bright dark eyes—"and think passionately of trapping your prey, if your hunger is a great gnawing within you, immobilizing you until the moment when you become a rocket of appetite to consume what swims near—"

"What do they want?" Pat's shadow fell across the rock. I turned to see that he was standing now, staring down the beach at the Yurok men.

They'd taken several paces toward us. They seemed to be watching the woman.

She was on a roll, didn't even notice. "Then you don't ride the river into the idle mouth, the appetite without intelligence, the hunger that happens without knowing itself."

Pat's anoraked arm reached over me and plucked the paper cup from her hand. "You better leave now."

"What is your problem, Patrick?" I jumped to my feet. Big damn kid, Jesus Christ. Scared by legends, by champagne talk on a beach! "Mellow the hell out."

My words wiped the martial look off his face. A marveling betrayal replaced it. "You think you're so smart, Maggie, you think you know everything! But you're really just a sheltered little housewife."

I was too angry to speak. I maybe hadn't earned much over the years, but I was a *writer*.

His lips compressed, his eyes squinted, his whole freckled Scot's face crimped with wronged frustration. "But I guess the Mature One has seen more than a child like myself. I guess it takes an Artist to really know life."

"Oh, for Christ sake!" I spoke the words with both arms and my torso. "Are you such a white-bread baby you can't hear a little bit of Yurok metaphor without freaking out?"

He turned, began to clamber down the rock. He was muttering. I caught the words "princess" and "know everything," as well as some serious profanity.

I turned to find the Yurok woman sitting on the blanket, drinking sedately, her posture unabashedly terrible. I remained standing for a few minutes, watching Patrick jerk along the beach, fists buried in his pockets.

"He doesn't want my friends to join us," she concluded correctly. From the look of it, he was marching straight over to tell them so.

The men stood waiting. A hundred yards behind them, desperate eels wriggled from their sand pits like the rays of a sun.

I had a vision of roasting eels with the Yuroks, learning their legends as the waves crashed beside us. What a child Pat was. Just because we'd fought a bit in the car.

"I know why he thinks I'm crazy," the woman said.

I sat with a sigh, pulling another paper cup out of the old backpack and filling it. I handed it to her, feeling like shit. So what if the men wanted to join us for a while? Patrick and I had the rest of the afternoon to fight. Maybe the rest of our lives.

"We came out here to decide if we should get married," I told her. I could feel tears sting my eyes. "But the trouble is, he's still so young. He's only seven years older than my oldest daughter. He doesn't have his career together—he just got laid off. He's been moping around all month getting in my way. He's an engineer—I met him when I was researching a science-fiction story. All he knows about politics and literature is what I've made him learn." I wiped the tears. "He's grown a lot in the last year, since we've been together, but it's not like being with an equal. I mean, we have a great time unless we start talking about something in particular, and then I have to put up with all these half-baked, college-student kind of ideas. I have to give him articles to read and tell him how to look at things—I mean, yes, he's smart, obviously, and a quick learner. But fifteen years, you know."

She nibbled a bit more salmon. "Probably he saw the van on the road coming down."

"What van?"

"Our group."

"The Yurok?"

She wrinkled her nose. "No. They're up in Hoopa on the reservation, what's left of them. They're practically extinct."

"We assumed you were Yurok. You're all so dark. You know how to do that whip-spear thing."

"Yeah, we're all dark-haired." She rolled her eyes. "But jeez, there's only five of us. You're dark-haired. You're not Yurok." Her expression brightened. "But the whipstick, that's Yurok, you're right. Our leader"—she pointed to the not-Yuroks on the beach, I wasn't sure which one—"made them. We're having an out-of-culture experience, you could say."

Patrick had reached the group now, was standing with his shoulders up around his ears and his hands still buried in his pockets.

"How did you all get so good at it?"

"Good at it?" She laughed. "The surf's absolutely crawling with eels. If we were good at it, we'd have hundreds of them."

"What's the group?"

Patrick's hands were out of his pockets now. He held them out in front of him as he began backing away from the four men.

"You didn't see the van, really?"

"Maybe Pat did. I was reading the map." I rose to my knees, watching him. Patrick was still backing away, picking up speed. Up here, showing fear of a ranting woman, he'd seemed ridiculous. Down on the beach, with four long-haired men advancing toward him, his fear arguably had some basis. What had they said to him?

"The van scares people." She nodded. "The slogans we painted on it."

"Who are you?" I asked her, eyes still locked on Patrick.

"I was going to say before your fiancé huffed out: what about the sea lions? They get fat with no effort, just feasting on the self-enslaved, black-souled little eels. Do they get away with it?"

The sky was beginning to darken. The sea was pencil-lead gray now, with a bright silver band along the horizon. Patrick was running toward us across the beach.

Two of the men started after him.

I tried to rise to my feet, but the woman clamped her hand around my ankle.

"No," she said. "The sea lions aren't happy very long. They're just one more fat morsel in the food chain. Offshore there are sharks, plenty of them, the mightiest food processors of all. This is their favorite spot for sea lion sushi."

"What are they doing? What do your friends want?" My voice was as shrill as the wind whistling between the rocks.

"The Yurok were the eels, kings of the river, stealthy and quick and hungry. But the obsessions of history washed them into the jaws of white men, who played and gorged in the surf." She nodded. "The ancient river meets the thing that is much bigger, the thing the eel can't bear to understand because the knowledge is too bitter."

She'd said that more than once, almost the same way. Maybe that's what scared Pat: her words were like a litany, an incantation, some kind of cultish chant. And the men below had mirrored her gestures.

I knocked her hand off my ankle and started backward off the rock. All she'd done was talk about predation. She'd learned we were alone and not expecting company, and she'd signaled to the men on the beach. Now they were chasing Patrick.

Afraid to realize what it meant, too rattled to put my shoes back on, I stepped into a slick crevice. I slid, losing my balance. I fell, racketing over the brutal jags and edges of the smaller rocks we'd used as a stairway. I could hear Patrick scream my name. I felt a lightning burn of pain in my ribs, hip, knee. I could feel the hot spread of blood under my shirt.

I tried to catch my breath, to stand up. The woman was picking her way carefully down to where I lay.

"There's another kind of hunter, Maggie." I could hear the grin in her voice. "Not the eel who waits and strikes. Not the seal who finds plenty and feeds. But the shark." She stopped, silhouette poised on the rock stair. "Who thinks of nothing but finding food, who doesn't just hide like the eel or wait like the sea lion but who quests and searches voraciously, looking for another—"

Patrick screamed, but not my name this time.

"Looking for a straggler." Again she raised her arms and her chin to the heavens, letting her dark hair fly around her. Patrick was right: she did look crazy.

She jumped down. Patrick screamed again. We screamed together, finally in agreement.

I heard a sudden blast and knew it must be gunfire. I watched the woman land in a straddling crouch, her hair in wild tendrils like eels wriggling from their pits.

Oh, Patrick. Let me turn back the clock and say I'm sorry.

I looked up at the woman, thinking: too late, too late. I rode the river right into your jaws.

Another shot. Did it hit Pat?

A voice from the sand cliff boomed, "Get away!"

The woman looked up and laughed. She raised her arms again, throwing back her head.

A third blast sent her scrambling off the small rocks, kicking up footprints in the sand as she ran away. She waved her arms as if to say goodbye.

I sat painfully forward—I'd cracked a rib, broken some skin, I could feel it. Nevertheless, I twisted to look up the face of the cliff.

In the blowing grass above me, a stocky man with long black hair fired a rifle into the air.

A real Yurok, Pat and I learned later.

A Scandal in Winter

GILLIAN LINSCOTT

Gillian Linscott (b. 1944) was born in Windsor, England, the daughter of a shoe shop manager and a shop assistant. Holding an Oxford degree in English language and literature, she worked as a newspaper journalist in Liverpool and Birmingham between 1967 and 1972, moved to the *Guardian* (Manchester and London) until 1979, then turned to broadcast journalism, reporting on Parliament for the British Broadcasting Corporation, for which she has also written radio plays. Her first novel, *A Healthy Grave* (1984), was set in a nudist camp and introduced her short-lived series character Birdie Linnet, a former policeman whom she described to *Contemporary Authors* (volume 128, 1990) as being no super sleuth: "in fact . . . [he] is remarkable chiefly for getting the point later than anybody else on the page. He's well-meaning, none too intelligent, and frequently hit on the head." As this description suggests, Linscott does not take the detective-story form too seriously, liking it because "it's not pompous. In my view there are few books that couldn't be improved by dumping a body in them somewhere. The mystery novel is a very artificial creation and I'm not greatly concerned with realism." Linscott achieved her greatest renown, as well as possibly greater realism, when she moved from contemporary whodunnits to historicals, first with *Murder, I Presume* (1990), set in the 1870s, then with the series about early-twentieth-century suffragette Nell Bray, beginning with *Sister Beneath the Sheets* (1991).

One prominent sub-category of historical mystery fiction is the Sherlock Holmes pastiche, once relatively rare and, for whatever reason, usually written by men. In recent years, following the best-selling success of Nicholas Meyer's *Seven-Per-cent*

Solution (1974), new Holmes novels have become a cottage industry and several original anthologies have been filled with shorter adventures for the Baker Street sleuth. Some of the best of these have been written by women, including the work of L. B. Greenwood at novel length and June Thomson in a series of short-story collections. With her knowledge of the Victorian and Edwardian eras, Linscott was a natural to write a Holmes pastiche. "A Scandal in Winter," one of the best stories in the Christmas Sherlockian anthology *Holmes for the Holidays* (1996), gains some of its freshness and originality from the use of a narrator other than Dr. Watson.

At first Silver Stick and his Square Bear were no more to us than incidental diversions at the Hotel Edelweiss. The Edelweiss at Christmas and the new year was like a sparkling white desert island, or a very luxurious ocean liner sailing through snow instead of sea. There we were, a hundred people or so, cut off from the rest of the world, even from the rest of Switzerland, with only each other for entertainment and company. It was one of the only possible hotels to stay at in 1910 for this new fad of winter sporting. The smaller Berghaus across the way was not one of the possible hotels, so its dozen or so visitors hardly counted. As for the villagers in their wooden chalets with the cows living downstairs, they didn't count at all. Occasionally, on walks, Amanda and I would see them carrying in logs from neatly stacked woodpiles or carrying out forkfuls of warm soiled straw that sent columns of white steam into the blue air. They were part of the valley like the rocks and pine trees but they didn't ski or skate, so they had no place in our world—apart from the sleighs. There were two of those in the village. One, a sober affair drawn by a stolid bay cob with a few token bells on the harness, brought guests and their luggage from the nearest railway station. The other, the one that mattered to Amanda and me, was a streak of black and scarlet, swift as the mountain wind, clamorous with silver bells, drawn by a sleek little honey-colored Haflinger with a silvery mane and tail that matched the bells. A pleasure sleigh, with no purpose in life beyond amusing the guests at the Edelweiss. We'd see it drawn up in the trampled snow outside, the handsome young owner with his long whip and blond mustache waiting patiently. Sometimes we'd be allowed to linger and watch as he helped in a lady and gentleman and adjusted the white fur rug over their laps. Then away they'd go, hissing and jingling through the snow, into the track through the pine forest. Amanda and I had been promised that, as a treat on New Year's Day, we would be taken for a ride in it. We looked forward to it more eagerly than Christmas.

But that was ten days away and until then we had to amuse ourselves. We skated on the rink behind the hotel. We waved goodbye to our father when he went off in the mornings with his skis and his guide. We sat on the hotel terrace drinking hot chocolate with blobs of cream on top while Mother wrote and read letters. When we thought Mother wasn't watching, Amanda and I would compete to see if we could drink all the chocolate so that the blob of cream stayed marooned at the bottom of the cup, to be eaten in luscious and impolite spoonfuls. If she glanced up and caught us, Mother would tell us not to be so childish, which, since Amanda was eleven and I was nearly thirteen, was fair enough, but we had to get what entertainment we could out of the chocolate. The truth was that we were all of us, most of the time, bored out of our wits. Which was why we turned our attention to the affairs of the other guests and Amanda and I had our ears permanently tuned to the small dramas of the adults' conversation.

"I still can't believe she will."

"Well, that's what the headwaiter said, and he should know. She's reserved the table in the corner overlooking the terrace and said they should be sure to have the Tokay."

"The same table as last year."

"The same wine, too."

Our parents looked at each other over the croissants, carefully not noticing the maid as she poured our coffee. ("One doesn't notice the servants, dear, it only makes them awkward.")

"I'm sure it's not true. Any woman with any feeling . . ."

"What makes you think she has any?"

Silence, as eye signals went on over our heads. I knew what was being signaled, just as I'd known what was being discussed in an overheard scrap of conversation between our parents at bedtime the night we arrived: "... effect it might have on Jessica."

My name. I came rapidly out of drowsiness, kept my eyes closed but listened.

"I don't think we need worry about that. Jessica's tougher than you think." My mother's voice. She needed us to be tough so that she didn't have to waste time worrying about us.

"All the same, she must remember it. It is only a year ago. That sort of experience can mark a child for life."

"Darling, they don't react like we do. They're much more callous at that age."

Even with eyes closed I could tell from the quality of my father's silence that he wasn't convinced, but it was no use arguing with Mother's certainties. They switched the light off and closed the door. For a minute or two I lay awake in the dark wondering whether I was marked for life by what I'd seen and how it would show, then I wondered instead whether I'd ever be able to do pirouettes on the ice like the girl from Paris, and fell asleep in a wistful dream of bells and the hiss of skates.

The conversation between our parents that breakfast time over what she would or wouldn't do was interrupted by the little stir of two other guests being shown to their table. Amanda caught my eye.

"Silver Stick and his Square Bear are going skiing."

Both gentlemen—elderly gentlemen as it seemed to us, but they were probably no older than their late fifties—were wearing heavy wool jumpers, tweed breeches, and thick socks, just as Father was. He nodded to them across the tables, wished them good morning and received nods and good-mornings back. Even the heavy sports clothing couldn't take away the oddity and distinction from the tall man. He was, I think, the thinnest person I'd ever seen. He didn't stoop as so many tall older people did but walked upright and lightly. His face with its eagle's beak of a nose was deeply tanned, like some of the older inhabitants of the village, but unlike them it was without wrinkles apart from two deep folds from the nose to the corners of his mouth. His hair was what had struck us most. It clung smoothly to his head in a cap of pure and polished silver, like the knob on an expensive walking stick. His companion, large and square shouldered in any case, looked more so in his skiing clothes. He shambled and tended to trip over chairs. He had a round, amiable face with pale, rather watery eyes, a clipped gray mustache but no more than a fringe of hair left on his gleaming pate. He always smiled at us when we met on the terrace or in corridors and appeared kindly. We'd noticed that he was always doing things for Silver Stick, pouring his coffee, posting his letters. For this reason we'd got it into our heads that Square Bear was Silver Stick's keeper. Amanda said Silver Stick probably went mad at the full moon and Square Bear had to lock him up and sing loudly so that people wouldn't hear his howling. She kept asking people when the next full moon would be, but so far nobody knew. I thought he'd probably come to Switzerland because he was dying of consumption, which explained the thinness, and Square Bear was his doctor. I listened for a coughing fit to confirm this, but so far there'd been not a sign of one. As they settled to their breakfast we watched as much as we could without being rebuked for staring. Square Bear opened the paper that had been lying beside his plate and read things out to Silver Stick, who gave the occasional little nod over his coffee, as if he'd known whatever it was all the time. It was the *Times* of London and must have been at least two days old because it had to come up from the station in the sleigh.

Amanda whispered: "He eats."

The waiter had brought a rack of toast and a stone jar of Oxford marmalade to their table instead of croissants. Silver Stick was eating toast like any normal person.

Father asked: "Who eats?"

We indicated with our eyes.

"Well, why shouldn't he eat? You need a lot of energy for skiing."

Mother, taking an interest for once, said they seemed old for skiing.

"You'd be surprised. Dr. Watson's not bad, but as for the other one—well, he went past me like a bird in places so steep that even the guide didn't want to try it. And stayed standing up at the end of it when most of us would have been just a big hole in the snow. The man's so rational he's completely without fear. It's fear that wrecks you when you're skiing. You come to a steep place, you think you're going to fall and nine times out of ten, you do fall. Holmes comes to the same steep place, doesn't see any reason why he can't do it—so he does it."

My mother said that anybody really rational would have the sense not to go skiing in the first place. My ear had been caught by one word.

"Square Bear's a doctor? Is Silver Stick ill?"

"Not that I know. Is there any more coffee in that pot?"

And there we left it for the while. You might say that Amanda and I should have known at once who they were, and I suppose nine out of ten children in Europe would have known. But we'd led an unusual life, mainly on account of Mother, and although we knew many things unknown to most girls of our age, we were ignorant of a lot of others that were common currency.

We waved off Father and his guide as they went wallowing up in the deep snow through the pine trees, skis on their shoulders, then turned back for our skates. We stopped at the driveway to let the sober black sleigh go past, the one that went down the valley to the railway. There was nobody in the back, but the rugs were ready and neatly folded.

"Somebody new coming," Amanda said.

I knew Mother was looking at me, but she said nothing. Amanda and I were indoors doing our holiday reading when the sleigh came back, so we didn't see who was in it, but when we went downstairs later there was a humming tension about the hotel, like the feeling you get when a violinist is holding his bow just above the string and the tingle of the note runs up and down your spine before you hear it. It was only mid-afternoon but dusk was already settling on the valley. We were allowed a last walk outside before it got dark, and made as usual for the skating rink. Colored electric lights were throwing patches of yellow, red, and blue on the dark surface. The lame man with the accordion was playing a Strauss waltz and a few couples were skating to it, though not very well. More were clustered round the charcoal brazier at the edge of the rink where a waiter poured small glasses of mulled wine. Perhaps the man with the accordion knew the dancers were getting tired or wanted to go home himself, because when the waltz ended he changed to something wild and gypsy sounding, harder to dance to. The couples on the ice tried it for a few steps then gave up, laughing, to join the others round the brazier. For a while the ice was empty and the lame man played on to the dusk and the dark mountains.

Then a figure came gliding onto the ice. There was a decisiveness about the way she did it that marked her out at once from the other skaters. They'd come on staggering or swaggering, depending on whether they were beginners or thought themselves expert, but staggerers and swaggerers alike had a self-conscious air, knowing that this was not their natural habitat. She took to the ice like a swan to the water or a swallow to the air. The laughter died away, the drinking stopped and we watched as she swooped and dipped and circled all alone to the gypsy music. There were no showy pirouettes like the girl from Paris, no folding of the arms and look-at-me smiles. It's quite likely that she was not a particularly expert skater, that what was so remarkable about it was her willingness to take the rink, the music, the attention as hers by right. She wasn't even dressed for skating. The black skirt coming to within a few inches of the instep of her skate boots, the black mink jacket, the matching cap, were probably what she'd been wearing on the journey up from the station. But she'd been ready for this, had planned to announce her return exactly this way.

Her return. At first, absorbed by the performance, I hadn't recognized her. I'd registered that she was not a young woman and that she was elegant. It was when a little of my attention came back to my mother that I knew. She was standing there as stiff and prickly as one of the pine trees, staring at the figure on the ice like everybody else, but it wasn't admiration on her face, more a kind of horror. They were all looking like that, all the adults, as if she were the messenger of something dangerous. Then a woman's voice, not my mother's, said, "How could she? Really, how could she?"

There was a murmuring of agreement and I could feel the horror changing to something more commonplace—social disapproval. Once the first words had been said, others followed and there was a rustling of sharp little phrases like a sledge runner grating on gravel.

"Only a year . . . to come here again . . . no respect . . . lucky not to be . . . after what happened."

My mother put a firm hand on each of our shoulders. "Time for your tea."

Normally we'd have protested, begged for another few minutes, but we knew that this was serious. To get into the hotel from the ice rink you go up some steps to the back terrace and in at the big glass doors to the breakfast room. There were two men standing on the terrace. From there you could see the rink and they were staring down at what was happening. Silver Stick and Square Bear. I saw the thin man's eyes in the light from the breakfast room. They were harder and more intent than anything I'd ever seen, harder than the ice itself. Normally, being properly brought up, we'd have said good evening to them as we went past, but Mother propeled us inside without speaking. As soon as she'd got us settled at the table she went to find Father, who'd be back from skiing by then. I knew they'd be talking about me and felt important, but concerned that I couldn't live up to that importance. After all, what I'd seen had lasted only a few seconds and I hadn't felt any of the things I was supposed to feel. I'd never known him before it happened, apart from seeing him across the dining room a few times, and I hadn't even known he was dead until they told me afterward.

What happened at dinner that evening was like the ice rink, only without gypsy music. That holiday Amanda and I were allowed to come down to dinner with our parents for the soup course. After the soup we were supposed to say good night politely and go up and put ourselves to bed. People who'd been skating and skiing all day were hungry by evening so usually attention was concentrated discreetly on the swing doors to the kitchen and the procession of waiters with the silver tureens. That night was different. The focus of attention was one small table in the corner of the room beside the window. A table laid like the rest of them with white linen, silver cutlery, gold-bordered plates, and a little array of crystal glasses. A table for one. An empty table.

My father said: "Looks as if she's funked it. Can't say I blame her."

My mother gave him one of her "be quiet" looks, announced that this was our evening for speaking French and asked me in that language to pass her some bread, if I pleased.

I had my back to the door and my hand on the breadbasket. All I knew was that the room went quiet.

"Don't turn round," my mother hissed in English.

I turned round and there she was, in black velvet and diamonds. Her hair, with more streaks of gray than I remembered from the year before, was swept up and secured with a pearl-and-diamond comb. The previous year, before the thing happened, my mother had remarked that she was surprisingly slim for a retired opera singer. This year she was thin, cheekbones and collarbones above the black velvet bodice sharp enough to cut paper. She was inclining her elegant head toward the headwaiter, probably listening to words of welcome. He was smiling, but then he smiled at everybody. Nobody else smiled as she followed him to the table in the far, the very far, corner. You could hear the creak of necks screwing themselves away from her. No entrance she ever made in her stage career could have been as nerve-racking as that long walk across the hotel floor. In spite of the silent commands now radiating from my mother, I could no more have turned away from her than from Blondin crossing Niagara Falls. My disobedience was rewarded, as disobedience so often is, because I saw it happen. In the middle of that silent dining room, amid a hundred or so people pretending not to notice her, I saw Silver Stick get to his feet. Among all those seated people he looked even taller than before, his burnished silver head gleaming like snow on the Matterhorn above that rock ridge of a nose, below it the glacial white and black of his evening clothes. Square Bear hesitated for a moment, then followed his example. As in her lonely walk she came alongside their table, Silver Stick bowed with the dignity of a man who did not have to bow very often, and again Square Bear copied him, less elegantly. Square Bear's face was red and flustered, but the other man's hadn't altered. She paused for a moment, gravely returned their bows with a bend of her white neck, then walked on. The silence through the room lasted until the headwaiter pulled out her chair and she sat down at her table, then, as if on cue, the waiters with their tureens came marching through the swinging doors and the babble and the clash of cutlery sounded as loud as war starting.

At breakfast I asked Mother: "Why did they bow to her?" I knew it was a banned subject, but I knew too that I was in an obscurely privileged position, because of the effect all this was supposed to be having on me. I wondered when it would come out, like secret writing on a laurel leaf you keep close to your chest to warm it. When I was fourteen, eighteen?

"Don't ask silly questions. And you don't need two lumps of sugar in your café au lait."

Father suggested a trip to the town down the valley after lunch, to buy Christmas presents. It was meant as a distraction and it worked to an extent, but I still couldn't get her out of my mind. Later that morning, when I was supposed to be having a healthy snowball fight with boring children, I wandered away to the back terrace overlooking the ice rink. I hoped that I might find her there again, but it was occupied by noisy beginners, slithering and screeching. I despised them for their ordinariness.

I'd turned away and was looking at the back of the hotel, thinking no particular thoughts, when I heard footsteps behind me and a voice said: "Was that where you were standing when it happened?"

It was the first time I'd heard Silver Stick's voice at close quarters. It was a pleasant voice, deep but clear, like the sea in a cave. He was standing there in his rough tweed jacket and cap with earflaps only a few yards away from me. Square Bear stood behind him, looking anxious, neck muffled in a woolen scarf. I considered, looked up at the roof again and down to my feet.

"Yes, it must have been about here."

"Holmes, don't you think we should ask this little girl's mother? She might . . ."

"My mother wasn't there. I was."

Perhaps I'd learnt something already about taking the center of the stage. The thought came to me that it would be a great thing if he bowed to me, as he'd bowed to her.

"Quite so."

He didn't bow, but he seemed pleased.

"You see, Watson, Miss Jessica isn't in the least hysterical about it, are you?"

I saw that he meant that as a compliment, so I gave him the little inclination of the head that I'd been practicing in front of the mirror when Amanda wasn't looking. He smiled, and there was more warmth in the smile than seemed likely from the height and sharpness of him.

"I take it that you have no objection to talking about what you saw."

I said graciously: "Not in the very least." Then honesty compelled me to spoil it by adding, "Only I didn't see very much."

"It's not how much you saw, but how clearly you saw it. I wonder if you'd kindly tell Dr. Watson and me exactly what you saw, in as much detail as you can remember."

The voice was gentle, but there was no gentleness in the dark eyes fixed on me. I don't mean they were hard or cruel, simply that emotion of any sort had no more part in them than in the lens of a camera or telescope. They gave me an odd feeling, not fear exactly, but as if I'd become real in a way I hadn't quite been before. I knew that being clear about what I'd seen that day a year ago mattered more than anything I'd ever done. I closed my eyes and thought hard.

"I was standing just here. I was waiting for Mother and Amanda because we were going out for a walk and Amanda had lost one of her fur gloves as usual. I saw him falling, then he hit the roof over the dining room and came sliding down it. The snow started moving as well, so he came down with the snow. He landed just over there, where that chair is, and all the rest of the snow came down on top of him, so you could only see his arm sticking out. The arm wasn't moving, but I didn't know he was dead. A lot of people came running and started pushing the snow away from him, then somebody said I shouldn't be there so they took me away to find Mother, so I wasn't there when they got the snow off him."

I stopped, short of breath. Square Bear was looking ill at ease and pitying but Silver Stick's eyes hadn't changed.

"When you were waiting for your mother and sister, which way were you facing?"

"The rink. I was watching the skaters."

"Quite so. That meant you were facing away from the hotel."

"Yes."

"And yet you saw the man falling?"

"Yes."

"What made you turn round?"

I'd no doubt about that. It was the part of my story that everybody had been most concerned with at the time.

"He shouted."

"Shouted what?"

"Shouted 'No.'"

"When did he shout it?"

I hesitated. Nobody had asked me that before because the answer was obvious.

"When he fell."

"Of course, but at what point during his fall? I take it that it was before he landed on the roof over the dining room or you wouldn't have turned round in time to see it."

"Yes."

"And you turned round in time to see him in the air and falling?"

"Holmes, I don't think you should . . ."

"Oh, do be quiet, Watson. Well, Miss Jessica?"

"Yes, he was in the air and falling."

"And he'd already screamed by then. So at what point did he scream?"

I wanted to be clever and grown-up, to make him think well of me.

"I suppose it was when she pushed him out of the window."

It was Square Bear's face that showed most emotion. He screwed up his eyes, went red, and made little imploring signs with his fur-mittened hands, causing him to look more bear-like than ever. This time the protest was not at his friend, but at me. Silver Stick put up a hand to stop him saying anything, but his face had changed too, with a sharp V on the forehead. The voice was a shade less gentle.

"When who pushed him out of the window?"

"His wife, Mrs. McEvoy."

I wondered whether to add, "The woman you bowed to last night," but decided against it.

"Did you see her push him?"

"No."

"Did you see Mrs. McEvoy at the window?"

"No."

"And yet you tell me that Mrs. McEvoy pushed her husband out of the window. Why?"

"Everybody knows she did."

I knew from the expression on Square Bear's face that I'd gone badly wrong, but couldn't see where. He, kindly man, must have guessed that because he started trying to explain to me.

"You see, my dear, after many years with my good friend Mr. Holmes . . ."

Yet again he was waved into silence.

"Miss Jessica, Dr. Watson means well but I hope he will permit me to speak for myself. It's a fallacy to believe that age in itself brings wisdom, but one thing it infallibly brings is experience. Will you permit me, from my experience if not from my wisdom, to offer you a little advice?"

I nodded, not gracious now, just awed.

"Then my advice is this: always remember that what everybody knows, nobody knows."

He used that voice like a skater uses his weight on the blade to skim or turn.

"You say everybody knows that Mrs. McEvoy pushed her husband out of the window. As far as I know you are the only person in the world who saw Mr. McEvoy fall. And yet, as you've told me, you did not see Mrs. McEvoy push him. So who is this 'everybody' who can claim such certainty about an event which, as far as we know, nobody witnessed?"

It's miserable not knowing answers. What is nineteen times three? What is the past participle of the verb *faire*? I wanted to live up to him, but unwittingly he'd pressed the button that brought on the panic of the schoolroom. I blurted out: "He was very rich and she didn't love him, and now she's very rich and can do what she likes."

Again the bear's fur mitts went up, scrabbling the air. Again he was disregarded.

"So Mrs. McEvoy is rich and can do what she likes? Does it strike you that she's happy?"

"Holmes, how can a child know . . . ?"

I thought of the gypsy music, the gleaming dark fur, the pearls in her hair. I found myself shaking my head.

"No. And yet she comes here again, exactly a year after her husband died, the very place in the world that you'd expect her to avoid at all costs. She comes here knowing what people are saying about her, making sure everybody has a chance to see her, holding her head high. Have you any idea what that must do to a woman?"

This time Square Bear really did protest and went on protesting. How could he expect a child to know about the feelings of a mature woman? How could I be blamed for repeating the gossip of my elders? Really, Holmes, it was too much. This time too Silver Stick seemed to agree with him. He smoothed out the V shape in his forehead and apologized.

"Let us, if we may, return to the surer ground of what you actually saw. I take it that the hotel has not been rebuilt in any way since last year."

I turned again to look at the back of the hotel. As far as I could see, it was just as it had been, the glass doors leading from the dining room and breakfast room onto the terrace, a tiled sloping roof above them. Then, joined onto the roof, the three main guest floors of the hotel. The top two floors were the ones that most people took because they had wrought-iron balconies where, on sunny days, you could stand to look at the mountains. Below them were the smaller rooms. They were less popular because, being directly above the kitchen and dining room, they suffered from noise and cooking smells and had no balconies.

Silver Stick said to Square Bear: "That was the room they had last year, top floor, second from the right. So if he were pushed, he'd have to be pushed over the balcony as well as out of the window. That would take quite a lot of strength, wouldn't you say?"

The next question was to me. He asked if I'd seen Mr. McEvoy before he fell out of the window and I said yes, a few times.

"Was he a small man?"

"No, quite big."

"The same size as Dr. Watson here, for instance?"

Square Bear straightened his broad shoulders, as if for military inspection.

"He was fatter."

"Younger or older?"

"Quite old. As old as you are."

Square Bear made a chuffing sound and his shoulders slumped a little.

"So we have a man about the same age as our friend Watson and heavier. Difficult, wouldn't you say, for any woman to push him anywhere against his will?"

"Perhaps she took him by surprise, told him to lean out and look at something, then swept his legs off the floor."

That wasn't my own theory. The event had naturally been analyzed in all its aspects the year before and all the parental care in the world couldn't have kept it from me.

"A touching picture. Shall we come back to things we know for certain? What about the snow? Was there as much snow as this last year?"

"I think so. It came up above my knees last year. It doesn't quite this year, but then I've grown."

Square Bear murmured: "They'll keep records of that sort of thing."

"Just so, but we're also grateful for Miss Jessica's calibrations. May we trouble you with just one more question?"

I said yes rather warily.

"You've told us that just before you turned round and saw him falling you heard him shout 'No.' What sort of 'No' was it?"

I was puzzled. Nobody had asked me that before.

"Was it an angry 'No?' A protesting 'No?' The kind of 'No' you'd shout if somebody were pushing you over a balcony?"

The other man looked as if he wanted to protest again but kept quiet. The intensity in Silver Stick's eyes would have frozen a brook in mid-babble. When I didn't answer at once he visibly made himself relax and his voice went softer.

"It's hard for you to remember, isn't it? Everybody was so sure that it was one particular sort of 'No' that they've fixed their version in your mind. I want you to do something for me, if you would be so kind. I want you to forget that Dr. Watson and I are here and stand and look down at the ice rink just as you were doing last year. I want you to clear your mind of every-thing else and think that it really is last year and you're hearing that shout for the first time. Will you do that?"

I faced away from them. First I looked at this year's skaters then I closed my eyes and tried to remember how it had been. I felt the green itchy scarf round my neck, the cold getting to my toes and fingers as I waited. I heard the cry and it was all I could do not to turn round and see the body tumbling again. When I opened my eyes and looked at them they were still waiting patiently.

"I think I've remembered."

"And what sort of 'No' was it?"

It was clear in my mind but hard to put into words.

"It . . . it was as if he'd been going to say something else if he'd had time. Not just no. No something."

"No something what?"

More silence while I thought about it, then a prompt from Square Bear.

"Could it have been a name, my dear?"

"Don't put any more ideas into her head. You thought he was

going to say something after the no, but you don't know what, is that it?"

"Yes, like no running, or no cakes today, only that wasn't it. Something you couldn't do."

"Or something not there, like the cakes?"

"Yes, something like that. Only it couldn't have been, could it?"

"Couldn't? If something happened in a particular way, then it happened, and there's no could or couldn't about it."

It was the kind of thing governesses said, but he was smiling now and I had the idea that something I'd said had pleased him.

"I see your mother and sister coming, so I'm afraid we must end this very useful conversation. I am much obliged to you for your powers of observation. Will you permit me to ask you some more questions if any more occur to me?"

I nodded.

"Is it a secret?"

"Do you want it to be?"

"Holmes, I don't think you should encourage this young lady . . ."

"My dear Watson, in my observation there's nothing more precious you can give a child to keep than a secret."

My mother came across the terrace with Amanda. Silver Stick and Square Bear touched their hats to her and hoped we enjoyed our walk. When she asked me later what we'd been talking about, I said they'd asked whether the snow was as deep last year and hugged the secret of my partnership. I became in my imagination eyes and ears for him. At the children's party at teatime on Christmas Eve the parents talked in low tones, believing that we were absorbed in the present-giving round the hotel tree. But it would have taken more than the porter in red robe and white whiskers or his largesse of three wooden geese on a string to distract me from my work. I listened and stored up every scrap against the time when he'd ask me questions again. And I watched Mrs. McEvoy as she went round the hotel through Christmas Eve and Christmas Day, pale and upright in her black and her jewels, trailing silence after her like the long train of a dress.

My call came on Boxing Day. There was another snowball fight in the hotel grounds, for parents as well this time. I stood back from it all and waited by a little clump of bare birches and, sure enough, Silver Stick and Square Bear came walking over to me.

"I've found out a lot about her," I said.

"Have you indeed?"

"He was her second husband. She had another one she loved more, but he died of a fever. It was when they were visiting Egypt a long time ago."

"Ten years ago."

Silver Stick's voice was remote. He wasn't even looking at me.

"She got married to Mr. McEvoy three years ago. Most people said it was for his money, but there was an American lady at the party and she said Mr. McEvoy seemed quite nice when you first knew him and he was interested in music and singers, so perhaps it was one of those marriages where people quite like each other without being in love, you know?"

I thought I'd managed that rather well. I'd tried to make it like my mother talking to her friends and it sounded convincing in my ears. I was disappointed at the lack of reaction, so brought up my big guns.

"Only she didn't stay liking him because after they got married she found out about his eye."

"His eye?"

A reaction at last, but from Square Bear, not Silver Stick. I grabbed for the right word and clung to it.

"Roving. It was a roving eye. He kept looking at other ladies and she didn't like it."

I hoped they'd understand that it meant looking in a special way. I didn't know myself exactly what special way, but the adults talking among themselves at the party had certainly understood. But it seemed I'd overestimated these two because they were just standing there staring at me. Perhaps Silver Stick wasn't as clever as I'd thought. I threw in my last little oddment of information, something anybody could understand.

"I found out her first name. It's Irene."

Square Bear cleared his throat. Silver Stick said nothing. He was looking over my head at the snowball fight.

"Holmes, I really think we should leave Jessica to play with her little friends."

"Not yet. There's something I wanted to ask her. Do you remember the staff at the hotel last Christmas?"

Here was a dreadful comedown. I'd brought him a head richly crammed with love, money, and marriages and he was asking about the domestics. Perhaps the disappointment on my face looked like stupidity because his voice became impatient.

"The people who looked after you, the porters and the waiters and the maids, especially the maids."

"They're the same . . . I think." I was running them through my head. There was Petra with her thick plaits who brought us our cups of chocolate, fat Renata who made our beds, gray-haired Ulrike with her limp.

"None left?"

"I don't think so."

Then the memory came to me of blond curls escaping from a maid's uniform cap and a clear voice singing as she swept the corridors, blithe as a bird.

"There was Eva, but she got married."

"Who did she marry?"

"Franz, the man who's got the sleigh."

It was flying down the drive as I spoke, silver bells jangling, the little horse gold in the sunshine.

"A good marriage for a hotel maid."

"Oh, he didn't have the sleigh last year. He was only the under porter."

"Indeed. Watson, I think we must have a ride in this sleigh. Will you see the head porter about booking it?"

I hoped he might invite me to go with them but he said

nothing about that. Still, he seemed to be in a good temper again—although I couldn't see that it was from anything I'd told him.

"Miss Jessica, again I'm obliged to you. I may have yet another favor to ask, but all in good time."

I went reluctantly to join the snowballers as the two of them walked through the snow back to the hotel.

That afternoon, on our walk, they went past us on their way down the drive in Franz's sleigh. It didn't look like a pleasure trip. Franz's handsome face was serious and Holmes was staring straight ahead. Instead of turning up toward the forest at the end of the hotel drive they turned left for the village. Our walk also took us to the village because Father wanted to see an old man about getting a stick carved. When we walked down the little main street we saw the sleigh and horse standing outside a neat chalet with green shutters next to the church. I knew it was Franz's own house and wondered what had become of his passengers. About half an hour later, when we'd seen about Father's stick, we walked back up the street and there were Holmes and Watson standing on the balcony outside the chalet with Eva, the maid from last year. Her fair hair was as curly as ever but her head was bent. She seemed to be listening intently to something that Holmes was saying and the droop of her shoulders told me she wasn't happy.

"Why is Silver Stick talking to her?"

Amanda, very properly, was rebuked for staring and asking questions about things that didn't concern her. Being older and wiser, I said nothing but kept my secret coiled in my heart. Was it Eva who pushed him? Would they lock her up in prison? A little guilt stirred along with the pleasure, because he wouldn't have known about Eva if I hadn't told him, but not enough to spoil it. Later I watched from our window hoping to see the sleigh coming back, but it didn't that day. Instead, just before it got dark, Holmes and Watson came back on foot up the drive, walking fast, saying nothing.

*

Next morning, Square Bear came up to Mother at coffee time. "I wonder if you would permit Miss Jessica to take a short walk with me on the terrace."

Mother hesitated, but Square Bear was so obviously respectable, and anyway you could see the terrace from the coffee room. I put on my hat, cape, and gloves and walked with him out of the glass doors into the cold air. We stood looking down at the rink, in exactly the same place as I'd been standing when they first spoke to me. I knew that was no accident. Square Bear's fussiness, the tension in his voice that he was so unsuccessful in hiding, left no doubt of it. There was something odd about the terrace, too—far more people on it than would normally be the case on a cold morning. There must have been two dozen or so standing round in stiff little groups, talking to each other, waiting.

"Where's Mr. Holmes?"

Square Bear looked at me, eyes watering from the cold.

"The truth is, my dear, I don't know where he is or what he's doing. He gave me my instructions at breakfast and I haven't seen him since."

"Instructions about me?"

Before he could answer, the scream came. It was a man's scream, tearing through the air like a saw blade, and there was a word in it. The word was "No." I turned with the breath choking in my throat and, just as there'd been last year, there was a dark thing in the air, its clothes flapping out round it. A collective gasp from the people on the terrace, then a soft thump as the thing hit the deep snow on the restaurant roof and began sliding. I heard "No" again and this time it was my own voice, because I knew from last year what was coming next—the slide down the steep roof gathering snow as it came, the flop onto the terrace only a few yards from where I was standing, the arm sticking out.

At first the memory was so strong that I thought that was

what I was seeing, and it took a few seconds for me to realize that it wasn't happening that way. The thing had fallen a little to the side and instead of sliding straight down the roof it was being carried to a little ornamental railing at the edge of it, where the main hotel joined onto the annex, driving a wedge of snow in front of it. Then somebody said, unbelievingly: "He's stopped." And the thing had stopped. Instead of plunging over the roof to the terrace it had been swept up against the railing, bundled in snow like a cylindrical snowball, and stopped within a yard of the edge. Then it sat up, clinging with one hand to the railing, covered from waist down in snow. If he'd been wearing a hat when he came out of the window he'd lost it in the fall because his damp hair was gleaming silver above his smiling brown face. It was an inward kind of smile, as if only he could appreciate the thing that he'd done.

Then the chattering started. Some people were yelling to get a ladder, others running. The rest were asking each other what had happened until somebody spotted the window wide open three floors above us.

"Her window. Mrs. McEvoy's window."

"He fell off Mrs. McEvoy's balcony, just like last year."

"But he didn't . . ."

At some point Square Bear had put a hand on my shoulder. Now he bent down beside me, looking anxiously into my face, saying we should go in and find Mother. I wished he'd get out of my way because I wanted to see Silver Stick on the roof. Then Mother arrived, wafting clouds of scent and drama. I had to go inside of course, but not before I'd seen the ladder arrive and Silver Stick coming down it, a little stiffly but dignified. And one more thing. Just as he stepped off the ladder the glass doors to the terrace opened and out she came. She hadn't been there when it happened but now in her black fur jacket, she stepped through the people as if they weren't there, and gave him her hand and thanked him.

*

At dinner that night she dined alone at her table, as on the other nights, but it took her longer to get to it. Her long walk across the dining room was made longer by all the people who wanted to speak to her, to inquire after her health, to tell her how pleased they were to see her again. It was as if she'd just arrived that afternoon, instead of being there for five days already. There were several posies of flowers on her table that must have been sent up especially from the town, and champagne in a silver bucket beside it. Silver Stick and Square Bear bowed to her as she went past their table, but ordinary polite little nods, not like that first night. The smile she gave them was like the sun coming up.

We were sent off to bed as soon as we'd had our soup as usual. Amanda went to sleep at once but I lay awake, resenting my exile from what mattered. Our parents' sitting room was next to our bedroom and I heard them come in, excited still. Then, soon afterward, a knock on the door of our suite, the murmur of voices and my father, a little taken aback, saying yes come in by all means. Then their voices, Square Bear's first, fussing with apologies about it being so late, then Silver Stick's cutting through him: "The fact is, you're owed an explanation, or rather your daughter is. Dr. Watson suggested that we should give it to you so that some time in the future when Jessica's old enough, you may decide to tell her."

If I'd owned a chest of gold and had watched somebody throwing it away in a crowded street I couldn't have been more furious than hearing my secret about to be squandered. My first thought was to rush through to the other room in my nightdress and bare feet and demand that he should speak to me, not to them. Then caution took over, and although I did get out of bed, I went just as far as the door, opened it a crack so that I could hear better and padded back to bed. There were sounds of chairs being rearranged, people settling into them, then Silver Stick's voice.

"I should say at the start, for reasons we need not go into, that Dr. Watson and I were convinced that Irene McEvoy had not pushed her husband to his death. The question was how to prove it, and in that regard your daughter's evidence was indispensable. She alone saw Mr. McEvoy fall and she alone heard what he shouted. The accurate ear of childhood—once certain adult nonsenses had been discarded—recorded that shout as precisely as a phonograph and knew that strictly speaking it was only half a shout, that Mr. McEvoy, if he'd had time, would have added something else to it."

A pause. I sat up in bed with the counterpane round my neck, straining not to miss a word of his quiet, clear voice.

"No—something. The question was, no what? Mr. McEvoy had expected something to be there and his last thought on earth was surprise at the lack of it, surprise so acute that he was trying to shout it with his last breath. The question was, what that thing could have been."

Silence, waiting for an answer, but nobody said anything.

"If you look up at the back of the hotel from the terrace you will notice one obvious thing. The third and fourth floors have balconies. The second floor does not. The room inhabited by Mr. and Mrs. McEvoy had a balcony. A person staying in the suite would be aware of that. He would not necessarily be aware, unless he were a particularly observant man, that the second-floor rooms had no balconies. Until it was too late. I formed the theory that Mr. McEvoy had not in fact fallen from the window of his own room but from a lower room belonging to somebody else, which accounted for his attempted last words: "No . . . balcony.""

My mother gasped. My father said: "By Jove . . ."

"Once I'd arrived at that conclusion, the question was what Mr. McEvoy was doing in somebody else's room. The possibility of thieving could be ruled out since he was a very rich man. Then he was seeing somebody. The next question was who. And here your daughter was incidentally helpful in a way she is too young to understand. She confided to us in all innocence an overheard piece of adult gossip to the effect that the late Mr. McEvoy had a roving eye."

My father began to laugh, then stifled it. My mother said "Well" in a way that boded trouble for me later.

"Once my attention was directed that way, the answer became obvious. Mr. McEvoy was in somebody else's hotel room for what one might describe as an episode of *galanterie*. But the accident happened in the middle of the morning. Did ever a lady in the history of the world make a romantic assignation for that hour of the day? Therefore it wasn't a lady. So I asked myself what group of people are most likely to be encountered in hotel rooms in mid-morning and the answer was . . ."

"Good heavens, the chambermaid!"

My mother's voice, and Holmes was clearly none too pleased at being interrupted.

"Quite so. Mr. McEvoy had gone to meet a chambermaid. I asked some questions to establish whether any young and attractive chambermaid had left the hotel since last Christmas. There was such a one, named Eva. She'd married the under porter and brought him as a dowry enough money to buy that elegant little sleigh. Now a prudent chambermaid may amass a modest dowry by saving tips, but one look at that sleigh will tell you that Eva's dowry might best be described as, well . . . immodest."

Another laugh from my father, cut off by a look from my mother I could well imagine.

"Dr. Watson and I went to see Eva. I told her what I'd deduced and she, poor girl, confirmed it with some details—the sound of the housekeeper's voice outside, Mr. McEvoy's well-practiced but ill-advised tactic of taking refuge on the balcony. You may say that the girl Eva should have confessed at once what had happened . . ."

"I do indeed."

"But bear in mind her position. Not only her post at the hotel but her engagement to the handsome Franz would be forfeited. And, after all, there was no question of anybody being tried in court. The fashionable world was perfectly happy to connive at the story that Mr. McEvoy had fallen accidentally from his window—while inwardly convicting an innocent woman of his murder."

My mother said, sounding quite subdued for once: "But Mrs. McEvoy must have known. Why didn't she say something?"

"Ah, to answer that one needs to know something about Mrs. McEvoy's history, and it so happens that Dr. Watson and I are in that position. A long time ago, before her first happy marriage, Mrs. McEvoy was loved by a prince. He was not, I must admit, a particularly admirable prince, but prince he was. Can you imagine how it felt for a woman to come from that to being deceived with a hotel chambermaid by a man who made his fortune from bathroom furnishings? Can you conceive that a proud woman might choose to be thought a murderess rather than submit to that indignity?"

Another silence, then my mother breathed: "Yes. Yes, I think I can." Then, "Poor woman."

"It was not pity that Irene McEvoy ever needed." Then, in a different tone of voice: "So there you have it. And it is your decision how much, if anything, you decide to pass on to Jessica in due course."

There were sounds of people getting up from chairs, then my father said: "And your, um, demonstration this morning?"

"Oh, that little drama. I knew what had happened, but for Mrs. McEvoy's sake it was necessary to prove to the world she was innocent. I couldn't call Eva as witness because I'd given her my word. I'd studied the pitch of the roof and the depth of the snow and I was scientifically convinced that a man falling from Mrs. McEvoy's balcony would not have landed on the terrace. You know the result."

Good nights were said, rather subdued, and they were shown out. Through the crack in the door I glimpsed them. As they came level with the crack, Silver Stick, usually so precise in his movements, dropped his pipe and had to kneel to pick it up. As he knelt, his bright eyes met mine through the crack and he smiled, an odd, quick smile unseen by anybody else. He'd known I'd been listening all the time.

When they'd gone Mother and Father sat for a long time in silence.

At last Father said: "If he'd got it wrong, he'd have killed himself."

"Like the skiing."

"He must have loved her very much."

"It's his own logic he loves."

But then, my mother always was the unromantic one.

Murder-Two

JOYCE CAROL OATES

In John Guare's play *Bosoms and Neglect,* two deeply neurotic characters are discussing neglected writers. When one advances the name of Joyce Carol Oates, the other demands (paraphrasing), how can she be neglected when she writes a book a week? From the publication of her first novel *By the North Gate* (1963), Joyce Carol Oates (b. 1938) has been the most prolific of major American writers, turning out novels, short stories, reviews, essays, and plays in an unceasing flow as remarkable for its quality as its volume. Writers who are extremely prolific often risk not being taken as seriously as they should—if you can write it that fast, how good can it be? Oates, however, has largely escaped that trap, and even her increasing identification with crime fiction, at a time that the field has attracted a number of other mainstream literary figures, has not damaged her reputation as a formidable serious writer.

Many of Oates's works contain at least some elements of crime and mystery, from the National Book Award winner *Them* (1970), through the Chappaquiddick fictionalization *Black Water* (1992) and the Jeffrey Dahmer–inspired serial-killer novel *Zombie* (1995), to her controversial 738-page fictionalized biography of Marilyn Monroe, *Blonde* (2000). The element of detection becomes explicit with the investigations of amateur sleuth Xavier Kilgarvan in the 1984 novel *The Mysteries of Winterthurn* which, the author explains in an afterword to the 1985 paperback edition, "is the third in a quintet of experimental novels that deal, in genre form, with nineteenth- and early-twentieth-century America." Why would a serious literary writer like Oates choose to work in such "deliberately confining structures?" Because "the formal discipline of 'genre' . . . forces us inevitably to a radical re-visioning of the world and the craft of fiction." Oates, who numbers among her honors in a related genre the Bram Stoker Award of the Horror Writers of America, did not establish an explicit crime-fiction identity until *Lives of the Twins* (1987; British title *Kindred Passions*) appeared under the pseudonym Rosamund Smith. Initially intended to be a secret, the identity of Smith was revealed almost immediately, and later novels were bylined Joyce Carol Oates (large print) writing as Rosamund Smith (smaller print).

Among the key attributes of the astonishingly versatile Oates is her insight into deeply troubled adolescents, a quality "Murder-Two" demonstrates, along with her vivid descriptive style and her unconventional way with a crime-fiction situation.

This, he swore.

He'd returned to the town house on East End Avenue after eleven p.m. and found the front door unlocked and, inside, his mother lying in a pool of squid ink on the hardwood floor at the foot of the stairs. She'd apparently fallen down the steep length of the stairs and broken her neck, judging from her twisted upper body. She'd also been bludgeoned to death, the back of her skull caved in, with one of her own golf clubs, a two-iron, but he hadn't seemed to see that, immediately.

Squid ink?—well, the blood had looked black in the dim foyer light. It was a trick his eyes played on his brain sometimes when he'd been studying too hard, getting too little sleep. An *optic tic.* Meaning you see something more or less, and valid, but it registers surreally in the brain as something else. Like in your neurological programming there's an occasional bleep.

In Derek Peck, Jr.'s, case, confronted with the crumpled, lifeless body of his mother, this was an obvious symptom of trauma. Shock, the visceral numbness that blocks immediate grief—the unsayable, the unknowable. He'd last seen his mother, in that same buttercup-yellow quilted satin robe that had given her the look of an upright, bulky Easter toy, early that morning, before he'd left for school. He'd been away all day. And this abrupt, weird transition—from differential calculus to the body on the floor, from the anxiety-driven jokes of his Math Club friends (a hard core of them were meeting later weekdays, preparing for upcoming SAT exams) to the profound and terrible silence of the town house that had seemed to him, even as he'd pushed open the mysteriously unlocked front door, a hostile silence, a silence that vibrated with dread.

He crouched over the body, staring in disbelief. "Mother? *Mother!*"

As if it was he, Derek, who'd done something bad, he the one to be punished.

He couldn't catch his breath. Hyperventilating! His heart beating so wildly he almost fainted. Too confused to think, *Maybe they're still here, upstairs?* for in his dazed state he seemed to lack even an animal's instinct for self-preservation.

Yes, and he felt to blame, somehow. Hadn't she instilled in him a reflex of guilt? If something was wrong in the household, it could probably be traced back to *him.* From the age of thirteen (when his father, Derek Senior, had divorced his mother, Lucille, same as divorcing *him*), he'd been expected by his mother to behave like a second adult in the household, growing tall, lank, and anxious as if to accommodate that expectation, and his sand-colored body hair sprouting, and a fevered grimness about the eyes. Fifty-three percent of Derek's classmates, girls and boys, at the Mayhew Academy, were from "families of divorce," and most agreed that the worst of it is you have to learn to behave like an adult yet at the same time a lesser adult, one deprived of his or her full civil rights. That wasn't easy even for stoic streetwise Derek Peck with an IQ of, what was it?—158, at age fifteen. (He was seventeen now.) So his precarious adolescent sense of himself was seriously askew: not just his *body image* (his mother had allowed him to become overweight as a small child, they say that remains with you forever, irremediably imprinted in the earliest brain cells), but more crucially his *social identity.* For one minute she'd be treating him like an infant, calling him her baby, her baby-boy, and the next minute she was hurt, reproachful, accusing him of failing, like his father, to uphold his *moral responsibility* to her.

This *moral responsibility* was a backpack loaded with rocks. He could feel it, first fucking thing in the morning, exerting gravity even before he swung his legs out of bed.

Crouched over her now, badly trembling, shaking as in a cold wind, whispering, "Mommy?—can't you wake up? Mom-*my*, don't be—" balking at the word *dead* for it would hurt and incense Lucille like the word *old*, not that she'd been a vain or frivolous or self-conscious woman, for Lucille Peck was anything but, a woman of dignity it was said of her admiringly by women who would not have wished to be her and by men who would not have wished to be married to her. *Mommy, don't be old!* Derek would never have murmured aloud, of course. Though possibly to himself frequently this past year or so seeing her wan, big-boned, and brave face in harsh frontal sunshine when they happened to descend the front steps together in the morning, or at that eerie position in the kitchen where the overhead inset lights converged in such a way as to cruelly shadow her face downward, bruising the eye sockets and the soft fleshy tucks in her cheeks. Two summers ago when he'd been away for six weeks at Lake Placid and she'd driven to Kennedy to pick him up, so eager to see him again, and he'd stared appalled at the harsh lines bracketing her mouth like a pike's, and her smile too happy and what he felt was pity and this, too, made him feel guilty. *You don't pity your own mother, asshole.*

If he'd come home immediately after school. By four p.m. Instead of a quick call from his friend Andy's across the park, guilty mumbled excuse left on the answering tape, *Mother? I'm sorry guess I won't make dinner tonight okay?—Math Club— study group—calculus—don't wait up for me, please.* How relieved he'd been, midway in his message she hadn't picked up the phone.

Had she been alive, when he'd called? Or already . . . dead?

Last time you saw your mother alive, Derek? they'd ask and he'd have to invent for he hadn't seen her, exactly. No eye contact.

And what had he *said*? A rushed schoolday morning, a Thursday. Nothing special about it. No premonition! Cold and windy and winter-glaring and he'd been restless to get out of the house, snatched a Diet Coke from the refrigerator so freezing his teeth ached. A blurred reproachful look of Mother in the kitchen billowing in her buttercup-yellow quilted robe as he'd backed out smiling *'Bye, Mom!*

Sure she'd been hurt, her only son avoiding her. She'd been a lone woman even in her pride. Even with her activities that meant so much to her: Women's Art League, East Side Planned Parenthood Volunteers, HealthSty Fitness Center, tennis and golf in East Hampton in the summer, subscription tickets to Lincoln Center. And her friends: most of them divorced middle-aged women, mothers like herself with high-school or college-age kids. Lucille *was* lonely, how was that his fault?—as if, his senior year in prep school, he had become a fanatic about grades, obsessed with early admission to Harvard, Yale, Brown, Berkeley, just to avoid his mother at that raw, unmediated time of day that was breakfast.

But, God, how he'd loved her! He had. Planning to make it up to her for sure, SAT scores in the highest percentile he'd take her to the Stanhope for the champagne brunch then across the street to the museum for a mother-son Sunday excursion of a kind they hadn't had in years.

How still she was lying. He didn't dare touch her. His breathing was short, ragged. The squid-inky black beneath her twisted head had seeped and coagulated into the cracks of the floor. Her left arm was flung out in an attitude of exasperated appeal, the sleeve stained with red, her hand lying palm-up and the fingers curled like angry talons. He might have noted that her Movado watch was missing, her rings gone except Grandma's antique opal with the fluted gold setting—the thief, or thieves, hadn't been able to yank it off her swollen finger? He might have noted that her eyes were rolled up asymmetrically in her head, the right iris nearly vanished and the left leering like a drunken crescent-moon. He might have noted that the back of her skull was smashed soft and pulpy as a melon but there are some things about your mother out of tact and delicacy you don't acknowledge seeing. *Mother's hair, though*—it was her only remaining good feature, she'd said. A pale silvery-brown, slightly coarse, a natural colour like Wheaties. The mothers of his classmates all hoped to be youthful and glamorous with bleached or dyed hair but not Lucille Peck, she wasn't the type. You expected her cheeks to be ruddy without makeup and on her good days they were.

By this time of night Lucille's hair should have been dry from her shower of so many hours ago Derek vaguely recalled she'd had, the upstairs bathroom filled with steam. The mirrors. Shortness of breath! Tickets for some concert or ballet that night at Lincoln Center?—Lucille and a woman friend. But Derek didn't know about that. Or if he'd known he'd forgotten. Like about the golf club, the two-iron. Which closet? Upstairs, or down? The drawers of Lucille's bedroom bureau ransacked, *his* new Macintosh carried from his desk, then dropped onto the floor by the doorway as if—what? They'd changed their minds about bothering with it. Looking for quick cash, for drugs. That's the motive!

What's Booger up to, now? What's going down with Booger, you hear?

He touched her—at last. Groping for that big artery in the throat—cateroid?—car*toid?* Should have been pulsing but wasn't. And her skin clammy-cool. His hand leapt back as if he'd been burnt.

Jesus fucking Christ, was it possible—Lucille was *dead?*

And *he'd* be to blame?

That Booger, man! One wild dude.

His nostrils flared, his eyes leaked tears. He was in a state of panic, had to get help. It was time! But he wouldn't have noticed the time, would he?—11:48 p.m. His watch was a sleek black-faced Omega he'd bought with his own cash, but he wouldn't be conscious of the time exactly. By now he'd have dialed 911. Except thinking, confused, the phone was ripped out? (*Was* the phone ripped out?) Or one of them, his mother's killers, waiting in the darkened kitchen by the phone? Waiting to kill *him?*

He panicked, he freaked. Running back to the front door

stumbling and shouting into the street where a taxi was slowing to let out an elderly couple of neighbors from the adjoining brownstone and they and the driver stared at this chalk-faced grief-stricken boy in an unbuttoned duffel coat, bareheaded, running into the street screaming, "Help us! Help us! Somebody's killed my mother!"

EAST SIDE WOMAN KILLED
ROBBERY BELIEVED MOTIVE

In a late edition of Friday's *New York Times*, the golf club–bludgeoning death of Lucille Peck, whom Marina Dyer had known as Lucy Siddons, was prominently featured on the front page of the Metro section. Marina's quick eye, skimming the page, fastened at once upon the face (middle aged, fleshy yet unmistakable) of her old Finch classmate.

"Lucy! *No*."

You understood that this must be a *death photo*: the positioning on the page upper center; the celebration of a private individual of no evident civic cultural significance, or beauty. For *Times* readers the news value lay in the victim's address, close by the mayor's residence. The subtext being *Even here among the sequestered wealthy, such a brutal fate is possible.*

In a state of shock, though with professional interest, for Marina Dyer was a criminal defense attorney, Marina read the article, continued on an inside page and disappointing in its brevity. It was so familiar as to resemble a ballad. *One of us* (Caucasian, middle-aged, law-abiding, unarmed) surprised and savagely murdered in the very sanctity of her home; an instrument of class privilege, a golf club, snatched up by the killer as the murder weapon. The intruder or intruders, police said, were probably looking for quick cash, drug money. It was a careless, crude, cruel crime; a "senseless" crime; one of a number of unsolved break-ins on the East Side since last September, though it was the first to involve murder. The teenaged son of Lucille

Peck returned home to find the front door unlocked and his mother dead, at about eleven p.m., at which time she'd been dead approximately five hours. Neighbors spoke of having heard no unusual sounds from the Peck residence, but several did speak of "suspicious" strangers in the neighborhood. Police were "investigating."

Poor Lucy!

Marina noted that her former classmate was forty-four years old, a year (most likely, part of a year) older than Marina; that she'd been divorced since 1991 from Derek Peck, an insurance executive now living in Boston; that she was survived by just the one child, Derek Peck, Jr., a sister, and two brothers. What an end for Lucy Siddons, who shone in Marina's memory as if beaming with life: unstoppable Lucy, indefatigable Lucy, good-hearted Lucy: Lucy, who was twice president of the Finch class of 1970, and a dedicated alumna: Lucy, whom all the girls had admired, if not adored: Lucy, who'd been so kind to shy stammering wall-eyed Marina Dyer.

Though they'd both been living in Manhattan all these years, Marina in a town house of her own on West Seventy-sixth Street, very near Central Park, it had been five years since she'd seen Lucy, at their twentieth class reunion; even longer since the two had spoken together at length, earnestly. Or maybe they never had.

The son did it, Marina thought, folding up the newspaper. It wasn't an altogether serious thought but one that suited her professional skepticism.

Boogerman! Fucking fan-tas-tic.

Where'd he come from?—the hot molten core of the Universe. At the instant of the Big Bang. Before which there was *nothing* and after which there would be *everything*: cosmic cum. For all sentient beings derive from a single source and that source long vanished, extinct.

The more you contemplated of origins the less you knew. He'd studied Wittgenstein—*Whereof one cannot speak, thereof one must be silent.* (A photocopied handout for Communication Arts class, the instructor a cool youngish guy with a Princeton Ph.D.) Yet he believed he could recall the circumstances of his birth. In 1978, in Barbados where his parents were vacationing, one week in late December. He was premature by five weeks and lucky to be alive, and though Barbados was an accident yet seventeen years later he saw in his dreams a cobalt-blue sky, rows of royal palms shedding their bark like scales, shriek-bright-feathered tropical birds; a fat white moon drooping in the sky like his mother's big belly, sharks' dorsal fins cresting the waves like the Death Raiders video game he'd been hooked on in junior high. Wild hurricane nights kept him from sleeping a normal sleep. Din of voices as of drowning souls crashing on a beach.

He was into Metallica, Urge Overkill, Soul Asylum. His heroes were heavy metal punks who'd never made it to the Top Ten or if they did fell right back again. He admired losers who killed themselves OD'ing like dying's joke, one final FUCK YOU! to the world. But he was innocent of doing what they'd claimed he'd done to his mother, for God's sake. Absolutely unbelieving fucking fantastic, *he, Derek Peck, Jr.,* had been arrested and would be tried for a crime perpetrated upon his own mother he'd loved! perpetrated by animals (he could guess the color of their skin) who would've smashed his skull in, too, like cracking an egg, if he'd walked in that door five hours earlier.

She wasn't prepared to fall in love, wasn't the type to fall in love with any client, yet here is what happened: just seeing him, his strange tawny-yearning eyes lifting to her face, *Help me! save me!*—that was it.

Derek Peck, Jr., was a Botticelli angel partly erased and crudely painted over by Eric Fischl. His thick, stiffly moussed, unwashed hair lifted in two flaring symmetrical wings that framed his elegantly bony, long-jawed face. His limbs were monkey-long and twitchy. His shoulders were narrow and high, his chest perceptibly concave. He might have been fourteen, or twenty-five. He was of a generation as distant from Marina Dyer's as another species. He wore a T-shirt stamped SOUL ASYLUM beneath a rumpled Armani jacket of the color of steel filings, and pinstriped Ralph Lauren fleece trousers stained at the crotch, and size-twelve Nikes. Mad blue veins thrummed at his temples. He was a preppy cokehead who'd managed until now to stay out of trouble Marina had been warned by Derek Peck, Sr.'s, attorney, who'd arranged through Marina's discreet urging for her to interview for the boy's counsel: probably psychopath-matricide who not only claimed complete innocence but seemed actually to believe it. He gave off a complex odor of the ripely organic and the chemical. His skin appeared heated, of the color and texture of singed oatmeal. His nostrils were rimmed in red like nascent fire and his eyes were a pale acetylene yellow-green, flammable. You would not want to bring a match too close to those eyes, still less would you want to look too deeply into those eyes.

When Marina Dyer was introduced to Derek Peck, the boy stared at her hungrily. Yet he didn't get to his feet like the other men in the room. He leaned forward in his chair, the tendons standing out in his neck and the strain of *seeing, thinking*, visible in his young face. His handshake was fumbling at first, then suddenly strong, assured as an adult man's, hurtful. Unsmiling the boy shook hair out of his eyes like a horse rearing its beautiful brute head and a painful sensation ran through Marina Dyer like an electric shock. She had not experienced such a sensation in a long time.

In her soft contralto voice that gave nothing away, Marina said, "Derek, *hi*."

It was in the 1980s, in an era of celebrity-scandal trials, that Marina Dyer made her reputation as a "brilliant" criminal defense lawyer; by being in fact brilliant, and by working very hard, and by playing against type. There was the audacity of drama in her positioning of herself in a male-dominated courtroom. There was the startling fact of her physical size: she was a "petite" size five, self-effacing, shy-seeming, a woman easy to overlook, though it would not be in your advantage to overlook her. She was meticulously and unglamorously groomed in a way to suggest a lofty indifference to fashion, an air of timelessness. She wore her sparrow-colored hair in a French twist, ballerina style; her favored suits were Chanels in subdued harvest colors and soft dark cashmere wools, the jackets giving some bulk to her narrow frame, the skirts always primly to midcalf. Her shoes, handbags, briefcases, were of exquisite Italian leather, expensive but understated. When an item began to show signs of wear, Marina replaced it with an identical item from the same Madison Avenue shop. Her slightly askew left eye, which some in fact had found charming, she'd long ago had corrected with surgery. Her eyes were now direct, sharply focused. A perpetually moist, shiny dark-brown, with a look of fanaticism at times, but an exclusively professional fanaticism, a fanaticism in the service of her clients, whom she defended with a legendary fervor. A small woman, Marina acquired size and authority in public arenas. In a courtroom, her normally reedy, indistinct voice acquired volume, timbre. Her passion seemed to be aroused in direct proportion to the challenge of presenting a client as "not guilty" to reasonable jurors, and there were times (her admiring fellow professionals joked about this) that her plain, ascetic face shone with the luminosity of Bernini's St. Teresa in her ecstasy. Her clients were martyrs, their prosecutors persecutors. There was a spiritual urgency to Marina Dyer's cases impossible for jurors to explain afterward, when their verdicts were sometimes questioned. *You would have had to be there, to hear her, to know.*

Marina's first highly publicized case was her successful defense of a U.S. congressman from Manhattan who'd been charged with criminal extortion and witness tampering; her second was the successful, if controversial, defense of a black performance artist charged with rape and assault of a druggie-fan who'd come uninvited to his suite at the Four Seasons. There had been a prominent, photogenic Wall Street trader charged with embezzlement, fraud, obstruction of justice; there had been a woman journalist charged with attempted murder in the shooting-wounding of a married lover; there had been lesser-known but still meritorious cases, rich with challenge. Marina's clients were not invariably acquitted but their sentences, given their probable guilt, were considered lenient. Sometimes they spent no time in prison at all, only in halfway houses; they paid fines, did community service. Even as Marina Dyer shunned publicity, she reaped it. After each victory, her fees rose. Yet she was not avaricious, nor even apparently ambitious. Her life was her work and her work her life. Of course, she'd been dealt a few defeats, in her early career when she'd sometimes defended innocent or quasi-innocent people for modest fees. With the innocent you risk emotions, breakdown, stammering at crucial moments on the witness stand. You risk the eruption of rage, despair. With accomplished liars, you know you can depend upon a performance. Psychopaths are best: they lie fluently, but they believe.

Marina's initial interview with Derek Peck, Jr., lasted for several hours and was intense, exhausting. If she took him on, this would be her first murder trial; this seventeen-year-old boy her first accused murderer. And what a brutal murder: matricide. Never had she spoken with, in such intimate quarters, a client like Derek Peck. Never had she gazed into, for long wordless moments, any eyes like his. The vehemence with which he stated his innocence was compelling. The fury that his innocence should be doubted was mesmerizing. *Had* this boy killed, in such a way?—"transgressed?"—violated the law, which was Marina Dyer's very life, as if it were of no more consequence than a paper bag to be crumpled in the hand and tossed away? The back of Lucille Peck's head had literally been smashed in by an estimated twenty or more blows of the golf club. Inside her bathrobe, her soft naked-flaccid body had been pummeled, bruised, bloodied; her genitals furiously lacerated. An unspeakable crime, a crime in violation of taboo. A tabloid crime, thrilling even at second or third hand.

In her new Chanel suit of such a purplish-plum wool it appeared black as a nun's habit, in her crisp chignon that gave to her profile an Avedon-lupin sharpness, Marina Dyer gazed upon the boy who was Lucy Siddons's son. It excited her more than she would have wished to acknowledge. Thinking. *I am unassailable, I am untouched.* It was the perfect revenge.

Lucy Siddons. My best friend, I'd loved her. Leaving a birthday card and a red silk square scarf in her locker, and it was days before she remembered to thank me though it was a warm thank-you, a big-toothed genuine smile. Lucy Siddons who was so popular, so at ease and emulated among the snobbish girls at Finch. Despite a blemished skin, buck teeth, hefty thighs, and waddling-duck walk for which she was teased, so lovingly teased. The secret was, Lucy had *personality.* That mysterious X-factor which, if you lack it, you can never acquire it. If you have to ponder it, it's out of your reach forever. And Lucy was *good, good-hearted.* A practicing Christian from a wealthy Manhattan Episcopal family famed for their good works. Waving to Marina Dyer to come sit with her and her friends in the cafeteria, while her friends sat stonily smiling; choosing scrawny Marina Dyer for her basketball team in gym class, while the others groaned. But Lucy was good, so good. Charity and pity for the despised girls of Finch spilled like coins from her pockets.

Did I love Lucy Siddons those three years of my life, yes I loved Lucy Siddons like no one since. But it was a pure, chaste love. A wholly one-sided love.

His bail had been set at $350,000, the bond paid by his distraught father. Since the recent Republican election-sweep it appeared that capital punishment would soon be reinstated in New York State, but at the present time there was no murder-one charge, only murder-two for even the most brutal and/or premeditated crimes. Like the murder of Lucille Peck, about which there was, regrettably, so much local publicity in newspapers, magazines, on television and radio, Marina Dyer began to doubt her client could receive a fair trial in the New York City area. Derek was hurt, incredulous: "Look, why would *I* kill her, *I* was the one who loved her!" he whined in a childish voice, lighting up another cigarette out of his mashed pack of Camels. "—*I was the only fucking one who loved her in the fucking universe!*" Each time Derek met with Marina he made this declaration, or a variant. His eyes flamed with tears of indignation, moral outrage. Strangers had entered his house and killed his mother and *he* was being blamed! Could you believe it! His life and his father's life torn up, disrupted like a tornado had blown through! Derek wept angrily, opening himself to Marina as if he'd slashed his breastbone to expose his raging palpitating heart.

Profound and terrible moments that left Marina shaken for hours afterward.

Marina noted, though, that Derek never spoke of Lucille Peck as *my mother* or *Mother* but only as *her, she.* When she'd happened to mention to him that she'd known Lucille, years ago in school, the boy hadn't seemed to hear. He'd been frowning, scratching at his neck. Marina repeated gently, "Lucille was an outstanding presence at Finch. A dear friend." But still Derek hadn't seemed to hear.

Lucy Siddons's son, who bore virtually no resemblance to her. His glaring eyes, the angular face, hard-chiseled mouth. Sexuality reeked about him like unwashed hair, solid T-shirt, and jeans. Nor did Derek resemble Derek Peck, Sr., so far as Marina could see.

In the Finch yearbook for 1970 there were numerous photos of Lucy Siddons and the other popular girls of the class, the activities beneath their smiling faces extensive, impressive; beneath Marina Dyer's single picture, the caption was brief. She'd been an honors student, of course, but she had not been a popular girl no matter her effort. Consoling herself, *I am biding my time. I can wait.*

And so it turned out to be, as in a fairy tale of rewards and punishments.

Rapidly and vacantly Derek Peck recited his story, his "alibi," as he'd recited it to the authorities numerous times. His voice resembled one simulated by computer. Specific times, addresses; names of friends who would "swear to it, I was with them every minute"; the precise route he'd taken by taxi, through Central Park, on his way back to East End Avenue; the shock of discovering *the body* at the foot of the stairs just off the foyer. Marina listened, fascinated. She did not want to think that this was a tale invented in a cocaine high, indelibly imprinted in the boy's reptile-brain. Unshakable. It failed to accommodate embarrassing details, enumerated in the investigating detectives' report: Derek's socks speckled with Lucille Peck's blood tossed down a laundry chute, wadded underwear on Derek's bathroom floor still damp at midnight from a shower he claimed to have taken at seven a.m. but had more plausibly taken at seven p.m. before applying gel to his hair and dressing in punk-Gap style for a manic evening downtown with certain of his heavy-metal friends. And the smears of Lucille Peck's blood on the very tiles of Derek's shower stall he hadn't noticed, hadn't wiped off. And the telephone call on Lucille's answering tape explaining he wouldn't be home for dinner he claimed to have made at about four p.m. but had very possibly made as late as ten p.m., from a SoHo club.

These contradictions, and others, infuriated Derek rather than troubled him, as if they represented glitches in the fabric of the universe for which he could hardly be held responsible. He had a child's conviction that all things must yield to his wish, his insistence. *What he truly believed, how could it not be so?* Of course, as Marina Dyer argued, it *was* possible that the true killer of Lucille Peck had deliberately stained Derek's socks with blood, and tossed them down the laundry chute to incriminate him; the killer, or killers, had taken time to shower in Derek's shower and left Derek's own wet, wadded underwear behind. And there was no absolute, unshakable proof that the answering tape always recorded calls in the precise chronological order in which they came in, not 100 percent of the time, how could that be proven?

(There were five calls on Lucille's answering tape for the day of her death, scattered throughout the day; Derek's was the last.)

The assistant district attorney who was prosecuting the case charged that Derek Peck, Jr.'s, motive for killing his mother was a simple one: money. His $500 monthly allowance hadn't been enough to cover his expenses, evidently. Mrs. Peck had canceled her son's Visa account in January, after he'd run up a bill of over $6,000; relatives reported "tension" between mother and son; certain of Derek's classmates said there were rumors he was in debt to drug dealers and terrified of being murdered. And Derek had wanted a Jeep Wrangler for his eighteenth birthday, he'd told friends. By killing his mother he might expect to inherit as much as $4 million and there was a $100,000 life-insurance policy naming him beneficiary, there was the handsome four-story East End town house worth as much as $2.5 million, there was a property in East Hampton, there were valuable possessions. In the five days between Lucille Peck's death and Derek's arrest he'd run up over $2,000 in bills—he'd gone on a manic buying spree, subsequently attributed to grief. Derek was hardly the model preppy student he claimed to be either: he'd been expelled from the Mayhew Academy for two weeks in January for "disruptive behavior," and it was generally known that he and another boy had cheated on a battery of IQ exams in ninth grade. He was currently failing all his subjects except a course in Postmodernist Aesthetics, in which films and comics of Superman, Batman, Dracula, and *Star Trek* were meticulously deconstructed under the tutelage of a Princeton-trained instructor. There was a Math Club whose meetings Derek had attended sporadically, but he hadn't been there the evening of his mother's death.

Why would his classmates lie about him?—Derek was aggrieved, wounded. His closest friend, Andy, turning against him!

Marina had to admire her young client's response to the detectives' damning report: he simply denied it. His hot-flamed eyes brimmed with tears of innocence, disbelief. The prosecution was the enemy, and the enemy's case was just something they'd thrown together, to blame an unsolved murder on him because he was a kid, and vulnerable. So he was into heavy metal, and he'd experimented with a few drugs, like everyone he knew, for God's sake. *He had not murdered his mother, and he didn't know who had.*

Marina tried to be detached, objective. She was certain that no one, including Derek himself, knew of her feelings for him. Her behavior was unfailingly professional, and would be. Yet she thought of him constantly, obsessively; he'd become the emotional center of her life, as if she were somehow pregnant with him, his anguished, angry spirit inside her. *Help me! Save me!* She'd forgotten the subtle, circuitous ways in which she'd brought her name to the attention of Derek Peck, Sr.'s, attorney and began to think that Derek Junior had himself chosen her. Very likely, Lucille had spoken of her to him: her old classmate and close friend Marina Dyer, now a prominent defense attorney. And perhaps he'd seen her photograph somewhere. It was more than coincidence, after all. She knew!

She filed her motions, she interviewed Lucille Peck's relatives, neighbors, friends; she began to assemble a voluminous case, with the aid of two assistants; she basked in the excitement of the upcoming trial, through which she would lead, like a warrior-woman, like Joan of Arc, her beleaguered client. They would be dissected in the press, they would be martyred. Yet they would triumph, she was sure.

Was Derek guilty? And if guilty, of what? If truly he could not recall his actions, was *he* guilty? Marina thought, *If I put him on the witness stand, if he presents himself to the court as he presents himself to me . . . how could the jury deny him?*

It was five weeks, six weeks, now ten weeks after the death of Lucille Peck and already the death, like all deaths, was rapidly receding. A late-summer date had been set for the trial to begin and it hovered at the horizon teasing, tantalizing, as the opening night of a play already in rehearsal. Marina had of course entered a plea of not guilty on behalf of her client, who had refused to consider any other option. Since he was innocent, he *could not* plead guilty to a lesser charge—first-degree, or second-degree, manslaughter, for instance. In Manhattan criminal law circles it was believed that going to trial with this case was, for Marina Dyer, an egregious error, but Marina refused to discuss any other alternative; she was as adamant as her client, she would enter into no negotiations. Her primary defense would be a systematic refutation of the prosecution's case, a denial seriatim of the "evidence"; passionate reiterations of Derek Peck's absolute innocence, in which, on the witness stand, he would be the star performer; a charge of police bungling and incompetence in failing to find the true killer, or killers, who had broken into other homes on the East Side; a hope of enlisting the jurors' sympathy. For Marina had learned long ago how the sympathy of jurors is a deep, deep well. You would not want to call these average Americans fools exactly, but they were strangely, almost magically, impressionable; at times, susceptible as children. They were, or would like to be, "good" people; decent, generous, forgiving, kind; not "condemning," "cruel." They looked, especially in Manhattan, where the reputation of the police was clouded, for reasons not to convict, and a good defense lawyer provides those reasons. Especially they would not want to convict, of a charge of second-degree murder, a young, attractive, and now motherless boy like Derek Peck, Jr.

Jurors are easily confused, and it was Marina Dyer's genius to confuse them to her advantage. For the wanting to be *good*, in defiance of justice, is one of mankind's greatest weaknesses.

"Hey: you don't believe me, do you?"

He'd paused in his compulsive pacing of her office, a cigarette burning in his fingers. He eyed her suspiciously.

Marina looked up startled to see Derek hovering rather close beside her desk, giving off his hot citrus-acetylene smell. She'd been taking notes even as a tape recorder played. "Derek, it doesn't matter what I believe. As your attorney, I speak for you. Your best legal—"

Derek said pettishly, "No! You have to believe me—*I didn't kill her.*"

It was an awkward moment, a moment of exquisite tension in which there were numerous narrative possibilities. Marina Dyer and the son of her old, now deceased, friend Lucy Siddons shut away in Marina's office on a late, thundery-dark afternoon; only a revolving tape cassette bearing witness. Marina had reason to know that the boy was drinking, these long days before his trial; he was living in the town house, with his father, free on bail but not "free." He'd allowed her to know that he was clean of all drugs, absolutely. He was following her advice, her instructions. But did she believe him?

Marina said, again carefully, meeting the boy's glaring gaze. "Of course I believe you, Derek," as if it was the most natural thing in the world, and he naive to have doubted. "Now, please sit down, and let's continue. You were telling me about your parents' divorce . . ."

"'Cause if you don't believe me," Derek said, pushing out his lower lip so it showed fleshy red as a skinned tomato, "—I'll find a fucking lawyer who *does.*"

"Yes, but I do. Now sit down, please."

"You *do?* You *believe*—?"

"Derek, what have I been saying! Now, sit down."

The boy loomed above her, staring, For an instant, his expression showed fear. Then he groped his way backward, to his chair. His young, corroded face was flushed and he gazed at her, greeny-tawny eyes, with yearning, adoration.

Don't touch me! Marina murmured in her sleep, cresting with emotion. *I couldn't bear it.*

Marina Dyer. Strangers stared at her in public places. Whispered together, pointing her out. Her name and now her face had become media-sanctioned, iconic. In restaurants, in hotel lobbies, at professional gatherings. At the New York City ballet, for instance, which Marina attended with a friend . . . for it had been a performance of this ballet troupe Lucille Peck had been scheduled to attend the night of her death. *Is that woman the lawyer? the one who . . . ? the boy who killed his mother with the golf club . . . Peck?*

They were becoming famous together.

His street name, his name in the downtown clubs, Fez, Duke's, Mandible was "Booger." He'd been pissed at first, then decided it was affection not mockery. A pretty white uptown boy, had to pay his dues. Had to buy respect, authority. It was a tough crowd, took a fucking lot to impress them—money and more than money. A certain attitude. Laughing at him, *Oh, you Booger man!—one wild dude.* But now they *were* impressed. *Whacked his old lady? No shit! That Booger, man! One wild dude.*

Never dreamt of *it*. Nor of Mother, who was gone from the house as traveling. Except not calling home, not checking on him. No more disappointing Mother.

Never dreamt of any kind of violence, that wasn't his thing. He believed in *passive-ism*. There was the great Indian leader, a saint. *Gandy*. Taught the ethic of *passive-ism*, triumphed over the racist British enemies. Except the movie was too long.

Didn't sleep at night but weird times during the day. At night watching TV, playing the computer, "Myst" his favorite he could lose himself in for hours. Avoided violent games, his stomach still queasy. Avoided calculus, even the thought of it: the betrayal. For he hadn't graduated, class of ninety-five moving on without him, fuckers. His friends were never home when he called. Even girls who'd been crazy for him, never home. Never returned his calls. *Him, Derek Peck! Boooogerman.* It was like a microchip had been inserted in his brain, he had these pathological reactions. Not being able to sleep for, say, forty-eight hours. Then crashing, dead. Then waking how many hours later dry-mouthed and heart-hammering, lying sideways on his churned-up bed, his head over the edge and Doc Martens combat boots on his feet, he's kicking like crazy like somebody or something has hold of his ankles and he's gripping with both hands an invisible rod, or baseball bat, or club—swinging it in his sleep, and his muscles twitched and spasmed and veins swelled in his head close to bursting. *Swinging swinging swinging!*—and in his pants, in his Calvin Klein briefs, he'd *come.*

When he went out he wore dark, very dark, glasses even at night. His long hair tied back rat-tail style and a Mets cap, reversed, on his head. He'd be getting his hair cut for the trial but just not yet, wasn't that like ... giving in, surrendering ... ? In the neighborhood pizzeria, in a place on Second Avenue he'd ducked into alone, signing napkins for some giggling girls, once a father and son about eight years old, another time two old women in their forties, fifties, staring like he was Son of Sam, sure okay! signing *Derek Peck, Jr.,* and dating it. His signature an extravagant red-ink scrawl. *Thank you!* and he knows they're watching him walk away, thrilled. Their one contact with fame.

His old man and especially his lady-lawyer would give him hell if they knew, but they didn't need to know everything. He was free on fucking bail, wasn't he?

In the aftermath of a love affair in her early thirties, the last such affair of her life, Marina Dyer had taken a strenuous "ecological" field trip to the Galápagos Islands; one of those desperate trips we take at crucial times in our lives, reasoning that the experience will cauterize the emotional wound, make of its very misery something trivial, negligible. The trip was indeed strenuous, and cauterizing. There in the infamous Galápagos, in the vast Pacific Ocean due west of Equador and a mere ten miles south of the Equator, Marina had come to certain life-conclusions. She'd decided not to kill herself, for one thing. For why kill one*self,* when nature is so very eager to do it for you, and to gobble you up? The islands were rockbound, stormlashed, barren. Inhabited by reptiles, giant tortoises. There was little vegetation. Shrieking sea birds like damned souls except it was not possible to believe in "souls" here. *In no world but a fallen one could such lands exist,* Herman Melville had written of the Galápagos he'd called also the Enchanted Isles.

When she returned from her week's trip to hell, as she fondly spoke of it, Marina Dyer was observed to devote herself more passionately than ever, more single-mindedly than ever, to her profession. Practicing law would be her life, and she meant to make of her life a quantifiable and unmistakable success. What of "life" that was not consumed by law would be inconsequential. The law was only a game, of course: it had very little to do with justice, or morality; "right" or "wrong"; "common" sense. But the law was the only game in which she, Marina Dyer, could be a serious player. The only game in which, now and then, Marina Dyer might win.

There was Marina's brother-in-law who had never liked her but, until now, had been cordial, respectful. Staring at her as if he'd never seen her before. "How the hell can you defend that vicious little punk? How do you justify yourself, morally? He killed his *mother*, for God's sake!" Marina felt the shock of this unexpected assault as if she'd been struck in the face. Others in the room, including her sister, looked on, appalled. Marina said carefully, trying to control her voice, "But, Ben, you don't believe that only the obviously "innocent" deserve legal counsel, do you?" It was an answer she had made numerous times, to such a question; the answer all lawyers make, reasonably, convincingly.

"Of course not. But people like you go too far."

" 'Too far?' 'People like me—?' "

"You know what I mean. Don't play dumb."

"But I don't. I don't know what you mean."

Her brother-in-law was by nature a courteous man, however strong his opinions. Yet how rudely he turned away from

Marina, with a dismissive gesture. Marina called after him, stricken, "Ben, I don't know what you mean. Derek *is* innocent, I'm sure. The case against him is only circumstantial. The media . . ." Her pleading voice trailed off, he'd walked out of the room. Never had she been so deeply hurt, confused. Her own brother-in-law!

The bigot. Self-righteous bastard. *Never* would Marina consent to see the man again.

Marina?—don't cry.
They don't mean it, Marina. Don't feel bad, please!
Hiding in the locker-room lavatory after the humiliation of gym class. How many times. Even Lucy, one of the team captains, didn't want her: that was obvious. Marina Dyer and the other last-choices, a fat girl or two, myopic girls, uncoordinated clumsy asthmatic girls laughingly divided between the red team and the gold. *Then, the nightmare of the game itself.* Trying to avoid being struck by thundering hooves, crashing bodies. Yells, piercing laughter. Swinging flailing arms, muscular thighs. How hard the gleaming floor when you fell! The giant girls (Lucy Siddons among them glaring, fierce) ran over her if she didn't step aside, she had no existence for them. Marina, made by the gym teacher, so absurdly, a "guard." *You must play, Marina. You must try. Don't be silly. It's only a game. These are all just games. Get out there with your team!* But if the ball was thrown directly at her it would strike her chest and ricochet out of her hands and into the hands of another. If the ball sailed toward her head she was incapable of ducking but stood stupidly helpless, paralyzed. Her glasses flying. Her scream a child's scream, laughable. It was all laughable. Yet it was her life.

Lucy, good-hearted repentant Lucy, sought her out where she hid in a locked toilet stall, sobbing in fury, a bloodstained tissue pressed against her nose. *Marina?—don't cry. They don't mean it, they like you, come on back, what's wrong?* Good-hearted Lucy Siddons she'd hated the most.

*

On the afternoon of the Friday before the Monday that would be the start of his trial, Derek Peck, Jr., broke down in Marina Dyer's office.

Marina had known something was wrong, the boy reeked of alcohol. He'd come with his father, but had told his father to wait outside; he insisted that Marina's assistant leave the room.

He began to cry, and to babble. To Marina's astonishment he fell hard onto his knees on her burgundy carpet, began banging his forehead against the glass-topped edge of her desk. He laughed, he wept. Saying in an anguished choking voice how sorry he was he'd forgotten his mother's last birthday he hadn't known would be her last and how hurt she'd been like he'd forgotten just to spite her and that wasn't true, Jesus he loved her! the only person in the fucking universe who loved her! And then at Thanksgiving this wild scene, she'd quarreled with the relatives so it was just her and him for Thanksgiving she insisted upon preparing a full Thanksgiving dinner for just two people and he said it was crazy but she insisted, no stopping her when her mind was made up and he'd known there would be trouble, that morning in the kitchen she'd started drinking early and he was up in his room smoking dope and his Walkman plugged in knowing there was no escape. And it wasn't even a turkey she roasted for the two of them, you needed at least a twenty-pound turkey otherwise the meat dried out she said so she bought two ducks, yes *two dead ducks* from this game shop on Lexington and Sixty-sixth and that might've been okay except she was drinking red wine and laughing kind of hysterical talking on the phone preparing this fancy stuffing she made every year, wild rice and mushrooms, olives, and also baked yams, plum sauce, corn bread, and chocolate-tapioca pudding that was supposed to be one of his favorite desserts from when he was little that just the smell of it made him feel like puking. *He* stayed out of it upstairs until finally she called him around four p.m. and he came down knowing it was going to be a true bummer but not knowing how bad, she was swaying-drunk and her eyes smeared and they were eating in the dining room with the chandelier lit, all the fancy Irish linens and Grandma's old china and silver and she insisted *he* carve the ducks, he tried to get out of it but couldn't and Jesus! what happens!—he pushes the knife in the duck breast and there's actual blood squirting out of it!—and a big sticky clot of blood inside so he dropped the knife and ran out of the room gagging, it'd just completely freaked him in the midst of being stoned he couldn't take it running out into the street and almost hit by a car and her screaming after him *Derek come back! Derek come back don't leave me!* but he split from that scene and didn't come back for a day and a half. And ever after that she was drinking more and saying weird things to him like he was her baby, she'd felt him kick and shudder in her belly, under her heart, she'd talk to him inside her belly for months before he was born she'd lie down on the bed and stroke him, his head, through her skin and they'd talk together she said, it was the closest she'd ever been with any living creature and he was embarrassed not knowing what to say except *he* didn't remember, it was so long ago, and she'd say yes oh yes in your heart you remember in your heart you're still my baby boy *you do remember* and he was getting pissed saying *fuck it, no; he didn't remember* any of it. And there was only one way to stop her from loving him he began to understand, but he hadn't wanted to, he'd asked could he transfer to school in Boston or somewhere living with his dad but she went crazy, *no no no* he wasn't going, she'd never allow it, she tried to hold him, hug and kiss him so he had to lock his door and barricade it practically and she'd be waiting for him half-naked just coming out of her bathroom pretending she'd been taking a shower and clutching at him and that night finally he must've freaked, something snapped in his head and he went for the two-iron, she hadn't had time even to scream it happened so fast and merciful, him running up behind her so she didn't see him exactly— "It was the only way to stop her loving me."

Marina stared at the boy's aggrieved, tearstained face. Mucus leaked alarmingly from his nose. What had he said? He had said . . . *what*?

Yet even now a part of Marina's mind remained detached, calculating. She was shocked by Derek's confession, but was she *surprised*? A lawyer is never surprised.

She said, quickly, "Your mother Lucille was a strong, domineering woman. I know, I knew her. As a girl, twenty-five years ago, she'd rush into a room and all the oxygen was sucked up. She'd rush into a room and it was like a wind had blown out all the windows!" Marina hardly knew what she was saying, only that words tumbled from her; radiance played about her face like a flame. "Lucille was a smothering presence in your life. She wasn't a normal mother. What you've told me only confirms what I'd suspected. I've seen other victims of psychic incest—I know! She hypnotized you, you were fighting for your life. It was your own life you were defending." Derek remained kneeling on the carpet, staring vacantly at Marina. Tight little beads of blood had formed on his reddened forehead, his snaky-greasy hair dropped into his eyes. All his energy was spent. He looked to Marina now, like an animal who hears, not words from his mistress, but sounds; the consolation of certain cadences, rhythms. Marina was saying, urgently, "That night, you lost control. Whatever happened, Derek, it wasn't you. *You are the victim*. She drove you to it! Your father, too, abrogated his responsibility to you—left you with *her,* alone with *her,* at the age of thirteen. Thirteen! That's what you've been denying all these months. That's the secret you haven't acknowledged. You had no thoughts of your own, did you? For years? Your thoughts were *hers,* in *her* voice." Derek nodded mutely. Marina had taken a tissue from the burnished-leather box on her desk and tenderly dabbed at his face. He lifted his face to her, shutting his eyes. As if this sudden closeness, this intimacy, was not new to them but somehow familiar. Marina saw the boy in the courtroom, her Derek: transformed: his face fresh scrubbed and his hair neatly cut, gleaming with health; his head uplifted, without guile or subterfuge. *It was the only way to stop her loving me.* He wore a navy-blue blazer bearing the elegant understated monogram of the Mayhew Academy. A white shirt, blue-striped tie. His hands clasped together in an attitude of Buddhistic calm. A boy, immature for his age. Emotional, susceptible. *Not guilty by reason of temporary insanity.* It was a transcendent vision and Marina knew she would realize it and that all who gazed upon Derek Peck, Jr., and heard him testify, would realize it.

Derek leaned against Marina, who crouched over him, he'd hidden his wet, hot face against her legs as she held him, comforted him. What a rank animal heat quivered from him, what animal terror, urgency. He was sobbing, babbling incoherently, "—Save me? Don't let them hurt me? Can I have immunity, if I confess? If I say what happened, if I tell the truth—"

Marina embraced him, her fingers at the nape of his neck. She said, "Of course I'll save you, Derek. That's why you came to me."

English Autumn—American Fall

MINETTE WALTERS

Minette Walters (b. 1949), born Minette Jebb in Bishop's Stortford, England, to an army captain and an artist, attended Godolphin and Latymer School and spent six months as a volunteer in Israel before attending Durham University, where she took a degree in French. The mother of two sons with husband Alexander Walters, she lists her pre-writing careers as magazine journalism in London, PTA work, and standing for local elections in 1987.

Walters is one of the most critically acclaimed new writers to debut in the 1990s. Indeed, her first three novels were all award-winners: *The Ice House* (1990) won the British Crime Writers' Association's John Creasey Award for Best First Novel; *The Sculptress* (1993) won the Edgar for Best Novel from the Mystery Writers of America; and *The Scold's Bridle* (1994) won the Gold Dagger Award from the Crime Writers' Association for best novel. Most frequently compared to Ruth Rendell, to whose success she attributes her own opportunity to be published, Walters is a traditionalist with a difference, emphasizing family relationships and the importance of a puzzle but disclaiming, indeed denouncing coziness.

Walters has written few short stories, apart from some romance novelettes done in her magazine days under unrevealed pseudonyms. "English Autumn—American Fall" is an example of the short-short, demonstrating how much character and suggestion can be packed into a very brief tale.

remember thinking that Mrs. Newberg's problem was not so much her husband's chronic addiction to alcohol as her dreary pretense that he was a man of moderation. They were a handsome couple, tall and slender with sweeps of snow-white hair; always expensively dressed in cashmere and tweeds. In fairness to her, he didn't look like a drunk or, indeed, behave like one, but I cannot recall a single occasion in the two weeks I knew them when he was sober. His wife excused him with clichés. She hinted at insomnia, a death in the family, even a gammy leg—a legacy of war, naturally—which made walking difficult. Once in a while an amused smile would cross his face as if something she'd said had tickled his sense of humour, but most of the time he sat staring at a fixed point in front of him, afraid of losing his precarious equilibrium.

I guessed they were in their late seventies, and I wondered what had brought them so far from home in the middle of a cold English autumn. Mrs. Newberg was evasive. Just a little holiday, she trilled in her birdlike voice with its hint of Northern Europe in the hard edge she gave to her consonants. She cast nervous glances toward her husband as she spoke, as if daring him to disagree. It may have been true, but an empty seaside hotel in a blustery Lincolnshire resort in October seemed an unlikely choice for two elderly Americans. She knew I didn't believe her, but she was too canny to explain further. Perhaps she understood that my willingness to talk to her depended on a lingering curiosity.

"It was Mr. Newberg who wanted to come," she said sotto voce, as if that settled the matter.

It was an unfashionable resort out of season, and Mrs. Newberg was clearly lonely. Who wouldn't be with only an uncommunicative drunk for company? On odd evenings a rep would put in a brief appearance in the dining room in order to fuel his stomach in silence before retiring to bed, but for the most part conversations with me were her single source of entertainment. In a desultory fashion, we became friends. Of course, she wanted to know why I was there, but I, too, could be evasive. Looking for somewhere to live, I told her.

"How nice," she said, not meaning it. "But do you want to be so far from London?" It was a reproach. For her, as for so many, capital cities were synonymous with life.

"I don't like noise," I confessed.

She looked toward the window where rain was pounding furiously against the panes. "Perhaps it's people you don't like," she suggested.

I demurred out of politeness.

"I don't have a problem with individuals," I said, casting a thoughtful glance in Mr. Newberg's direction, "just humanity en masse."

"Yes," she agreed vaguely. "I think I prefer animals as well."

She had a habit of using non sequiturs, and I did wonder once or twice if she wasn't quite "with it." But if that were the case, I thought, how on earth had they found their way to this remote place when Mr. Newberg had trouble negotiating the tables in the bar? The answer was straightforward enough. The hotel had sent a car to collect them from the airport.

"Wasn't that very expensive?" I asked.

"It was free," said Mrs. Newberg with dignity. "A courtesy. The manager came himself."

She tut-tutted at my look of astonishment. "It's what we expect when we pay full rate for a room."

"I'm paying full rate," I said.

"I doubt it," she said, her bosom rising on a sigh. "Americans get stung wherever they go."

During the first week of their stay, I saw them only once outside the confines of the hotel. I came across them on the beach, wrapped up in heavy coats and woolen scarves and sitting in deck chairs, staring out over a turbulent sea which labored beneath the whip of a bitter east wind from Siberia. I expressed surprise to see them, and Mrs. Newberg, who assumed for some reason that my surprise was centered on the deck chairs, said the hotel would supply anything for a small sum.

"Do you come here every morning?" I asked her.

She nodded. "It reminds us of home."

"I thought you lived in Florida."

"Yes," she said cautiously, as if trying to remember how much she'd already divulged.

Mr. Newberg and I exchanged conspiratorial smiles. He spoke rarely but when he did it was always with irony. "Florida is famous for its hurricanes," he told me before turning his face to the freezing wind.

After that I avoided the beach for fear of becoming even more entangled with them. It's not that I disliked them. As a matter of fact, I quite enjoyed their company. They were the least inquisitive couple I had ever met, and there was never any problem with the long silences that developed between us. But I had no wish to spend the daylight hours being sociable with strangers.

Mrs. Newberg remarked on it one evening. "I wonder you didn't go to Scotland," she said. "I'm told you can walk for miles in Scotland without ever seeing a soul."

"I couldn't live in Scotland," I said.

"Ah, yes. I'd forgotten." Was she being snide or was I imagining it? "You're looking for a house."

"Somewhere to live," I corrected her.

"An apartment then. Does it matter?"

"I think so."

Mr. Newberg stared into his whiskey glass. "*Das Geheimniß, um die größte Fruchtbarkeit und den größten Genuß vom Dasein einzuernten, heißt; gefährlich leben,*" he murmured in fluent

German. " 'The secret of reaping the greatest fruitfulness and the greatest enjoyment from life is to live dangerously.' Friedrich Nietzsche."

"Does it work?" I asked.

I watched him smile secretly to himself. "Only if you shed blood."

"I'm sorry?"

But his eyes were awash with alcohol and he didn't answer.

"He's tired," said his wife. "He's had a long day."

We lapsed into silence and I watched Mrs. Newberg's face smooth from sharp anxiety to its more natural expression of resigned acceptance of the cards fate had dealt her. It was a good five minutes before she offered an explanation.

"He enjoyed the war," she told me in an undertone. "So many men did."

"It's the camaraderie," I agreed, remembering how my mother had always talked fondly about the war years. "Adversity brings out the best in people."

"Or the worst," she said, watching Mr. Newberg top up his glass from the liter bottle of whiskey which was replaced, new, every evening on their table. "I guess it depends which side you're on."

"You mean it's better to win?"

"I expect it helps," she said absentmindedly.

The next day Mrs. Newberg appeared at breakfast with a black eye. She claimed she had fallen out of bed and knocked her face on the bedside cabinet. There was no reason to doubt her except that her husband kept massaging the knuckles of his right hand. She looked wan and depressed, and I invited her to come walking with me.

"I'm sure Mr. Newberg can amuse himself for an hour or two," I said, looking at him disapprovingly.

We wandered down the esplanade, watching seagulls whirl across the sky like windblown fabric. Mrs. Newberg insisted on wearing dark glasses, which gave her the look of a blind woman. She walked slowly, pausing regularly to catch her breath, so I offered her my arm and she leaned on it heavily. For the first time I thought of her as old.

"You shouldn't let your husband hit you," I said.

She gave a small laugh but said nothing.

"You should report him."

"To whom?"

"The police."

She drew away to lean on the railings above the beach. "And then what? A prosecution? Prison?"

I leant beside her. "More likely a court would order him to address his behavior."

"You can't teach an old dog new tricks."

"He might have a different perspective on things if he were sober."

"He drinks to forget," she said, looking across the sea toward the far-off shores of Northern Europe.

I turned a cold shoulder towards Mr. Newberg from then on. I don't approve of men who knock their wives about. It made little difference to our relationship. If anything, sympathy for Mrs. Newberg strengthened the bonds between the three of us. I took to escorting them to their room of an evening and pointing out in no uncertain terms that I took a personal interest in Mrs. Newberg's well-being. Mr. Newberg seemed to find my solicitude amusing. "She has no conscience to trouble her," he said on one occasion. And on another: "I have more to fear than she has."

During the second week, he tripped at the top of the stairs on his way to breakfast and was dead by the time he reached the bottom. There were no witnesses to the accident, although a waitress, hearing the crash of the falling body, rushed out of the dining room to find the handsome old man sprawled on his back at the foot of the stairs with his eyes wide open and a smile on his face. No one was particularly surprised, although, as the manager said, it was odd that it should happen in the morning when he was at his most sober. Some hours later a policeman came to ask questions, not because there was any suggestion of foul play but because Mr. Newberg was a foreign national and reports needed to be written.

I sat with Mrs. Newberg in her bedroom while she dabbed gently at her tears and explained to the officer that she had been sitting at her dressing table and putting the finishing touches to her makeup when Mr. Newberg left the room to go downstairs. "He always went first," she said. "He liked his coffee fresh."

The policeman nodded as if her remark made sense, then inquired tactfully about her husband's drinking habits. A sample of Mr. Newberg's blood had shown a high concentration of alcohol, he told her. She smiled faintly and said she couldn't believe Mr. Newberg's moderate consumption of whiskey had anything to do with his fall. There was no elevator in the hotel, she pointed out, and he had had a bad leg for years. "Americans aren't used to stairs," she said, as if that were explanation enough.

He gave up and turned to me instead. He understood I was a friend of the couple. Was there anything I could add that might throw some light on the accident? I avoided looking at Mrs. Newberg, who had skillfully obscured the faded bruise around her eye with foundation. "Not really," I said, wondering why I'd never noticed the scar above her cheek that looked as if it might have been made by the sharp corner of a bedside cabinet. "He told me once that the secret of fulfillment is to live dangerously, so perhaps he didn't take as much care of himself as he should have done."

He flicked an embarrassed glance in Mrs. Newberg's direction. "Meaning he drank too much?"

I gave a small shrug which he took for agreement. I might have pointed out that Mr. Newberg's carelessness lay in his failure to look over his shoulder, but I couldn't see what it would achieve. No one doubted his wife had been in their room at the time.

She bowed graciously as the officer took his leave. "Are English policemen always so charming?" she asked, moving to the dressing table to dust her lovely face with powder.

"Always," I assured her, "as long as they have no reason to suspect you of anything."

Her reflection looked at me for a moment. "What's to suspect?" she asked.

BOOKS BY ELIZABETH GEORGE

WRITE AWAY
One Novelist's Approach to Fiction and the Writing Life
ISBN 0-06-056044-4 (paperback)

Elizabeth George offers would-be writers exactly what they need to know about how to construct a novel. She provides a detailed overview of the craft and gives helpful instruction on all elements of writing, from setting and plot to technique and process.

A MOMENT ON THE EDGE
100 Years of Crime Stories by Women
ISBN 0-06-058821-7 (hardcover)

A stunning collection of 26 crime stories, selected by Elizabeth George, from some of the best practitioners of the genre, who also happen to be some of the most successful women writers of our time.

"From start to finish, a first-rate anthology."

—Booklist

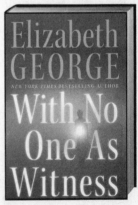

NEW IN HARDCOVER

WITH NO ONE AS WITNESS
ISBN 0-06-054560-7 (hardcover)

When an adolescent boy's nude body is found mutilated on the top of a tomb, it takes no large leap for the police to recognize the work of a clever killer, a psychopath who does not intend to be stopped. Scotland Yard's Thomas Lynley is on the case.

ISBN 0-06-056330-3
(abridged audio CD)

ISBN 0-06-056329-X
(unabridged audio CD)

ISBN 0-06-075940-2
(large print)

**Don't miss the next book by your favorite author.
Sign up for AuthorTracker by visiting *www.AuthorTracker.com*.**

Available wherever books are sold, or call 1-800-331-3761 to order.